MW00534193

ARCANE KNIGHT

AN EPIC LITRPG FANTASY BOOK 1

ARCANE KNIGHT

AN EPIC LITRPG FANTASY

ORDER & CHAOS
BOOK 1

TIMOTHY MCGOWEN

ILLUSTRATED BY
RICHARD SASHIGANE

RISING
TOWER
BOOKS

Fantasy / LitRPG / Gamelit

ALSO BY TIMOTHY MCGOWEN

Haven Chronicles

Haven Chronicles: Eldritch Knight

Short Stories/Novellas

Dead Man's Bounty

Exiled Jahk

Last Born of Ki'darth

Reincarnation: A Litrpg/Gamelit Trilogy

Rebellion: A Litrpg/Gamelit Trilogy

Retribution: A Litrpg/Gamelit Trilogy

Order & Chaos

Arcane Knight Book 1: An Epic LITRPG Fantasy

REVIEWS ARE IMPORTANT

Please remember that reviews are the life blood of authors, consider leaving one on amazon and share with others how much you enjoyed the book.

Join my Facebook group and discuss the books
https://www.facebook.com/groups/234653175151521/

SPECIAL THANKS

I wanted to give a special thanks to those that helped bring this book to its current state.

Candace Morris - Alpha Reader, Beta Reader, Editor, and Proofer

Dantas Neto - Editor, Proofer

Sean Hall - Proofer

To my kids, Avery and Chandler. I write stories so that this world can have just a touch more adventure. One day I hope you can escape into my books and find joy in the reading.

CONTENTS

Prologue – Battle of Lynsteen Pass   1

1. Daily Grind   7
2. Knight on the Road   19
3. Drinks with Friends   25
4. Gone Hunting   37
5. My Arm Hurts   45
6. Trespasser   51
7. Just a baby   63
8. A New Day   73
9. Big Secrets in a Big Keep   79
10. Gifts   83
11. Fun Times   95
12. Secrets and Shadows   101
13. Fun and Games   105
14. Cut off what?   113
15. Marketplace   127
16. Gilfoy's Emporium   137
17. Time to Eat   151
18. Romantic Vistas   163
19. Meetings   171
20. Library   189
21. Nearly Ready   199
22. Journey Home   207
23. Gone Shop'n   225
24. Hunting Rats of Unusual Size   241
25. That's a Fat Rat   259
26. Healing up   271
27. Hope Falters   277
28. Sign on the Line   285
29. One Touch is all it Takes   295

30. System Activate! 303

31. Dinner and Dessert Divine 315

32. Finding a Map 331

33. Fred and Fran 337

34. Magical Maps 349

35. That was Unexpected 359

36. Explosion in the Night 365

37. Follow the Lights 373

38. Mommy's Here 381

39. Bloody Roots 385

40. Death, Guts, and Loot 389

41. Hunting for Fae Hearts 399

42. Cliffs of Fire 415

43. Chaos Wurm 423

44. Dire Bear 433

45. Owl Bears 447

46. Ambush off the Road 465

47. Sea Serpent Hunting 471

48. An Unlikely Ally 485

49. Arcane Knight 493

50. New Abilities and a Profession 505

51. Side Quest 519

52. Noble Reporting 543

53. Professions and Essence 555

54. First Dungeon Run 573

55. Argh there be Pirates here! 581

56. Slay the Kraken 603

57. Goodbyes and Character Sheets 627

58. Full Circle 633

Leave a Review 645

About the Author 647

LitRPG Group 649

Learn More About LitRPG/Gamelit Genre 651

PROLOGUE – BATTLE OF LYNSTEEN PASS

S hadow fire slammed down all around my party, but we stood steadfast in the face of utter demise. There was zero chance that we would leave this battle without suffering heavy casualties. The battlefield before us was a sea of ivory skeletons, armored Chaos knights, and even a few dread lords—hulking giants of spikes and armor—standing tall above the sea of invaders.

None of that mattered though, the combined might of the nations of Newaliyn, Eldah'ren, and the few able to escape Lynsteen before the invasion began, would wash against the horde, a mix of steel, bone, and death. My party and I had a greater mission.

"Warrick," I turned to my closest friend, an old wiry wizard in billowing grey robes. "Have you located him?"

"Yes, indeed I have," his warm baritone voice was comforting to my ears. I hoped this wouldn't be the last I'd hear it.

"Then make ready," I said, my voice rising above the din of

battle. "The king himself has appointed us and we cannot fail. It's time to kill a lich!"

Byron, the stout dwarf, pumped his battle axes into the air. The grim snarl that escaped his lips was expected, considering we stood outside the walls of his homeland. No one, the dwarves most of all, expected the Eastern kingdoms to send such a powerful lich against Lynsteen Pass.

Nicole, the swift ranger with her mighty black panther, matched my gaze, inclining her head. Her elven features sharp and her eyes keen.

Sneal, the cunning rogue, flipped his deadly poisoned daggers and gave me a wink. Though his stature as a gnome was often seen as a weakness, he was quick to end the lives of those who underestimated him with a quick flash of his daggers.

And lastly, Penear, the holy priest of Vanir, lifted his chin defiantly against the dark horde that stood before us. He would be the one to keep us alive and sheltered from the lich's deadly dark influences. His golden aura blazed brightly, a torch against the darkness that threatened to crush us with its dreary gloom.

Between the six of us, nothing would stand in our way.

Warrick waved his gnarled staff in front of our party and the air stirred. Moments later the space in front of us took on a translucent glass-like texture. Just inside the forming portal flanked by two massive drakes, all black scales and wilting mist, was a single man. He wore simple clothing, a loose white tunic, black slacks, a common brown belt, and boots, and atop his head sat a mess of black curls.

His youthful appearance gave me pause; he looked not much older than my son.

"Warrick," I spoke barely above a whisper. "If the worst were to happen."

He cut me off, putting a hand on my shoulder. "We will prevail," he declared, but I ignored him and continued.

"If I fall this day." I held out my right hand, my sword materializing into my grip and lightning dancing down the blade. "Take care of my boy and watch over my family. I can feel my son's potential, but he mustn't walk this path. Suppress his *Spark* if you can, this is no life for my sweet boy."

Warrick didn't answer, but I knew he would honor my request if I fell. I loved my family dearly and had no plans to perish this day. The portal stopped shifting and solidified in front of us, a window to our enemy.

"To battle!" I yelled, charging forward with my sword raised, ready to kill the Lich of Lynsteen.

The corpses of Byron and Nicole lay at my feet. Rage, unbridled and furious, boiled within me as I turned my attention to the drake that had killed my friends. To my left, Warrick traded magical blows with the lich; Penear chanted behind him, pushing back the darkness. Sneal was nowhere to be seen.

I activated my arcane barrier, a blue sheen of magical energy forming around me, and charged the drake. It squared off against me, turning its bulk at the last moment, thinking to take me across the chest with its tail. But I wasn't Byron or Nicole, I was one of the strongest to walk these lands. With a grin I lifted my sword, lightning dancing out from the tip and striking the drake's back leg, while simultaneously letting loose a stream of fire from my free hand. The drake reeled from the attack, but I wasn't finished.

I took up position and waited for the monster of Chaos to charge, when it did, I ran headlong towards it. Mighty jaws opened to consume me, but a quick burst of lightning reflected from the ground pushed the large draconic head upward, giving me the space I needed. My blade cut into the soft underbelly as I slid beneath it and out again, its guts falling free. The drake let out a mighty bellow of fire and roared, but the combined damage my companions had inflicted plus having its guts spilled out, was enough to bring it down. Moments later the foul monster fell silent, dying next to the bodies of my friends.

"Die, you fiend!" Warrick's voice cut through the din of battle, and I turned just in time to see the lich wave a hand, black energy arcing through the air, knocking both Warrick and Penear to the ground.

A shimmer of air behind the Lich of Lynsteen gave me hope and I charged forward, throwing ball after ball of fire at it. I now knew where Sneal had gone, and I had to buy him time.

The lich turned towards me, his eyes black orbs of swirling red, staring back at me. Somewhere deep down I felt a trickle of worry. We'd assumed this man had been a lich, a being in the service of Chaos, and his army of dark creatures the result of a compact with a Chaos Lord. I knew enough lore to recognize what we were up against, an actual Chaos Lord. The most powerful of all Chaos beings.

"Take this!" I screamed at the Chaos Lord, throwing a few smaller fireballs. He waved a casual hand, deflecting the attacks. I stopped midstride and began pushing my mana into one massive attack. My fireball spell allowed any amount of mana to be channeled into it, so I emptied myself, my rings, and the gem on my blade. I heard the ring's gem crack first, completely empty, then the sword's gem, and finally I felt my aura dissipate —leaving me vulnerable.

A fireball the size of a small cottage formed above my head;

both my arms stretched upward as high as I could, my sword clattering to the ground beside me. Even with my natural heat resistance, I could feel the flesh on my arms begin to boil and burn.

"Deflect this, you bastard!" I screamed, arching my back and body forward. The massive attack roared through the air and sped towards the Chaos Lord. He had a subtle grin on his face, but it was soon followed by a look of shock as a dagger slammed into his spine. As fast as Sneal appeared behind him he blinked away, using his shadow step ability to return to my side.

"You looking to kill us all, eh?" he said, wiping black blood from his dagger.

I didn't get a chance to respond, the air around us exploded from the force of my attack as it connected with the deadly Chaos Lord.

Warrick appeared at our side, chanting words of a spell of shielding. A blue iridescent globe formed around us. Mere moments later a wall of flames spread out around us, consuming the corpses of all those who had fallen. Penear hadn't been able to get behind the wall Warrick erected, and I saw him put up a golden light shield around himself through the orange tint of the fire. But it flickered and failed. I sensed his essence leave him and a portion traveled into me.

It made me feel sick to my stomach to gain essence from a fallen friend, but I did what needed to be done. Several long moments later the fire cleared, and Warrick fell to his knees, exhausted.

"You did what you had to do," Warrick said between heavy breaths, echoing my own thoughts. He knew me well enough to know my mind on the matter.

"It isn't over yet," I said. In front of us a charred figure stood at the center point of the attack. It raised a hand towards us, and a ball of black and red energy formed. Reaching into my satchel I downed a mana potion and charged forward, my blade materializing in my hands.

The ball of Chaos energy sped through the air, and I swiped at it with my blade. My sword shattered against the chaotic energy, deflecting it into the side of a nearby cliff and knocking debris into the air.

Still holding firm to the hilt of my ruined sword, I plunged the three inches of jagged blade into the chest of the charred figure. A satisfying squelch and spray of blood confirmed that this monstrosity could indeed be killed.

"You fool," it said, the voice eerily calm and clear considering the damage he'd been dealt. Pain lanced through my hand, and I looked down just in time to see my flesh beginning to char away.

The world around me slipped into a sudden quiet calm and my surroundings shifted. I stood at the edge of a familiar lake, a voice speaking nearby, capturing my attention.

"We need to talk," the Chaos Lord said, his voice the same eerily calm tone as moments ago.

CHAPTER 1
DAILY GRIND

The trill of a sparrow went suddenly still, a victim of our tomcat, Munster, no doubt. The early morning had gone, and the afternoon's heat filled my small bedroom, finally motivating me enough to crawl out of bed. I'd gotten into the habit of getting up an hour before the sun rose to knock out my most vital chores; milk the cow, feed Breanna the donkey, and if I felt up to it, pick a few bushels of kelt fruit. After which, I promptly returned to the comfort of my bedsheets for a few extra hours of sleep.

In the kitchen I heard the tumble of dishes, my mother had gotten up before me. That was surprising. She usually slept well into the late afternoon. Another crash, this one further off, informed me that the twins, Grace and Gregory, had also made it out of bed.

I couldn't help but smile. The last ten years had been hard, and my mother was finally approaching a semblance of normal behavior on most days. She'd taken my father's death really hard, and the gifts and glory that came from my father's service to the crown didn't last as long as we'd hoped.

It could have, but I'd made several bad financial decisions while trying to step into the role of head of the family, and without a steady influx of coin, we could no longer afford the expensive elixirs my mother needed to help her mind sickness.

The twins, bless them, were only three years old when our father died, and while they held a few faint memories of their father, it was hard for them to understand the pressure I dealt with not having him around. The last ten years had all but scrubbed his memory from their minds.

"Have you finished your chores?" My mother's voice carried over the laughs of my siblings and through the small cabin.

Hurriedly splashing water onto my face, I sighed. There were few feelings so sweet as waking up to chilled water on a warm day. I'd dressed earlier, so it was just a simple matter of slipping on my shoes before I was ready for the day. Our narrow hallways were dim, and the wood creaked under my feet as I moved into the kitchen.

The twins ran past me, chasing each other for one reason or another, their faces and hands stained purple. They'd gotten into the kelt fruit I'd picked for the market.

"Come here," I said, using my best 'older brother' voice. "You little turds are going to replace the fruit you ate, and you better not have spilled the rest on the ground; they'll spoil!"

In response, Grace and Gregory each shot me a look, racing from the room seconds later, hopped up on the sugary kelt fruit.

My mother spoke without turning away from whatever she was doing at the counter. "I gave them the fruit for breakfast."

I smiled; I couldn't help it. Today was going to be a great day. Walking to the counter, I wrapped her in a hug.

"Thank you," I said, peeking over her shoulder to see what

she was doing. She had pulled out a dozen kelt fruit from the bushels I'd picked and was cutting them into small pieces. The purple flesh contrasted against the deep red of the fruit's skin.

"Mother," I said, my brow furrowing. "Why are you preparing so much fruit?"

"You know your father likes to have fresh kelt fruit when he gets home," she said, her voice as cheery as it ever had been. "He will be home any moment now."

I sighed, releasing my hug. Today was not going to be a good day.

"I'm going to bring the twins over to the Heddal's place for a few days," I said, my voice losing all feeling. "Mrs. Heddal will send over Jill, you remember Jill, right mother?"

"Oh yes, their little girl, I remember her beautiful blonde curls."

Jill was nearly thirty years old, five years older than me.

"Uh yeah," I struggled to keep my voice clear. "Well, she will stop by and make sure you are doing okay. I'm going to be leaving for a while. Do you remember why?"

"Of course I do," she said, looking at me with her brow furrowed. "You are going hunting with your father."

She was half correct. I was going hunting, but not with my father. He had died nearly ten years ago fighting for the king.

"Yes mother," I said, letting her see my smile as I spoke. "It will be a few days at least, but we need the meat to sell if we are going to make it to winter."

"You worry too much," she said, reaching over and pinching my face like she did when I was younger. "My little Caldor, always being too serious. Your father will bring in plenty of coin when he's finished with whatever dungeon he has left to clear out."

I couldn't disagree with her and from experience, I knew it

didn't help. So, I continued to smile and let her go back to her work. She had been doing better, but today it was like her mind was in a completely different time.

Taking one last look at her, I turned her towards me and gave her a deep hug.

"I love you, mother." I stared deep into her eyes, searching for a *Spark* of recognition. Her sparkling green eyes stared back, not truly seeing me as I was.

Beams of sunlight ran across my face as I walked from the kitchen into the small living room and out the door. We had a covered porch with my father's favorite rocking chair sitting empty to the left and the twins playing sword fighting with sticks just ahead. They were immature for their age, sheltered from the rigors of our worsening finances in a vain attempt to keep their innocence intact.

At their age, they would soon need to take on greater responsibilities.

I walked through the dirt, kicking up dust as I went.

"Help me pick some fruit and then I'm taking you both over to Mrs. Heddal's. Mother isn't feeling well," I said, my tone meant to be fatherly, but coming out tired.

"She was talking about father again," Grace said, looking up at me, her eyes filled with concern. She had his eyes, a deep gray color.

"Mother will be fine," Gregory said, puffing out his chest. "She's strong just like us." He held his head high, as if doing so made him appear stronger.

"Jill will come over and check on her," I said, smiling down at them. I wish I had any feeling behind the smile, but I didn't know what to do about our mother. I just prayed, Vanir willing, that her mind stayed together enough that I could continue to care for her.

It was an odd kind of pressure having them rely on me for so much, my mother included. I had always planned to become an adventurer like my father, but I wasn't as lucky as he had been. I didn't have the *Spark*.

The twins helped hold the baskets so I could pick and fill them. After an hour of work, we left, traveling down the road to our closest neighbors.

After filling the Heddals in on my mother's current condition, I paid Joe Heddal two silver, letting him know I'd be gone for longer than normal and to please watch over my brother and sister. Like always, he tried to give the coin back, but I held firm. Mrs. Heddal—she preferred I call her Emma, but it didn't feel proper—would help watch the kids, and Joe, though I told him it wasn't needed, always took the time to tend to our orchards when I was gone. The two silver I gave him was a pittance when put against the help they offered.

Making my way outside, I checked the contents of the wagon and when I was satisfied everything was secure, I walked over and checked the harness on our donkey.

Breanna the donkey, she'd been around for as long as I could remember, hee-hawed at me and I scratched her behind the ears. My father had joked many times that my mother named the trusty pack animal after one of my father's many admirers, saying that her namesake was a proper jackass, so they might as well use the name.

It wasn't long before Breanna and I were winding ourselves down the dusty road heading towards Creeshaw, the closest town to our little farmhouse. The heat of the day seemed to pulse down on us in waves, my tunic sticking to my chest as sweat trickled down my neck.

"You know what, Breanna," I said, turning to address the donkey that followed behind me at a lazy pace.

In response she shook her head, the flies temporarily giving her peace, before swarming around her face again.

I let out a frustrated sigh. "Yes, I agree. We should stop at Warrick's tower and see if he has anything refreshing to drink. And perhaps..." I let the words trail off, my index finger raising to my lips and tapping against them. "Perhaps we can take lunch with him, and I can read more of that new volume he purchased last week. What was the title, Book of Monsters, or something?"

Breanna didn't offer an answer, but I knew her mind. She wanted a break from this accursed heat as much as I did. It didn't take long to reach Warrick's tower, being almost exactly the middle point between our farm and Creeshaw.

For those who didn't know where to look, the turn off into the dense woods was nearly invisible. Just ahead of me among a sea of black oaks, stood a single purple leafed tree. What type of tree it was, I hadn't asked, but knew from experience this was the entrance to Warrick's grove.

Breanna, as she always did, gave me trouble while passing the tree; something about it seemed to not sit right with her. I attributed it to the fact that she had once eaten from its blossoms and spewed forth violent diarrhea for days after.

We made it past the tree and she visibly relaxed, her ears perking up as the tower came into sight.

Warrick's tower sat directly in the middle of a perfectly spherical grove of trees ringing the outer edge. No bushes or briers grew inside the circle, just a pleasant-smelling field of mint. A path of white stone cut through the mint and led to a single dark wooden door affixed to a blue iron frame. The tower where the door sat was a most peculiar sight, rising well above the tree line.

I remember commenting on how odd it was that it wasn't

visible from a distance, being so much higher than the trees, but Warrick never provided a suitable answer, instead just giving me his trademark shrug and a wink.

The tower was built of a dark marble set so perfectly together that you'd swear it was a single stone. No handhold or edge could be seen, and only a single window high above the ground stood out against the sea of dark marble. The tower was topped with a conical roof made of simple wood tiles and at its peak a metal rod. These facts were shared to me by Warrick, as I couldn't see the top well enough to make out any of those details.

Breanna hee-hawed at me excited to be loose. I released her reins and let her graze. She had a special love for mint and Warrick had never expressed any disfavor about letting her eat from his field.

A voice called out, startling me. "The ice is melting, and I haven't the energy to create more. You best come in and enjoy lunch with me while it's worth eating." Warrick's smooth baritone voice had a hint of humor in it as he spoke. "You'll be wanting time to peruse my library before you leave. I've received a new tome. It speaks of dragons."

"Thanks, Warrick," I said, pushing past Breanna and down the path to meet my father's longtime friend. We'd grown close since my father's passing. I think Warrick felt sorry for me at first, but now, several years later, we had developed our own close friendship. Despite not having the *Spark*, I spent as much of my free time studying the lore of monsters and magic. Paying special mind to anything I could find written about *Sparked* and *Awakenings*—the process of going from a *Sparked* to a full fledged adventurer. I had many fond memories of my weekly visits to Warrick's tower, curled up on a soft chair reading and sipping at his favorite lemon sour tea. It was bitter and sour, but he insisted I drink a cup every time I visited, droning on endlessly about the many health benefits it provided.

His tower was much larger and expansive than it appeared on the outside, but that was normal for Warrick. He was a man of many mysteries. My father used to tell me stories about how he and Warrick, along with a few other party members, had slain great monsters and cleared the most dangerous dungeons. He made Warrick seem like a being that could rival a god in power.

I often wondered why Warrick hadn't been able to save my father from the lich if he were as strong as everyone professed. But I quickly pushed that thought away. If Warrick had been able to save my father he would have, this I knew with a certainty.

Ahead of me lay a grand open entryway, filled to the brim with velvet carpet, wall hangings of kingdoms so old that most history books had forgotten their names, and towards the back, a varied array of preserved and mounted monsters. I'd heard the story of each one, how they'd been defeated by one of my father's swift and powerful attacks. Warrick always spoke highly of my father's power in battle.

It felt good being in Warrick's home. Here I wasn't a farm boy who had to take care of his family. No, when I was in Warrick's tower, I could pretend to be whatever I liked. So, most days I let myself believe that I still might have the *Spark* within me. It was silly, of course; I was over twenty years old by this point and it was rarer than seeing a noble at market than a *Spark* to be unlocked this late in life. It does happen though, I reminded myself.

His tower was my home away from home, where I studied

magic and trained with the sword. Warrick was no good with a blade, but he had many books on the subject.

Following my father's footsteps, I yearned to be an Arcane Knight as he had been. Both a master of the blade and evocation. Warrick described him as a demon on the field of battle, able to match both Warrior and Wizard alike in combat.

"What's the weather like up there?" Warrick asked, his voice echoing from a side room that I quickly followed him into.

"Weather?" I slipped into a small sitting room with two comfortable maroon couches.

"Yes, weather, my boy," Warrick said with a chuckle and a wave of his hand. Teacups appeared on the small table in front of me. "You have your head in the clouds, no doubt. Come down for a while and perhaps we can speak."

"Anything in particular or can I suggest a topic," I quipped back. Warrick gave me a soft smile and sat next to me. I examined the room we sat in, there were shelves with a variety of glass jars containing powders, roots, and what looked like an animal heart, still bloody. I'd never been in this room before, the only room that ever stayed relatively the same was his main entrance hall. Even the library changed layout and location each time I visited.

Warrick fidgeted and seemed uncharacteristically nervous. "Perhaps we should enjoy our tea and you can get a spot of reading done before we speak. Heavy matters have no place during greetings."

"Seriously?" I asked, grunting my displeasure. "You can't say something like that and not expect me to want to hear about it right away." I began to mimic his voice. "*What heavy matters are we to discuss this day?*"

He didn't laugh and his brow tightened. Perhaps I'd been too free with my joke.

"Drink your tea," Warrick said, his face relaxing. "It is nothing too terrible. I will be leaving for a time to investigate some important matters. My tower will be open to you when I am gone, but I'm not sure when I will have the opportunity to return."

I spit out a mouthful of tea and nearly dropped my cup. "You're leaving?" My voice came out much shriller than I had intended. Clearing my throat, I tried again. "You can't leave. You are basically my only friend." I hadn't said what I meant, that he was my only friend left that had also been friends with my father.

"What if you," I struggled to get the words out. "What if you don't come back?" My eyes began to sweat, but I forced away the leaks. First my father and now Warrick. Taking a deep breath, I pulled myself together enough to look up at Warrick.

A warm smile and glistening orbs of deep blue looked down at me.

"I will return." His voice warm and reassuring. "I haven't need to leave for another few minutes, so enjoy some refreshments and my company, for whatever it might be worth." His face shifted and he seemed to consider something. "You will begin to feel different in the upcoming weeks. Don't fight the feeling."

It was my turn to scrunch my brows. What in the Wyrd was he talking about? "I don't understand," I said simply. He reached over and pulled me into the warmth of his side.

"You will," Warrick said before finishing his tea and standing to leave. "On second thought, it would be best if I departed now. Stay sharp, young master." I watched him go, a hollowness in my chest.

Warrick left, and I was alone.

"I need a book," I declared to the empty room, leaving my tea and sandwiches unfinished.

It only took ten minutes this time to find the library. I ignored the new book Warrick had placed on the reading table, instead grabbing a tome on theories of *Sparked* by Merlin of Eldar.

The usual joy I felt when reading felt dull and lifeless. After only an hour, I left, this visit being the shortest weekly trip I'd ever had at Warrick's tower. I'd been so beside myself that I only drank a few sips of my tea. If Warrick had stayed, he would have insisted I finish the entire cup. He really liked tea.

CHAPTER 2
KNIGHT ON THE ROAD

The road into town was not as well maintained on this side of the Blackwood Forest. It teemed with life and activity; travelers, farmers, merchants and even beggars crowded the bustling road. I knew by experience that most would take the northern path a mile ahead, heading for larger towns and cities, but Creeshaw still saw its fair share of travel. Through the town was the safest path to Redridge Lake, a place I'd frequented with my father. In the past ten years, I could count on one hand the times I'd made it out there.

Ahead of me an oddly armored adventurer—because who else would dress in mismatched armor—spoke with a farmer I recognized but couldn't recall his name. The armored man sat upon a bulky black horse, saddled with various items; bedroll, a sword, and what appeared to be half a dozen goblin heads, dry and shriveled, tied together by their stringy black hair. He had a bag of apples slung over one shoulder and handed over a few copper coins to the farmer. He turned to make his way back onto the main road, and I caught a look at his face—the helmet on his head not constructed in a way that provided any facial protection.

I urged Breanna forward, tugging on her reins, deepened my voice, and called out. "Emory Fadel, is that you or has a pile of horse shit learned to ride!"

As much as I tried to mask it, my voice cracked with humor, laughter escaping as Emory turned toward me. His face was a mix of confusion and anger, until his eyes met mine and a wicked grin split his face.

He pulled his sword half out of its scabbard and deepened his own voice. "You're a slimy son of a bitch," he said, in mock offense. Returning his voice back to its usual youthful cadence, he continued. "If it isn't the one and only Caldor Miles, you haven't changed a bit in the last year!"

With a soft clink, his blade slid back into its scabbard. He approached me, weaving through the sea of travelers, his black horse flicking its head at him but following, nonetheless.

I might not have changed much, but he had.

Gone was the slim-framed youth from only a year ago. Now he looked more like his father than not. He wore a tarnished iron chest plate painted yellow—whether by magical means or his design I couldn't tell—his arms were exposed to the heat of the day.

In place of his wiry arms from only a year before, he had developed two appendages that rippled with muscle, the kind you only ever saw on someone who had been *Awoken* or been a blacksmith their entire lives.

Even his hands looked bigger, his palms worn into calluses. The rest of his armor was a mismatched set of leather pants with boiled plates providing average coverage, a hideous orange tower shield hanging on his back, and on his head, a light blue helmet that was partially translucent. The helmet was by far his best-looking item, and my mind raced with questions about what kind of magical item it could be.

The mismatched attire was topped off by a billowing faded purple cloak. It was more rag than cloak, holes and rips running up and down the length. It was notable in that it was billowing while no breeze currently blew.

"You look ridiculously awesome," I said, laughing and slapping him on the shoulder. I was slightly taller than Emory, but he had filled out physically enough that it looked like he'd be able to lift me over his head without issue.

Emory wasn't offended; he laughed and slapped my back. "You'd be surprised at how damned difficult it is to find matching armor when your items come from random dungeon drops. It costs far too much to have custom armor crafted or have an artisan adjust the look of dropped gear, but I'm getting there!" He smacked a small pouch on his belt, it jingled with the ring of coins.

"I was only teasing, Emory," I said. It was good to see him after so long. It brought back memories of stealing crops from old Grady's farm while he set his dogs loose on us, all for the adventure of it. The only thing that was missing was having Ismene with us.

As if he had read my mind, Emory responded, "I'm about to meet Ismene for a drink. You should join us!"

I pulled Breanna up closer, Emory reached out and scratched behind her ears. She made an affectionate mulling noise. Traitor. "Breanna and I have some business to attend to first, but after I offload some goods, I'd love to meet up. You guys doing drinks at Merlin's or the Bearded Lady?"

Emory took a bite into a delicious-looking red apple and spoke with his mouth still half full. "I thought Merlin was shutting down his place last summer?" he asked, swallowing the remaining apple bite.

I reached into Emory's bag of apples and snatched one for myself, he made no move to stop me, so I took a bite. After enjoying two mouthfuls myself, I answered him. "He did. I even heard he got a cozy job working as a chef for the Lord of Variyn. They say that he was granted equal proxy levels so he could retain the perks he'd earned at his pub."

"No shit?" Emory asked, taking another large bite of his apple. He shook his head appreciatively. "He wasn't even that old. Wonder how he nabbed such a prestigious job." Emory paused, seeming to consider, then asked, "If he's gone, why'd you ask if we were going to eat there?"

"An elderly man bought it up," I answered, holding the apple in front of my face, ready for another bite. "But get this," my voice went soft to keep prying ears from overhearing. "Warrick, my dad's old friend, says he recognizes the old man. I still haven't gotten a name, but the old man tells everyone it's Merlin. What are the chances someone buys a place and already has the same name as the last owner? Anyways, Warrick swears to me that this guy used to be a wizard, but if it is the same man, he hasn't been seen in over a hundred years."

Emory laughs. "How old is Warrick if he knows the guy? Come on man, don't feed me this load of crap."

"It's what I heard," I said defensively, shaking my head.

Emory stopped laughing suddenly and tilted his head in my direction. At the same moment, I felt something stir inside of me, and my stomach went queasy. Then as fast as it came, the feeling was gone again.

"Whoa, head rush," I said, wobbling on my feet.

Emory shot out a hand and steadied me. "That was the strangest thing," he said, his eye pinched into a serious stare. "I could have sworn for a fraction of a second that I sensed mana from you."

"Now who is feeding who full of shit?" I asked, standing up straight as my balance returned to me.

"Yeah, I must have been imagining it," Emory said, not looking fully convinced by his own words. "I got a new skill recently, and it messes with my sight."

"I need to get these goods into town before they spoil from the heat," I said, gesturing to the load Breanna the donkey carried.

"Fine, fine," Emory said. He scratched his chin as if deep in thought. "I had planned on going to the Bearded Lady, but now I think I will tell Ismene we are meeting at Merlin's. I want to see this new guy; if he hasn't set up a way to block it, I can Inspect him, it usually gives me at least a name."

"It's a plan," I announced, pulling Breanna the donkey's reins, eager to get into town. Emory rode past me on his large battle horse, and a thought occurred to me. I needed to remember to ask him how his adventuring had been going. He received his *Spark* much later than most, having only *Sparked* last year. It gave Ismene and me hope that perhaps we'd become *Sparked* as well, but a year had come and gone with neither of us showing the telltale signs.

I filed the thought away for later and trudged down the road towards town.

CHAPTER 3
DRINKS WITH FRIENDS

"That is three coppers less a bushel than last time," I complained to Phillip, the owner of the largest fruit stand in town.

"Supply and demand, my young friend," Philip said, his large stomach jiggling as he spoke.

Supply and demand, my ass. There was only one other orchard that produced kelt fruit as high of a quality as us, and I knew for a fact that they sold directly to Variyn.

"I won't accept lower than a silver and fifteen coppers a bushel," I insisted, grabbing one of the bushels of fruit and loading it back into my uncovered wagon. Philip squirmed, and I knew I'd gotten his attention.

He reached out a hand to stop me. "Let's not be hasty now," he said, scratching at his chin as if considering things again. "I can do a silver and fifteen copper, but just this time. Fewer and fewer adventurers are passing through my shop, and no one else pays the higher price for kelt fruit."

I nodded along knowingly, putting the fruit back on his large wooden table. He was right, kelt fruit was sweet and nourishing, but its real value came from the benefits it gave to *Sparked* who had *Awoken*. Though not able to experience it myself, I knew that it helped them recover.

"Same half-dozen bushels next week?" I asked, a nervous chuckle escaping as I presented my best smile.

Philip let out a frustrated sigh, running his hands through what was left of his white greasy hair. "It depends if I am able to move these before they spoil. But I'd be willing to commit to four bushels at one silver and ten copper each." He held out his hand in informal agreement.

I shook his outstretched hand, doing my best to hide my frustration. After unloading the remaining fruit, Phillip paid me seven silver, and I gave him the difference of ten copper.

Kelt fruit's harvesting season was nearly over. If I couldn't find a way to sell our remaining harvest before it spoiled, we wouldn't have enough coin to buy supplies to get us through winter, much less the rest of the year till the next harvest season. I could ask Warrick if he'd be able to store a large portion for us with some preservation magic, but I knew the ingredients for a spell like that cost more than the fruits' value and I didn't want to put that burden on Warrick. Besides, I had no idea when he'd return, even if I wanted to ask him. That meant I'd need to gather more meat from my hunt, perhaps stay out longer until I found a larger buck, or I could try to bag a dire boar.

Thoughts of hunting brought my mind to my father, who'd taught me to hunt in the first place. He had given his life to save the Wyrd, pushing back the Chaos. I often wondered what he would think about his family having to get by on scraps after all he did. His words echoed in my mind.

I do what must be done, not for gold, prestige, or even honor, but because it is the right thing to do, son.

His 'do good for the sake of good' attitude meant he only took as much as he felt we needed to get by. So, when he died, we had only enough to get by for that month, maybe two. Warrick had given us a small amount of money that was meant to be my father's share of the reward, but it didn't last.

Warrick helped where he could, but he didn't adventure anymore, using the little amount of money he made from selling his research to the Variyn's Council of Sages to purchase more books to continue his personal research.

I had asked about items, armor, or anything left over from my father's possessions, but as most high-level adventurers did, he had a special sanctum that only he could enter. It was a spell you could learn after you'd *Awoken*, but only those given special permission could enter the area, and without a *Spark* I'd be unable to enter even if he'd selected me as someone who could enter.

I'd read somewhere that you could also bind the spell and entry to an item, but if my father had done that, it had been destroyed with him when he fell. With my father dead and no one, not even Warrick, having been given permission, we were left to fend for ourselves.

The main street of Creeshaw was cobbled and, despite a street sweeper working diligently not far away, covered in dust from the several miles of farmland that bordered the town. The heat of the day was subsiding into a cool night, the sun slipping behind the Korthak mountains to the East. The main street bustled with activity, even as the day came to a close.

Shop lights flickered through the windows, and stalls were being emptied, the goods being carried inside. The street was wide, and there was enough room for two full wagons to travel side by side, but only the occasional horse and smaller cart, like the one my donkey pulled, ventured down the main path. I walked Breanna the donkey close behind me towards Merlin's pub.

Before getting there, I noticed that the scrying stone didn't have a line and I redirected her to check on my proxy stats.

It was a pedestal of pure silver with the likeness of an open book sitting atop it. Releasing Breanna's reins, I placed my hand on the surface and it flickered to life.

The faintest white light spelled out my basic information. It had my name and the name of the mayor who I earned my proxy levels under. After a quick scan, I saw that our orchard had finally made it to level 5, which meant I could pick a new perk.

I pressed the perk icon and didn't even need to look over the available options, because I'd spent countless sessions reading them all over, so I picked the one I knew we needed and let out a satisfied sigh.

The perk I chose was called Longevity. It had two main benefits. The first was it allowed fruit harvested from our orchard to last several days longer before spoiling, and the second allowed us an additional month added to our harvest season. So now, as long as we didn't pick the fruit, it would last us into the first few weeks of winter without spoiling.

Satisfied that I'd made the right decision, I checked my personal proxy level. My overall level was just seven, but I had levels in farming, hunting, fishing, and a few other odds and ends. None of the levels had reached five yet, but for my age that was better than most and gave me significant passive bonuses when farming or hunting. For instance, I could see tracks about ten percent easier than someone without the hunting skill. Satisfied in what I saw, I turned back towards Merlin's pub.

Several people were leaning against the nearby alley, talking loud enough for everyone to hear. They discussed the rise in prices, saying that they likely wouldn't return next season. With the help of the low light of a nearby streetlamp, I took a closer look. They were adventurers, each wearing armor of some kind or another. Weapons hung at their waist, and one leaned heavily on a withered old staff with a dimly glowing blue stone atop it.

I ached to bombard them with questions. My studies and access to Warrick meant that I had a vast well of knowledge beyond what someone normally would regarding *Sparked*, *Awakenings*, and adventures, but that only seemed to add fuel to the fire of my curiosity.

Not giving in to the temptation, I walked past them and into the alley. Ahead a lantern hung from a small stable that was empty aside from a single large black horse. I took Breanna to stand beside the steed and tied her to the post. Then taking the empty cart, I wheeled it down the alley a bit further, confident that it'd be left alone.

Scratching Breanna behind the ears, I said, "You two play nice." I then turned to join my friends inside Merlin's pub.

The sign out front had a carved image of a large conical hat crossed with a smooth shafted staff with a gem set into the top. The tavern door had been changed out when the new owner took over. Instead of a simple thin wooden door, it now held a thick heavy black oak door banded together in cast iron. At the center of the door was a clear crystal. It didn't flicker with magic or even reflect the light very well, probably some cheap glass inserted to look magical.

It swung light and easy with a simple push and the sounds of the tavern poured out into the street as I entered. I caught sight of Emory first, his large ugly yellow shield leaning against a table meant to seat four. Beside him sat Ismene. She wore a simple blue dress with a black ribbon cinching just below her breast. Her black hair was braided tight and hung over her shoulder. She looked up, and her deep purple eyes caught sight of me.

She was devastatingly beautiful, and her simple clothes stuck out in stark contrast. As beautiful as she was, she rarely wore dresses or cared to be prim or proper. She wanted nothing more than to be *Sparked*. We both did. Her mother had been a Ranger and her father a Paladin. They both perished at the Battle of Lynsteen Pass, along with my father.

I understood her need to be something greater, we weren't meant for a life of farming and ordinary living. And yet destiny had another idea, forcing us both into obscurity.

I held our gaze, her eyes a deep purple, mine a brilliant blue.

Emory stopped talking after seeing that Ismene stopped paying him anymore attention. He turned and saw me.

He stood and waved me over. "Caldor! Get over here and stop ogling over Ismene!"

I smiled but said nothing. The tavern was a sprawling open room, brightly lit by two simple fireplaces on each side. At the back of the room was a staircase that led to several rooms that could be rented for the night, and just to the side of the staircase was the main bar area. An old gray-haired man stood there, his sharp dark eyes scanning the room as he polished a mug with a cloth rag. That was Merlin, or at least he claimed his name was Merlin. You really couldn't know.

He caught my eye as I finally made it to the table with my friends and winked at me. I checked behind me, but I stood alone. By the time I looked back, his gaze had settled elsewhere. The tavern was packed tonight and by the garb that everyone wore I'd have to guess that most of the visitors were adventurers.

I pulled out a chair and sat. At the table were three bowls of a light-colored stew, steam wafting up from them, and three large mugs of foaming beer.

I slapped my hands together and licked my lips. "Got here just in time." My stomach rumbled and I grabbed my spoon digging into my stew. Ismene and Emory continued whatever conversation they had been having before I arrived.

"Like I was saying," Ismene's voice was soft and sweet. "Mr. Fawlkner, the owner of the magic trinket shop, hired me earlier this year to help manage his inventory, but he is considering moving the shop to the Capital. He says there isn't as much business here anymore, so he has been gone a lot this month, looking for a new shop to move into in Variyn and trying to acquire a transfer stone."

I slurped on my soup, listening intently.

Emory slapped the table, causing me to spill some soup. "I thought he was a wizard, so he wouldn't need to worry about transferring his perks. What a shame. He's been here for years; he must have all his perks maxed," Emory said.

I cut in and asked, "Would you move with him? If he finds a new place?"

My eyes flipped from Emory and then back to Ismene.

She smiled and shook her head. "I honestly don't know. My whole life is here, but there are more adventures to be had in a bigger city. What if I could figure out how to unlock my *Spark*." She blushed and glanced down. "Maybe, I don't know."

"If you figure that out, be sure to tell me," I spouted, soup dribbling down my chin. I really needed to slow down eating, but the soup was so delicious, thick, and hearty.

"Both of you need to move on with your life," Emory said, his tone turning serious.

Ismene and I glared at him, but I spoke first.

"Easy for you to say," I said, leaning forward. "You were one of us just a year ago, wishing and hoping to get the *Spark*. Do you know how rare it is to have your *Spark* manifest at twenty-four? About as rare as it is for it to manifest at twenty-five. If it can happen to you, it can still happen to us."

Ismene smiled, nodding along. "Yeah, what he said."

In answer, Emory took a long pull on his drink. "Do you all want to hear about my adventures or not?" he asked, slamming down his mug and waving to a bar maiden for another.

The rest of the night was spent with Ismene, and I enraptured as Emory told the tale of his first few dungeon dives.

"And after all that hassle, I only made it to level nine. Nine levels in a year, can you believe my shitty luck?"

In all the books I'd read I didn't recall any going into the specifics of how fast you could level, only vague mentions that you gained levels faster at first and each succeeding level being harder than the last.

"Why only nine?" Ismene asked.

"Oh right, you noobs don't know about the bonuses at the end of dungeons," Emory said, lifting his chin haughtily. "You see, since all my groups failed epically and we never got to the end of a single dungeon, we never got the massive essence boost. It's like eating the appetizer for every meal. Sure, I got essence, loot, and plenty of coin, but never enough. I should be at least level twelve or thirteen."

"So, what now?" I asked. Emory succeeded in catching my full attention. "Are the dungeons in Variyn too hard? Will you hunt roaming monsters instead?"

Emory nodded along as I spoke. "Something like that.

Except that I wasn't doing dungeon runs in Variyn, I moved south to House Thouca, because I'm a gullible twit. A healer I met early on assured me that it would be better to skip the lower leveled dungeons and go straight for ones that were more challenging. Part of why we didn't make it very far."

"Well, I could have told you that was a bad idea," Ismene scoffed.

"Oh yeah?" Emory asked, raising his eyebrows questionably.

"Yeah," I said, cutting into the argument. Ismene's dungeon knowledge was probably only second to mine outside of experienced adventurers. "Almost all dungeons have several floors that get harder as you dive deeper. Many scholars theorize the reason you can't enter a dungeon until level five is because you are just barely strong enough to clear the first floor and maybe a room or two on the next. It's a natural progression. If you had cleared lower leveled dungeons and progressed through it instead, you probably would have been level ten or higher in half the time."

"Seemed like a good idea at the time," Emory muttered. "Stronger monsters equal stronger essence gains. I gathered enough after clearing three rooms to make it to level six. If we'd been able to clear any more rooms, it would have been epic."

"But you didn't," Ismene said. She seemed to be enjoying herself, a large smile on her lips. "Imagine if all three of us received our *Spark*. We'd be unstoppable!"

The thought was exciting, but highly unlikely. It wouldn't stop either of us from wishing that it would happen. "What is your class exactly?" I asked Emory, realizing he hadn't really said. It was obviously some kind of tanking class, filling the role of keeping the monsters' attention and shielding the physically weaker party members.

Emory perked up at the question, scooting his chair in and speaking low enough that only we could hear. "I'm a Vanguard. I try not to tell too many people because it is a purely defensive class and I've been wanting to try my hand at a more offensive party spot, you know, like a damage dealer."

"Vanguard," I said, letting my mind filter through what I'd read about the class. "You can use defensive skills that divert damage from other party members, able to numb the pain you feel from incoming attacks at the cost of your own offensive capabilities. I think one of the core abilities is shield block; able to erect a physical barrier within twenty feet of your current location."

"Damn," Emory hissed. "Keep it down. Also, what the hell, man? I know you read, but how could you know all that?"

"I've been studying every book I could get my hands on about adventurers since I could read," I said flatly, as if that explained it all.

Ismene chuckled across the table. "I thought I was a nerd; you are a super nerd." She teased.

"Well, you know the basics," Emory said, "I had very few choices when I was *Awoken*. I guess we all have certain inborn affinities towards certain skills and magic. But I learned a new ability that should increase my damage capabilities. Maybe when I get to a high enough level, I can fill more of an off-tank role."

"Vanguards are almost always the main tank," I began to say, but Emory lifted a hand to quiet me.

"I'll be the first if I have to be," he announced. Just then, the bar maiden came by, dropping off a round of beers. I had only made my way through half of mine, so I quickly gulped it down and grabbed a new one, smiling at the cute brunette.

"Did you use that skill on Merlin yet?" I asked, suddenly remembering our earlier conversation.

"You planning on attacking me in my own establishment?" A creaky old voice rung out behind me.

Realizing that I'd just outed Emory's plan to the very person he was wanting to practice the skill on, left me feeling sick. I turned in my seat and saw that Merlin was indeed standing just behind me.

"Not attack," Emory sputtered. "I got a skill that helps me get information about people and monsters. It wouldn't have hurt."

"Oh, wonderful. You've learned how to use the Inspect skill. Go ahead then, try it out on me," Merlin said, his tone shifting and sounding almost jovial at the idea.

Emory scrunched his brow and I swear I could see some sweat forming on his forehead. After a solid three seconds of this he stopped, looking confused.

"I didn't get anything," Emory said, shaking his head. Then turning to a random adventurer sitting at the table beside us, he scrunched his brow again. "Well, it worked on that guy. His name is Dale, and he is a level twelve Fire Brand. Whatever that class does."

Fire Brand wasn't a class I was familiar with, but Merlin spoke up surprising us all. "Fire Brand is just a fancy name for a monk/sorcerer hybrid."

"How do you know that?" I asked, looking up at the old man appreciatively.

"I've met all types and I imagine I'll meet a few more unique folks with interesting classes before I die," Merlin said, his eyes going from Ismene and then to me. Winking at me again, he turned away and walked back to the bar.

The rest of the night was a blur of drinking, laughing, and

at one point, an arm-wrestling match where Emory showed off his new strength, completely destroying me and several lower-leveled adventurers.

After walking Ismene home, Emory and I rented a room with two beds and promptly fell asleep. By the time I awoke, headache blazing like the noonday sun, Emory had already left. A note on a rickety end table told me he was traveling to find a dungeon group to join up with to challenge some lower leveled dungeons.

Smart man, I thought as I devoured a plate of bacon and eggs, sipping my coffee between mouthfuls. I was going hunting today, and I couldn't wait to be out among the trees.

CHAPTER 4
GONE HUNTING

Books are my escape, but hunting is something special. The chance I get to pit myself against nature and test my meager skills. I left Breanna with old man Ferdel, paying him a few extra coppers to deliver the goods I picked up after selling our fruit. My father had used Ferdel as a farmhand years back, when our orchards had stretched much further than they currently do.

My father's income from adventuring had purchased the land, but without the steady flow coming in after his death and my failed attempts to spend our coin wisely, I had to sell off much of the land and now Ferdel owned a small section of it not far from where we lived. I let my mind wander through these random facts as I avoided thinking about what was really on my mind.

Where had Warrick gone? In all the years since my father was killed, Warrick had never been gone for more than a few days at a time.

I moved through the forest as silently as I could, letting my mind calm and my thoughts go still. There were tracks of all kinds to be found if you knew how to look, so I picked up some deep-set dire boar prints. I had never successfully taken one down while hunting by myself, always being able to rely on my father, or one of his party members on the rare occasion one came along.

This hunt would be different. I would prove to myself that I had the strength and skill required to be an adventurer. So what if I didn't have the *Spark*. There had to be successful adventurers that didn't rely on having a Class. There were obvious advantages to becoming stronger, leveling up, gaining access to magic, and becoming physically strong enough to match brute strength with literal monsters, but was that the only thing that set them apart?

Okay, maybe I wouldn't be able to be the best adventurer without a *Spark*, but I'll be damned if I didn't at least try. I studied, I practiced with a blade, a bow, and kept my body strong and fit, no one could stop me from being what I was meant to be. I felt it deep inside that I was meant to be more than a farm boy.

As I went over my grandiose plans, the wind shifted, and a cool breeze brushed against my face. The streams of sweat helped to cool me. The heat of the day penetrated through the thick canopy; the shade only provided a measure of comfort.

The rest of the day was spent tracking the boar, back-tracking to ensure I was, in fact, following the correct tracks, and then more tracking. I camped for the night, using my flint and steel to start a small fire. There wasn't much to be worried about in these woods. A healthy population of adventurers passed through here, so the monster population was almost nonexistent, and the wildlife stayed clear of fires for the most part.

I was a light sleeper and had a very large knife held firmly in my grip as I slept. I felt safe.

The night passed without incident, and the next, and the next after that. I had traveled far, but I was certain I still knew my way back. My sense of direction was strong, and more importantly, I was closing in on the boar. In my previous hunts I killed rabbits, deer, and even a few foxes, but they traveled along predictable trails and so I could always post up in a tree stand and get lucky. This boar didn't follow any such predictive path and I needed to prove I could take down a dire boar. It roamed back and forth but always in the same general direction, which is why I was able to keep tracking it.

The stillness of the forest was split by a loud angry snuffling and then a snorting roar. My bow was off my shoulder and nocked within seconds. Had the wind shifted, and the boar caught my scent? My eyes scanned the line of trees ahead, but I saw no movement. I pushed forward, using the large black oaks to hide my approach. The angry snuffling filled my ears again. Not far ahead through a split in the trees, I could almost make out a massive black hairy form.

The wind had died down enough that it shouldn't be able to catch my scent, but I needed to get up into a tree before I took the shot. Dire boars were tough, and if I didn't hit it with a kill shot to the brain or heart, then I would most certainly be running for my life.

Memories of hunting with my father flickered through my mind. Even he had insisted that we do things 'the right way' as he called it. Getting up into a tree blind and ensuring our safety. Hunting was about getting food for my family, not showing off.

The boar was screeching at something ahead, but I couldn't make out what. It wasn't moving forward though, and as I carefully and slowly crept forward, I saw why. Ahead, the tree line ended in a circular fashion in front of two massive stone doors set into a rocky outcrop.

A dungeon entrance!

I slipped up a tree at the edge of the clearing and found a comfortable spot to perch ten feet up. As I examined the boar, I decided to go up an extra few feet, because it was massive. It was so big, that I wondered if it was normal at all. But I saw no signs of mutation that would mark it as mana infused, just a huge damn beast. Sometimes nature created beings that could match power with some low-level monsters, this boar was probably among them.

The boar's behavior was strange. It kept charging the dungeon entrance, to what end I couldn't figure out. Maybe the boar needed a lesson on dungeon mechanics?

You see boar, I began to wordlessly lecture the giant pig, dungeons are direct creations of the magic of the Wyrd and the ancient designs of the Ordu. The Ordu are beings of Order and only those given the ability to level up by the Ordu can enter a dungeon. You, as a pig, do not have the right kind of levels and as such, you cannot enter.

Satisfied that I had educated the swine, I raised my bow and readied to end it. If I was careful and lucky, I could kill it in a single shot. I wasn't hopeful though; the boar was very agitated, it fidgeted and moved constantly. The best I was going to be able to do was just aim center mass and put as many arrows into it as I could before it ran. Then I'd have to track its blood trail to see where it fell before field dressing it.

I sighted the boar, pulled my bow string back, and released the arrow all in a fluid motion. It whistled through the air, going high and hitting it in the upper shoulder. The arrow broke on the boar's tough hide. My eyes went wide and

ARCANE KNIGHT

my butt-cheeks tight. My arrow hadn't even penetrated its hide!

As fast as I could, I nocked another arrow and let it fly. The boar had already turned and found my location, but instead of running as I assumed it would, it charged the tree. My next arrow had more success, hitting low into the softer tissue of its back leg.

It let out a cry of pain, squealing and snorting, but it didn't slow, it didn't go down, and it was coming straight for me and my tree.

It wouldn't be able to knock the tree over, would it? The question had barely filled my mind when the boar collided with the tree. With a deafening crack the tree shook but stood firm. I, however, wasn't as lucky. Even perched as I was, legs wrapped tight around a large branch, the blow dislodged me, and I fell.

My bow and arrow slipped from my grip as I reached out for anything to hold onto. With a painful grunt I managed to grab hold of a lower branch. Loud snorting and squealing told me that I had just barely kept myself from the boar's tusks.

Boars will eat anything, and by the looks of it, I was firmly on the menu now.

Pulling myself up and over the branch I looked down, seeing that the boar had moved off a bit.

I quickly turned and hugged the thick tree trunk. "Oh shit," I said as the boar once again collided with the tree. It shook violently and began to tilt. This tree was going down. "How are you so strong you monstrous swine, damn you!" I cursed down at the pig as it turned and readied for another run.

There was a wild ferocity in its eyes that I didn't remember seeing when I'd hunted boar with my father. We'd also never encountered a beast so large in our hunts.

My bow had survived the fall, next to it lay several arrows, their shafts intact as well. I was going to have to make a hasty retreat somehow. Without my bow all I had was my hunting knife, and while the blade was longer than average, it would barely make it through the fatty layer of this boar.

Smash!

Another mighty attack and the tree tilted further, I kept my footing, but I knew the time to act was now. As soon as the boar got far enough away and turned to charge once more, I leapt from the tree and fell into a roll.

Beside me lay my bow, I scooped it up along with four arrows. The boar charged, squealing in glee and frustration at me as it came. As fast as I could, I let my arrows fly. There was no way I'd outrun this beast.

My first arrow hit it just below the neck, blood spurting out around the wound, but it didn't slow. The next arrow went high, deflecting off its hard skull and doing no damage.

Panic shot through me and one of my last two arrows fell from my grasp. The boar was only feet away! I drew back the final arrow, something crackled inside of me, and I felt power pulse as I released my bowstring. I didn't have time to think or see if my shot had landed true, instead I leapt out of the boar's path.

My timing was off, and the boar's tusk ripped into my arm as I moved through the air. Intense pain shot through me and for the moment there was only the pain. More pain rippled through me as I landed on my wounded arm.

Stars played across my vision and the edges of my sight went black. *Get up and fight!* I screamed at myself.

"Ahhhhrrrr!" I screamed in pain and frustration as I rolled into a crouch, my dagger out and ready. The same odd crackling feeling rose deep in my chest and my breathing became ragged.

The boar lay in a pile of brush and broken branches at the foot of the black oak where I'd been just moments before. It wasn't dead, I could see its chest rising and falling, so I pushed myself forward, knife in hand ready to put it out of its misery.

My blade dug deep into the boar's brain, and its cries were silenced.

CHAPTER 5
MY ARM HURTS

I was in pain, but I knew better than to let meat go to waste. I laid out a thin leather blanket, pulled out my rope, and set aside several other items to help me field dress the boar. I had the special salt Warrick had made for me to help with the preservation process, but before I could do that, I needed to bleed it out as best I could, then gut it, and slice it into workable parts.

Normal meat salts would preserve the meat if kept cold enough for longer periods of time, Warrick's was much better. With his special touch of magic, meat salted and wrapped, even in the heat of this awful summer, would be preserved and ready to consume within hours instead of weeks. It was one of the few preservation spells he knew that required easily found ingredients, or least that is what he told me when he gifted me the salt.

There was no way I could lift this wagon-sized boar without help, so I fashioned a makeshift pulley system. Using a longer section of rope, I tied one end to a thick branch and the other between a 'V' section of branch. Taking the shorter length of rope, I tied the boar's feet up nice and tight, then fastened the end to the middle section with several strong knots. After that, it was just a matter of pulling with all my might. Once the swine was high enough that it wasn't brushing against the ground, I tied off the rope on a thick tree trunk.

Blood dripped from the wounds I'd given it so far, but I needed to slit its throat and get a steady bleed going. I noticed the arrow in its face. At first, I had thought it had gotten it in the eye. Looking again, I'd hit it square in the forehead, the same place that had deflected my previous arrow.

The wound was blackened and scarred, as if from something hot. I ran my finger over the wound, maybe the scarring and burns had already been here...surely, I hadn't done that. There was no time to focus on it right now, the meat would spoil if left too long in this heat.

I went to work, cutting its throat, gutting it, and cutting the meat into mostly equal parts on the leather blanket. I took out the blue salt and began to rub each piece, it *Sparked* as I rubbed, a normal occurrence when using it, the mana leaking free of the salt. It didn't take long before I had more meat than I could carry, prepped and ready to go.

I wiped sweat from my brow and cursed, "Damnit." This monster of a boar had given me close to five hundred pounds of meat. Warrick's special salt rub would keep the meat without any special cooling or protection for weeks, but if I left it out here someone would surely take off with it, be it adventurers coming for the dungeon or predators roaming the forest.

While thinking through my options I remembered the dungeon, the meat would last long enough for me to explore the entrance at the very least.

The leather blanket was held tight with my rope, keeping it from unfolding. The day had begun to grow colder, not so cold that I needed to worry, but the heat had finally broken enough that I could enjoy the shade. The sun was barely dipping below the horizon, but I could see well enough in the light.

I moved through the trees until I reached the entrance to the dungeon. Dungeons were strange, almost all that I had read about had doors set into little mounds of rock, even out here in the forest where the closest mountain range loomed in the distance. This particular dungeon was no different.

Two massive stone doors stood before me, rocky protrusions all around. In the dim light, I could clearly see several runes glowing a faint blue. The runic language was something I had tried to study, but Warrick had little literature on them, and what he did have was beyond my level of magical understanding.

I knew enough to know that these runes acted as wards to keep unwanted visitors from entering the dungeons. They were meant for those that had been *Awoken*, powers unlocked within a Prime Mana Shrine. *Awoken* beings had access to the unique ability to Level up. Each level pushed you further above the strength, speed, power, and magical ability of a normal person.

Each race had their natural talents, elves being swifter and longer-lived, dwarves with their hardy constitutions, and humans with their ability to have children nearly as fast as bunnies. I laughed, but that was an actual passage from a book I'd read and of course it didn't include every race of Wyrd, but I always enjoyed recalling that author's ideas on racial differences and bonuses.

I reached out to feel the surface of the dungeon door. The stone was warm beneath my touch. Holding my breath, I pushed.

To my shock it swung open.

I stepped back from the dungeon door and pinched myself. Ouch! There was no doubt, I was awake. It made no sense for a dungeon door to open for me, I wasn't *Awoken* and even if I had been, there was no way I'd be level five even if I had gone through the *Awakening*.

My heart raced and pounded in my chest. Stepping forward I pushed the door a few more feet and stepped into the dungeon.

There was an even glow to the room providing enough light to see by, but without any single source of light illuminating it. I took a deep breath and my heart calmed. The air inside the dungeon had an almost sweetness to it. Walking forward I stepped down a small corridor and into a natural cavern.

In the middle of the fifty-by-fifty pace room was a pedestal with water, like a bird bath. This would be mana infused water that dungeon divers could drink to replenish themselves between floors. I was in the dungeon's staging room, commonly known as a 'rest area'.

My arm chose that moment to remind me it had been injured. The wound tingled and itched. Walking up to the mana infused water I cupped my good hand and scooped a measure of water, pouring it on my wounded arm. I could feel the healing begin the moment the chilled water hit my wound; the itching increased but the pain lessened. Taking another handful, I applied it to my wound. Then for good measure, I cupped both hands and took a long pull of water, drinking until I felt refreshed.

"I know I'm not meant to be in here, but I appreciate the healing," I said to the empty room. I'd read one theory about dungeons being sentient beings and figured it wouldn't hurt to be polite. Not getting any kind of response, I walked the perimeter of the wall and was shocked at what I found. The way I had come in was the only way in or out.

Ismene was the real dungeon expert, but I knew enough to expect to find a swirling archway that led to the first floor of the dungeon. I found no such archway and after filling myself with more mana infused water I turned and left the way I came.

The doors shut behind me with a gentle thud and I went back to the task at hand, figuring out how I'd be moving such a large portion of meat back to civilization. I knew one thing for certain, it would be much easier now that my wound had healed.

CHAPTER 6
TRESPASSER

My walk home was slow, the heavy salted meat of the wild boar weighing me down. I'd fashioned a makeshift sled, having not expected to down such an enormous prize during my hunt. Adjusting my bow to better sit over my shoulder, I paused. The constant buzz of nature around me had suddenly gone still, not a cricket could be heard, nor the call of a wild bird. Just as I pulled my bow free and nocked an arrow, my eyes scanned the perimeter for whatever predator could be lurking in the shadows. Suddenly a sound cut through the dense forest. It was a bloodcurdling scream, the sound rattling me deep in my bones.

Without a second thought or hesitation, I was off in a sprint, leaving my boar meat. My father had taught me well and I knew that to be a true hero one must act fast, but also with care. So, as I ran, I began to go over scenarios in my head.

The scream had been female, or a very scared shrill man. It wasn't the scream of someone being startled or frustrated, there had been a terror in that sound that I could still feel deep in my bones. Whatever the situation, the person who cried out was in real danger.

Another bone chilling scream broke through the trees, I was close. It came from just ahead. I raised my arms to give myself a measure of protection against the wiry branches that whipped at my face as I ran. The air was cool, like most nights this close to the summer solstice, the sun having grown tired of baking us during the daylight hours.

The tree leaves had turned various shades of orange and yellow, and the trunks of the trees in this part of the forest were covered in thick black bark that had an odd white marbling. The sudden realization of where I had gone hit me and I nearly turned back. I'd roamed further than I had planned during my hunt, and it was quite possible that the large boar I had left behind was not mine to hunt. This was House Variyn land, I was in Shadowcrest Forest—land reserved for hunting by nobles of House Variyn.

Heroes don't abide any boundaries. Heroes go where they are needed most.

My father's words echoed through my head, lending motivation and speed to my legs.

A final row of trees passed me by as I entered a small clearing, just off the side of one of the most well-maintained roads I'd ever laid eyes on. The road, with its smooth cobblestones and dust free surface only held my attention for a fraction of a second as the scene before me came into focus.

A creature of legend, covered in black thick scales, with dagger-like teeth and a powerful muscled four-legged body, tore into a brown horse, ripping free a large chunk of flesh. It paused in its feasting, large orange eyes with sharp black eye slits inspecting me, before turning its attention back to its meal.

It was a drake, it had to be! Its draconic features were unmistakable. Thick scales, muscled body, horned head, spikes running down the spine and ending at the tip of the tail. The last thing I needed to confirm would be-

The drake opened its maw and a steady stream of fire shot forth, burning the meat to a black crisp, before it began to eat once more.

Yep, that was a drake all right. Which was weird considering the last of the Chaos beasts were supposed to have been driven from the land after my father killed the Lich of Lynsteen.

Moments after the fire spewed from the drake's mouth, another scream ripped me back to reality. Now was not the time to ponder on the academic study of monsters and magic, I reminded myself.

My eyes quickly scanned the rest of the scene before me. A girl, noble by the look of her finely sewn silk dress, lay at the base of a tree. Lying on the ground around her were three dead armored guards and an unarmed young man. The young man had medium length white hair and wore grey robes, he was alive, his back rising and falling as he breathed slow and steady, but blood pooled around him. He wouldn't be alive for long if someone didn't help him.

At the woman's feet, between her and the drake, stood an Astral Wolf. It's back stood nearly five feet tall, large swaths of white and blue hair shifting in the breeze. It was lowered into a defensive stance in front of its ward. I quickly went over what I knew about Astral Wolves.

Astral Wolves are not easily trained and can be vicious attackers. However, since the last Vielkrea (Great war between Order and Chaos), nobles have been imprinting pups to their children, creating an unbreakable bond between the pair. Full-

53

grown wolves can reach six feet tall, often being used as mounts when they reach adulthood. Their lifespans are estimated to range from eighty all the way to two hundred years in rare cases.

This one would be only twenty, maybe twenty-five years old based on the size. Which was troubling, because if any of the old legends were true it would be no match for even a baby drake, which I guessed this Chaos monster was based on the size. Well *Spark* or no *Spark*, I'll do what needs to be done.

My eyes ran over the bodies of the four fallen guards, they wouldn't have had the *Spark,* more likely trained in combat with proxy levels and based on the runes that glowed on their weapons and armor they would be a match for most average level adventurers. How would I be able to help if all of these trained fighters with magical gear had failed?

No. Push those thoughts aside, I admonished myself. *Think, act, use your head.*

For whatever reason the drake seemed unconcerned with all three of us, the girl, her pet, and me. It was possible it had dispatched everything it considered a threat and would allow us to leave. It was a theory worth testing.

I held my bow up, an arrow already strung and ready to be drawn and loosed if necessary. Did I really think that my iron tipped arrows stood a chance against the drake's scales? Well, no, but I could always get lucky and pierce an eye. The thought wasn't comforting as I steadily moved towards the Astral Wolf and the downed girl.

Her eyes were milky white and moved erratically. She held a hand against her leg, blood spewing all around her hand from a vicious gash. Moving closer I saw that the wolf had also sustained several injuries.

There was something slimy on her face and she didn't seem to be able to see me, but she must have heard me coming. "Protect me, Vash!" The girl's hand rose towards the Astral Wolf, and it immediately turned its attention towards me, shifting its weight as if ready to pounce. "Anaru es tuc va el!" The girl's words came out as a whisper but there was power behind them that stirred the air.

She was a caster! I'd been around enough mana users to feel the shift of power. I didn't, however, recognize the words of power she had used, but the context was clear when I next looked at her. A sphere of iridescent power had formed around her, some type of shielding spell.

I frowned, glancing at the drake and back to the Astral Wolf, neither had moved to attack yet. "I come in peace. I'm trying to help." I lowered my bow to add weight to my words.

Uncertainty played across the girl's face, but she reached out a hand towards her companion and said, "Hold." It came out in a huff of air, and she grimaced, either under the weight of the spell she'd erected or from pain, I couldn't tell, but the result was the same. The spell faltered and faded. The casting of the spell and her weakened condition became too much, and she went limp, slipping back against the tree.

A low growl pulled my attention away from the noble girl. The drake had finished its meal and was eying the pair of us.

I wouldn't be able to pick up the girl and run now. The wolf must have had a similar thought, because it let out a fierce growl, its back crouching low before opening its mouth. A beam of rippling blue energy spewed forth, smashing towards the advancing drake.

The beam of energy met a gout of fire, and my vision went white from the heat of it all. Moments later as my vision began to clear, I watched as the drake stepped through a cloud of dust.

Ribbons of black smoke spilled from both sides of the

drake's mouth. Even from thirty feet away I could see the damage done, and it wasn't much. The uniform sea of black scales was disturbed in one place, a fist-sized area showed pink flesh. Maybe the Astral Wolf wasn't as outclassed as I had originally thought.

As I stood watching the two beasts square off, I couldn't help but feel insignificant against their terrible power. The drake lunged forward directly at the Astral Wolf. The large white and blue wolf held its ground, its maw ready to clamp down on the draconic aggressor.

I had three arrows left that hadn't been damaged beyond use, but now wasn't the time to use them. Moving to the passed-out woman, I pulled out a bandage strip from my satchel and quickly covered the wound. The blood drenched the bandages within seconds, and I realized my mistake. Standing quickly, I untied my belt and drew it tight around her leg just above the wound.

The tree just above us exploded in a shattering spray of wood and splinters. I barely had a chance to look up when I saw the drake open its maw and a stream of brilliant red-white flame spewed forth. I could feel a power gathering in my body, and I latched hold of it. Time appeared to slow, and I threw myself atop the injured woman to protect her from the blast. My vision went white, and pain lanced through my body as I was engulfed in flame.

I repeated my father's words in my head for inspiration.

I'll protect the weak, be a shield against the darkness, when I am needed, I will answer the call.

I had no room for any other thoughts, instead I pictured him in his rune scribed glowing armor and wielding his powerful sword. He never feared death, I never saw him afraid.

But I was afraid right now. Doubt flitted through my mind and as it did, I felt the pain of the flames increase.

Of course, he didn't fear, he was *Sparked* and one of the most powerful adventurers in all of the Wyrd. The flames around us stopped and I was surprised that somehow, I was still alive.

I looked to my arms, expecting to see burnt and mangled flesh. Instead, my arms, now bare, let off a steady stream of smoke, but otherwise were unharmed. I realized, as I stood and my clothing fell in a tattered burnt heap at my feet, that the fire had only burnt away my clothing on my back. The woman in front of me and the section of tree directly behind her was also somehow unharmed by the all-consuming flames.

A growl erupted behind me, and I watched as a white blur soared over the pair of us and sunk its teeth into the drake.

The Astral Wolf was more bloody wounds than it was white and blue anymore, but still it fought on with a fierceness that left me breathless. Like a mother bear protecting its cubs it clawed, bit, and did all it could to keep the drake from getting any closer to the woman.

The feeling that burned deep in my chest pulsed and I knew what had happened. I had read so many first-hand accounts of *Sparked* that there was no doubt in my mind anymore.

I was *Sparked*.

There was an intuitive feeling behind it all, but I knew that being a *Sparked* who hadn't been *Awoken* yet I had access to a dangerous and wild magic. It wasn't until the Prime Mana Shrines tempered the magic and gave it order that levels and spells became a reality.

Despite the chaos around me I shut my eyes. I could hear the battle of the two powerful monsters less than ten feet away, but I pushed it away and reached down deep into myself. I searched, pulled, connected until I found what I was looking for.

The power wasn't really something you could grasp hold of, but I did my best to impart my desire into it. The magic was a part of me and answered my call.

My eyes snapped open just as the Astral Wolf took a nasty bite to its neck and fell still. The drake flung its opponent aside and lifted its narrow slits. The terrible gaze promised death, but I would make it break that promise.

Keeping my eyes locked on the drake, I knelt and retrieved my bow and a single arrow that survived the inferno. The drake didn't move, it just watched me, waiting to see what I'd do. As I pulled back my bow string and aimed at one of the many small wounds the Astral Wolf had inflicted, I realized something. The drake did not fear me.

Big mistake.

My arrow loosed and I urged a portion of the power pulsing inside of me to go with it. Mid-flight the arrow ignited, blue energy crackling down the length like lightning. I grinned, the intoxicating rush of power inside me making me feel as if I'd already won this battle.

But to my surprise and utter astonishment the drake opened its maw and chomped down on the speeding missile. Shit. I was in over my head.

The drake made a coughing noise that sounded eerily like a laugh and began to walk towards me, smoke starting to trickle from its maw once more.

Fire erupted from its mouth, spiraling towards me. I held my hands outstretched in front of me willing the power to protect me. It answered my call, a luminescent blue wall of energy sprung between the drake's attack and my naked body.

As fire met the wild blue magic, I had the oddest sense that my power wasn't growing weaker from use but stronger. There was a vast store of power inside me, it came as a trickle at first, but as whatever was holding it back completely broke away, a new surge of magic filled me.

The night was dark as the fire stopped, burning black barked trees lit our surroundings, but I stood out like a sun in the darkness.

I let off an intense blue mist that hung just a hair's width above my skin. It was impossible to describe the ecstasy and joy I felt. Not only was I a *Sparked*, but I'd never read anything about this kind of fierce wild magic from a newly *Sparked*.

As the dust and smoke cleared, a wind having picked up in the clearing beside the road, I caught sight of the drake. It wasn't doing that hissing laugh anymore, instead, if I didn't know any better, I would say it looked confused. The large spiked draconic head tilted to the left and it suddenly reminded me of a dog, confused by the actions of its master.

It was time to end this threat. I had no way of knowing how long this power would burn inside of me or what my limits were yet, so I needed to act. Pulling free my dagger from my boot, I willed my newfound power into it and the blade began to glow.

The drake's mouth once more began to smoke, but I wasn't going to give it a chance to spew fire at me again. I sprinted forward and to my surprise in only a matter of moments, I was in front of the drake, it appeared to be moving in slow motion as its jaw opened and red fire slowly began to leak out.

I slammed my dagger in between two damaged scales, forcing the drake's head upward, the flames shot into the sky creating a bright beacon of light. The power that pulsed and crackled within me had made me stronger, faster, but the drake wasn't a legendary Chaos monster for nothing. Its head came down hard and I was thrown to the ground.

Before I could push the stars from my vision, a heavy sharp taloned foot slammed onto my chest. Whatever the magic was that burned inside of me, it flared to life keeping me alive, but the pain was terrible.

The blow evacuated all the air from my lungs, and I gasped and squirmed trying to fill them. I needed to formulate a plan and attack, but I could barely keep a thought together before the pain increased as the drake tried to crush the life from me.

Then I heard a string of words that I couldn't quite understand. A spell chant. "Ahk mor dun, el tram oh gor!" Golden light in the shape of a brilliant spear smashed into the drake, pushing it back several feet. My naked form spun from the sudden crushing and raking of the drake's claws as it was pushed backwards.

At some point, the magic shielding me must have failed, because blood trickled down my chest and three large gashes lay open and bleeding. The drake looked injured now, the golden lance having hit a spot where the scales had been removed by the Astral Wolf. I didn't wait to look behind me and see if whoever had aided me was still in the fight. I needed to take advantage of the drake's weakened state before it burned me alive.

As I ran, the power inside of me answered my call. I moved with a terrible speed; my dagger held aloft ready to strike. Aiming for the bloody charred flesh that the light lance had hit, I stabbed with as much power and force as I could.

My momentum sent me crashing into the drake, but I was able to hit my target. Pain erupted as it closed its maw around my shoulder. The magic wasn't strong enough to stop the powerful teeth from cutting into me. Bones crunched and I knew pain beyond any that I had previously felt.

A wildness took over and I stabbed and stabbed and stabbed. At one point I vaguely remember my dagger breaking against the scales of the drake as my wild attacks missed their target, but I kept stabbing. The broken blade and my hand piercing deeper and deeper into the drake until the grip of its jaw slackened.

But the terrible wildness continued, and I stabbed and stabbed until the edges of my vision went black and I passed out from exhaustion, pain, and blood loss.

CHAPTER 7
JUST A BABY

I slipped in and out of consciousness, voices sounding around me as I drifted through fever dreams and reality.

"Are you sure you are alright, m'lady?" A gruff voice somewhere in the dark spoke.

"Yes, I assure you that I am quite well." It was a female voice, sweet and gentle. I felt a hand caress my forehead. "If not for this one, Vash, Zander, and I would be dead. Though, how Zander survived so long after having his entrails spilled out on the forest floor I couldn't say."

"This weakling has no level, no class," the gruff voice again. "How could he have helped, when three of my strongest guards fell to the beast. And how did it get the better of you m'lady, you were a match for the three guards I sent with you."

"Remember whom you speak with, Galt." There was reprimand in her voice. "Forgive me, I am worn thin. You misunderstand the situation. That baby drake was not what dispatched us, though it was likely a match for my power. No. It was a full-grown monster of Chaos. It left its baby behind to finish us off and feed while it slipped through a portal of darkness. It was unlike any portal I've witnessed; it was as if time and space were ripped asunder so that it could pass between."

"I knew I should have gone with you! You faced off against an adult creature of Chaos? How is that possible, that shouldn't be..." The gruff man's voice cut off as pain lanced through my shoulder and I cried out.

A hand stroked my forehead once more. "There, there," the sweet female voice said. "I've stabilized you, but healers more adept than I, will tend your wounds soon enough."

I couldn't answer, a wave of heat thrummed over me, and I went still once more, the pain easing noticeably.

Consciousness lost all substance, and my fever dreams took full hold of my mind. I saw the great Chaos dragons floating in the black void, among the stars. From their mouth power flowed, filling the gaps between giant balls of rock and water, making pathways. My vision shifted and the dragons were gone, in their place were great metallic warriors. They held a variety of grand devices and with those, they shaped planets. Cutting from the chaotic rubble of space, places of life and order.

A voice pierced through the darkness, and I woke up. "That should do it. He has a very strong core, healing him— even with such extensive damage—was a simple task." My eyes flickered open, and I saw a female elf, tall, slender, and strikingly beautiful, standing above me. "How are you feeling, young hero?"

My attempt to speak was blocked by a throat dryer than the Eastern Kingdoms. Without having to signal to the healer she understood, handing me a glass of cool water from a bedside table.

The room was brightly lit by a large fireplace burning opposite of where I lay. Extravagantly decorated tapestries depicting famous battles of the past hung on the walls. I recognized a few, but one in particular, stood out. It was a deep maroon color with golden thread depicting the Ordu walking among the races of the Wyrd and fighting at the head of our combined armies against the might of the black dragons. The battle of Order and Chaos, or Vielkrea as it came to be known.

After completely draining the cup of water I was given, I set it aside. "I feel like I wrestled a dire bear."

"I think it was a drake," the elf quipped, not missing a beat.

I smiled and sat up in the bed, groaning as I stretched the stiffness out of my back. "It's all coming back to me. Did I win?" I asked, running my hand through my hair and out of my face.

"You did indeed," she said, patting me on the shoulder. "It gave as good as it got, I imagine." She gestured to my chest. Looking down I saw what she meant.

My hand ran over my left shoulder and chest, jagged thick scars ran like a spider's web covering the majority of my left side. I moved my left arm, testing my mobility and was disappointed with the results.

"It'll be stiff for the first few days, but I have an ointment that should help loosen the skin up, but it'll never be as perfect as it was before the scarring. One of the risks of the trade. My name is Elandel, I serve in the Variyn house as their head physician."

"Nice to meet you Elandel," I said, nodding my head to her. "My name is Caldor. Caldor Miles."

"Miles?" She repeated the name letting it draw out as if she was tasting it. "Any relation to Elkor Miles, the famous knight who defeated the Lich of Lynsteen?" Her tone suggested she was just joking, but I was surprised that she knew my father's last name.

"That was my father," I said, Elandel had turned her head away, but it snapped back, and she gave me a questioning look. Her eyes bore into me, and a look of recognition crossed her face.

"By the old gods and the Ordu, you surely are, aren't you? I knew your father in his early days. We used to run dungeon dives together in our youth. I'm sorry for your loss, but I'm proud to meet you. You are just like him, risking your life in one impossible way or another. Not even *Awoken* yet and risking life and limb to save someone you couldn't possibly know."

My cheeks grew hot, I didn't know what to say to her words. "Thanks," I finally settled on, but the words didn't feel like enough. I wanted to ask her what my father had been like when he had first *Awoken* or why she stopped running dungeons with him, but just then someone entered the room.

"My daughter's hero has recovered?" The voice rung deep and vibrated with power. Whomever this man was, he had the same raw power that I used to feel from my father, one of the highest-level adventurers in the land.

"Yes, Lord Variyn," Elandel said, bowing her head. She approached the man and whispered several words in his ear that I couldn't hear. He nodded his head and dismissed her, she left without another word.

The man had a thin silver crown atop his neatly combed salt and pepper colored hair. A short, cropped beard covered his lower face and purple eyes pierced through me. He was dressed in white and golden thread hemmed robes, with a fur-lined cloak resting on his shoulders. At his waist hung a golden ornate scepter. I knew the face, though I'd only ever seen him once before in person, his likeness adorned the gold coins in this part of the kingdom. It was Lord Variyn, he ruled over one of the smaller kingdoms inside of a cluster of kingdoms known as the nation of Newaliyn and was said to be the greatest healer of his generation.

I absently wondered why he hadn't healed me if he was as great as everyone claimed. Perhaps my arm wouldn't still be so scarred if I'd warranted his care and not his servants.

"Tell me." Lord Variyn came to stand next to the bed. "How is it that you found yourself in Shadowcrest Forest and in a position to save my daughter and nephew?"

My butt-cheeks clenched as I tried to come up with a suitable lie. When nothing came to mind, I told the truth.

"I was tracking a boar," I said. "I followed its trail for several days and found myself outside a dungeon before I was able to catch it."

"And you were able to kill this boar?" Lord Variyn asked, his face showing no signs of his thoughts.

"Yes, barely," I said, then remembering the meat I'd left behind I sat up straighter. "I left a large amount of meat behind, I was going to sell it and feed my family. If I leave now, I might be able to still retrieve some of it."

"Your goods were found," he said, putting a hand on my shoulder and lightly pushing me back down. "We did an extensive search to be sure all traces of the Chaos abominations had been collected. In doing so, we found boar meat, tainted by Chaos. If that meat you collected had been given to the general populace, the results would have been disastrous. We also retrieved a broken bow, a shattered dagger, and half burnt clothing, but they were disposed of, and suitable replacements will be provided, if we can come to an understanding."

I scrunched my brow in confusion. "What understanding?" I asked, sitting up a little straighter in the bed. Though I knew I didn't stand a chance against this high-level healer and Lord, there was something innately threatening in his manner now, and I'd fight my way out of this bed if it came to it.

"Settle down," Lord Variyn said, shifting his weight into a more neutral stance. "I am merely about to suggest a mutually beneficial arrangement. You see, Caldor." He turned to the door, his hands moving up and twisting about, a soft white arcane circle appeared on the far door before sizzling out. "That should provide us a measure of privacy. As I was saying."

My eyes strained to see the symbols that had appeared on the door, but they dissipated too quickly. "What spell was that?" I asked, unable to help myself.

Lord Variyn's mouth turned up into a smile and he chuckled. "We will have plenty of time to discuss spells and such, for now you must listen to me." The insistence in his voice caught me off guard and I met his eyes, ready to listen.

"That's better," he said, taking a deep breath. "As I was saying, I have a mutually beneficial arrangement for the both of us. You see, hunting within the Shadowcrest forest is punishable by loss of property, imprisonment, or perhaps even death. And though I try to be a benevolent ruler, it is the rule of law that has kept our borders intact for these many years. But I have a solution!"

Lord Variyn's emotions were impossible to guess, but mine were plainly displayed on my face. I couldn't believe that he would consider punishing me after I helped his daughter. My mind raced, guessing one thing or another but each supposed solution I imagined was sillier than the last.

"You will be appointed a House Variyn position, which grants you full hunting rights, among other things. That will take care of our little issue of unlawful entry into House Variyn lands."

Of the dozen or so solutions I'd imagined, this was not one of them. My jaw went slack as I stared up at him. He smiled again, a friendly warmth radiating from him.

"I hate to ask a favor from someone who has already put himself in great peril for my own blood, but I'm afraid I must." Lord Variyn's visage shifted, and he appeared almost sad to have to ask anything of me.

"I will do what needs to be done. How may I serve?" I asked, still stunned at the direction of the conversation.

"Tomorrow we are having a small celebration in honor of the team that I assembled to eliminate the Chaos monster's incursion into my lands. As far as anyone need know, you were an original member of this party. A powerful *Sparked* who had learned to harness the sleeping magic within him."

Several questions raced through my mind, but I settled on the simplest. "Why?" I asked, not waiting for an answer I continued, my mouth unable to keep itself shut. "That doesn't make any sense. If you knew there were Chaos monsters in your lands, why would you send someone who hasn't even *Awoken* yet? Will anyone believe that."

"I worried about that myself, but was willing to take the risk, however Elandel has put that worry to rest. Son of Elkor, the Slayer of Chaos. I had no idea Elkor had a son, but if you have even a thread of the power your father displayed then not a single soul will doubt that I'd send you, *Awoken* or not, against a Chaos beast."

My mind raced and several emotions flitted over my face as I considered Lord Variyn's words. He was willing to make me a member of his house, which I think meant I'd be considered nobility or at least noble adjacent. All this for helping his daughter, surely, I could go along with a small white lie. None of my father's words or proverbs gave me clear direction in this decision.

Sure, I knew that he'd insist that he did not want or need a position in a noble house, but when the alternative was being put up on charges, I really didn't see any other option. My decision was made, and I smiled up at the kind, purple eyes of Lord Variyn, nodding my head.

"I will do as you said," I answered, then biting my lip added. "But if it isn't asking too much, I have a few conditions."

Lord Variyn's face gave no sign of his thoughts. "I'm listening," he said.

"Any wages entitled to the position should be sent to my mother. I want to be able to *Awaken* and be given basic gear and weapons. Oh, and unlimited access to your library!" I lifted my finger as I spoke about the library, having nearly forgot to ask about it.

Lord Variyn laughed. I wasn't sure what I had said that was so funny, but I felt my face grow hot.

"All you have asked for and more will be granted to you, young one. Hear me out and you will find that there are many more benefits to be had."

He gave in too quickly; I should have asked for more. I squished the greedy thought down and focused on Lord Variyn's words.

"You will be named a Knight, a Protector of the Realm. Some might scoff at a title given to someone who has yet to *Awaken*, but if what my daughter has told me about the intensity of the power you wield has any truth to it, they will accept you. I will have to let it slip to the various councils, and lords of the guilds, that you are the son of a previous Protector of the

Realm. The very one that slew the Lich of Lynsteen, that accursed Chaos bringer."

I hadn't known that my father was a knight, but it made sense now that I thought about it. He was often called to important meetings with nobility and even royalty on occasion, to deal with one monster or another. I shook my head; my father had kept his adventuring life such a mystery. But he was the best of fathers, when he was home, he was one hundred percent with you. It was a rare occasion that I could get him to tell me a story of his adventures, usually it was his party members singing his praise and him trying to downplay his part.

"Beyond the title of Knight, Protector of the Realm, I will also appoint you as a personal vassal to House Variyn. It will require that you swear fealty to me and in turn be granted several acres of land to do with as you please. There is a keep that sits at the most eastern edge of my domain. Its name is Blackridge Keep and the prior vassal given Lordship over it failed to protect it. I'm afraid it'll be a bit of work to wrest it free from the unsavory types who've taken residence. I would also add that you would be wise to gather a group of fellow adventurers before attempting to retake your keep, as well as employing guards who can gain proxy levels beneath you. In return, you will come to all required meetings, celebrations, and once you've reached sufficient strength you will need to serve a small period of time every five years on the front lines. We manage to keep most border assaults from our neighboring Lords to a minimum, but it is the way of Newaliyn that we should fight with our brothers."

My jaw hit the floor. What was happening? I must be dreaming, why would Lord Variyn be giving me a keep and a title? Having most likely watched my jaw drop to the floor, Lord Variyn spoke up again.

"These are troubled times," he said, his gaze shifting to the window and out to the horizon of his domain. "I have held these lands together since King Newaliyn granted them to my great grandfather, but times are changing and I need to change with them. This isn't the first Chaos monster to find its way into our lands and it won't be the last. If you are half as powerful as your father was, then I'll need adventurers like you fighting for me. Do you accept my offer?"

"Yes." I spoke without a second thought. With land of my own, and a steady influx of gold coming in, my mother and siblings would be set for life.

Lord Variyn's smiled down at me. "Welcome to my House, Caldor Miles. You have a great potential, do not let it go to waste."

A thought occurred to me. "Can you send word to my mother that I'm okay?"

"What's her name and where can I find her?"

"Emilia Miles and we live in an orchard farm outside Cree-shaw," I paused, considering. "Don't tell her that I've received my *Spark* or any of the matters we've discussed, not yet. Also, if it isn't too much trouble, she suffers from a mind sickness, and we haven't been able to afford her tonic for some time."

"Mind sickness? I will dispatch someone immediately. I have a Priest in my employ who's chosen profession is alchemy. He is very skilled and will do what he can for your mother, and I will see that she is informed of your good health and nothing more. Rest easy and in the morning, you will join a celebration in honor of those who slew the Chaos monster."

Sleep came easy that night and I drifted off with a smile on my lips.

CHAPTER 8
A NEW DAY

I awoke to sunlight in my face, the morning rays filtering through sheer curtains hanging loose over the window. For several long moments I was lost in the haze of waking and grasped wildly around for my dagger. But, as with all mornings, my mind cleared and memory of the nightmarish dreams that plagued my sleep faded.

I had unlocked my *Spark* and been given a keep! I suddenly found myself unable to stop smiling. Leaping from the bed I hooted loudly and pumped my fists in the air. An achy tightness was present in my left shoulder, but it didn't matter. Wound or no wound, I was a freaking *Sparked* now!

Like my father before me I would *Awaken* and become a mighty Arcane Knight and hero of the people. Watch out Chaos, here I come!

What little clothing that hadn't been burnt off my body, was missing. No one had seen fit to dress me while I slept. As I stood in front of the window looking out into the rolling green hills in the distance and the sprawling city just outside the keep walls, the sound of the door opening startled me.

I grasped for the bedsheet but was too slow. A burly guard dressed in a neatly pressed uniform, shiny breastplate, and helmet, with the emblem of house Variyn, a black star on a field of white with an ivory skull at the center of the star, stood half in the room, a grin on his face.

"Didn't mean to catch a glimpse of yer serpent, young lord," he said tipping his helmet in my direction. "The Lady Alayna means to come fetch you within the hour and take you down to the celebration. There's water in the basin if you wish to freshen up and Miss Elandel informed me that she left you clothing to wear in the chest at the foot of your bed, move swiftly Chaos Slayer."

Before I had a chance to respond he slipped out of the room. He must be keeping guard, I wondered if that was meant to keep me inside or keep others out. And what had he called me, *Chaos Slayer?* What had that been all about? A gentle breeze from the window reminded me that I was still completely naked and in need of dressing.

Moving to stand in front of the chest, I admired the craftsmanship. It was made of a beautiful brown wood and polished to a lacquered shine. Reaching down I flipped the top up and laid out the contents on the bed.

My chest tightened as I examined the black silk shirt. On the breast of the garment, over the heart, was a symbol I'd seen hundreds of times embroidered in a brilliant blue thread. A double circle of equal thickness with the Evoker's flame swirling around a knight's blade, a simple long sword tapered to a point on one end. My father told me that it was the symbol of an Arcane Knight, the protectors of Order.

I'd read no book or heard any mention of the truth of his words, but I knew the sign of the evoker branch of magic was a flame and I'd read about the symbols of both Order and Chaos.

I dressed without thinking after that, a hollowness pressing into my chest.

The entire outfit was a mix of deep blue cotton, black silk, and dark brown dyed leather all with touches of golden thread on the seams and edges. As a final touch they'd even provided white gloves that, somehow, fit perfectly and had the symbol of Order on one hand and the symbol of Chaos, a double ring broken by five cracks moving out from the center, on the other. This entire outfit, down to the golden belt buckle was what my father wore to formal occasions.

The last time I saw him wear a similar outfit was when the Kings of Newaliyn, Lynsteen and Eldah'ren had called a meeting of the strongest beings on the continent of Wyrd. Any *Sparked* who had reached level fifty or higher had been requested to attend. I remember my father explaining that the Prime Mana Shrine in Variyn had given him a quest that required he attend, and my father would sooner cease existing than reject a quest given from the Ordu.

A soft knock on the door drew my attention. Reaching down, I grabbed the last item on the bed and fastened it to my belt. An elegant arming sword, the blade nearly thirty inches long, with small arcane runes carved into the fuller. On the cross-guard, directly in the center, was the emblem of House Variyn. Clicking the blade in place, I examined where the cross-guard met the chape, the polished golden metal at the mouth of the scabbard and realized there was a small button release on the edge.

What an ingenious way to get a sword stuck in a scabbard, I thought as I tested it several times to ensure I could in fact get the blade free if I wanted. It worked fine, releasing with a barely audible click each time I applied firm pressure.

Having dressed and armed myself with the weapon they'd

provided me, I stood tall in front of the window—letting the rays of the morning sunlight warm my face. "Come in," I said in my deepest and manliest voice. I felt silly a moment after doing it, but it couldn't be helped.

A beautiful young woman, and she was younger than I had once believed, entered the room. She couldn't be older than her mid-twenties, her rosy-red cheeks, wavy blonde hair, and kind smile captured my attention faster than Arcanum's Study of Magical Theory and its effect on monster evolution, my favorite book.

She had a portion of her hair tied atop her head, and vibrant purple eye makeup highlighted her brilliant violet irises. Her dress was black and modern, cut just under the clavicle, but not so low that it exposed any part of her bosom. Her family's crest was embroidered into the dress, a shield of white behind a black star and a white skull, with one minor change. A golden crown sat atop the skull, what it signified I honestly wasn't sure.

I'd been to the city Variyn a few dozen times in my life, but all my studying had related to matters of magic and monsters. Not once had I picked up a book on family crests and their variations.

"You clean up nicely, Chaos Slayer," the woman who must be Alayna Variyn, daughter of Lord Variyn said. "My name is Alayna Variyn, the half dead girl you saved yesterday."

I grinned stupidly, my eyes wandered up and down her form. "Nice to meet you Alayna, my name is Caldor Miles. You are here to take me to a celebration?" I asked, grinning stupidly all the while.

Alayna caught my eyes and grinned back. "I am!" She exclaimed. "But first we should do something with your hair. It looks like you just awoke."

I laughed nervously. "I did just wake up," I said. Why had I said that she didn't need to know that? My cheeks burned red, and I found myself wishing I'd read books on how to talk to beautiful women. It wasn't like I hadn't found time to spend with women. Ismene and I had dated years back after my father passed, and I'd been with one or two women since, but none of them as strikingly beautiful or powerful as Alayna.

I stood with a stupid grin on my face while the daughter of Lord Variyn, the heir to the seat of power in a domain of thousands, wet her hands in the water basin and attempted to tame my hair.

I had no way of knowing what level she had achieved, but I could feel power thrumming off her in waves. Her gentle touch on my forehead brought back the memories of the conversation she'd had with the one she'd called Galt.

"Did you really fight off an adult Chaos monster, forcing it to retreat?" I asked, my admiration and respect for her building with each passing moment.

"Hah," she said, her purple eyes meeting mine and her smile disappeared. "It reflected everything I sent at it and hit us with a single attack, killing my three guards while my cousin hid behind them, even so, he barely survived. If it hadn't been for my protection spell and my bond with Vash, I'd have died just as quick. That *thing* was an abomination. And it left its child to feed on what was left of us. If you hadn't showed up when you did, there is no doubt in my mind that I'd be dead." She held my gaze, her purple eyes searching for something in mine, before scrunching her brow and declaring my hair fixed.

"Without your light lance attack, I wouldn't have killed it," I said, checking my hair in the mirror. My wavy brown curls were swept to one side, most of the tangles tamed. "I'm not even sure how I did any of that. I've read so many books on

Sparked, but I've never come across any passage that talk about harnessing wild magic before an *Awakening* and directing it to shield or lashing out offensively." My words grew more and more excited as I talked.

She stopped just inside the door and regarded me. "I don't know either, but I can tell you what I saw. You were moving your aura around, somehow directly shifting it without any spells or abilities. And for someone who hasn't *Awoken* and been given a class, I have to say, you have a silly amount of raw power. I can see it now, shifting around you like an invisible cloud of smoke." Her eyes unfocused as she looked me up and down. I knew enough that she must be using an *Awakened* ability or spell to detect my aura.

I squirmed under her gaze before coughing to get her attention. "If you're done ogling me, we should probably leave. I don't want to be late for whatever Lord Variyn has planned."

"We have time," she said, turning to the door and swinging it wide. "It will take a while to walk to the main gathering hall. Follow me!" Her dress swished as she glided out the door and into the hall.

CHAPTER 9
BIG SECRETS IN A BIG KEEP

"So, is it true? You're the son of the mighty Elkor, the famous Arcane Knight?" Alayna asked, as we walked side by side in the large stone keep. Every hallway had at least one guard and torches adding to the light that streamed in from the narrow-slit windows.

"Yes," I said, proud that my father's memory lived strong among the people here in Variyn. In my hometown people rarely spoke of him, so busy with the everyday tasks of their mundane lives. Even the adventurers that commonly passed through Creeshaw were almost all lower level and only seemed interested in talking about their latest monster kill or magical loot that dropped from the nearby dungeon.

"What was he like?" Alayna asked. She looked over while asking and I caught her gaze. For a moment we paused while staring deep into each other's eyes. The purple depths of color were pools that I could easily get lost in.

"What was who like?" I asked, realizing that I'd gotten lost in her gaze.

She giggled, a cute sound.

"Your father, silly, what was he like? It must have been exciting having one of the most powerful adventurers as a father!"

"Well, honestly?" I asked, she nodded. "He was the best man I knew. When he was home, he was just my father. Sure, I was able to get a few tales of his adventures out of him and he lectured me on the importance of doing what was right when the opportunity arose, but all of that was second to just having him there as my father."

"Oh, right. That makes sense," she said, offering me an apologetic smile. "I still can't believe I didn't know Elkor had a family, I mean why wouldn't he, but it just isn't something the bards sing about when they tell his tales."

"People sing about my father?" I asked, that was news I hadn't heard before. We got a few entertainers traveling to Creeshaw and with my busy schedule I hadn't really been able to attend any of the nights when they performed.

"You haven't heard the saga of the Arcane Knight? It tells of some of the most epic fights your father fought in. How he slew the Elite Adult Owlbear in High Mountain, or that time he slew the Shadow Serpent on the coast of the Elven city, Calenrah, and rescued a half dozen griffon eggs from its grasp. No? Oh wow, well I'm sure you got first-hand accounts, that must have been just as exciting."

I hadn't heard of either of those battles. The majority of the stories my father shared were about the quests that he'd accomplished, purifying the water source for a group of forest elves, helping a group of beastkin to recover a sacred artifact of their people. But nothing about slaying serpents or owlbears.

"He told me so many stories, it's hard to recall any singular one," I lied, for some reason I didn't want to share that my father had apparently been sheltering the more exciting parts of his adventures from us.

"How exciting!" Alayna said, she wasn't at all what I expected a Lord's daughter to be like, very relaxed and not at all stuck up like the princesses in the few fiction stories I'd read.

"Tell me about yourself, how long have you had your class unlocked?" I asked to change the subject.

If it were possible, she seemed to perk up even more. "Like most nobility I had my *Spark* unlocked just after my sixteenth birthday, right before the monthly *Awakening* Ceremony."

I'd read somewhere about that, a footnote about prime mana shrines, they were most powerful at a certain time each month, enabling *Sparked* to start their *Awakening* trials. What had she meant by having her *Spark* unlocked? She spoke of it like it was something you could just go do, I decided to ask her.

"You had your *Spark* unlocked?" I asked, trying to catch her eye as we walked.

She blanched, her face going white. "Oh, what I meant was I uhm." She looked behind us, a pair of guards followed, but not close enough that they would be able to overhear us. She moved closer, looping her arm so that we walked linked together. Her touch was warm, and I found myself wanting to pull her closer.

"I am horrible at keeping secrets," she whispered to me, guiding me down a turn. "But father says you are being given a House title, so you'll be privy to this knowledge anyways. I don't want to go into details here out in the open, but unlocking a *Spark* is something that doesn't happen naturally for everyone. We can't all have auras the size of a small sun." She smiled at that, falling into a fit of nervous giggles.

I stopped dead in my tracks, pulling her to a stop next to me. Was she truly saying what I thought she was? All this time

I'd assumed that being *Sparked* was a matter of luck or chance, but the nobles knew of a way to guarantee they became *Sparked*. While the rest of the world had to deal with the reality that one in a hundred would show signs of being *Sparked*, the noble houses just followed some secret recipe. What in the actual hell?

My emotions flitted from rage, to confusion, to wonder, before settling into acceptance. That is fine, I reassured myself. I may be getting a House title and not need the secrets of their *Awakening*, but I was going to find out what it was, and everyone would learn of it. I would make sure of that.

"Are you okay, Caldor?" Alayna asked, her hand coming up to my cheek, turning my face to meet hers. "I'm sorry if I said something to upset you. Let's hurry, we're almost there." She pushed me along in silence, my mind wandering aimlessly, thinking about what other secrets the nobles could be hiding.

CHAPTER 10
GIFTS

Massive oak doors banded with polished gold colored metal swung open as we approached. Inside was a sea of people, more than I'd ever seen packed into a single place. Alayna had mentioned that we'd be dining and celebrating inside a banquet hall with a few of her father's closest friends. Her father must have a different definition of close friends than me because this was ridiculous.

Alayna appeared to be surprised as well, leaning over, and whispering in my ear. "It appears plans have changed, and he invited half the kingdom." She let out a quiet giggle and I couldn't help but smile.

It was hard to stay mad at someone so kind and sweet. After all, she hadn't been keeping any secrets from me, in fact, she was the only reason I knew about nobles cheating the people out of being *Sparked*. I could save my contempt for other nobles; she didn't deserve it.

The banquet hall turned out to be a massive room supported by stone columns that stretched a hundred feet up to a domed ceiling. Intricate carvings covered every visible surface, from commonly used Ordu imagery, large beings with simple flat features, to overly detailed depictions of dragons, drakes, wurms, and other common Chaos monsters.

Every wall was adorned with more banners depicting famous battles, deadly monsters being defeated by heroic adventurers, and even a few showing images from one of the local dungeons; a fact I only knew because it had a team of adventurers squaring off against a Displacer Cat and the only ones said to exist are the ones found in dungeons, or at least I had read as much in a book.

Alayna cleared her throat, getting my attention. I looked in her direction, she nodded her head towards a plump man in black dress clothing and white undershirt, some kind of butler or servant.

He was looking at me expectantly. I blinked at him.

The plump man let out an exaggerated sigh before saying. "I asked for you to please provide me with a name so I might announce you and Lady Variyn." His voice was stuffy, as if someone was pinching his nose and forcing him to talk.

I took a deep breath and said, "I'm Caldor Miles, son of Elkor Miles, the Arcane Knight who fought against the Lich of Lynsteen and fell in battle to save the Wyrd."

The stuffy man turned and walked a little way off, announcing me to the room.

"I introduce to my Lord and Lady of House Variyn, Caldor Miles, son of Elkor Miles, the Arcane Knight, accompanied by the Defender of Light, Lady Alayna Variyn, heir to the throne of Variyn."

He left out the rest of my pronouncement and it made me angry for some reason. A gentle jab into my ribs brought my attention back to Alayna, she leaned in towards me, looking up.

"You know," She whispered, "you don't need to be so serious. Take a deep breath and relax a bit, the day is just beginning."

I smiled and whispered back, "Thank you, I'll try."

Alayna straightened and dragged me towards a high table set into the back wall. The room had several long tables, food had been spread out on almost all of them, but no one was sitting or eating, except for Lord Variyn and his wife, Lady Variyn.

We walked through a sea of colors. Dresses of purple, pinks, deep reds, and soft blues. The men wore darker more muted colors, but the combination of the female attire and the male attire created a pleasant variety of shades.

Nearly all the men wore styles I wasn't familiar with, Creeshaw being one of the smaller towns, we rarely saw many styles outside of the practical—unless you counted the adventurers like Emory who wore a mismatch of colored armor from dungeon drops.

The most popular styles among the men consisted of long sleeve shirts that billowed out around the arms, and tight vests that looked like they hindered mobility. Each vest appeared to be trying to outmatch the next with how much gold, silver, or white threaded embroidery they could fit on the front. Meanwhile, their slacks were of a more functional design, nearly all being straight legged pants that tied up the side, tucking into an equally diverse array of footwear designs.

I had worried that my silk clothing would make me stand out, and while I did stand out when put against this crowd, it wasn't because I was too fancy. My clothing compared to theirs was simple and in my opinion much more elegant. My father had style; I could give him that at least.

The sea of people parted, making room for us to stand unimpeded in front of the Lord and Lady's table. Alayna released my arm, standing tall and proud. Her humorous manner replaced with a fierce look of pride.

Another man stepped up next to us. He had colorless white hair, tied into a bun atop his head and a sneer on his face. I recognized his hair and decided this must be Alayna's cousin that had fallen in battle, but not died. His skin was nearly as white as his hair, whether from the major loss of blood or perhaps his normal complexion I couldn't decide. Despite his sickly pale complexion, he stood strong.

He was perhaps a few inches taller than me and wore simple black clothing with an ivory-colored breast plate, leg plates, bracers, greaves, and boots. The emblem of House Variyn, the black star with a skull in the center, was painted on his chest. I noticed he wore a leather headband and in the center of it was the shape of a shield made of a blue metal that clashed with the rest of his armor's color.

I felt drawn to the headpiece and as I looked at it, it shimmered with golden light. A strong magical item, I decided.

Turning my attention back to Lord and Lady Variyn, I examined them both. Lord Variyn looked much the same as before, however his demeanor was grimmer than it had been during our meeting.

Lady Variyn was beautiful, but in a different way than her daughter. She had red hair, like my mother, and her eyes were a deep green. Her face was passive, almost bored, as her eyes ran slowly over the three of us standing before the table. Her clothing similar in majesty to her husband's; furs, golden embroidery, and a thin silver crown with jewels set into them, sat upon her head.

"We have gathered here," Lord Variyn's voice boomed, easily carrying through the entire room and all the chatter quieted in response. "To celebrate the first of many victories against the encroaching Chaos. Yes, the rumors are true. Several Chaos monsters have been sighted within the domain of House Variyn, but rest assured it is a threat that is being dealt with. These three," he gestured to the three of us. "Are the first of many who will make it their priority to hunt down and destroy any remnants of Chaos that find their way into our domain."

The room was filled with polite clapping and a rush of whispers. Lord Variyn waited for the noise to die down before continuing.

"My daughter and nephew need no introduction, as their deeds and titles speak for themselves, but allow me to introduce you to another. You heard right when he was announced as the son of one of the previous protectors of the realm, Elkor the famed Arcane Knight. And though the young warrior has yet to *Awaken*, he possesses a powerful aura and the ability to wield that power in the defense of the realm. I would present him with a gift. Step forward, Caldor, son of Elkor."

I stepped forward, the table where Lord Variyn sat was lifted above the rest and I was forced to strain my neck to see them. From the side came the same nasally man who had announced me, carrying black cloth folded neatly in his arms.

He stepped behind me and I heard the cloth unfurl, then craned my neck to watch as he attached a silver clasp around my shoulders. The butler turned and walked away after he finished. My hand grabbed the edge of the cloak, and I examined it. The inside was lined with tiny white feathers that were soft to the touch. The outer layer I recognized immediately, and my eyes shot up to Lord Variyn, who was smiling down at me.

"From the hide of the Chaos monster, I have had a cloak

fashioned with a few other properties added for comfort and utility. Use this gift in defense of house Variyn and for the destruction of the Chaos."

The room buzzed with hushed whispers and some polite clapping once more.

My hand ran down the outer edge of the hundreds of drake scales that had been fashioned into the cloak. They weren't stiff at all like I expected but shifted and bent as easily as cotton. Iridescent light shimmered down the length of the cloak, it was enchanted or possessed with some type of magical enhancement, that much I was certain. I let the corner of the cloak go and it swooshed and fell still behind me.

Lord Variyn stood and stepped down from his high table, stopping in front of me. He drew his sword, and the room went deadly silent. I wasn't sure what he had planned, but it took all my restraint not to reach my hand to the sword at my waist.

"Kneel before me, Caldor Miles, son of Elkor the Arcane Knight," he said, his sword sweeping to the side as he spoke.

Begrudgingly I did as he said, thinking I might have an idea what he was planning now, and no longer fearing he meant to take my head.

Lord Variyn swept his gaze across the crowd, and no one stirred, the silence deepening as he stretched the moment out. "As is my right as Lord of House Variyn, I name you, Caldor Miles, a Knight, Protector of the Realm and Vassal of Blackridge Keep."

The room erupted in chatter, some angry but most just sounding shocked. Lord Variyn paid no attention to the ruckus and lifted his blade, tapping my shoulders and head with his sword while speaking an ancient language I didn't recognize. I felt a rush of power enter me but had no idea what it could be.

"Rise, Caldor. Knight of House Variyn and Lord of Black-ridge Keep."

I rose, meeting Lord Variyn's gaze. The room still rumbled with discussion and whispers. I wasn't sure what being a Knight and Vassal really meant, but I supposed that made me a part of the Nobility, which was a hard thought to process. As Lord Variyn moved to seat himself at his high table, I heard the pale young man scoff and mutter something I couldn't make out.

Alayna huffed and glared at him, but from what I could tell, he didn't notice, his gaze firmly fixed towards me. His face was twisted into a sneer, and he did not look happy to see me.

I smiled a big toothy grin at him and nodded, turning my head back up towards the Lord and Lady before he had a chance to react to my greeting.

Lord Variyn tried to speak, but the crowd had grown louder with each passing minute. A heavy thwack sounded from above and the room quieted.

"That's better," he said, clearing his throat. "There will be time at council when things can be discussed, for now, it is time to eat. Please sit and enjoy the feast."

Lord Variyn sat and began to follow his own orders, taking a bite from the leg of some type of large bird, bigger than any chicken leg I'd ever had the pleasure of eating.

"I'm supposed to sit up with my father," Alayna said, then leaning in, she whispered. "The white-haired boy is Zander, my cousin. He can be a bit much, but your place is at the same table as him, so follow his lead. Good luck." She gave me a quick smile, before her face reverted to the proud serious look she'd held when standing at attention.

Oh, this should be fun, I thought, turning to see that Zander had already walked off. Luckily, he stood out like a glowing white specter in the dark of night. Pushing through the crowd I found him sitting at a full table, with only a single spot open, the one directly across from him.

Sighing, I made my way around and sat, his stony gaze greeting me with another sneer, which I returned with a pleasant smile.

"Zander, was it?" I asked, still smiling. "It's good to see you've regained some color from the last time we met."

If it was possible, he turned a paler white.

"I'm unsure what you mean, peasant," Zander said, a grin of his own forming. "We ventured out together and with our combined might, took down the Chaos monster. Unless you remember things differently?"

Everyone within ear shot paused in their eating and turned their eyes to us. I really should have asked either Lord Variyn or Alayna if there was a certain narrative that I was meant to keep to. He had suggested that I play along as if I was originally sent out with the party, but were we also lying about Zander not being injured?

I decided to play on the side of caution until I could question Alayna about how her father wished the story to be told. But I couldn't just let him get away with talking down to me, not right after I was given the honor of Knighthood and Vassalship.

"Well, if you remember, Zander," I said, drawing out his name. "You took that nasty hit to the midsection when you weren't fast enough to evade the drake's fire, but lucky for you I was there to pull you out of harm's way. And I'm not sure if you heard, but I'm not a peasant, I'm a Knight of House Variyn and Vassal of Blackridge Keep."

Zander let out an exacerbated laugh. "More like Blackridge ruins. That shithole and its surrounding lands are infested with monsters and bandits. The only reason House Attra hasn't claimed it for themselves is my father's trade agreements have forbidden them to encroach any further into House Variyn land, but that could easily change."

"You wouldn't know a trade agreement if it bit you in the arse, son," a large man, with skin pale, but not quite so pale as Zander's, said. He regarded what was obviously his son and shook his head. "Don't make a fool of yourself. This is the son of Elkor and if he is anything like his father, then you'd do good to ally yourself to him as my brother has wisely done."

The older man, his hair a peppered black and white like his brother's, turned his attention to me before speaking again. "I'm Lord Variyn's brother, Bren Variyn. It was wise of Ceon to make a friend of you, I can sense the power of your aura without use of a spell. I see a bright future for you boy. You will make a fine Knight and a powerful resource for House Variyn."

Zander scoffed again but went quiet after his father glared at him once more.

"Nice to meet you," I said, tilting my head respectfully towards Bren Variyn. For whatever reason, I hadn't known Lord Variyn's first name was Ceon. "Blackridge Keep is really that bad?" I asked, between sips of a sweet malt ale.

Bren Variyn looked up, a large hunk of meat in his mouth. He tried to speak anyways but failed to say anything intelligible, he held up a finger until he finished. "Aye, that much is true. Nearly a dozen of our Keeps stand unoccupied and in ruins near the borders of our lands. House Variyn took some of the hardest losses in the Battle of Lynsteen Pass, you'd know it as the place your father fell. But not before he ended that wretched lich." His voice held a measure of pride as he spoke, and I wondered something.

"Did you fight at that battle?" I asked, taking a long swig of my ale, hoping to numb some of the feelings trying to push to the surface.

"I did, as did my brother. We are both powerful templars and held the backline, healing as many as we could." He paused, his fingers rubbing his temples and his face tightening. "I still remember the moment the battle turned. We'd been losing ground for days to the horde of undead, demons, and dragon kind; drakes, wurms, and the like. Then all at once the killing stopped. The monsters just turned and left, all racing to escape into Lynsteen Pass. They even collapsed the tunnels after they made it through. We learned later the cause of their retreat. Your father killed that wretched lich."

"And the lich killed him," I said, lowering my eyes. "He saved so many, but in the end, he couldn't save himself."

"You lost a father," Bren said, speaking over the low buzz of conversation around us. "There isn't anything I can say to change that, but I'll be damned if you don't get every chance to fill his shoes. If I'd have known he had a son, and a *Sparked* no less, you'd have been training under the best the kingdom had to offer. It is a damned shame that he kept his family a secret. This entire kingdom owes you a debt of gratitude."

Zander let out an exaggerated sigh and scoffed. "Could we eat in peace?" He said, sounding annoyed. What happened next shifted the mood of the table and had me struggling to keep a chuckle from escaping.

Bren gave his son a hard look, before swinging his arm out and knocking his chair backwards, causing a loud crack as the chair broke from the blow.

"Damn you boy, learn a measure of respect." Bren rose from his chair and hauled the boy up. "Go check on your mother and see if you can keep from shaming me for a few hours."

The look on Zander's face swept away any desire to laugh from my chest. He was an asshole for sure, but the public humiliation left him close to tears. I wasn't sure he deserved to be treated like that, but at the same time I found it difficult to feel any pity for him. He insulted me and my father, maybe his father putting him straight would help him be a decent human being, but probably not.

At our table the rest of the meal passed in awkward silence. No one close enough to me seemed willing to talk, and Bren excused himself shortly after throwing his son to the ground.

The food was something else altogether. Just in front of me there were at least three different kinds of meat, a large bird, a whole boar—not nearly as big as the one I'd killed, but bigger than I was used to—, and some large steak cuts from a cow I guessed. All around the meat were trays of vegetables, fruits, and several starches, including a purple potato dish that I'd never come across before.

After it was clear no one else wanted to talk, I dug in. Plate after plate I ate myself to a level of full that I had never achieved before in my living memory. To my astonishment, the food was cleared after a time to be replaced with an assortment of desserts, puddings, cakes, and frozen sweet milk. I didn't have space for more than a bite, but I did my best to find room. By the time the eating was over, I felt like a light breeze could cause me to expel all I'd eaten.

CHAPTER 11
FUN TIMES

Alayna appeared suddenly in front of me, the crowd parting for her as she walked. "Would you care for a dance, Knight Caldor, Vassal of Blackridge Keep?" she asked, holding her hand out.

A small group of instrumentalists had entered the hall, sitting to the side on a raised platform, one of only two in the room. The music was springy and light, a few people had taken to the dance floor already, doing a variation to a dance that was popular even in the isolated town of Creeshaw. We called it the noble's strut, and it was often done in jest with overly stiff movements and noses held high.

This was the first time I'd seen it done by actual nobles, and I was pleasantly surprised to find the dance actually held a certain amount of elegance when not being done in mock fun.

"I would love to dance," I said, doing my best to appear confident. I watched the others, trying to absorb enough of how they moved that I'd avoid falling into the stiff movements I was used to doing during town festivals and celebrations.

Alayna smiled and reached out her hand. I took it and we walked to the dance floor.

"Sorry you had to see Zander and my uncle fight," Alayna whispered, tilting her head closer to me as we walked. "Poor Zander is always getting picked on by Uncle Bren."

"Yeah, poor Zander," I said, not doing a good job of hiding my disdain.

Alayna didn't seem to notice and just nodded along.

We began to dance, and I had to use all my focus to not fall into the stiff movements. But after several minutes, I got the hang of it. A twirl here, and hand off there as we changed partners. Before I knew it, I was having fun.

My mind drifted to my friends. If Emory or Ismene could be here they'd be having a great time. That thought reminded me of something Alayna had said earlier in the morning about nobles knowing how to unlock a *Spark*.

My mood soured at the thought, but just then Alayna came back into view. I was, at least in some part, a noble now and I vowed that I'd share their secrets to any who wanted to know. I just had to figure out what the secret was first.

The music changed to a slower waltz. Alayna spun one last time, landing in my arms.

"Do you know how to waltz?" She asked, leaning into my chest and looking up at me with her sparkling purple eyes.

I nodded, mesmerized by her beauty and carefree attitude. This day felt like a dream. My *Spark* unlocked, the nobility with their endless connections and gold opened to me, and a keep of my own handed down as if it were a simple gift.

I took her in my arms, and we began to dance. The couples around us swished and turned like colorful brushstrokes on a masterwork painting. I was far less practiced in doing a formal waltz, but I did my best, holding Alayna closer than was proper in a waltz, but she made no attempt to pull away, instead leaning her head into me as we slowly made our way around the dance floor.

Much too soon the music ended, and someone approached.

"May I cut in and have this next dance, Lady Alayna?" A smooth voiced noble asked. He was around our age, mid-twenties if I had to guess, and wore a black vest with gold and purple embroidery. His fire red hair slicked back on his head.

"Yes, of course," Alayna said, her tone returning to the prim and proper façade that she presented in front of her father and other nobles. "If you will excuse me, Sir Caldor of Blackridge." She gave me a small curtsy, a wink, and a grin, before turning to begin dancing with the new gentlemen.

I made it half a dozen steps before two older men barred my path, each holding wine glasses and large smiles plastered on their faces.

"Might we have a word," the fatter of the two asked. Each wore the overly tight vests, one strikingly skinny while the other overflowed his vest with an excess of fat. Neither looked less than fifty years old, but their features held the timeless look of someone that reached the minimum level to slow aging. Making it anyone's guess how old these two would be.

"I was just going to get a quick drink," I said, trying to slip by them. The skinnier of the two snapped his fingers and a drink appeared in his empty hand in a puff of blue smoke.

"Here you are," he said, passing the drink to me. I took it but didn't drink it. "Allow us to introduce ourselves. I am Bagard Veslmy and this is my good friend Dunst Alvera. We were hoping you could enlighten us about your role for House Variyn. What plans do you have to hedge this new threat of Chaos monsters infiltrating this deep into the kingdom? And why would Lord Variyn choose one so young as you? Of course, it is well known that many of our strongest adventurers fell at Lynsteen Pass or left for stronger Houses, but why you?"

I blinked and struggled to process his words. He had spoken so fast and said so much that I wasn't sure which question exactly he wanted me to answer. To hell with it, I thought, downing the drink the two had provided in a single gulp.

"My, ...uh, ...role in the recent Chaos monster," I had barely gotten the words out when someone grabbed my arm. I turned to see a bald man wearing a plain black long coat that covered him from his upper neck down to a few inches from the ground. His eyes blazed a deep crimson as they passed over the two men that were attempting to question me.

"That will be enough," he said, both men visibly cowered at the sight of the black-clad figure. "Come with me young Caldor, we have much to speak of."

With an iron grip that I wasn't sure I'd be able to break if I wanted to, he led me to a side door, and we slipped out of the main hall into a smaller sitting room. There was a pair of plush, emerald green couches on the far end of the room and portraits of Lord and Lady Variyn on the walls.

"Sit and allow me to introduce myself," The bald, red-eyed man said.

I felt a wave of something hit me and I was compelled to follow his instructions, sitting immediately. My face screwed up in concentration while I tried to resist the force holding me. The power inside me stirred and pulsed, freeing me suddenly from whatever was trying to hold me back.

I stood, my hand going to the hilt of my sword. "I'd prefer to stand," I said facing the man.

The bald man just smiled and said, "Sit." His voice echoed in my head and before I could stop myself, I sat. "Very good.

Now don't be alarmed. I just wanted to test for myself if you had a measure of control over the forces inside yourself. Very few can resist my spell of control, even when I cast the weakest version, like I just did on you the first time. What you are feeling now is my spell being cast at Rank 2. I think with a bit of training you could resist even that, but there is no need. I am Non, the master of whispers for House Variyn."

Non waved his hand, and I felt the compulsion fade away. I stood, my thumb flicking the release and my sword coming free.

"What the hell!" I yelled, unable to control the rage I felt from someone so easily controlling me. I couldn't remember the last time I felt so violated. Blue energy began to *Spark* around my hand, and my breathing became ragged.

"No," Non said, and the blue energy dissipated. It felt as if my connection to the force inside was just out of reach. My rage faded along with the power.

"Please, I mean you no harm," Non said, raising white-gloved hands in mock surrender. "In fact, I have a task for you, but first, I need to debrief you on a few matters of House Variyn."

CHAPTER 12
SECRETS AND SHADOWS

"The narrative that Lord Variyn wishes you to keep is as follows," Non said, sitting opposite of me on the sofa. A wave of exhaustion had taken over me and all I could do to keep my eyes open was to sit and listen.

"You were chosen due to your potential and heritage to join the party sent to investigate rumors of Chaos monsters in the area. Lady Alayna, Zander, and yourself were part of a smaller group meant to observe and report. However, things went sideways when the elite strike force made up of Leon Eldris's band the Leonites, had to pursue an adult drake through a spatial tear."

My eyebrows raised at that; Leon Eldris was a famous adventurer that I'd heard a lot of lately from tavern rumors brought in by adventurers. He was said to be a rising star amongst adventurers, having formed a powerful party around himself and challenging some of the strongest dungeons in the land. Last I'd heard, they'd been far east along the mountain range of High Peak.

"You really have Leon Eldris fighting for you?" I asked,

unable to hide my excitement at the idea of meeting such a powerful adventurer.

Non gave me a blank stare and shook his head. "What? No, the idiot was up east and got himself and his party killed less than a week ago. I am certain that I am one of the only ones to have obtained this secret so we can use the narrative to our advantage. Plus, it makes more sense than us telling the entire realm that we sent a trio of kids to deal with one of the dead-liest threats to the realm, son of Elkor or not, you are lucky to be alive."

I sunk back into the couch, shock rippling through me again. So much for meeting Leon Eldris. Before I could dwell on the fate of the powerful adventurer, Non continued.

"You will communicate to any who ask that the three of you fought hard and, in the end, were victorious. Do not go into the details, say only that it was a tough fight, and you were glad for the assistance the Noble family was able to provide. The more mysterious we leave the encounter, the better. Let the slithering braggarts decide on the finer details themselves."

"I don't understand why it matters what we tell people," I said, shifting in my seat and un-bunching the cloak behind my back. "I mean, who cares what happened? Why is everyone making a big deal out of it? I'm sure some adventurers will come across any Chaos monsters and kill them before it's a problem."

"I would think that you, of all people, would understand the importance of controlling the narrative," Non said, a sly smile creeping onto his lips. "After all, your father made sure that very few knew of you and your family. He knew that as he got stronger, someone might look to his family as a way to get to him. It is the same here. If House Variyn is seen as weak in the eyes of the other Houses, then we will fall. They will come for us all. Having even a single Chaos monster running rampant inside our borders will be reason enough for the Houses to begin to encroach on us. But if we can show them that we responded swiftly and with deadly resolve, they will hold back, for now."

I knew of course that wars between Houses were commonplace throughout Newaliyn, but I hadn't experienced it myself, as House Variyn was renowned for being one of the most peaceful territories within the kingdom. How Lord Variyn accomplished this, I honestly didn't know, and hadn't given it much thought up until this point.

"Got it," I said, nodding along to Non's explanation. "You mentioned having a task for me?"

"Yes, I did," Non said, running his hand over his bald head. "You will be approached by representatives of one kind or another, it matters not what they call themselves, but when this happens, I need you to report to me and tell me who it was that approached you and the offer they extended. House Variyn has many enemies within and without. Will you help House Variyn in this matter?"

"All you want me to do is report to you if someone tries to recruit me for anything?" I asked, not hiding my confusion. "That seems rather vague, what if someone decides they want me to join the Adventurer's Guild? That doesn't seem out of place."

"Lord Variyn is the head of the Adventurer's Guild in the city, and all smaller charters report to him, so yes if someone asks you to join the Adventurer's Guild, I would find that suspicious."

"Oh, I didn't know that," I said, rubbing at the back of my neck. "So, does that mean I get access to the Adventurer's

Guild? I hear they have an expansive library here in the city. How do I go about visiting?"

Non harrumphed. "You do have access, as a Knight and Vassal of Blackridge Keep there is little that you can't find your way into if you wish. However, you'd be wise to wait until you've *Awoken* before diving into the library, as there is a certain measure of essence you can gain by studying. And although it is possible to gather essence before you *Awaken*, there is no way of knowing if you are doing so effectively."

"Wait. You can gather essence as a *Sparked* just by reading books?" I asked, thrilled at the prospect.

"You will see," Non said, "But we should return you to the party before your absence is noticed. Leave out the same way we entered, and remember, I will be watching."

I turned my attention back to Non to ask what he meant by that, but he was gone. The room had one exit, and I stood in front of it, but somehow Non had disappeared.

CHAPTER 13
FUN AND GAMES

After my conversation with Non, I was disappointed to discover that Alayna had left, as well as Lord and Lady Variyn. Several nobles approached wanting more information on the events leading to my knighthood, but I brushed them all off, giving small explanations as Non had instructed.

Searching for a place the nobles weren't congregating, I located a suitable area. I sat down on a free chair next to a small staging area the servants were using to refill and pour new drinks.

"These things can be a bit much, eh Chaos Slayer?" A deep voice intoned to my left. I looked up and regarded the man. He had dark piercing eyes, ink-black hair, and a witty smile.

"Just call me Caldor," I said. This man wasn't dressed as either servant or noble. His garb was simple, but of foreign design. He wore a light blue collared shirt that ruffled like silk but gave off an iridescent shimmer.

His shirt was tucked tight into a pair of black slacks, but instead of ties running up the leg, it had a silver button keeping it tight around his waist. A stiff purple belt hung around his hips with a large triangular black leather pouch attached, a curved handle sticking out the top attached to a shiny metal device.

"Well, Caldor," the stranger said. "I am Da- well no, let's say, I am Mah'kus, a guide to the lost, dead god, keeper of my brother, teller of tales, and well, yeah I guess that is it. Sorry, this is all very new to me, and I am still adjusting."

I looked at the tan-skinned gentleman with his cunning eyes and stood, ordering a stiff drink.

"Nice to meet you Mah'kus. Is this another game of the nobles? Confuse the silly peasant with drunken ridiculousness?" I asked, not feeling up to dealing with more of the mess. My special and exciting day was quickly turning into a nightmare.

"Not at all," Mah'kus said, "In fact, I came here to speak with you, but somehow, I think I'm too early. As I said, I am new to all this, you'd think being a god, even a dead one, would grant a certain omniscience." He paused, and his eyes rose to the ceiling as if he was waiting or listening for something. "Oh, shut up already. I will do as I please. You all had your chance, and now I must do what must be done."

This man was insane. I stood and began to walk away.

"I'll do it right this time, see you in...hmm a few months or was it years? Damn this is hard to get right," his words dropped in volume as he spoke until fading to silence. I turned and looked over my shoulder.

He was gone. Scanning the rest of the room I saw no place he could have gone. Sighing, I downed what was left of my drink and decided I would head back to my room before I hallucinated something else. There were far too many disappearing people in this castle.

The edges of my vision blurred. Whatever I had drank was

several times more potent than I was used to. But eventually, I got to a part of the keep that I was sure I remembered from my walk with Alayna.

I liked Alayna. Noble or not, she was a lovely girl. No, not a girl, a woman! A beautiful woman.

My mind wandered, and I stumbled my way towards my room.

Suddenly something crashed into me, knocking me straight off my feet. Someone was atop me; raining blows down on my chest. The haze of drunkenness faded as adrenaline shot through me.

With a quick shove, I was able to move the attacker off me, but before I could bring my left arm free, I felt the hot sting of steel cutting my flesh.

"Son of a harpy, get the fuck off me!" I screamed, my *Spark* reacting to my urgent commands, a blue flash of light slamming into my attacker.

I got a decent look at him as he stood and began to run away. He was of medium build, wearing the black clothing of a servant, but his boots didn't match what I'd seen them wearing, instead they were worn and torn. The leather of many miles walked.

He made it around the corner before I could stand. I examined my wrist as I stood. It was a mess of blood, but upon closer inspection, the cut was barely skin deep. A clatter of footsteps caught my attention, and I called my *Spark* to shoot out towards it.

A bolt of raw blue energy barely missed a guard's head, going wide. I recognized him as the guard that stood outside my room this morning.

"You alright? We heard a scuffle and came running." The guard said, his hand on his sword, but it hadn't yet been drawn.

"I'm uh," I said, standing to look up and down the hallway. Whoever it had been was long gone now. "I'm fine. Can you show me the way to my room?" I asked, ready for sleep.

"Aye, follow me," he said, the other two guards falling into step behind us.

"Name's Mick," the guard said, "Nice to formally meet you."

"Hey Mick," I said, looking up at the tall guard. His skin looked like leather left out in the sun too long, but his smile and eyes were kindly, and I couldn't help but smile back at him.

"So, you get into a scuffle?" Mick asked, pointing at the bloody line on my wrist. "Looks like a cat decided your wrist was its next meal."

"Yeah," I said, chuckling, "Something like that."

I was surprised when we turned a corner, and we were already at the room I'd been staying in. Whoever attacked me had been snooping close by. Outside my door was the deskside table from inside my room, a mess of cards sitting atop it, with several bronze and silver coins spread out.

Mick quickly stepped up to the table and scooped up the coins.

"We'll get this table put back right away," Mick said, a wide grin on his hide-like face. "We were just enjoying a few hands of cards while we waited for the nobles to finish drinking the night away."

"Yeah, could you bring it inside," I said, my voice growing serious. "Because I want to play too, but I'd prefer to lay on the bed while we play. Whatever I drank at that party hit me like a ton of bricks."

Mick laughed and slapped me on the back. "That-a-boy! You heard him boys. Let's get inside and finish our game."

The other two guards didn't hesitate, grabbing the two

sides of the small table and coming into the room while Mick held the door wide. As my adrenaline began to fade, I felt the dizzy drunkenness begin to grip me again. But I wasn't going to let it ruin my night.

"What are the chances of getting a keg or something brought in here so I can keep my lips wet? Perhaps some...honey ale?"

"You are a man of my own kind," Mick said through a hearty chuckle. "Hey Barny, you still seeing that kitchen wench? What's her name, Smooty?"

"It's Susan you dumb ass, and what of it?" The largest of the guards, Barny, I presume, took his helmet off and gave Mick a hard stare.

"Well, she's working tonight, right? See if you can go fulfill our little Lord's request and get us something to drink."

"Sure thing, Captain, give me a few minutes and I'll be back with refreshments," Barny said, putting his cap back on and slipping out the door.

I took my gloves and new cloak off before laying back on the bed, waiting to drown out my drunkenness with more drunkenness.

I awoke to the door opening and Barny entering carrying a cask of ale as big as his chest, followed closely by a petite servant girl. She seemed sweet, dropping off the mugs and blushing when Barny gave her a passionate kiss in front of all of us.

I smiled, happy to see someone was having fun already.

"Okay boys, deal them out before the Lordling changes his mind," Mick said, dealing out cards atop the table at the end of my bed.

"I'm not a real Lord. Shit, you guys have lives more glamorous than I've had up until today. Now give me a mug of ale, your Lord commands it." I laughed, doing my best not to slur my words, but it was hard.

The game used a forty-nine-card deck with seven distinct cards, each numbered one through seven. There were other card decks that were popular as well, but the seven-by-seven pattern was the oldest and most widely used. I was familiar with a few games, but they were playing the simplest, four-card draw. Mick threw me a small pouch of coins before we started.

"One of my boys found this in your nightstand here," Mick gestured to a small drawer set into the wood. "It ought to give you a few coins to play with."

I gave him a puzzled look, but instead of accusing him of stealing money that I wasn't even sure was mine in the first place, I just took a long pull of my ale and accepted the pouch. With a clink and a smile, I put my first bet on the table.

I was one hundred percent bluffing, but they didn't know that. Apparently, I was wrong, and they did. I spent the next hour losing money and winning only twice.

"You guys like working as guards?" I asked, my words coming out significantly more slurred than I cared to admit.

The quiet one, his name was Sam if I remembered right, spoke up. "It'd be a mite better if they paid more than the shit wage we get."

"Hey!" Barny hollered, half laughing as he did so, and slapping Sam upside the head. "Cap'n is right there. You ever want to get paid more, then stop being such an ignorant ass."

"Nah, he's right," Mick said, laughing. "The pay is shit for me too. One silver a week barely keeps my belly full."

"No!" I yelled, my drunkenness getting the better of me. "They only pay you a damned silver? I'd pay you better than that. Shit, you guys seem like wonderful guards. I'd give you

one gold a week. Come join me out at that keep they gave me...
shit what did they call it, white...uhg oh Blackridge!"

All three laughed, and Sam put his cards down, showing a
winning hand.

"You'd have to pay one gold a week to live that far out, but
if you are serious, I bet you'd find a handful willing to join
you," Mick said, his voice somehow remaining completely
steady as if unaffected by the several mugs of ale he'd
consumed.

The rest of the night slipped into a blur of laughter and
fun. At some point, probably halfway through a mug of ale, I
slipped off to sleep.

CHAPTER 14
CUT OFF WHAT?

The cruel bite of the morning buzz of activity assaulted me from every possible angle. Able to ignore it no longer, I pulled the sheets free. Searing beams of intense sunlight did their best to burn any reason from my mind. Stumbling to the water basin, I sought refuge inside the chilled water. Cool and biting water surrounded my head. It felt good.

I still wore the formal outfit I'd been given the day before, but I didn't care. Pushing through the room in a mild haze now that the water had *Awakened* my senses a bit more, I found my shoes, my sword, and the cloak I'd been given.

"Food?" I muttered to the guard outside my room as I stepped through the door. A cacophony of sound assaulted my senses once more. The clang of plates, footfalls of busy servants, and the ting of armor against armor as the guard shifted to regard me.

"Huh? Oh right," the guard whose name I couldn't recall turned his full attention on me. "Took in a bit more than you could handle last night, eh? Ha I can have Miss Meldry bring you a wittle cup of tea and a breakfast plate if you are too fragile to leave your room, or if you're made of hearty stuff, I can show you the way to the kitchen?"

"The kitchen please." My words were still all mutters and filled with the fatigue only a night of drinking can bring. I knew the guard was making fun of me, but I didn't even care. I wanted to say his name was Mick, but the previous night continued to fade from my memory along with his name. I wasn't some pampered noble that needed to have his hangovers nursed by whomever this Miss Meldry was meant to be.

"Good man," Maybe Mick said, slapping me firmly on the back. My world shattered momentarily as I considered plunging my sword into maybe Mick's face.

"What's your name?" I asked, trailing just a few steps behind the guard as he led me through the maze-like halls of Variyn Keep.

"You forget me already, eh? It's Mick. Barny and Sam played cards with us last night after you'd gotten yourself escorted from the fancy party. Don't be trying to escape the debt you got yourself into." Mick laughed deep and hearty, causing needles to pierce my skull. "I'll be taking that two gold from you one way or another.

"I'm good for my debts," I said, raising my head and risking the brightness of the hallway to regard Mick. How I'd ended up owing him two gold I didn't know and was fairly shocked that I'd been so irresponsible with money that I didn't have, but on the same note, my new life as an adventurer should enable me to pay him and care for my family's financial needs.

He wore the guard uniform & armor I'd previously seen on the guards walking through the keep. But Mick's was a bit worn for wear and held a noticeably less cared for shine to his breastplate. Still, he walked tall and strong. His skin was like leather left out in the sun, and his hair— from what little I could see escaping his helmet—was a sun-stained blonde nearly devoid of any color.

His sword sat on his left hip, just next to me, but I noticed he'd added an additional scabbard holding a knife the length of his forearm. The vaguest of memories surfaced as we walked. A game of cards and dice ending when Mick pulled his large dagger and saying something to the effect of 'This is a knife'.

The memories were anything but clear, so I let them fade while I focused on getting my head to stop hurting so much.

"So, Mick," I said as we turned a corner, more servants hurrying with trays of food to waiting nobles, I was sure. "You going to give me a chance to earn back my gold tonight?"

Mick laughed, once more slapping me on the back and testing my ability to not stab him as a reaction to the pain that lanced through me.

"Right. If you want to lose more of your coin I won't stand in your way," Mick said, then seeming to consider something, he met my gaze but quickly turned his eyes forward.

"What is it?" I asked. It was obvious to me he wanted to say something.

"Is it true what you said last night? You'd take those of us that were willing as guards for your new keep? I'm no one's fool, everyone says things when they've got the drink in them, but for a gold a week we'd follow you, even to Blackridge Keep, the place be damned."

I stopped dead in my tracks. My brain straining to recall that particular conversation. It came back to me in flashes and glimpses, but I definitely said something to that effect after they'd told me they only earned a silver a week as House Guards.

My hands padded around my waist until I found my coin purse. Fishing into it I found that I'd been given a small fortune along with the clothing, nearly thirty gold coins total. I fished out five and handed them to Mick.

"For my debt and the first week of service," I dropped the coin into Mick's outstretched leather glove. "There are a few conditions and things I ought to mention first, the most important being that I haven't any clue how to successfully run a keep or area of land. I'm an orchard farmer, so don't expect glory and riches beyond your wages. Second, is I'm not sure what occupying force currently holds the keep, but when the time comes, you'll be expected to fight to free the keep, but in return you are free to build on a small plot of land and live with a bit of freedom. We can work those details out later."

"That we can, my Lord," Mick said, bringing his fist up into a salute, banging it against his chest. "I will inform the boys and pass the word along to any other who might be thirsty for adventure and higher wages. You have a number you're looking for or should I test the waters for interest?"

My hand rubbed behind my neck as I considered how many guards I would likely need but decided upon a completely arbitrary number. "No more than twenty-five for now." The thought of paying even twenty-five guardsmen a gold a week made me shudder. I did not know what my drunken self was getting me into, but I would stand by my word.

"Twenty-five it is," Mick said. "I will see if we can grab a few elite guards, though they'll be more expensive to enlist, possibly two gold per head. How does twenty and five sound? Twenty guards like me and five elite."

"What is an elite guard?" I asked.

"I forget you aren't *Awoken* yet," Mick said, shaking his head while he chuckled. "As a landowner you can imbue a certain status on normal folk like us without *Sparks*. Normal guardsmen like us range from levels one to twenty, elite guardsmen have increased their power and reputation to levels higher than twenty, but no higher than forty. I'm no expert, but I'm fairly certain the twenty and five is the max you'll be able to command at Rank one as a Ruler of a keep."

My mind reeled and I considered Mick's words. I really needed to study up on this and so many other things my knowledge was severely lacking. Ask me about monsters, or certain runic variations and I could tell you the difference between a Dire Owlbear and a plain old Owlbear. But all these noble houses, land ruling things were a completely new subject for me.

I checked around us and pulled Mick into a deserted passage. "How do guard levels work? And what would you do if you could be *Awoken* instead of serving as a guard?"

Mick raised an eyebrow at my words and took a moment to consider before speaking. "Guards don't have proxy levels the same way as other professions, farmers, merchants and such. Guard levels are like levels gained while serving in military service, they stay with you no matter where you end up, along with the combat skills and perks you earn. So, if you're worried we might all reset to level one upon entering your service, we won't. We guards gain levels through a mixture of training and as we learn from the job. As to what we'd do if we could be *Awoken*, I can't speak for the rest, but I'm at peace with my lot in life, but if lady fate offered me a blessing, I'd not turn her away. I can't speak for all my guards, but I imagine most would be of like mind."

I stared up into his light brown eyes and considered what I'd vowed and how it could help him and so many others. "I can't say much now as I don't really know what I know and what I don't, but I'll remember what you said here."

"You are a strange Lordling, young one," Mick said, punching me lightly in the arm as we entered back into the busy hallway.

"Well Mick," I said, turning to my future new guard. "If you are up for it and when the time comes, how'd you like to be my Captain of the Guard?"

"I could be convinced," Mick said, rubbing his fingers together and smiling. "For the right price."

I tossed another gold coin up to him. "Keep me apprised of your recruiting efforts."

With a smile and a nod Mick grabbed the coin from the air. "As you command. Go through that door there and ask for Miss Meldry, she will set you up nice."

I gave Mick a nod, wishing I hadn't a moment later. The quick movement brought another wave of pain into my skull. Stumbling into the kitchen I surveyed the area.

It was an expansive room, several cooking fires burning in stone ovens and two long counters running the length. Nearly two dozen men and women moved here and there filling plates, platters, and pitchers.

"You'd best be ready to work if you enter my kitchen," a raspy voice called out from the side. I turned and saw who had spoken. A stout short woman with a wide waist and a sneer on her face regarded me. She had white wiry hair, tied into a neat bun. Her age was difficult to guess, her hair made her seem older, her skin, while plump, seemed well taken care of and younger than she first appeared. "Well, what it'll be, you working on getting out the way?"

"I have nothing against a little work," I said, my fingers coming up to my temples as I failed to subdue my headache. "However, I was hoping for a bite to eat first. Could you direct me to a Miss Meldry, Mick sent me?"

Her gaze softened and she looked at me more closely.

"Oh," she said suddenly, sounding apologetic. "My young Noble, I'm sorry. I uh, I only thought you were a roaming servant boy."

I quickly raised a hand, shaking my head. "I might as well be a servant boy, and I'm not really a noble, not in the sense that you're used to. Please, I'm pretty hung over. Could you help me find a spot to eat?"

"I'm Miss Meldry and I'll get you a plate, just sit tight." The plump woman turned and barked orders. Before long I had a plate of hot steaming food headed my way.

"Thank you," I said, my words disturbed by the large amount of saliva beginning to build up in my mouth.

"Don't mention it," she said, chuckling as a drop of saliva fell from my half open mouth. I quickly wiped it away and straightened my back.

"Are you Knight Caldor by chance?" She asked. I nodded between mouthfuls of toast and greasy bacon. "I think you are expected at breakfast with the King and Queen, but I can pass your regards if you would rather finish your food here with us." Without speaking, I nodded, and she got the message, sending off a servant to inform the Lord.

I found a worn wooden bench to sit on while I hurriedly consumed not one, but two full plates of food. By the time I was finished I could feel my stomach bulging and my headache receding.

The kitchen staff left me alone with my thoughts as I tried to digest all the events that I'd been a part of over the last two days.

Just days ago, I was struggling with the idea that I'd be stuck forever as an orchard farmer, but now? Now I was finally going to live the dream. So why did I have such a pit in my stomach? I thought about my siblings and my mother's condition, but why was that bothering me? I had taken care of it, hadn't I?

My position in House Variyn, new as it might be, would entitle me to provide for my family better than my father had during the height of his career. We'd never been very well off, my father only ever seemed to bring in just enough for us to get by. He was a powerful and respected adventurer, and it made me wonder.

Had my father had access to even more than I would have as a Knight and Vassal to House Variyn? I knew for a fact he'd been called on by the King not once but several times. Surely the rewards for service rendered to the King would outweigh that of a House Lord.

My father's words echoed in my mind. He'd often spoke of how serving others and being a hero to them wasn't about rewards but about doing right for the sake of right. Did that make accepting the title and rewards a bad thing?

I didn't think so. As much as I strived to be like my father, the idea of refusing help that could finally give my mother a measure of peace wasn't something I could consider. Regardless of what I told myself, the pit in my stomach remained.

I'd finished most of my food and was working on a hot glass of tea when Alayna glided through the door, her brows scrunched as her eyes scanned the kitchen. Her gaze found me, and she smiled.

Alayna wore a simple blue dress, the edges hemmed with white lace. "Your first day in my father's service and you are already skipping appointments," she said, speaking in a clearly mock serious tone, then giggled. She went suddenly still, seeing the kitchen staff looking their way.

I smiled up at her and drained what was left of my tea. "Should we take a walk," I suggested, standing.

Keeping her lips pressed together, she nodded. Alayna took my arm, leaning in and whispered to me. "I don't know why but it is so difficult to be serious around you." She giggled again and I saw her cheeks redden.

I didn't know if I should be insulted by her comment, as I saw myself as a hero just beginning his journey, not a silly buffoon meant to entertain a young noble girl. But I wasn't offended, and it was hard to see Alayna as anything but a sweet and caring woman. Even having only met her days before, I liked her a lot.

"It must be my dazzling personality," I suggested, being sure to speak loudly enough that several servants and guards gave us peculiar looks as we walked past.

Alayna's face reddened and she straightened her back, pushing me away. She shot me a look and I raised my hands in surrender.

We turned a corner and walked down a hallway free of any servants or guards. She immediately turned on me, raising her finger. For a moment, I thought she was truly angry at me, but she had a wide grin on her face. "You are going to get us both in trouble."

I laughed, shaking my finger back at her, her carefree attitude bringing out my sillier side. "And why is that, princess?"

Her face went deadpan. "Don't call me that."

"Oh, sorry, princess."

I expected her to laugh or giggle at least, but instead, she glared at me. "I am not a princess, and I don't want to take over for my father. I don't even want to be Lady Variyn." She said her title with mock annoyance.

"You'd prefer to be a peasant?" I asked, tilting my head and giving her a flat look. "Trust me, there is nothing exciting about having to work for everything and still not making enough to barely scrape by."

Her expression changed from angry to passive and then to confusion. "You're right. I'm not happy with my lot in life, but that doesn't mean I've got it as bad as others. That brings me back to my point. You are a Knight now and a Vassal. You are expected to act a certain way."

"You mean more like you?" I asked, my grin stretching the sides of my face.

"Well," she bit her lip before huffing out a lung full of air. "Yes, like me. I have to be prim and proper around everyone, well not you and maybe a select few others, but my father says appearances are important. One wrong move or show of weakness could mean his title, land, and the peace he has kept for so long. Peace I'm meant to maintain one day as Lady Variyn."

As she spoke her countenance changed, growing more serious as if her words solidified the facts in her mind.

"You, okay?" I asked, reaching out and touching her arm. She leaned into me, her eyes closing momentarily. When they opened, they burned with a fiery determination.

"I'm fine," she assured me, pulling her arm back. "Meet me outside the keep gates in half an hour. I have a few matters to attend to, but I wanted to show you around the city and fill in some details about your upcoming *Awakening*."

"Oh," I said, "Yeah sure, I can meet you outside. Maybe I'll go clean up a bit myself and change into less formal attire."

She gave me a brisk nod and glided away.

Had I done something to offend her? My thoughts retraced our conversation as I traced my steps back to my room. Mick stood guard, leaning outside the door frame, seemingly snoozing.

Just as I opened the door, though, he spoke. "Elandel stopped by looking for you. She left you a tonic she wants you to drink and told me to tell you that she has seen to your mother's potion and not to worry. It also looked like she dropped you off some clothes. Might think about changing into those because you smell like ale and piss." Mick reached up and tipped his conical helmet towards me, lowering it back over his eyes.

"Thanks, Mick," I said, patting him on the shoulder as I passed into my room.

Sure enough, there was a change of clothing, a tonic, and a note from Elandel saying pretty much what Mick said, on the bed in a bundle. Stripping out of my clothes, I found a cloth and gave myself a quick wipe down and a thorough sniff. Despite what Mick had said, I smelled fine, but the cold cloth bath was refreshing in its own way.

I was minding my own business walking to what I hoped was the way outside of the keep to meet Alayna, when a familiar face turned the hallway, eyes boring into me.

Galt, the head guardsmen, barreled straight for me in a fast walk.

"Hey there, Galt," I began to say, but he grabbed hold of my shoulder, and roughly pulled me into a broom closet. In his left hand, he held a torch he'd pulled free from the wall. The bright flames licked at my face as he held it close, his face resembling something from nightmares.

"Who in the fuck do you think you are?" He roared in my face; I could see his veins pulsating rapidly on his forehead as he pressed me hard against the stone wall. The increasing pressure was beginning to hurt. In response, I felt the power inside me flare to life, but I didn't reach for it yet.

"My name is Caldor," I said, pushing hard and managing

to dislodge him, my hand sliding to the hilt of my sword. "Son of Elkor, Knight of House Variyn and Vassal of Blackridge Keep." My tone was petulant, but I didn't care. Whether Knight, Vassal, peasant, or orchard farmer, I didn't let anyone talk to me like that.

Galt reeled at my words and tone, but quickly recovered, moving closer but not touching me. "I don't care if you are a fucking Ordu come down to save us from Chaos itself." Spittle flew as he spoke, and I got more than a little spit on my face. "You don't go poaching my men from under me! I've had twenty-five damn good guardsmen telling me they plan on signing up to serve under you because you promised them gold."

Well, that was fast. Mick wasted no time spreading the word that I needed guards. I slowly wiped the spittle off my face, wiping my hands on my tunic before turning my eyes up to Galt. "You're mad that I am planning to pay them so much, or that you are losing so many guards?" I asked, wanting clarification before I spoke any further.

"You won't be able to pay them that kind of coin!" Galt roared. "But fuck all if I care how much you pay them. These are men I've hand-picked and trained since young lads. I won't see their lives thrown away by some low-born peasant who seeks glory and riches."

I reeled back, Galt had raised a fist up to his chest and I wasn't going to be able to pull my weapon before he struck me. But he held back, his grizzled old form looking tough as iron.

"You don't know me," I said simply. "But you do know what little I've done. When I heard screams, I came running, ready to help. When I was offered a position as a Knight and Vassal, I accepted, ready to serve. When Mick and several other guards complained of boredom and low pay, I offered an alternative. Sure, I don't know how easy it'll be to pay their wages, but I will find a way. Their lives aren't meaningless objects for me to move around on a game board. I can't promise them safety, but neither can you."

Galt's breathing slowed, his chest rising and falling slower with each breath. "You should have come to me. You are new to these nobles' games, and you've overstepped. I will grant you leave to take eight normal ranked guards and two elite, no more. If after they've served and been paid for three months, I'll consider allowing the rest to join you."

"That sounds fair," I said, holding out a hand. Galt took it and we shook, meeting eyes. His were hard and dark, the eyes of a man who has seen too much. I'm sure that my gaze seemed frail and childlike in comparison.

But whatever he saw in my eyes seemed to appease him, and he nodded, squeezing my hand hard.

"Come to me when you are ready to lay claim to Blackridge Keep and I will personally release the guards I've chosen to aid you. I suggest you grow stronger and reach at least level fifteen or twenty before you attempt it."

"Thank you, Galt," I said. "And I'm sorry for the misunderstanding."

"Oh, and another thing," Galt said, his expression changing from the ever-present sneer to a wicked grin. "You bed Lady Alayna, and I'll cut your bits off."

For that, I had no response, just a look of utter terror as he turned and left me alone in the dark broom closet.

CHAPTER 15
MARKETPLACE

The warmth of the rising sun as it peeked over the distant shops and houses was comforting. Leaving the cold stone and politics of Keep Variyn behind me felt just as comforting. How had I already entwined myself in the middle of so much? I shook my head as I crossed over the lowered drawbridge, looking down into the churning water of the moat.

Glancing behind me, I marveled at the size of the keep. If I was any good at eyeballing the size of things, this keep looked like it could fit most of Creeshaw inside it. The scale of the castle was massive.

The sound of early morning activity buzzed in my ears as I got further from the keep and closer to the distant wall that wrapped around the castle grounds. I passed several guards, a few standing erect and some patrolling. I was surprised when a few tipped their helmets to me and shared a shit-eater grin or a friendly slap on the shoulder as I walked.

Mick's words about me being willing to pay guards more

than the average salary had gotten around, or Variyn's guards were very friendly. I decided it must be a mix of both.

Standing just outside the gate was a cloaked figure in tans and browns, with their hood up. I approached the man cautiously, wondering who it could be. It wasn't until I was within several feet that the figure looked up and I saw sparkling purple eyes staring back at me.

"Ready to explore?" Alayna asked, a mischievous grin spreading across her face.

"I'm ready," I announced, pulling up beside her. She didn't move to latch arms as we'd done while inside the keep, instead adjusting her hood to keep her face concealed and turning left to walk down the street at a brisk pace.

I had to hurry to catch up with her, and she didn't as much as look up as she pushed onward. After a minute or two of walking in silence I had matched her pace enough to be able to speak to her.

"So, are you going to show me to a bookstore or something?" I asked, putting forth what I considered to be the best possible scenario.

She turned, a dumbfounded look on her face, before saying between heavy breaths. "What, no. My father has a few extra gifts for you, and I decided I owed you something to make us even."

"You don't—" I began to say, but she cut me off.

"I do," she said. We turned the corner into a wide cobbled stone street, she slowed her pace significantly as there was a thick sea of people moving from building to building here.

We'd entered a marketplace, but it was far grander than any I'd ever visited. The street we'd entered led into a large open courtyard and in the middle of it all, a spiral of canvas-covered booths. But that wasn't what made it stand out to me, no, it was the dozen or so three-story buildings that ringed around the outer edge. Each one had various shop signs and symbols hanging from them.

It was like the biggest shop vendors gathered and began to sell things only nobles or rich merchants could afford. For instance, at one of the many open-air shop stands, there was a jeweler polishing a large gem while finely dressed men and women admired his hundreds of rings, necklaces, and earrings. Next to his twelve-foot-long table was another deeper and longer booth.

Behind this table stood an elderly man with a long white wispy beard, a blue starred hat and glowing blue eyes. His tables were filled with ornately decorated scrolls of gold, silver, and metallic green. He was obviously some kind of powerful wizard selling equally powerful spells. I beelined for his booth, forgetting I'd traveled here with Alayna. Finding a scroll with a few runes I thought I recognized, I picked it up and took a closer look.

"Welcome young Lord," the elderly man said, his eyes gazing forward as if looking deep into time itself. "You have need of Zerondak's powerful sorcery?" His voice had a slight echo to it, lending to the awesome presentation of it all. Then Zerondak looked down at me. His voice changed instantly to a nasally annoying sound. "Dear gods, who let the damned peasant thieves in here. Guards! Guards!"

I took a step back, alarmed. The scroll was still in my hands, so I hurriedly put it back on the table. Sure, I didn't have my nice formal clothing on anymore, but I thought I looked rather dashing in my simple tunic and brown canvas pants. Shoot, I even decided to wear the nice black leather boots from the night before and had the fancy-looking drake cloak over my shoulders. How out of my depth must I be if this is what peasants dressed like in the city?

A rough hand grabbed my arm and a guard—not a keep guard, but a plainly dressed guard with simple chainmail armor and neatly cleaned gambeson showing from beneath it—glared down at me. Atop his head was an iron helmet painted white with a wide brim all around the edges.

Before he had a chance to speak, I reacted. My previous encounter with Galt had me on edge and my power answered my faintest desire, a blue light *Sparking* out and throwing the guard from his feet.

The guard cried out in alarm, and I saw three more appear as if from nowhere as the crowd parted around us in a wide circle.

"Oh," I said, raising my hands as if I might be able to signal an apology when the words failed to come.

"Get him!" Cried the guards, one pulled a sword, but the other two leveled large halberds in my direction. Things were quickly getting out of hand.

My hand moved to the hilt of my blade. I couldn't leave myself defenseless. Either one of those halberds were likely to split me down the middle before I had a chance to react.

And as if the universe had some sick sense of humor, before my blade was halfway out of its scabbard, a halberd flashed downward right at my head. But instead of splitting me wide open, it glanced harmlessly off a golden shield that flickered to life inches from my face.

Out of the corner of my eye I saw golden light flash as Alayna stepped out of the crowd. She was chanting a spell, one hand held outstretched towards me—most likely maintaining the shielding spell—the other making odd gestures in the direction of the guards, chanting all the while. All at once, the guards froze and slammed down to their knees, weapons falling harmlessly beside them.

I looked closer and could see dozens of small chains made of golden light holding each of them down. My blade fell back into the scabbard, and my heart fluttered at the show of magic. She was powerful, and although she didn't use the kind of magic my studies normally centered around, I was intrigued at her casual show of strength.

The hand that had been pointing towards me relaxed and the shield flickered away. Alayna pulled down her hood, showing her face, making sure each guard in turn saw her, before she stopped her chanting and the chains flickered away.

One of the guardsmen, this one wearing an iron chest piece and not just chainmail, approached Alayna. I moved to stand by her side, giving the guards a large berth just in case any of them still had any ideas.

"Lady Alayna Varyin, Defender of Light," the guard said, his voice lazy and sarcastic. He saluted by slamming his gauntleted hand against his chest and inclining his head to her. "Please excuse my brashness but explain why you've interfered with a matter of the city Guardsmen's Guild. Your name holds great power, but we operate independently, and General Daris will not be pleased to hear of this."

"You think to remind me," Alayna began to say, her eyes pulsing a golden light as her voice rose in volume. "Of the operations of this city? Give me your name, rank, and direct superior." The guard seemed stunned momentarily by the wrathful response, and while he stuttered, Alayna bore into him. "Now!"

"Yes, sir," the guard said. "I mean ma'am or Lady Alayna right away. My name is Veltrees Gother, my rank is Lieutenant of the central corridor, and my direct superior is Captain Markus Rull."

My eyes zipped back and forth between the pair during their confrontation. Things sure had gone to shit quickly.

"Gather your men and take that man into custody," Alayna said. For a moment, I thought she meant me, and I stepped back reflexively, thinking I had another fight on my hands. But her finger pointed past me towards Zerondak, the scroll vendor.

His eyes went wide, and I noticed they were no longer glowing. In their place were sunken brown eyes that were currently bulging wide as the guards approached, not waiting for their lieutenant's command.

"What crime has he committed?" Veltrees Gother asked, his tone much more respectful now.

Her eyes ran over the older man, now being led over in the arms of two burly guards. "Several, it would seem. First, he instigated this entire unfortunate mishap against Caldor Miles, Knight and Vassal of Blackridge Keep, and honored guest of Lord Variyn my father."

The lieutenant's eyes shifted to me, giving me a look that seemed to say, this guy is important? I returned his gaze with a shrug and a look that answered, I'm as surprised as you are, man.

"Secondly, you will want to speak to the Master of Goods at the Tradesmen's Guild. He will be interested to know that he has a charlatan selling fake scrolls in his famed Spiral Market."

Several of the nearby crowd gasped at this, and I couldn't

help but laugh a little. This entire scenario was more dramatic and sillier than I'd experienced my entire life up to this point. These merchants and nobles needed to loosen their clothing a little. They were rung up way too tight.

Alayna seemed to be enjoying herself. I studied her face during the exchange, and several times I saw the hint of a grin threatening to turn up the side of her very serious-looking face.

"We will look into this matter right away, Lady Variyn," Veltrees Gother said, motioning to his guards to bring the elderly man, while a single guard stood behind to watch over the abandoned booth that overflowed with arcane scrolls.

Faster than what seemed normal, the square fell back into a bustle of activity. People buying, booths selling, vendors calling out their wares.

"That was weird," I said, looking over to Alayna—her hood had already been put back into place, her expression hidden.

"As much as I enjoyed that," she said, turning to face me. "You've just forced me to stir up a good bit of trouble. Between the Guardsmen Guild, the Tradesmen Guild, and then there was my accusations against that vendor."

"Wait," I said, still grinning despite the serious tone Alayna had; my voice dropped to a whisper. "Was Zerondak not selling fake goods?"

"How should I know?" She said, grabbing my hand in hers and walking us towards one of the larger buildings. "He wasn't an *Awoken* though, he was using an enchanted item to add the eye glow and voice distortion. I could see the glow from an amulet under his clothing."

"Remind me not to make you mad," I said, looking up at the building she was leading us towards. It was identical to the others, in all ways but one. This building only had a single sign, meaning—I guessed—that a single shop owner ran all three floors.

The sign was larger and grander than the others, with golden painted letters spelling out a phrase in the runic language. What it meant I wasn't sure, but below the words were several words I could understand.

"Gilfoy's Emporium, magical items crafted by House Gilfoy," I read the words aloud. "There is a 'House' Gilfoy?" I asked, pulling Alayna to a stop outside the door. The foot traffic here wasn't as bad, so we weren't in the way.

"You should pick up a history book while we are out shopping," Alayna said sarcastically. "You really haven't heard of House Gilfoy?"

"No," I said slowly. "Should I?"

"House Gilfoy was once the largest of all the houses, probably two hundred years ago? They led a rebellion against the king after uniting all the houses under their banner. They failed, and their lands were stripped from them, along with any credible use of their name, but in recent years they've made a new name for themselves as expert craftsmen."

"What does the King think about House Gilfoy using their title again?" I wondered aloud.

"A House title can't be completely removed without all current Houses agreeing, and that was never going to happen. So, I guess the King just deals with it. They aren't a threat anymore. Garyus Gilfoy was killed during the rebellion and without his voice to unite the Houses, no one was willing to keep it going. None of his brothers or sisters had the passion he did for bringing down the monarchy."

"I do need to pick up a history book," I said, wondering what other interesting facts about my homeland I didn't know.

"Come on," Alayna said, "I sent a messenger ahead so your items should be already set aside."

"Lead the way," I said, gesturing wide with my arm as if inviting her forward and trying but failing to look as proper as those that passed by us.

CHAPTER 16
GILFOY'S EMPORIUM

The outside of the building was built with various shades of red brick, creating a veritable sea of color. It was broken only by the windows, a door, and the ash gray mortar used between the bricks. While other buildings had painted their sides white, or in one particular case, gold, this appeared to be the only unpainted building. It made it stand out in a rustic way that I found visually pleasing.

Just as with the outside, the interior proved to be simple, yet elegant. At one side of the open floor plan was a row of black oak checkout counters, each one manned by a neatly dressed man or woman. The rest of the open space was filled with neat rows of merchandise, a mix of tall bookshelves and wide tables all covered with items. They held anything from small red vials neatly placed in stands, to wicked looking swords —some even glowing or letting off an aura.

Lining the left side, away from the tall windows that filled the area with light, were various armor stands, each covered with a unique armor set. I continued to scan the aisles but didn't catch sight of any books, despite the many bookshelves being used to hold items.

"Welcome to Gilfoy's Emporium, we are having a buy two and get a third potion for free sale today. Are you a specialty member or would you care to sign up?"

A very monotone and steady voice sounded from a suit of armor that had been setup next to the door. I jumped back a measure, very confused and startled. Upon closer examination I realized it wasn't just a suit of armor, it was living armor.

I'd read about the creation of basic golems by magic practitioners, mostly about ones that had gone rogue and become monster mobs, but this was something different altogether.

The armor was lined with hundreds, no thousands, of tiny glowing runes. They simmered and shifted as the thing adjusted its position to regard me, the closer I got to examine it.

"These are new," I heard Alayna say, I reached out to run a hand down the arm of the metal man.

"Please do not touch the Runeforged," a friendly female voice sounded out behind me. I turned to see a beautiful elven woman wearing the same simple white and black uniform as those helping people purchase their goods, standing behind me with a patient smile on her face.

She clasped her hands together just under her chin and continued. "Well met, my name is Ena, allow me to introduce this Runeforged model. This is the latest model, Runeforged Beta Five. They are built using advanced Rune Scripting and Arcane Forging methods, as well as our patented Summoner abilities to give the shell a bound elemental spirit. As such, it can follow a full range of commands, even serving as a competent dungeon companion. This particular unit was made with a rock spirit and is very durable. For the sum of five hundred thousand gold or, if you qualify for our specialty credit program, twelve monthly installments of forty-five thousand, and it can be yours today!"

"I doubt even my father would spend that much on a golem," Alayna said, her head shaking in disbelief.

"The elven royalty have purchased four dozen, and I believe King Newaliyn ordered several dozen specialty units constructed as well. Don't worry, though, we have a budget base model that we hope to begin mass production of in the coming months. Rumors say it'll still cost a hundred thousand gold, but they've said to have found a way to allow the Units to grow in strength, so less essence is needed for their initial construction, which cuts costs considerably. The only draw-back being, that you will have to supply it with a weekly dose of mana or come by one of our many locations to have it topped off for a small fee."

"That's pure genius," I said, admiring the construction of the Runeforged. "How do you keep them from acting independently? What if the elemental spirits used to animate them decide they are tired of following orders?"

"Our patented binding spells guarantee that such an event will never be an issue," Ena happily announced. "Would either of you be interested in becoming specialty members? You can get a ten percent discount on items you purchase more than once from Gilfoy's Emporium, excluding specialty created items of course."

"We are both members under the House Variyn account," Alayna announced. "However, my friend here, Caldor Miles, is a newly appointed Vassal, so if you could issue him a seal for future visits that would be greatly appreciated."

"Hmm, House Variyn? We have a specialty item and several small other purchases awaiting pickup, will you be handling that today?" She asked.

Alayna nodded.

"Perfect! If you could just show me your seal?" Alayna reached into a small satchel and pulled out a plain looking wooden token. She raised it and as I watched a Large 'G' appeared on the surface, glowing golden. "That will do, thank you, follow me to the third floor and we can retrieve your items."

Ena the elf turned on her heels and walked towards a door set into the side of the wall. She pulled on a lever, and I heard the clink and clank of gears.

"Thank you and have a nice day." The Runeforged's monotoned voice startled me, as I was still a nose's length from it, inspecting the runes.

"Come on," Alayna said. "There is no way I can justify buying that to my father, you'll have to use your own funds."

We joined Ena beside the wall, and just as we arrived next to her, the wall opened, two doors sliding free on their own accord. I couldn't help but think that it seemed very spooky.

Ena stepped through the door into an equally large and open room. As I moved to follow her, I noticed a barely perceivable shimmer in the air between the two rooms.

A portal, I realized.

Stepping through, I quickly moved to a window and sure enough, we'd just teleported from the first floor to the third. What a waste of a portal.

"How much gold is wasted because you all decided not to install stairs?" I asked Ena, moving quickly to catch up with the pair.

"None," Ena announced happily. "Gilfoy Emporium uses patented mana collectors in conjunction with some clever gear-work and spells to maintain one hundred percent mana free portals."

"How do I get a job working here," I asked, my mouth practically watering from all the advanced magical achievements I'd encountered during my short visit to Gilfoy's Emporium.

"Our recruitment offices are on the basement level if you are seriously considering employment," Ena said, her smiling never wavering.

"He's not," Alayna said a moment before I said, "I'm not."

There were wonderful magical achievements to learn about for sure, but I was going to be a great adventurer like my father, and nothing would stand in my way.

"Okay, wonderful. If you would wait here at the counter, I will go into the back room and fetch the items ordered."

She was only gone a few seconds before she came out with a small black box, no bigger than my fist. The box was fairly plain with a black lacquered colored sheen and copper edges reinforcing the sides.

"I hope you don't mind, but we stored the rest of your order inside the custom piece you ordered."

"That's fine," Alayna said, stepping forward to examine it. "How did you use it without having it bound and keyed yet?"

"The bound and keyed runes will click into place when you turn this piece here," Ena indicated a small copper circle on the one side of the box. "However, please be aware that once the runes have been set, they cannot be undone, so be careful to have whoever is meant to use the storage device ready to bind the box. Until that point, anyone will be able to retrieve the items."

"Very good," Alayna said, reaching out and taking the box. She flipped the small lid open, her eyes glazed over as if she stared into the distance at something I couldn't see. She held her hand open, and one moment it was empty, the next she held the edge of a leather breastplate with strips of overlapping metal on it.

I gasped. That was a dimensional box, or some Gilfoy's patented version of an incredibly rare dungeon drop known as an endless bag. The dungeon dropped version used a lost Ordu magic to create and store items in pockets of space, similar to the spell that created a personal sanctuary.

Alayna repeated her 'glazed-over' look and pulled several other items free, laying each on the counter in front of us until finally she shut the lid and set the box down as well.

Altogether, I saw roughly a dozen items. The first few were part of a set of armor, each made of simple leather with reinforced metal—upon closer inspection I saw that runes had been scratched into the surface of the metal strips. Each piece had the same repeating pattern, though what it meant I couldn't figure out.

In total, the armor consisted of a chest piece, leggings, gauntlets, gloves, boots, and even a simple helmet.

Alayna must have noticed my close inspection of the armor, because she said, "That is a set of Leather Banded armor of the Owlbear. It increases your Strength and Intellect attributes. I wasn't sure if you were planning on doing a mixed class like your father, but I assumed you might. If you go a different path, just let me know and we can exchange it for an attributed beginners set of armor that aligns with your chosen class."

An entire set of armor. I knew for a fact that Emory hadn't had the benefit of such armor when he started out. I still remember the extra hours he worked doing menial tasks for various shop owners to be able to afford a plain banded leather chest piece and a basic shoddy short sword. He was going to be so jealous when he heard about the crazy things that had happened over the last few days.

I ran my hand carefully over the armor, faint pulses of power emanated from it and from somewhere deep inside I could sense it.

"Thank you," I said, turning my head to face Alayna. "This is too much." I gestured to the items and the magical storage box.

"It doesn't come free of strings, Caldor," Alayna said, her eyes locking with mine. "My father is in need of powerful supporters, and you might not see it yet, but you have the potential to be a titan among men. Without even activating my 'Detect Magic' skill, I can feel it pulsing off you in waves. You're like a furnace burning red hot all the time."

"She's right you know. I'm relatively low level and never picked up the 'Detect Magic' skill, but you are like a beacon, practically glowing with power," Ena the Elf said, interrupting our conversation. Alayna glared in her direction, and she shrunk back. "I'll leave you two to your conversation. The charges have been added to House Variyn's account. I'll be back in a few minutes to key your membership token."

"That doesn't make any sense," I said, frustrated. "I literally became a *Sparked* days ago. I shouldn't be anything special, that isn't how it works. I've read plenty of academic studies of *Sparked* and none of what is happening to me lines up."

Alayna grabbed my hand and forced me to look in her eyes. "I told you that every Noble House has its secrets, and you understand that we know how to guarantee a *Sparked*, well maybe if I explain how we do it you can really understand why you are so special."

I met her stare but said nothing.

"What makes a *Sparked* a *Sparked* is the collection of essence at their core. Because everyone is different, we all collect and naturally use essence at different rates. People who never

'Spark' are those that are in a deficit with their natural expenditure of essence and rate of collection."

She took a deep breath, looking back and forth to make sure no one was close enough to listen in. "You seem to know a fair bit about monsters, what do you know about monster cores and the essence that they release upon death?"

I shrugged. "I know of monster cores, it is rare to find one undamaged after the death of a monster, the dust from the crystal formations are used as spell and crafting reagents. But I'm not well versed in how essence works other than the fact that adventurers kill monsters because they get essence that can be spent to increase their skills, spells, and levels."

Alayna brightened and took over the conversation. "Yes exactly! So, when a monster is killed it releases all its essence. Naturally, most of it just dissipates into the air, ground, water, and other elements around the broken core, but a portion will travel towards the pull of another core. For example, monsters will fight and kill each other until one stands at the head of the group, much stronger than the rest. Like that boar you killed, it was a dire boar, much stronger than a normal boar."

"But boars aren't monsters," I said, interrupting. "It's a normal beast."

"Until it becomes strong enough. Once it becomes a dire boar, it is a monster. Just as all beasts can become monsters if given enough essence or something else mutates them beyond their normal strength. In the case of the boar, my father and I think the Chaos monsters roaming the forest infected it with something that caused it to mutate."

"Okay, so are you telling me you mutate other nobles to become *Sparked*?" I asked, my understanding of the subject getting less clear as the conversation continued.

"No, humans, elves, beastkin, and the like, we are different," she assured me. "You see, one of the reasons why roaming monsters have been all but cleared out inside House Variyn territory is because we know the truth. All humanoids, at least the ones we've come across, can be *Sparked* and be *Awoken*. All they need is enough latent essence to interact with a Mana Shrine."

Alayna took a deep breath before continuing. "That's why most don't even try, they are naturally able to collect only enough to keep themselves living, but what they don't understand is that if they were to kill monsters that had a core or broke a core nearby, that extra essence would wrap around them and be added to their own. So, if you kill enough you can go from having the lowest essence gathering attribute and still become an *Awoken*."

"But I hadn't killed the dire boar yet and I am certain I showed signs of being *Sparked*," I said, furrowing my brow.

"From what I can tell of your aura you have an incredibly high Core attribute, possibly even Paragon level. You would have been showing signs of being *Sparked* before puberty. I can't explain why you are such a late bloomer, but the essence you must have pulled from that dire boar has brought you to an almost dangerous level of essence for an un-*Awoken*. Unfortunately, there won't be another Prime Mana Shrine ready for the *Awakening* ceremony for another week, so you will just have to hold yourself together until then."

"Why don't the nobles share the information around *Awakening* and *Sparked*? Wouldn't the world be better if all men and woman were equal?"

Alayna laughed. "You sound like Garyus Gilfoy, from what I've read he also thought everyone should be equal. If we gave equal power to everyone it would result in chaos and disorder. There isn't enough essence in the world to support a large population of *Sparked*, so eventually the dungeons would cease to work, runes would no longer be able to pull enough magic in to operate, and the world would lose access to the benefits of *Awakening*. It just can't support so many sources pulling from it at once."

"How do you know that?" I asked, unable to accept what I was hearing.

"Well," Alayna said, she fidgeted under my gaze for a few seconds before continuing. "Well, my father told me, and his father told him. It's a well understood fact by most nobles."

"Because someone said so," I said, closing my eyes in frustration. My hand rubbed behind my neck as I attempted to release some of the building tension.

"I don't have an exact text to point to, but my father wouldn't tell me something he didn't truly believe. I'll just have to take you to our library, and you can find out for yourself. We do have a week's worth of time to kill."

"I can't stay here the entire week," I said quickly. "I need to check on my mother and my siblings."

"I didn't know you had siblings!" Alayna said, the tension draining from her posture as she perked up. "How old are they? What are their names?"

I smiled, glad to have the conversation turn to more mundane topics. I told her my twin siblings' names and shared about my mother's condition all while inspecting the remaining items on the table.

There were three sets of three potion vials, red, blue and yellow. A bedroll and several ordinary items that would be useful during longer dungeon runs. Lastly, there was a box filled with powders, teeth, small horns, and other oddball items.

"That's a reagent box," Alayna informed me. "It carries

some of the more common items needed when *Awakening* to unlock certain classes, spells, and skills. However, it is impossible to know what the Shrine will require you to get for your quest, so I'd still expect you'll have to travel a bit gathering resources."

"Thank you," I said, not sure what to do with the items now that I had them. No matter how I touched the box it didn't respond to me.

"Oh, that won't work properly until you've had your *Awakening*. But I can put the items back for you, everything except the armor. You should put that on, it'll mark you as an adventurer to common folk like that wispy bearded scroll vendor."

I grabbed the chest piece and began to undo the buckle on the back so I could try to put it on, but Alayna stopped me with a hand on my shoulder. "They have dressing rooms," she said, pointing to a row of small rooms with cloth doors on the far wall. "Here, come on, I'll help you get it on."

Grabbing my hand, she pulled me into one of the dressing rooms and helped me into the armor. I ended up leaving my tunic on, but the legging armor worked as pants with armored sections, so I slipped out of the brown trousers I'd been given. I felt awkward wearing only undergarments in front of Alayna, but she was professional and in almost no time, I was dressed.

The helmet had a strap on it that allowed me to hook it to my belt, which I did. It would be hot enough outside wearing the armor, I didn't need to stick something atop my head as well.

The armor was surprisingly flexible and easy to move around in, I hadn't ever really worn any armor, so I wasn't sure what I expected, but it wasn't this. I found that even though I was covered head to toe in leather, I felt cool inside. Whether that was an effect of the armor's magic or some other circum-stance, I wasn't sure, and as long as I stayed cool, I didn't care.

We exited the dressing room together to find Ena the Elf smiling at us just outside the room.

"Hello!" She exclaimed, her smile widening. "Usually, the changing room is only for one guest at a time, but I won't tell anyone." She winked at Alayna who went beet red. "I have your House Variyn Token ready! I just need a drop of blood right here at the top to bind it to you."

I had to do a double take. "You want some of my blood?" I asked, stunned. Blood magic was something I'd spent a few weeks studying, but it was considered a forbidden branch of magic as it gave incredible control over mages who could obtain blood of their enemies.

"It isn't what you think," Ena the Elf said, holding her hands up as if to pacify me. "Because you aren't *Awoken* yet, I need something completely unique to you to bind it. Okay, I guess that technically makes it blood magic, but you will be keeping the item tagged with your blood, so there is nothing to worry about."

"I know he isn't *Awoken* yet, but I've seen him direct mana before. Maybe we could try just using a small bit of that instead?" Alayna offered.

"Hmm," Ena the Elf didn't seem convinced but shrugged her shoulders after a moment and said, "We can try!"

"So, what do I do?" I asked.

"Well, if you were *Awoken*, you'd touch the token, and it would ask you if you wanted to add mana into it. Since you can't do that, I'm not sure," Ena said.

Alayna pressed a finger against her lips in thought. "Do you remember how you felt when you flung that guard away from you?" she asked.

"Sort of," I said, my hand rubbing the back of my neck nervously. "It's like a force that churns inside of me and sometimes I can't keep it in check and a little bit escapes."

"Okay so touch the coin and let some out. Easy." Alayna said, biting her lip.

I reached out grabbing the wooden token. Nothing happened. Closing my eyes, I imagined the growing storm inside and tried to visualize a small amount releasing into the token. I heard a large crack and my eyes shot open. Looking around I followed Ena and Alayna's gaze to my feet and saw that the floor had been scorched black. Ena and Alayna had taken several steps back.

"It worked!" Alayna exclaimed excitedly.

My eyes shot to the coin, and I saw a brilliantly bright G glowing on its surface.

"You put a good deal more than was required and nearly blew me across the room, but you did it," Ena said, far less excited than Alayna. "That coin has enough mana in it to stay active for several lifetimes I'd wager. Is there anything else I can assist you with?"

"Nope, I think we are done for today," Alayna said, grabbing my arm and guiding me towards the portal door that was still open to the first floor. "I'm hungry. Let's go get some food."

I nodded, letting her drag me out of the shop. The Rune-forged bid us farewell as we passed it. At some point I really needed to get me one of those. The small black box containing my items bounced at my waist. I had put it into a medium size pouch that Alayna had provided, not knowing how else to carry around a magical box.

CHAPTER 17
TIME TO EAT

After only minutes of walking, we entered through a twenty-foot-high gate, into an open courtyard with various tables set up outside of an insane number of restaurants. It was like they had built the entire area just to cater to rich folks who wanted to eat various foods in a garden. I counted almost two dozen distinct signs denoting different types of food. In Creeshaw we had two main choices if we wanted to eat food prepared by someone else, and for such a town that size it was rare.

I noticed that this area had quite a few more adventurers, folks dressed in armor that glowed faintly with various colored runes, long flowing robes of wizards, mages, sorcerers, and even a few I was pretty sure were warlocks—their staffs glowing with a sinister purple light—but no one really seemed concerned, so I let it go, not that I was strong enough to challenge anything but the weakest of adventurers. I hadn't even been *Awoken* yet, I had no levels, no spells, abilities, skills, not even a single attribute that I could define like adventurers.

A tall and slender elf wearing brown leather and a green

cloak passed us by, a spectral tiger following closely behind—it's see-through form pulsating slowly in the light of the noon day sun. A thought suddenly occurred to me.

"Is your Astral Wolf okay?" I asked, turning to Alayna and catching her eye.

"Who, Vash?" Alayna asked, smiling. "Yeah, he's fine. I let him return to the astral plane to recover."

"The astral plane? I didn't know you could do that. Is that unique to Astral creatures like Vash or would that elf girl who passed us be able to let her spectral tiger go to a, uhh, spectral realm?" I had spent so little time learning about magical companions, ones that weren't technically monsters and existed —from what I can guess—in realms just outside of our own.

"I'm not an expert by any means, but yeah something like that," Alayna said. "Maybe I can set up a meeting with our master tamer. He is a bit eccentric, but he has a wealth of knowledge."

"I'd like that, thank you," I said, my hand came up and rubbed behind my neck as I scanned the available places to eat. There was one eatery that seemed to be attracting more adventurer types than any of the others and I began walking in that direction, Alayna followed behind me letting me take the lead and saying nothing.

A rustic wooden sign hung over the door, it read '*Awaken*er's Pub' a nondescript figure with a flaming aura pulsing upward depicted beneath the words. I squinted and focused on the sign, it was actually pulsing, the little adventurer powering up on the sign moved a little bit here and there and the aura danced like a live flame.

"That is cool," I said, pointing upward. "How did they manage that without some kind of..." I trailed off, seeing a thin line of crystalized sparkling light feeding into the sign. I followed the line up to a row of glowing gems. They'd set up a recharging gem mechanism, ingenious!

"Oh, I hadn't ever noticed that," Alayna said, her eyes finally seeing what had me all excited. "I've never eaten here before, I was thinking we could check out the Foradee Elama, they have the tastiest desserts."

"But look at this place," I said, my jaw hanging down a little.

"Okay but you have to promise to take me to Foradee Elama another time and we can share one of the desserts!" Alayna exclaimed; she was very excited about this Foradee Elama place. But I really wanted to go inside and see what else this magical *Awaken*er's Pub had going on.

"Why would we share?" I asked, scratching at the side of my head. "Are the portions really big or?" I was halfway through the sentence when it clicked. I awkwardly stole a glance over to Alayna who looked like she was about to burst into a fit of laughter at my expense. "Aw I get it. You think I'm handsome!"

"Stop," she laughed. "You are embarrassing yourself. Let's go eat, I'm starving."

I reached out and took Alayna's hand, leading her inside. She didn't pull away or resist so I let out a breath. Galt's words echoed in my mind, and I nearly let go of her hand, but fuck that guy. I gave Alayna's hand a squeeze and looked for an open table.

The inside was more magnificent than the cool magical sign had promised. Above our heads hundreds of glowing little butterflies flapped their wings, some landing on tables and exploding in a small pop and burst of light. In their place after they exploded were plates of food, or drink, and in one case a small piece of paper—a bill most likely.

The inside of the room was much bigger than its outer walls suggested, being easily twice the size as the outside dimensions. On the furthest wall, in front of several doors that led to the back kitchen, was a long sturdy bar. No less than twelve barkeeps walked up and down giving out drinks and taking orders.

The walls were painted in vibrant colored scenes depicting dungeon dives, battles against armies, monsters, and even a huge black dragon attacking a village. Each of the scenes moved, depicting the events in a slowed down replay. The scenes weren't more than a few minutes each, I gawked at them long enough to see them repeat.

"There's a table," Alayna said, pointing to a small two-person table just off the wall.

She must have assumed I was scanning the room for a table and not just enjoying the sights. This time she pulled me forward, our hands still holding tightly. There was something exhilarating about feeling the warmth of her skin that I couldn't really quantify. It had been some time since I'd been with a woman, but I was sure that it was more than just that. From what little I knew about Alayna, she was powerful, intelligent, and caring—a person I could really grow to care about.

I broke my grip from her hand and slipped in front of her, getting to the table in time to pull her chair out. She laughed at me and sat in the other chair. Feeling momentarily deflated, I gave into the nervous laughter and sat in the chair I'd pulled out.

"Rude," I said in mock offense.

"Caldor," Alayna said, her purple eyes catching mine. "I have spent the entirety of my life with servants trying to do everything for me. That isn't what I want when I'm outside that stuffy keep."

"Sorry," I said. "I guess I'm not used to being around noble women."

"Oh dear," she said, laughing. "Any other noble woman would probably be offended that you didn't let the 'help' pull out the chair and think you were some kind of barbarian for doing that lowly work. But I just want to be normal. I want to be an adventurer or a crafter, anything but head of House Variyn, like my father hopes I'll be."

Our conversation was cut off when someone approached our table. I looked up and stared into the yellow eyes of a cat woman. She must be a beastkin, I'd only ever met one or two and they'd looked like humanoid bears.

"Welcome to *Awaken*er's Pub, my name's Kate, can I take your order?" Her words came out quick and terse, like she'd said them hundreds of times just today.

Her features were more humanoid than cat, but her entire form was covered in grey and black hair, like a house cat. Her ears sat closer to the top of her head and her eyes were sharp and keen. She wore clothes, well armor really, like a normal person would, not that I expected her to be walking around in just her fur, but the bearkin I'd met barely had loin clothes on when I saw them back in Creeshaw.

She looked dressed for battle, wearing a leather breastplate and a sword at her waist, but the white apron she wore over it all spoke of her job as a waitress. She cleared her throat, and I looked up at her giving my best awkward smile.

Remembering that I was supposed to be ordering, I looked around and not seeing any menu or list, I gave Kate a blank look.

"The menu is being magically projected," Alayna said, she

seemed awed by this fact so it must not be a common thing. "We will take two kelt ales and two of your 'Hero' meals."

"Thanks, it'll arrive shortly," Kate said, giving me a confused look before turning and walking away, her tail moving with the swing of her hips as she walked.

"See something you like?" Alayna asked, bringing my attention off Kate's swaying hips and back to Alayna.

"Oh, uh no," I said, grinning stupidly. "It's just, we don't get many beastkin out in Creeshaw."

"They aren't very common here either," Alayna admitted, turning to look at Kate once more. "It's even weirder to see one working at a pub."

"Everyone has to make a living somehow," I said, raising my eyebrows to emphasize my point.

"Yeah, I get it," Alayna said. "I'm out of touch because I'm a rich noble. I'll have you know that most adventurers over level twenty are pretty well off too. Which begs the question, shouldn't you be rich? Your father was way beyond level twenty and the coin he could earn from a single of the more difficult dungeon runs could rival my father's monthly tax intake."

"What, really? How much gold does your father get from taxes each month?" I asked. My father had always told me that he only used as much as he needed and never anymore. He had said it like he was proud of doing so, but I hadn't had a frame of reference and usually just liked having my father home.

"Gold?" Alayna asked, laughing. "No, he collects a large amount of platinum each month, obviously most of it goes to upkeep, wages, and supplies, but he does well. I don't know the exact figures, but I imagine he has enough stored to purchase a Runeforged or two and could buy one from monthly proceeds after paying all his debts in half a year. Don't quote me about any of this, I'm not the treasurer."

My jaw dropped. A single platinum was equal to one thousand gold! With one hundred platinum I could have had my own castle built and pay the wages of an army of servants to keep it maintained for a few months. I really had no way of knowing if those amounts could truly go as far as my imagination thought they could, but I could dream. My mind raced as I tried to work out how much exactly the Lord of Variyn might collect.

"Are you joking?" I asked, deciding that was the only proper answer.

"No, I'm really not," Alayna said. "Obviously he would need to split his take with his group and find buyers for the armor and weapons to get the full value, but older dungeons are incredibly deadly and so the rewards for challenging them are immense."

At that exact moment, two small glowing butterflies landed with a poof and swish. As I watched, they were replaced with two purple ales. Kelt ale, I wasn't aware that kelt fruit was used in such a way. I took a tentative sip and let out a satisfied sigh. It was sweet but had a full body taste as well. I took another long swig before finally putting the glass mug down on the black oak table.

The buzz of conversation, laughter, and the occasional yell of frustration filled the room. Wide windows on the side of the building let in a constant stream of light, filling the room with a sense of majesty. I wondered how exactly the light from outside seemed to keep pouring in when I was almost completely certain the sun had been coming in at an angle before we arrived.

Staring at the windows I saw my answer. The windows

didn't let out into the square, but a mix of soft and hard light shone in like a wall. I couldn't stare for long as it began to hurt my eyes, and it made me wonder what would happen if someone jumped out one of those windows that didn't lead to the outside.

"Pretty cool, huh," Alayna said, she seemed to have noticed where my gaze was transfixed. "Some of the magic they accomplish these days makes me wonder if the days of old are returning."

Oh great, more history I thought, but smiled in response, doing my best to appear interested. "What do you mean?" I asked.

"The Ordu of course," she said, sounding flabbergasted.

I perked up, very interested now. The Ordu were the beings that are said to have organized magic and formed worlds like Wyrd, where we lived. The idea that others might be approaching the magical understanding of the Ordu gave me goosebumps.

"But from what I've read, the Ordu basically made magic, how could anyone else match their knowledge if they literally made the rules?" I asked, more to myself than to Alayna, trying to work out the logic in my head.

"No," Alayna said, she didn't laugh or giggle, but had a confused grin on her face. "Ordu didn't make magic, magic is magic. The Ordu organized the threads of magic, creating Order where there had only ever been Chaos. Starting the ancient battle between Order and Chaos. Or so that's what the good book says."

"The good book?" I asked, laughing. "What does that mean?"

"It's just what my father always calls the book of Vanir.

Don't you have a temple in...where did you say you were from again?" She asked, a puzzled look on her face.

"Creeshaw," I answered. "And no, we don't. The closest temple to the god Vanir is here in Variyn. But we do have some old shrines to the moon and sun deities, I think they are Elven, but like I said I'm no history buff. I prefer to stay in the here and now."

"Lunar and Solar!" Alayna exclaimed, raising her finger up like a wand. "Yeah, those are Elven gods, they almost have as many gods as the dwarves, beastkin, goblins, and orcs combined."

I smiled at that. There was no way that was true, the four races she mentioned were all more tribal in their worship: worshipping anything from seasons, to metals, to the rain and snow. I'd heard in the tavern that Orcs even worshipped the dirt.

I'd never met many non-humans living out in Creeshaw, but I had to hope that some of the stories I had heard were true. Nearly all of my information I got about the outside world was from tavern rumors or what little my father decided to share.

"So even if the Ordu only brought Order to the magic," I said, trying to get back on topic. "That would imply an insane understanding of how things worked. This pub is cool and all, but I just can't reconcile in my mind wizards today coming close to the fathomlessness of the Ordu."

I wasn't religious and didn't practice the Vanir faith, but I understood that the Ordu were as close to a race of gods as you could get. Something occurred to me then that I didn't understand even after reading a few passages on the subject.

"Well, you see," Alayna had begun saying something, but I cut her off, not realizing I had until I was already speaking.

"You use mana the same as other magic users, as a priest right?" I asked, then stopped realizing I had completely blown over her while she was talking. She frowned at me, but it slowly turned to a grin.

"Now who's the rude one?" she asked. "And yes, but also no. As a priest I must do daily prayers to infuse my mana pool for a certain extent of time with faith. So, while I expend mana, it reacts differently than the mana used by arcane types. I can't infuse runes after my daily prayers, for instance, which makes picking up certain professions difficult, but our spells are much more potent than an arcane user of the same level and rank."

"But mana is mana," I said, frowning. "From everything I've read and tried to understand, it made the most sense that mana works the same for everyone."

"Then how do you explain warriors, rogues, and rangers who use special abilities? They don't use direct mana, they aren't casting spells, but they are calling upon the same force to do their skills and abilities. You will understand more when you *Awaken*." She finally assured me, looking up as another pair of butterflies landed with a poof and a swish.

I looked down and my mouth began to water. Apparently the 'Hero' meal consisted of a plate nearly the size of my mid-section filled with a large portion of shredded beef with brown gravy, two fist-sized portions of mashed potatoes, several cuts of cheese next to three dinner rolls, a small fruit pie, and a mess of vegetables.

I wiped away saliva that began to drip down my chin as I examined the plate. Steam wafted up along with the smells of, what was possibly, the best meal I had ever been seated in front of.

"This is too much," Alayna said, she sounded annoyed and not nearly as excited as I did. "When it said enough to feed a hungry hero, I thought they'd serve things in several courses, not one huge plate."

I just smiled up from a mouth full of pleasantly hot shredded beef and nodded along. She could do what she liked, but I was going to do my damnedest to eat every last gravy dripping bite.

CHAPTER 18
ROMANTIC VISTAS

"I ate too much," I groaned, my feet struggling to keep up with Alayna's brisk pace. "Slow down, where are we going in such a hurry?"

"Nowhere," Alayna answered, giggling as she increased her speed. "I just want to show you something, and if we don't hurry, we will miss it!"

Letting out a heavy sigh, I increased my pace. It felt as if my midsection was trying to bust out of my armor, which, while being extremely comfortable before eating, felt more like a vice trying to squeeze me to death now. But with no way to access my magical spatial storage box, I was stuck wearing it until I found a place I could change.

"We are almost there," Alayna called behind her shoulder.

I scanned ahead, trying to see where it was she might be taking me, and spotted it. Atop an agonizingly steep walk, was a pavilion that overlooked the city.

Sweat dripped down my face. The cooling effect of my armor was not able to keep pace with the heat generated by my swift climb, while being overfilled with food. Meanwhile,

Alayna, who had finished not even one tenth of her plate, skipped merrily ahead of me whistling a tune.

My face twisted into a sneer; it was all I could do to keep myself from throwing up the entire contents of my stomach on the side of the path. Well-dressed couples passed us as we walked, looking annoyingly comfortable in the cool evening. Just ahead, I could see the sun was beginning to set, orange rays of light outlining the distant mountains.

"Hurry, we are missing the best part," Alayna said, running on ahead and reaching the top.

I did a quick check around and seeing no one looking in my direction, I retched into a bush just off the path. It wasn't pretty but I felt wonderfully normal afterwards. The food I had eaten tasted much better going in than it had been going out.

"That won't do mate," a voice from behind me said. I turned to find a middle-aged man all dressed in dark leathers and daggers at his side.

"Oh sorry," I began to say, but the gnome—I had never actually met one but his height and lack of dwarven bulk made it clear—shook his head and raised his hands.

"You misunderstand me, good sir," he said, pulling a metal tin from his black vest. "Have a mint. You can't go up there to kissing point with bile on your breath. Especially not if you are going with the Lady Alayna." The gnome winked, holding out his tin to me.

I grabbed one of the white chalky mints from inside and gave it a tentative sniff.

"How do I know this hadn't been messed with," I looked up to ask, but he'd already turned and was off walking down the path.

On the wind I heard his voice, but it was distant. "Don't

say I never did nothing for you." It was followed by a hearty laugh that slowly faded to the quiet of my surroundings.

"Well, that was a bit creepy," I said, looking down at the mint. If Alayna was truly taking me to some kind of 'kissing point' as the stranger had called it, I would definitely need a mint, but it just went against everything I knew to trust an odd stranger.

I risked it and gave it the quickest and smallest of licks. Waiting an excruciating two seconds, I didn't die, so I threw the entire thing into my mouth and ran to catch up with Alayna, who was practically shouting at me at this point.

"Finally," she huffed, and straightened out her cloak nervously with her hands. "Sit here, and we can watch what is left of the sunset." She pointed to a stone bench at the edge of the pavilion, then grabbed my hand pulling me down next to her.

I didn't resist, but a knot grew in my stomach, this one not from an overabundance of food. Did she really want to kiss me or was that gnome just playing a prank on me? I took a deep breath and decided to just let things happen naturally.

I turned my head discreetly and blew air into my hand, giving it a thorough sniff. Minty fresh, and I hadn't died, so that was good.

"You come here a lot?" I asked, my attention completely on Alayna while hers was stuck to the horizon watching the sun sink into the horizon.

Without looking up she said, "I've been a few times, but always alone. Galt is pretty good about letting me slip out, as long as I get in before dark, so I rarely get to sit up here above it all and enjoy the peace of watching another day come to an end."

"I wish this day didn't have to come to an end," I said.

Immediately I regretted my corny words, but Alayna just giggled and squeezed my hand.

"Me too," she said, turning her attention from the horizon to shoot me a grin.

Her purple eyes Sparkled in the light of the sunset, her blonde wavy hair rustling from a sudden breeze. A strand fell into her face, and I reached out to brush it aside.

As I did so, her eyes went wide for just an instant then she grinned and leaned forward, closing them. Realizing what was about to happen I took a deep breath and leaned in as well.

Her kiss was tender and her lips soft. I felt her hand reach up behind my head, pushing me in closer. I didn't resist, and after an acceptable amount of time, the kiss ended.

She was breathing heavily, catching her breath, and smiling from ear to ear, her face had the slightest flush of red as I stared into her beautiful eyes. I realized my breathing had accelerated as well and I took a deep breath, smiling back at her.

"Well, that was nice," I said, grinning like a fool.

"You've missed the sunset," she said, teasingly. I looked to the horizon and the sun had indeed fully set.

"There was plenty of beauty in the view I had," I said, pulling her into my chest. We sat there in silence for some time, before she eventually spoke.

"I want to be an adventurer," she said, her voice filled with longing.

"Then be one," I said, squeezing her against me to show my support.

"If it were only that easy."

"Why shouldn't it be," I retorted. She laughed and peeked her head back, purple eyes gazing into my own.

"Have you thought about what profession you will choose?" She asked, nuzzling her head back into my chest. The night air was beginning to chill and if it weren't for a few hanging oil lamps that had been lit, we'd be sitting in darkness, the moon failing to be bright this evening.

"In all my time spent wishing to be an adventurer," I said. "I never considered a profession. If I can be completely honest."

"Of course, you can," she whispered, she let out a cute sigh and reached behind me pulling my black drake cloak around her as well.

"I never really believed I'd become *Sparked*, but there was nothing that was going to keep me from being an adventurer."

"Well, you can't be an adventurer if you don't ever get your *Spark*," she said.

"I know, I know, but I figured if I studied monsters and magic long enough, I'd be able to learn their weakness and manage without ever going through an *Awakening*."

"Except the first time you took a monster down, you'd probably begin to *Spark*," Alayna said, her hand resting on my thigh.

"Well, I didn't know then that nobles were keeping all the best secrets to themselves."

She looked up at me again, shadows playing across her soft features and cute nose. "Not all nobles are bad. I'm a noble."

"I know," I said, reassuring her that I didn't in fact hate all nobles. "It's just, can you imagine wanting something so bad it hurts and then finding out there had always been an answer and things weren't as black and white as everyone told you?"

"I can understand the first part," she whispered, then saying aloud. "I want to take you to the library tomorrow."

"Oh yeah," I said, laughing. "You already know the way to my heart. I love books."

"So I'm beginning to understand," she shot back, followed by a laugh of her own.

"You should come with me on my first dungeon run," I said, having a sudden thought.

She snorted. "As if my father would ever allow that. Besides, I'm already level fifteen and you need to get to level five before you can enter a dungeon."

"I'll ask your father and if he says no, we will do it anyway," I said, speaking as if I was making a mock royal decree.

"Let me know what he says after he takes your title and lands away," Alayna said between laughs. "You know what though."

"What?" I asked, my hand slipping behind her back and around her waist, pulling her closer.

"My cousin Zander could probably go with you. He is a Templar of Light, so he can heal and do a decent amount of crowd control. He's only level 9 though, so not so high for someone just starting out."

"Your cousin is an asshole," I said, trying and failing to not sound mean while insulting her family.

"He can be a bit much," Alayna agreed. "But he really is sweet. His father is really rough on him."

"I noticed that," I said, giving her that much. "But I'm not sure I could count on him keeping me alive in a dangerous dungeon."

"Oh don't be dramatic, he wouldn't," she paused, seeming to consider. "Well, he might let you take a little bit of a beating, but he wouldn't let you die."

"Very convincing," I teased. "I'd prefer you to fight beside me and tend to my wounds."

"What role are you hoping to fill," Alayna asked, sitting up and adjusting her cloak around herself.

I sat up as well, my cloak falling free from around her. "Damage dealer most likely. I don't think I'm up to be the front-line tank or anything, but I could see myself being a hybrid like my father. I'm hoping I have the right attribute line up to become an Arcane Knight, like my father."

"I'm sure you will," Alayna said smiling as she stood. "We should start heading back before Galt sends out a search party for me."

"Just one more thing before we head back," I said, looking around me like I was searching for something, then stepping forward and pulling Alayna into a deep passionate kiss.

"Thank you for a wonderful day." I said as our lips parted.

"Thank you," Alayna said, her voice breathy as she staggered back half a step with a smile on her lips.

CHAPTER 19
MEETINGS

We arrived back at the keep and went our separate ways, promising to meet up the next day to visit the library. Oil lamps lit my way through the maze of corridors as I searched for my room. I knew I was going in the correct general direction, but I wasn't in a hurry to lay down.

My mind was awash with thoughts of Alayna and our time together. She was amazing. So smart, powerful, strikingly beautiful, and her lips. The thought of our kiss nearly had me turning back to see if I could find her again, but I restrained myself.

A guard approached from down the corridor, and I started, thinking it was Galt here to take off my dangling bits, but relaxed when I saw that it was a guard I didn't recognize. I nodded my head to him in greeting, but he didn't acknowledge me, continuing forward alone.

As he was passing me by, I realized that I'd very rarely seen guards walking alone in the keep, they almost always went in pairs. He must be on urgent business so he couldn't be bothered to interact with me, yeah that must be it.

I'd barely got the thought into my head when rough hands covered my mouth, and something hit my head hard. A flash of white then black, and I slipped into unconsciousness.

When I finally came to, my mouth was dry, and I broke into a coughing fit. My eyes flashed open, pain shooting through my skull as I coughed. Something was tied around my head, obscuring my vision.

"Oh good," a sinister oily voice said. "I was worried our messenger had done permanent damage and we would have to dispose of a body tonight."

I took several measured breaths. I had to stay calm and reach down to release my *Spark*. Down deep inside I felt it moving and I beckoned it to push outward. If I could lash out at those around me, I might be able to make a run for it. I wasn't an expert at using my *Spark*, but I could use the momentary surprise to my advantage.

Unfortunately, no matter how hard I tried, my *Spark* just wouldn't do anything. An utterly annoying laugh filled the corridor around me, at least two people.

"Did you see that?" A new voice said, this one distinctly female. "He tried to lash out with his tiny *Spark*. Keep trying boy, you can do it."

A third voice, this one low and deep spoke, "Don't patronize the boy. That *Spark* of his is anything but small. But listen, Caldor, it is our power against yours, that *Spark* of yours won't be able to budge while we're suppressing you. The fact that you tried while blindfolded and in obvious danger gives you my respect but listen carefully and you will leave here in one piece, you have my word of honor."

There was a soothing feeling coming from the newest speaker's voice and something told me he was lacing his words with magic, some type of emotional spell. But soothing spell or not, his words rang true.

I checked my hands and feet, both were bound. There was nothing I could do if they could truly keep my *Spark* from manifesting. But I had to try again. Reaching deep I grabbed hold of the power and ripped with all my might. This time I felt something.

It wasn't what I wanted to feel though, my head swam from the effort, and I threw up all over the front of myself.

"Damnit boy!" The first oily voice again. "I'm not cleaning that up, he can stew in his own filth."

"Caldor," the deep, almost elderly voice again. "You will hurt your ability to *Awaken* if you continue to rip at the seams of your very soul. I commend the effort and can't say I've ever encountered anyone in over a hundred years that could manipulate their own being like you've just tried but calm yourself and hear our words. We mean only to give you much needed information."

I spat out the bile from my mouth toward whomever was in front of me, not out of spite really, just to clear my mouth. The female voice scoffed, and I heard feet walking towards me, heels if I had to guess by the click against the stone. Then out of the darkness came a loud smack as a hand connected with my face.

"He isn't worth this effort," the female voice hissed just inches from my face. "Let's end him and be on with our night."

"I told you when I brought you in on this," the fatherly deep voice again. "That we wouldn't be harming him, not unless we had no other choice, so control your damned temper and sit down!" His voice reached a fever pitch, and the room went still.

Finally, I heard the click, click of heels and what must have been her sitting back down.

"Very well let's continue," the oily voice said. "We represent a certain group that has interest in helping you succeed over the coming months. You represent a possible shift in power, and we want that power."

No matter how hard I strained my eyes I couldn't make out any light or details beyond, so I focused all my attention on remembering their voices. Memorizing each inflection and vibration I could.

"He speaks crudely, but truthfully. Things aren't exactly as they seem. House Variyn's peace is under threat. With so many of the nation's most powerful adventurers dead following the events leading up to the Battle of Lynsteen Pass, the race is on to secure the rising generation's loyalty. There are many among our number that worry Lord Variyn will seek to end the peace and reach for new lands as he secures more and more potentially powerful allies. It was all but confirmed when he gave you Blackridge Keep, an old, dilapidated fortress at the very edge of what is considered House Variyn land."

"I think we are overestimating this child's value," the female voice, this time low and wrathful. "I vote we kill him and be done with it before it has a chance to be a problem."

"I think she could be right," the oily voice said.

"We will not kill the son of Elkor without cause, you slimy bastards. I would sooner have your own heads laid out before me!" I flinched at the fury in the deep-voiced man's words.

"You knew my father?" I asked. Who was this man, these three people who kidnapped me from inside the very heart of House Variyn's keep.

"Our request is simple, Caldor." The deep voice continued, ignoring my question. "Will you promise, when the time comes, you will refuse to join Lord Variyn in his conquest? As a vassal and a Knight in his service, you will be in a unique position to oppose the start of a bloody conflict."

The female voice interjected moments after the deep voice finished. "And don't you even think of recapturing Blackridge keep from whatever forces have taken control, that will bring only pain for you and anyone you take there."

"Enough," the deep voice snapped. "He can do as he wishes. In fact, I think it would be wise for him to begin to fortify himself an outpost. If he chooses to follow our warning, he might find himself in a position where he needs a fortress."

Two voices huffed at that but said nothing. The room fell into silence, and I realized they must be waiting for my response.

What did I think about what they'd said? It wasn't like I needed to commit to anything right now, and what did I care if House Variyn decided to push their borders? Every single house did the same, or so I heard from the tavern gossip. Personally, I didn't want to stop adventuring and dungeon diving to participate in a border war. Could I even bring myself to kill other adventurers, or even soldiers, for the whims of a House Lord? Deciding it was best to choose my words very carefully, I spoke.

"I don't know what conquest you are referring to, but I have no desire to get intertwined in a conflict among sentient races. I want nothing more than to be an adventurer, slaying monsters, defeating dungeons, and growing strong so that I can help those who cannot help themselves," I said, doing my best to not betray my own values but also not committing to anything.

"So much like your father," I was surprised to hear the oily voice say in a sneer.

"He is," the female voice agreed.

"Indeed, he is," the deep voice. "You will be a powerful asset when the time comes. Sleep now and be rested."

A calloused hand, as large as my head, closed over the front of my face. A sudden warmth spread across me, and I became very tired. The next thing I knew, I was sitting up in my bed and sunlight trickled in through the open curtains.

———

I sat on the edge of my bed; a wet towel slung over my neck. After waking up in my armor and an ache in my head, I'd stripped naked, putting my armor, sword, and cloak aside.

What had I gotten myself into? My emotions ran unchecked, from pleasantly happy when I thought about being an adventurer and my day with Alayna, to disturbed and fearful when I considered the implications of last night.

Lord Variyn obviously had enemies that were willing to strike out against those that would support him, but they hadn't killed me, hadn't even hurt me really. Was Lord Variyn actually planning on actively pushing for more land? I knew that border skirmishes happened, even in the peaceful borders of House Variyn, but there were rarely reported to be any deaths and the borders remained the same. Why did I have to be smack dab in the middle of it all.

If Lord Variyn had enemies, that meant those same people would be enemies to the future leader of House Variyn, Alayna. I made up my mind then and there. I would seek out Non, the Master of Whispers and tell him every detail I could remember. I was sure he would be better equipped to deal with all of the information.

As for myself, I still was going to focus on what was most

important to me, becoming an adventurer.

It took longer than it should have to finish washing myself with a cold cloth. Each stroke of the wet cloth brought with it another memory, another thought.

I was beginning to understand why my father decided to keep his life as an adventurer mostly obscured from us. If he got into half the twisted vines of plans and political maneuvers that I had in just days, he'd be able to do little else but deal with this crap.

I clasped my cloak to my armor and looked in the mirror. My hair was a mess, the waves turning to hard curls. It had been nearly three days since I'd had a proper bath, so still one more day before I'd normally take one.

Someone had been kind enough to leave a bottle of scented liquid for me, and I splashed it over my body before dressing. The scent of it itched at my nose as I did a final check before leaving. My box was tucked away in a small carrying bag I slung over my shoulder and under my cloak.

Stepping out of my door I saw Mick, leaning against the opposite wall, nearly asleep as usual.

"You got in late," Mick said, his voice emanating from the shadows of his helmet that lay tipped over his eyes.

"Yeah," I said, shrugging. "You know how it is, seeing the sights and all that."

"Well next time you spend the day out in the city with Alayna, you be sure Galt doesn't hear about it. Word is, he is looking for you."

My face blanched and I let out a groan of frustration. "Great."

"Ha, you'll be fine," Mick said, finally looking up and tilted his iron helmet back. "Just try not to look him in the eye, he has a wicked temper and doesn't care to be challenged."

"I need to find Non," I said, suddenly eager to get to the task and out of the hallways that Galt patrolled.

"Non?" Mick's eyes widened in surprise and shook his head while raising his hand. "You don't want to get entangled into any mess that Non has interest in, lad. Besides no one finds Non, he finds you."

"Well, that's unhelpful," I muttered, slapping Mick on the shoulder as I passed. "I'll see you tonight for some cards." I called back, moving down the hallway to begin my search.

I'd asked three different servants the location on Non, before the man appeared out of seemingly nowhere.

"You have word?" Non's voice came from behind me, and I jumped in surprise.

"Yeah, I have a few," I said sarcastically.

"Follow me and say nothing until I tell you," Non said, walking past me, his form all black cloth and silent footsteps.

I followed him down a narrow hallway, maybe some kind of servants' corridor, and to a room with a door without a handle. However, as we approached, I heard a click, and it swung open on its own accord.

Inside the room was a single long table, no chairs, and bookshelves overflowing with scrolls and books covering every wall. It was perhaps twenty feet long and half as deep. There were no windows and I saw no oil lamps burning, yet there was an even ever-present light filling the entire room.

Non slapped my hand as I reached for a book, the lure of untouched knowledge too much for me. Behind me I heard the door close and a click indicating a lock being thrown, all the while Non stood beside me, his face unreadable.

"Okay," Non said, his voice soft yet still loud in the eerie complete silence of the tomb-like room. "Tell me what is so important that you would go around throwing my name to every soul you meet."

"I was kidnapped last night," I said, meeting Non's eyes and searching his reaction for any trace of surprise, I saw none.

"I know," he answered, his expression not changing. "Tell me what you remember."

I recounted it all as close to word for word as I could remember. The entire time Non stood like a thing carved of granite, not moving and emotionless.

"This was expected, but I wonder what dealings they had with Elkor, to instill such a deep sense of restraint in the deep-voiced gentlemen." Non turned away from me and I saw his hand go up, possibly to scratch at his chin.

He walked forward and pulled a scroll from a stack on one of the higher shelves, seemingly at random. I watched as he pulled it open and began to read. Taking a step forward, I tried to get a glimpse of it. Unfortunately, it was in a language I had never seen before, it looked like one long squiggle.

"Don't waste your time looking over my shoulder. I've my own personal language I created to discourage prying eyes from diving into my secrets," Non said, not taking his eyes off the scroll he was intently reading.

"Aw I had forgotten this tidbit. Your father was quite the revolutionist it would seem."

"What do you mean?" I asked, moving to stand beside Non. "My father was an adventurer; he didn't mess with politics, or if he did, he never told me."

"I can imagine he had many secrets, but no, you are right. If my notes are accurate, he was as steady as the river, your father, he believed in what he believed in and did not waver from those ideals, all the way to his end. You see, your father was appointed as a Protector of the Realm by High King Newaliyn himself, not by a Lord who rules over a smaller House. So, when old 'golden crown' wanted a problem dealt with that he was too lazy to deal with himself, your father and his merry band of do-gooders were the first to answer that call."

I listened intently, and Non continued to talk, never taking his eyes from his scroll. "He could have, and was offered several times, a position as Lord, Vassal, Knight, even once it would seem Captain of the Royal Guard, meant to protect the King. But he turned down each offer, never giving a reason or expla- nation. An odd one your father was, that much you ought to know."

"My father was the most honorable, bravest, and strongest man I ever met." A righteous fury growing in my chest. Why did Non's words make me defensive? I took a deep breath and focused on what was upsetting me.

Perhaps hearing that my father had turned down so many titles while I accepted one before even becoming an *Awakened* stung a little. I wasn't the same as my father, but I would try my damnedest to be.

"Yes," Non said. "I'm sure that he was indeed. Well, that is enough for now, here is your reward for completing my little quest, but you will have to wait till your *Awakening* to claim any essence."

Non dropped a fist sized pouch into my hand. I opened the drawstrings to see a bag filled to the brim with silver.

"Thank you," I awkwardly mumbled, walking towards the door. It clicked and swung open as I approached. The hallway was darker than I remembered but stumbling about for a while I finally made my way into a corridor that I recognized.

I'd gone only ten more steps before Galt rounded the corner ahead of me, his eyes going wide when he saw me. I considered turning and running, but instead put my hand on the hilt of my blade while at the same time straightening my back. I didn't want him to think I was taking a fighting stance, but he needed to know I wouldn't allow him to rough me around anymore.

"There you are," Galt said, his voice unusually calm for a man that I thought wanted to kill me. "Lord Variyn requires your presence, come now." A cruel smile appeared on his lips, matched by a devious look in his eyes.

Damn, he got me.

"Show the way," I said, doing my best to keep my voice from showing my apprehension. Galt I could stand up to, but the Lord of House Variyn was a completely different story.

If half of what I'd heard about him was true, he could disintegrate me with the snap of his fingers. He was a powerful Light Templar, and I was nothing yet.

Galt led me to a large study, the walls lined with trophy heads of many different kinds of monsters as well as a few artifacts that pulsed with undeniable power. Behind a large wooden desk sat Lord Variyn, wearing the same silver crown and a cloak of black furs.

"You may go, Galt," Lord Variyn said, his eyes not lifting from a ledger that sat in front of him.

Galt flashed me a wicked grin before saluting Lord Variyn and leaving.

"Take a seat, we have matters to discuss," Lord Variyn said, gesturing to a simple chair that sat on the other side of his massive desk.

I sat, my eyes running from monster to monster, trying my best to identify each. Owlbear, Dire Camel, Blood Hawk, a Rock Elemental, and several that I couldn't identify.

One in particular pulled my attention, by far the largest of the displayed monsters, it was a large sphere with several dozen eyes spread out over its bulk, it had no limbs of any kind that I could see, just a huge ball of eyes. What skin I could see was a vibrant blue and had the rough look of leather left out in the sun.

I wondered how a mouthless monster like that could eat or if it had another means of digestion.

"Admiring some of my more exotic kills?" Lord Variyn asked, pulling my attention from the ball of eyes. "I had a very exciting youth, there were times I wanted to keep my life as an adventurer going, but I knew where I was truly needed. Respect for the way things are meant to be is important, wouldn't you say, Caldor?"

What did he know or was he always this cryptic? "I like to follow my father's way of thinking. He told me that being powerful held a responsibility to help those who couldn't help themselves. So, if being the Lord of House Variyn helps more people than you being an adventurer, then yes I agree," I said, carefully choosing my words.

"Your father was wise beyond his years," Lord Variyn said, his hand coming up to stroke his short beard. "What do you know about what it takes to run a city or a small part of a larger kingdom?"

I frowned. "Not much," I assured him, shrugging. "Up until a week ago I tended to my family's orchard, trying my best to make sure we had enough money to keep food on the table and the livestock fed."

"A farm boy then? How quaint. You've been whisked away into a fabulous adventure, filled with danger and excitement. How old are you?"

"Twenty-four," I answered after a few moments of thought, "Twenty-five next month."

"Your father did you a disservice," he said, taking a sip from a silver goblet to his left. "I'm not sure how it was done, but you've had your *Spark* suppressed. You have such a high natural affinity that you should have shown signs of being *Sparked* before puberty. I think your father figured out a way to suppress your natural talent, maybe a tonic of some sort, but you'd need to have been taking it weekly, if not more, to keep such power in check."

I was speechless and confused at how he would know any of this and decided to ask him just that. "How could you know anything about my natural affinity or that I've been suppressed. My father would never do that to me!"

"Easy," he said, taking another long drink. "I've had a few of my arcane councils spying on you, studying you. Except for a few hours last night, you'll have to tell me how you accomplished that, we've had our eyes on you since you arrived. You are quite the oddity after all."

"Since I arrived?" I asked, the room felt as if it was getting hotter. I could feel beads of sweat forming on my forehead.

"Yes, I am aware of your time with my daughter," Lord Variyn's voice showed a hint of humor. "But worry not, I care not for who my daughter chooses to spend her time or feelings for, but I would warn you to think before you speak of grand adventures with her. She has the same desires I had when I was young, but times are far too treacherous for her to be out on her own."

I considered telling him about my secret meeting, but I had told Non and that would have to be enough. Surely Non would inform him of things if he thought it necessary.

I pushed the thoughts about being watched from my mind and considered his other words. Could it be possible that my father had known that I was *Sparked* and tried to prevent me from *Awakening*? It went against everything I knew about him; besides he'd been gone for years now and I just barely *Sparked*.

He said I would have to have drunk the tonic weekly.

Oh no, oh no, it couldn't be.

Dread filled me and realization sank in. Warrick, my closest link to my father and someone I considered a dear friend, had insisted we meet weekly since my father's passing.

Maybe he didn't love tea as much as he claimed. Could he have truly been drugging me this entire time? Keeping me from my destiny?

I thought I knew him.

Warrick would do anything for his friends, and maybe that is exactly what he was doing. The air around me began to crackle with power, small arcs of blue lightning shot off my body as I began to see the truth.

Warrick was a good friend, closer than a brother to my father. If my father had told him to keep me from *Awakening*, he would do it. And if he had died, he would probably see it as honoring his dead friend's request, adding weight to the responsibility of it all.

Damnit father! Damnit, damnit, damnit. My fist clenched and it took all I had not to just scream aloud. Pressing my eyes shut I tried to calm the growing pulses of power building around me.

"Control yourself, Caldor. I'm sure that he had good intentions, whatever they might have been," Lord Variyn said, his voice fatherly and kind.

My eyes snapped open as something hit me hard, it wasn't a physical hit but hit on my very soul, my power constricted and was forced down. Looking up, I saw an older man with a long wispy beard had appeared, his hands pulsing blue as he stood over me.

"Control the power, do not let it control you," a deep voice said, it was vaguely familiar, but I couldn't place it. "If you continue to allow your power to rip out of you in such a chaotic way, you will not make it to next week's *Awakening*, young Chaos Slayer."

My eyes went wide as I placed the voice. The older man noticed my expression and he gave me a subtle nod, moving his head back and forth as if to say 'no'.

"Who are you?" I asked, storming to my feet, my power still unable to pulse outward, under the weight of whatever force this elderly old man was employing.

"Some call me," he paused scratching at his beard as if he couldn't remember what people called him. "Tim. I am high seat of the Council of Sages that serves House Variyn in all matters related to advising and control of magical objects."

These are the people Warrick had been selling research to all these years. Was Warrick in league with the people who kidnapped me? I didn't know, but I was going to be having a long talk with Warrick whenever I saw him next.

"He is also the wise wizard who has been keeping a keen eye on you these last few days," Lord Variyn said, regarding the elderly wizard with a warm expression.

"That's right," Tim said, bowing his head and a smirk appearing on his face. "I've seen *everything* you've done. In fact, I know you haven't eaten breakfast yet, so here, have a snack." With a wave of his hands, Tim produced a plate filled with fruit, cheese, and a few slices of sweet looking cake.

I didn't know what to do, so I took the plate and sat down. If I told Lord Variyn that the man he trusted to watch my 'every move' was in fact in league with a shadow council of some kind whose motivations were dubious at best, I'm not sure I'd make it out of the room alive.

I looked up to thank Tim for the food, still not knowing what I should do, but was surprised to find that he was no longer standing over me. The steady pressure around me, holding back my *Spark*, lessened, and then eventually faded. While still confused and fairly upset at the news I'd received, my rage had passed, and my *Spark* no longer threatened to lash out at those around me.

"That was all very exciting," Lord Variyn said. "But shall we get back on topic. I brought you here to tell you that I have a quest for you, once you've *Awakened* of course, but the information can't wait. Several more Chaos monsters have been spotted, a few slain, but most escaped. Will you make it your priority to deal with this threat and find what is bringing these Chaos beasts into my land?"

"Yes," I said, the words leaving my mouth before I had a chance to consider what I was agreeing to. My father might have kept secrets from me, even trying to stop me from fulfilling my destiny, but I still believed in him. I would do as he did and fight back the Chaos.

"Very well," he said, his eyes returning to his ledger. "I believe my daughter is awaiting you in the western library, if you hurry to the kitchen, perhaps you can bring her some food as well. Silly girl hasn't eaten anything yet either. Seems she has other things on her mind."

I blanched, expecting that any moment Lord Variyn would decide my interest in his daughter was misplaced or that her interest in me was equally misplaced, but he did nothing, just continued to study his ledger.

I stood and excused myself. Once more I felt a mixture of dread and excitement as I found my way to the kitchen to get a suitable breakfast for Alayna.

It didn't take long to find the same kitchen I'd been directed to the day before, but to my surprise I recognized someone.

"Merlin!" I called over the din in the bustling kitchen. It looked as if they had already started work on whatever would be served for lunch. Merlin, the former owner of 'Merlin's Pub' was calling out orders and rushing here and there. Having spent a fair amount of time in his establishment, I was certain he'd remember me.

He wasn't as old as the current owner of the establishment, being in his mid-forties if I were to guess, but he'd earned several long streaks of gray hair that I hadn't remembered him having a year back.

His clothing was the typical fashion of the kitchen staff, long white aprons, white caps that were yellowing from sweat, and black boots and trousers, however his hat was noticeably taller than the rest. His eyes were a brilliant yellow and they widened in surprise upon seeing me.

"Young Caldor?" He asked, squinting towards me. "Is that really you? I'd heard your name mentioned in rumors from the other staff but had yet to see you walking about. You still drinking pubs out of their casks of ale and leaving them penniless?"

I laughed, remembering a time Emory, Ismene, and I had partied a bit too hard, literally draining his entire stock. We'd only been able to pay a fraction of the bill and spent the next week working off our debt.

"Oh yeah," I said, my hand rubbing the back of my neck. "No, we've learned a measure of self-control since then. How's the new position been treating you?"

His eyes were sunken in with faint black circles. He looked tired, stressed, but content—a large smile on this face.

His hand lashed out like a snake, grabbing a small bit of meat off a large platter, one of the other servants—a young black haired boy—was carrying towards the door. "It isn't an easy job," he began to say, but stopped short to yell at the boy. "Get that back in here, we haven't glazed it yet. You want to be the one to tell Bren why his meat isn't sweet like he prefers?"

Just as quick as his voice raised into a roar it settled back to a normal tone and he turned back to me. "Like I was saying. It isn't easy, but the pay and benefits are beyond anything I'd ever had gotten in Creeshaw. How can I help you, Caldor? I hear you are a lordling yourself now."

"Not really a Lord," I assured him, my hands coming up to forestall him. Then moving closer I whispered, "I got my *Spark* and Lord Variyn made me a Vassal and Knight."

Merlin nodded. "I heard as much. You are either lucky or you are being played for a fool. Careful you find out which," he whispered back to me, his head swiveling to see if any of his staff had heard him. None had, from what I could see.

"Anyways," I said, making a point to raise my voice a touch above normal volume. "I need a meal for two, I'm bringing breakfast to Alayna."

"Oh, are you now?" Merlin asked with a sly smile crossing his face. "Give me ten minutes and I'll have it sent to you." He paused, eyeing me. "Your room?" He asked, winking.

I laughed aloud. "No," I answered my hands held in front of me to emphasize my point. "To the western library, please. Also, could you give me directions to the western library?"

Merlin chuckled, giving me a quick set of directions and a promise of food to be delivered.

CHAPTER 20
LIBRARY

I approached the door to the library and my face felt hot. It wasn't often that I felt nervous, but it was clear that I was being watched, not only by Lord Variyn, but by the people who had kidnapped me last night as well. Doubt scratched at my mind as I stood in front of the double doors into the library.

What if I was reading too much into it? Maybe it wasn't his voice after all. It had been late, and my head was hurting, it made very little sense for someone who worked so closely with Lord Variyn to be his enemy. If the wizard truly had ill intent, why wouldn't he just kill Lord Variyn?

I was bad at politics, things in my life had always been simple and straightforward. If I needed food, I'd tend to the farm or go hunting. If someone wronged me, I'd step right up and tell them as much. All this sideways talk, schemes, and dealings in the dark were such a foreign concept to me.

They had me doubting my appointment as a Knight and Vassal. Was I really just being set up as a pawn to be moved around by others? It left an uneasy pit in my stomach to consider such things, but this was my reality now and I needed to be as calculating in battle as I was in my interactions with those around me.

Letting out a long steady breath, I opened the doors. They creaked as I pushed, and Alayna's brilliant purple eyes looked up from a large tome to meet mine.

Her expression went from surprise to joy, as soon as she saw me. She stood and walked towards me. I let the doors close behind me with a soft, thud.

Alayna walked right up to me, and I put my arms around her as she fell into my embrace. We kissed then, it was shorter than I would have liked, but it sent electricity throughout my body at the touch of her lips.

"Good morning to you too," I said with a quick grin.

"I thought you'd forgotten our meeting," Alayna said, pulling free and taking my hand. "I hope that will help you remember me better in the future."

I was finally able to take my eyes off Alayna long enough to see the library.

Warrick had the largest library I'd seen so far in my life, it was an expansive room with nearly a hundred books, he traded and sold his supply for newer books all the time, so I always had plenty to explore.

But this library, the smaller of the two inside keep Variyn—Merlin had told me when giving me directions—held at least a thousand books, possibly more.

It was a domed room filled with reading tables, sofas, and a completely enclosed fireplace and a grand chimney with carvings all the way up its length, opening out the top of the domed room. The ceiling was made of a translucent material, maybe glass but I didn't know enough to say, and I could see a steady stream of smoke puffing from the large chimney's top.

The walls were lined with three levels of bookshelves, each with a walkway to give access. Several black iron staircases gave access to each level. I had to pick my jaw off the ground as I slowly twirled, taking in the sight of it all.

There were enough books here to keep me reading the rest of my natural life. Non's words echoed in my mind. Would it be possible to just level up by reading? The variety of books that were potentially held in this room set my mind alight.

"How do you ever leave this place?" I asked Alayna, walking slowly to the closest bookshelf and out of her grip. She said something in response, but I didn't hear it, my eyes scanning the titles.

History of Known Runecraft, Runecraft Theory by Aldwin Retch, Magical Runic Theory, and its many applications, A study of Monster Cores and Runic Engraving by Merlin Clearwater. I hadn't heard of a single one of these titles, most of my studying having centered around monsters and general magical theory, not the profession of runic theory.

A hand grabbed roughly on my shoulder and spun me about. Alayna was there, and before I could react, she kissed me again.

"Do I have your attention back?" She asked, venom in her voice, but the anger didn't reach her eyes. She was clearly amused by my obsession with books and not as hurt as she pretended, I hoped.

I gave her my best cheesy smile and said sorry, following her back to the desk. Just as we reached it, the door opened and the young black haired boy entered carrying two platters of food, covered by silver domed tops.

He gave us an awkward head nod, rushing to an adjacent table without any books, setting the dishes down.

"Your breakfast," he said, his voice quiet and his eyes downcast.

"Thank you," I began to say, then scratched at the back of my head. "I didn't get your name before. What is it?" I asked.

"My name is Jon, Jon Shettal, Lord," Jon said, his eyes still downcast.

I chuckled and held a hand for him to shake.

"Nice to meet you, Jon Shettal. My name is Caldor Miles," I said.

He saw my hand and looked up, his deep brown eyes traveling to meet mine. After an awkward few moments, my hand held out in front of me all the while, he reached out and took my hand, giving it a surprisingly firm shake.

"Nice to meet you, Caldor," he said as if tasting the sound of my name. He shot a nervous smile and then bowed to Lady Alayna before scurrying out of the room.

"I think you scared him," Alayna said, a contemplative look on her face.

"Your beauty made him nervous, I'm sure of it," I declared. I crunched up my face into a mock-serious look and gave her a few very stern nods of my head. "Yes, that must have been what happened."

"Quit teasing me," she said, laughing. "What'd you get for breakfast? I'd forgotten about eating entirely."

In response, I lifted the lids, and a small cloud of steam wafted up off the prepared meal. Small flat cakes, sausages, and under a separate glass dome, a variety of sliced fruits.

My stomach gurgled at the sight of it. I was used to eating leftovers from the night before for breakfast. On the rare occasion when we had extra time or money, some boiled oats, but this was unbelievable.

"Oh, my favorite!" Alayna cried, her face lighting up as she sat down and motioned for me to sit beside her.

A part of me wanted to ask if she ate like this every day, but I withheld the question, certain it would come across wrong. Instead, I smiled back at her and dug in.

We ate in relative silence, the entire library empty except for us. But it wasn't an awkward silence, instead it was pleasant. Between bites and drinks of a spiced wine that Jon brought, returning shortly after he left to say he'd forgotten it, we stole glances at each other.

Flirting with our eyes. I finished first and spent the next few minutes studying her face. She was strikingly beautiful, her blond curls falling free about her pale, freckled face. The rosy, red of her cheeks stood out among her delicate skin, and her purple eye makeup made her eyes seem larger than they actually were, drawing attention to the brilliant orbs.

"My father is using you," Alayna said, as she finished. Lifting her napkin out of her lap and placing it atop the remains of her food.

The sudden and odd change of topic startled me. "I know," I said, my hand lifting to rub the back of my head. "I mean, I was beginning to suspect. Also," I leaned in and whispered, "He has a wizard monitoring me, and he saw us last night."

It was Alayna's turn to be startled. Her face turned a vivid red, and her brow furrowed. "Is he now," she said, standing and marching over to the bookshelf on the east side of the room. She scanned several titles before pulling one free. Then without looking at me, she walked back to the table and grabbed the knife that had come with her meal.

"What are you going to do?" I asked, bolting up to follow her as she headed for the door.

"I am going to give us some privacy," she said, her voice eerily calm.

I watched as she went to work, copying runic symbols from a page of the book she had grabbed with shocking accuracy considering the tools she had at her disposal. After a minute or two, she had carved three interlocking circles of runes with three larger ones surrounding the smaller ones on the surface of the door.

Turning, she handed me the book *Magical Runic Theory and its many applications,* along with the knife. Both her hands rose, and she pressed them against the door, chanting loudly.

I couldn't recognize any of it, but it continued steadily for several minutes. With a flash of light, the runic symbols lit up, followed by a few trickles of black smoke. Then, after a long moment, they stabilized into a steady faint blue glow.

Her form visibly slackened from the effort, and I used my one free arm to steady her.

"Are you okay," I asked, but she had already recovered and stood, letting out a weary breath.

"I'm fine," she said, taking the book and knife back and walking to our table. "That will keep prying ears and eyes from listening in for the next few hours. We are lucky I haven't done my prayers yet. I had to invest a substantial amount of mana to ensure that my father's cronies couldn't just push through it."

"How'd you do that?" I asked, grabbing the book that she set down in front of us and leafing through it. It all made little sense at first glance.

"I chose Rune Smith for my profession," Alayna said as if that explained it all.

"I'm not really familiar with professions," I admitted, my hand rubbing at the back of my neck nervously.

"Oh yeah, that's right. Well, when you reach level ten, you

get to choose an *Awakened* profession. Most of them are based around mana infusion, but what sets them apart from a job any person could just pick up is the ability to gain essence, use perks, and complete complex tasks in a fraction of the time."

I nodded along, trying to understand what she meant. Was she saying if I had just carved the same symbols and pumped mana into them, it wouldn't have the same effect?

"For instance, House Variyn employs nearly a hundred blacksmiths, but only one Runic Blacksmith and one Enchanter. While the items they make are focused around utility and armor, they are essentially doing the same tasks as their un-*Awoken* tradesmen."

"So, one of them could make me a set of magical horse-shoes?" I joked.

Alayna didn't laugh and nodded along. "Yeah, in fact, my horse has a set that allows it to pass terrain several times better than a normal horse. And I have magically fashioned reins that keep my steed from tiring as fast as a normal horse. The perks can be huge, but mostly they are subtle. For instance, your armor, cloak, and sword all have subtle enchantments to them, as well as a few substantial ones."

"What about my armor, cloak, and sword?" I asked, my full attention focused on her now.

She gave me a wicked grin and shook her head. "No," she said. "I think that perhaps I will let you discover the nature of them yourself. I can't wait till you *Awaken*; the entire world will blossom before you."

I gave her a frustrated glare, but it turned into a wide smile in just moments.

"I can't wait," I declared.

"So now that we have some privacy," I said, glancing towards the door. "What do you want to do?"

"There were a few things I wanted to make sure you understood," Alayna said, her face reddening. "I'm not sure anything can come of us."

"What? Why not?" I asked, confusion taking over once more.

"Well, it's like I already told you. My father is using you, and if the incidents with the Chaos monsters continue, he will probably set you up as the person to take the blame. First, by raising you in public opinion as a capable, seasoned adventurer, then slowly announcing your failures. I've seen him do the same thing with other problems. He is a kind and noble soul, but his first thoughts are always how to keep House Variyn safe and at peace."

Someone should tell the shadow council that kidnapped me as much, I thought, trying to reconcile the man I'd met against everyone else's view of him.

"I'm not so sure, and something doesn't make sense about that," I countered, giving her a blank stare. "He announced both you and Zander as dealing with the threat as well."

"But did he give Zander a keep to rule over? Just watch," Alayna assured me, her eyes filled with concern. "I just want you to be careful. If we allowed ourselves to continue like this, it would only end badly."

"I don't care," I said, looking her straight in the eyes, my hands reaching out and holding hers. "To hell with all of that. Alayna, I have to tell you something that happened."

"About what?" She asked, her eyes softening.

I explained my kidnapping and my suspicion of who had done it, one of them at least.

"I don't know what it means, really. I'm no politician, but I plan on taking control of that keep, and I will build a town that will be free of the shadowy politics and manipulations."

Alayna didn't speak for several long moments. Her face had become a mask, and I couldn't make out what she could be thinking.

"Very well," she finally said, her eyes softening and giving me a cute smile. "I look forward to seeing what kind of home you build, and if I can find my way to you, I will. But that's enough politics for now. I brought you here so you could enjoy some books." Her hand waved about, gesturing to the large library.

I leaned in, and we shared a long passionate kiss.

"Thank you," I said as I turned and sat down, pulling the book about Runes she had grabbed to enchant the door. I gently turned the pages until I got to the start of the text.

The next several hours passed far too quickly. At some point, Alayna left, returning with food and then leaving again a few hours later and not returning. I'm sure she said her good-byes, but I was far too distracted to notice.

My research began with runes and ended with a book about folding runic carvings into metal during the smithing process. Very little of this information would be useful to me, but it was beyond fascinating.

After my eyes grew too heavy to stay open and light waned to nothing, I finally pushed my way from the desk and groggily shuffled my way to my room. To my surprise, I saw Mick and three other guards, two of which I recognized from the previous night of cards.

"Aye," Mick said as I entered. They'd pulled the small bed table over and used it to hold their bets while keeping their cards close to their chests. "Thought you'd forgotten about us."

I quickly splashed my face with water and found a place around the table, spending the next few hours drinking, laughing, and losing money to Mick. By the time they finally left, I had lost nearly ten gold but had plenty more tucked away. I collapsed on the bed, instantly falling into a dreamless sleep.

CHAPTER 21
NEARLY READY

The haze of sleep faded, and I felt the warm touch of the sun as I sat up in bed. The covers were soft, the pillows filled with actual feathers, and I marveled at the size of the room that I had stayed in for the past few days. I was fairly certain that it was nearly the size of our modest home.

Today it all ended. I would be leaving for home, but I would need to return in less than a week. A part of me wanted the dream of a life to continue, but I needed to visit my mother and see if the tonic was helping. And what of the twins? If the Heddals were still watching them they'd need to be paid a bit more.

Oh crap, I'd forgotten about my ass.

There was nothing to do now, but I hoped that Breanna the donkey was being tended to.

My life back in Creeshaw seemed like a faraway dream when compared to the exciting and fast-paced few days I'd had. And it was only going to get more exciting. Soon I'd join the ranks of adventurers out slaying monsters, casting magical spells, and discovering ancient secrets.

In less than a week, I'd be as my father was, or at least I'd try to be. There were restrictions based on your attributes to what class you could choose, but I had faith in my destiny. I was meant to be as my father was, a hero, a champion of the weak.

I held my father up in my head as a sentinel of truth and justice, but it was hard to forget some of the facts I'd learned. He had lied to me. Somehow, he had hidden what I was from the world. Or at least that is what I was meant to believe. Could I trust someone else's word over that of my father or Warrick? Again, I decided that I needed to speak with Warrick at the first available chance I had. He was my friend, and I knew he would tell me the truth if I asked.

A soft knock on the door grabbed my attention. I was dressed in a white tunic and my undergarments, all of which had been freshly washed the day before and left for me on my bed. Thinking it was probably just Mick or another guard, I swung the door open.

A tall and strikingly beautiful elf stood in the doorway. My face reddened, and I shifted my underpants to make sure nothing got loose. Elandel didn't seem bothered by my state of dress and let herself into the room, closing the door behind her.

"Alayna informed me that you would be leaving us today to return early next week for the *Awakening* ceremony?"

"Yeah, that's right," I said, walking towards the bed and grabbing a pair of tan pants, slipping them over my undergarments and tying them tight.

"Well, in that case, I've prepared a horse for you and will have a servant sent here to gather your belongings, as well as pack the horse. It won't be as swift as riding a griffon—it could make the distance in a matter of hours—but the journey shouldn't take you more than a day, however I will have three days' rations packed. Before you leave, you ought to bathe, your mother is excited to see you, but we wouldn't want her to think we are not providing the best for you."

"You've spoken with my mother," I said while attempting to sniff my armpits as slyly as I could. I didn't think I smelled that bad. Someone had left perfume in my room, and I'd been using it to contain the smell of my sweat and grime. Plus, I'd wiped myself clean each morning.

"Yes. I administered the mind tonic to her myself. And as Lord Variyn instructed, I'll deliver her a new supply each month," Elandel said.

"How is she?" I asked, stepping up to Elandel, my eyes wide and expectant.

"I did not know your mother before the sickness took her, but her behavior appeared normal, and she showed no signs of confusion after the second dose. It is important that she continue to take the medication. If the sickness progresses too far without treatment, it will become irreversible."

A wave of emotion washed over me. She was okay. She was going to be okay. I struggled to hold my emotions back. All of this would be worth it if she was going to be okay.

She's going to be okay, father. I will take care of our family. I will be the man of the house like you wanted.

I sent my thoughts into the endless void, hoping beyond hope that wherever souls went when they left this world that he'd be able to hear me.

Pulling myself together, I put on a serious face. I would be strong for my father, my mother, and my siblings.

"Did you tell her about me?" I asked. A sudden realization that since her mind had righted itself, she might be concerned about why I was gone and demand an answer.

"I told her only that you helped someone in dire need and that I personally had knit her boy back together. She was pacified by this and asked only when she could expect you to return. Also, your sweet brother and sister returned to her. I felt it was okay considering her stable condition."

"Yeah, that's fine," I said, my eyes staring into the distance, lost in thought. The Heddals would still check on my mother, I was sure of it. If she truly had recovered so quickly, they'd be safe with her. I turned to Elandel and held a hand out for her to shake. "Thank you. Truly, of all the gifts I've been given, this is the most precious."

She smiled and stepped forward, giving me a tight hug. I didn't resist and repeated my thanks, doing my best to keep the tide of emotions from overtaking me.

"You are welcome, Chaos Slayer," she said, releasing me. "I have one final message for you. Queen Elsena of the Elven Nation, Eldah'ren, invites you to visit her capital city of the same name on the shores of the endless waters. Further she extends the same privileges she granted your father, as she will of any of your bloodline, to enter into her nation and be among her people as long as you desire. She bids me tell you that her heart is light at the news that Elkor has an heir to walk in his footsteps and wishes you to take this blessing as a gift of welcome."

I knew my father had traveled among the lands of the Elves before but like in all things to do with his family, it would seem he chose to keep the details hidden. Elandel raised her hands before me but waited to catch my eye before beginning. I gave her a slight nod, not knowing what to expect from this blessing but unwilling to offend friends that my father had made.

Words of power, ancient and foreign to me, spilled from her lips, and she began to chant. A soft golden light emanated from her hands, and a warmth spread throughout my body.

As fast as it began, it was over. But the gentle warmth

remained, invigorating my senses. My body felt stronger, my mind more alert, and my eyes picked out details all around me that I wouldn't have thought to pay attention to. A spider in the upper corner of my room spun a bug up in its web. Motes of dust seemed strikingly clear as they passed through the rays of sunlight from my window.

"This feels amazing," I said, no adequate words coming to my tongue to express the joy of the gift I'd been given.

She smiled at me; her eyes soft. "It is a special gift that will remain unless revoked by the creator of the gift, my queen. You will find you can benefit to only a certain degree from this blessing until you *Awaken*, but all that will become clear in the coming weeks. I must depart now, but a servant will come to fetch you for a bath, then you must be off and see to your mother. It was a pleasure to meet you, Chaos Slayer, son of Elkor, and future Arcane Knight." She gave me a wink and slipped from the room.

I would be as my father before me, an Arcane Knight, defender of Order and enemy to Chaos.

True to her word, someone came to fetch me for a bath shortly after she departed. It had been some time since I'd bathed, and it had been cold water. What I experienced in the royal tub was not something I was sure I could even call bathing.

The servant girl had left shortly after we arrived, and I assumed that was the last I'd see of her. So, I was extremely surprised when she returned with two other beautiful young women, armed with sponges and more soap than I'd previously ever seen in my life.

Though I stayed immersed up to my shoulders, not out of

any sense of chastity, more out of being unfamiliar with the noble customs where people bathed you. The bath was built in a way that all three women could stand at the side of the tub and reach over without having to bend.

Any thought of it being an erotic experience fled the furthest reaches of my mind as they went to work. I wasn't sure who instructed them to bathe me, whether it was the King or Elandel but my mind began to lean towards the former. It hurt to be scrubbed so fiercely, my skin screamed for them to stop, much of it rubbed nearly raw.

They finished their torture and handed me a small red vial that had glowing motes of white light inside. With my father being an adventurer, I knew what it was, a health potion. Had they really just scrubbed me raw only to give me a health potion to heal from the process?

The oldest looking of the three saw the confusion on my face and spoke up. "Removal of the skin and subsequent healing will better prepare you for the *Awakening*. Princess Alayna specially requested that we do this for you, were you not informed?"

"I was not," I said, my mood lightening. If it was Alayna's idea, then it must have come from a place of care. "It's fine. Thank you for the...unusual experience."

I took the vial and downed it in one gulp. My inner chest turned with an icy cold feeling while my outermost skin began to burn and itch. It increased until the icy cold was overtaken, and my entire body was comfortably warm.

"Thank you," I said. I was feeling much better now. "I think I will soak for a bit longer before I leave."

"As you wish, Lord Caldor," the oldest one spoke again for the trio. "I will have fresh clothing brought to you, and your horse will be made ready."

"Thank you," I said. My eyes had closed, and I was soaking in every moment of warmth. I heard the quiet thump of the door closing and let myself sink below the surface of the water.

I didn't stay long under the water, my head soon breaking the surface, but I kept my eyes closed, enjoying every moment of the stillness. How long I stayed in the water became unclear, but my opinion of bathing had gone up several notches.

It was odd. No matter how long I stayed, the water didn't cool, and after a short while, it was cleared of my blood. It was as if it cleaned itself continuously.

CHAPTER 22
JOURNEY HOME

I left with much less trouble than when I arrived. Slipping out in the late morning and making it to the main road, then moved in a Southwest direction toward Creeshaw. Normally the ride would take close to three days, but the mount they'd provided moved swifter than any I'd previously used.

Several times during the trip I was worried that if I fell, I'd surely die, but the horse was well trained and had an even gait. It was the end of the first day, the sun or moon unable to provide decent light to see on, and I sat beside a small campfire.

Alone with my thoughts I had a chance to reflect over everything that'd happened to me in such a short period of time. I worried about Lord Variyn and his wizard councilor that led a secret group against him, but I had done well beyond my due diligence. The more I pondered, the more I narrowed in on what truly bothered me about the situation. It was much too early to say, but I think I was falling for Alayna pretty hard.

Whenever I thought of being around her, I couldn't help but smile. And then there was the way she acted around me versus most of the others she had to interact with. I got to see the goofy, fun, and sarcastic woman that hid beneath the solid and serious exterior. These thoughts led me to some of the final words we'd shared together. Why was she so ready to pull the plug on our blossoming relationship?

Perhaps she worried her father wouldn't approve? Why shouldn't he be okay with us, he said pretty convincingly that he had no issue with whomever his daughter chose. I was a Vassal and Knight of his land now. Shouldn't that make me worthy enough to at least be considered?

Maybe it wasn't her father that truly gave Alayna pause and it was something I did? Unfortunately, I couldn't pinpoint what it was about myself that made me so undesirable, and I soon fell asleep next to the warmth of the fire.

My dreams, as they often did, trailed off to distant places far beyond any imaginings that I thought myself capable of having. I first visited a place that felt far and distant, but that didn't truly describe things, it was as if it were separate from our own reality. Inside it, six beings fought for control while a seventh and creator of them all watched from afar. Next, my mind was bent even further, and I saw the beginning of all things. A great nothingness settled over everything one moment and the next, stars, planets, and the old ones came into being. The old ones created two forces, one of Order and one of Chaos.

I woke from my sleep covered in a deep sweat and breathing hard. Looking around I half expected a monster or beast to be close, but I was alone in the darkness. The fire had gone out, but my skin burned as if from a fever. I sat there, wide awake now, letting my mind run over the dreams I'd experienced until the sun rose over the horizon bringing forth the second day of my travels.

I rode in on a horse named Jill. She took care of me well during the two-day ride, and I wanted to ensure she got a nice long rub down. With that in mind, I headed for Merlin's pub—where I was fairly certain he employed someone to tend to the horses of guests. I didn't know much about horses, but the one they'd given me was a beautiful white with grey spots covering half her body.

After having a small lunch and letting Jill rest, I planned on moving swiftly to my farm. The eagerness I felt in wanting to check that mother was finally okay, nearly made me travel straight through, but that would be selfish. Jill had worked hard for me over the last two days and deserved a small rest, magically enchanted horseshoes or not.

Before I departed this morning, I'd donned my armor. What little heat was left of the waning summer became inconsequential under the effects of my armor's cooling. Cursing my stupidity at not wearing the armor on the first day of riding and having suffered through the heat and blistering winds when I could have just put the armor on and avoided most of the issue.

The side stables were empty, so I tied off Jill where she could reach the hay and headed inside to find the stable boy and get some food. Unlike the night I'd spent with Ismene and Emory, the pub was practically dead inside. I saw Joe sitting by himself and finishing up a plate of food, but other than that, the place was deserted.

Deciding I should find out how Breanna the donkey was doing I went to check in with Joe first.

"Hey there, Joe," I said, leaning against the chair opposite of him.

209

He looked at me, a confused and then startled expression on his face.

"By the Ordu above, Elkor?" Joe asked, then squinting and rubbing his eyes, he shook his head. "Damnit, Caldor, you are the spitting image of your father. For a second there, I thought I'd taken my last breath, and your father had come to guide me to the next place. Don't scare an old man like that, and where'd you get that armor?"

"It was a gift from Lord Variyn," I said, then quickly explained that I'd become *Sparked* and helped clear out a Chaos beast. I said it in a way that included the truth of the matter without admitting that I'd just happened to be in the area. Joe nodded along as I spoke, not seeming surprised at all that I'd become *Sparked*.

"You ask Marine! You just ask her. I was always telling her you'd be just like your father, and here you go getting *Sparked*. It was just as I'd said." Joe was smiling and shaking his head as he spoke. "She told me just last night that I was a fool to think it, and you were far too old now, but I have a nose for these things."

Not sure the best way to respond to the line of comments Joe was saying, I decided to turn the conversation. "I didn't expect to be gone this long, has Breanna been alright?" I asked, sitting down, my knees aching from the long ride.

"What's that? Oh yeah, she's been happy as a clam. When I heard your mum was feeling better, I had her delivered and gave Gregory a good talking to, so he knew how best to care for the temperamental woman. That was two days ago, but on my way into town today, I checked in, and he's doing right by her." Joe pushed his chair out as he finished eating and picked at his teeth with his pinky. "Speaking of which, I need to get back before the missus gives me a hard time." Turning his head and lifting a hand up to his mouth as if he were sharing a secret, he said, "Was only meant to be getting some fertilizer and some supplies to mend the old cart, but I couldn't resist stopping in for some sweet ale. This new Merlin fellow really knows how to brew."

"Thank you for looking after my donkey and your secret's safe with me," I assured him, as he stood and made his way to the door to leave.

Merlin walked in from the back and stopped in the middle of the bar to begin polishing a glass. His attention seemed to be elsewhere; his eyes glazed over as he stared at the far wall. Moving to the bar as noisily as I could so as not to startle the elderly man, I cleared my throat, finally getting his attention.

"You catching a sickness, Chaos Slayer?" Merlin asked, winking at me as he spoke. I was about to ask him if he had an issue with his eye that caused him to wink so much when what he called me registered in my brain.

"How could you know?" I asked, putting myself directly in front of his gaze. "Where did you hear that name?"

"Don't worry," Merlin assured me with a grin. "There have been rumors about the new House-appointed Chaos Slayer, but I've not heard a single whisper from anyone about who it was. They certainly don't suspect you yet, and I will keep your secret. I am very practiced at keeping secrets, you see, so it is a small thing for me."

"Okay," I said, drawing out the word. I didn't very well plan on keeping it a secret, but I wanted my family to hear the news from me and not some stray rumor. "I appreciate that. Could you have the stable boy tend to my horse in your stables? She needs to be brushed and given fresh hay." I pulled five silver from my coin purse and slid it across the bar.

"For five silver, I'll feed you and give you a room for the

night as well as have your horse tended to," Merlin said, picking up each coin one at a time, then sliding them into a pocket in his robes.

"I'll take the meal now but keep any extra as a tip and encourage the stable boy to be swift but thorough," I said, smiling.

"Let me grab your food and have your horse cared for," Merlin said. The conical hat with its wide brim slipped forward as he spoke. He left, disappearing to the back, and returned within a minute, holding a steaming plate of food. After setting it down, he poured me a honey ale and then took up his polishing of the same cup he'd been working on when I arrived.

"What do you know of the nature of Order and Chaos?" Merlin asked suddenly.

I was mid-bite, a large portion of roasted chicken in my mouth, so I had a moment to consider his words before I answered. Washing down the bite with a mouthful of ale, I cleared my throat.

"As much as anyone," I finally answered.

"So not much at all," Merlin said.

"The Ordu created and maintained the Order and the great dragons, and their minions try to throw the world into Chaos." My words came out as if regurgitating the words from a book I'd read. What book the passage belonged to eluded me for the moment, but it was likely a stray passage from one I'd read while in the western library.

"In a sense, you are correct," Merlin said, sighing. "You are to be a champion of Order, eh? Will you slay all Chaos beings you encounter?"

"As much as I'm able," I said, confused by the direction of the conversation. "I'm honestly not sure how much help I am going to be against any Chaos monsters at first or what expectations Lord Variyn has for me, but I'm going to try my best. If I can get together with a decent group, I should be able to level fast enough to help out some."

"You don't seem so confident in yourself, Chaos Slayer," Merlin said, his voice holding a hint of teasing.

I surprised myself when I didn't grow angry from the verbal poking. What did an old barkeep know of adventuring and dealing with Chaos monsters anyhow?

"I'm confident I need to get stronger, and that won't happen until I've *Awoken*. Until then, I'm just happy to be able to provide for my family," I said, smiling.

Merlin stared deep into my eyes, his expression one of consideration. "Two sides of a coin. Each must do their duty, neither able to harm the other. You will do right when the time comes. Yes. I am confident of it."

I blinked at Merlin and deliberately took another bite, filling my mouth with food instead of the words that came to my mind. The barkeep seemed to be suffering from a mind sickness of his own, but it wasn't my place to say such things to a man who—while very odd—had done nothing wrong by me.

A cloaked figure entered from the back of the room and spoke to Merlin.

"The task is complete," it spoke in a monotone, even voice. If this was the stable boy, he was no boy, easily big enough to be a full-grown man. The way it spoke itched at the corner of my mind and just as it turned, I caught a glimpse of its face, knowing exactly where I'd heard it before.

"You have a Runeforged!" I exclaimed standing from my stool and leaning forward to see as much of it as I could before it disappeared into the back.

"A what now?" Merlin asked, following my gaze. "Oh, is that what they call golems nowadays? Do you mean old rusty butt? It's been with me for ages. It comes in handy, managing all the tasks that cause my bones to ache and creak."

"Yours isn't one of Gilfoy's Emporium's models?" I asked, even more amazed that he had a custom created golem.

"They finally worked out how to use my design?" Merlin asked, his eye alight with interest. "I figured it would take them at least another decade to work out the finer details. Oh well, it was bound to happen eventually."

"Are you saying that you sold them the design for the Runeforged? That would mean you're an adventurer. That you've *Awoken*!" My excitement was barely containable. "What profession do you have that allows for the creation of golems?" I asked, finally settling on a single question.

"Profession?" Merlin asked, snapping out of whatever thought that had taken over his mind. "Oh right, I'm an Inscriptionist. It is similar to Rune Smith or a Gem Inscriptionist, but far less specialized."

"I have so many questions for you," I muttered, trying to organize the clutter in my head well enough to pick the next one. Just then, the door opened, and half a dozen people filed in, finding places to sit. The lunch rush must be beginning. Damn.

"I've got patrons to tend to now," Merlin said, setting his cup down and moving to the first table. "Feel free to ask me your questions another time." He called over his shoulder.

My excitement died down, but I didn't let it dampen my mood. I'd just met the man who'd created the design for the Runeforged, maybe I could pick the same profession as him and create my own golem. It would be nice to have someone around to help with menial tasks or to fight at my side in dungeons.

I found Jill still munching on hay in the alley stables and, after a quick check, determined the golem had done a fair job.

It was time to go see my family. I could barely contain my excitement.

The last leg of our journey came to an end as we approached our small farmhouse. The paint, what little was left, flaked off the sides of the wooden paneling, and one of the windows in the front had a hole, breaking the entire square panel.

Home sweet home, I thought. We'd finally have enough money to fix the place up a little. I'd checked my coin purse before leaving, and I now had twelve gold, fourteen silver, and thirty-six copper. Not much when trying to purchase items at Gilfoy's Emporium, but a literal fortune in Creeshaw.

We lived just close enough to gain the perks, buffs, and farmer improvements granted to those under an *Awakened* Mayor. And with several dungeons less than a day's ride from Creeshaw, we got our fair share of adventurers passing through.

I was surprised and relieved to see Breanna the donkey grazing on some hay thrown down just inside our barn to the left. From inside the house, I heard Gregory and Grace fighting about one thing or another. It was hard to separate the pair, but they sure did enjoy a good squabble.

After getting Jill set up in the barn with some fresh hay and refreshing the water in the trough with several buckets of water out of the well near the side of the farmhouse, I decided to take on some of the chores that had been neglected in my absence.

It wasn't long before I'd done all that made sense to avoid going into the house. Munster, the cat, appeared out of some shadowy place in the barn and rubbed his head against my leg.

Reaching down, I gave him a scratch and pet his back while I tried to understand my apprehension.

My mother was taking the tonic again and her mind would be clear. Ever since my father had died, she'd struggled. At first, she had enough tonic to keep her well, but losing her closest friend and companion hadn't been easy, so she'd withdrawn from us kids. However, as the mind sickness took over, it became harder, except on the rare days when her mind was clear, and she appeared not to remember that my father had died.

How would she be now?

There was nothing left to do but go in and find out for myself.

I stood, Munster running off to bother Breanna the Donkey, and walked towards the door of the farmhouse. The sounds of the twins fighting had faded, but I could hear the low chatter of voices within.

Making my way down the hall and into the dining room, I found my mother sitting at the table with Grace and Gregory. They were sharing freshly cut fruit and talking about going into town in the evening for sweets.

Seeing as my mother hadn't been into town in years, I had to pick my jaw off the floor and froze in place as I entered.

"Caldor!" Grace squealed. "We missed you! Look, momma's feeling better, and a nice lady said she would be back each month to help her with her head!"

I laughed and felt a swell of emotions threaten to overtake me. Of course, I knew that she'd been given the tonic and that as long as I continued in Lord Variyn's service, that Elandel would return with the tonic, but to see sweet Grace's joy at having her mother back nearly crippled me with emotion.

"I know, Grace," I said, "I've had such an adventure over the last week. But this is by far the best moment."

"You sound so much like him," my mother said, her eyes tearing up. "Kids!" She exclaimed, looking at the twins. "Take the fruit and play outside for a bit. I need to talk with Caldor."

The twins did what they were told, both of them trying to give excuses, but with a look from their mother, they cut off and went outside.

After several long moments of being alone, my mother stood and embraced me. The warmth of her hug was inviting and for the first time in many years, I felt safe in my mother's embrace.

"I love you," I said, hugging her tightly.

"I love you too, Caldor," she said. "But we need to talk about how you're able to afford Elandel's help. A member of the royal elven family doesn't come cheap, I'm sure."

I started at that and reeled back to look her in her eyes. sparkling green eyes stared back at me, a mix of love and questioning in them.

My mother looked significantly better than she had, both well rested and well dressed. Gone were the wild tangles of her hair. Now it was up in a bun, and each strand had been tamed. She wore a strikingly bright purple and gold dress, as well as having done her face makeup, something she had only done when her and father had gone to town for a night alone.

"I've *Sparked*," I whispered, my eyes turning away from hers for only a moment before I forced myself to watch her reaction.

To my surprise, her gaze didn't hold any of the emotions I expected. There wasn't anger, surprise, or confusion, just a steady, loving look.

"You knew?" I asked, my voice rising back from a whisper, but I controlled my temper.

"No," she said, her hand coming out to rest on my arm. "I suspected you were years ago, but your father was adamant that you were not, so I let it go. But now, I can see it. That same look in your eyes as your father had."

"You aren't mad?" I asked, all my mental preparation for this moment and not once did I consider my mother would react so calmly.

"Mad?" She asked in a surprised tone before pulling me into another tight hug. "You are my handsome boy. No, I'm not mad. I'm scared for you, and I have a few ideas of alternatives I'd like you to consider, but I could never be mad at you for something you have no control over."

"Alternatives?" I asked, releasing her from the hug and both of us sitting at the table.

"Yes," she said, smiling brightly. "I don't know what deals you've made with the elves for the tonic, but until you've *Awoken*, you can't make any magical binding agreements, so you can still back out. I've spoken with Mayor Ghoft. He is willing to apprentice you as the future Mayor and said he could help you reach level ten. Afterward, his only requirement would be that you choose the Scholar profession to become his apprentice. He assured me that even out here in Creeshaw, there are plenty of methods of gaining essence through your profession and being a Scholar would greatly increase those gains."

"I can't," I said, my voice as even as I could make it. "Mom, you don't understand."

"No, Caldor," My mother said, a fierceness in her voice I wasn't accustomed to. "You don't understand. I will not lose anyone else to this life. They can't make you keep whatever promises you've made. I'll go and speak to them myself if I must!" Her voice rose in determination, and tears poured down her face. "I won't. I can't lose you too."

"Please, just listen," I said, reaching across the table to take her hands.

I told her everything, not sparing a single detail of what had happened or what I'd learned.

"A Lord?" she asked after I finished. "He made you a Lord and a Knight? I'll kill that man and his traitorous wizard!"

She stood, and her face grew red with anger. "No one hurts my babies!"

In that moment, I felt a little afraid myself. The wrath of a mother was not something to idly ignore.

"Mother, please understand," I said. "I have a chance to make a difference. I can't turn it down. Besides, we can finally live comfortably again." I poured the coin out on the table, but her fierceness didn't lessen.

She grabbed a gold coin and threw it across the room. "No amount of coin is worth your life." Her voice had gone down to a whisper again, the ferocity burning out as she sat, tears starting to pour down her face once more.

"You are right," I said, my voice firming. "It isn't for the money. It is because I can help those who need me. They say I have the potential to be very strong. I will see that to the end. I will help those who cannot help themselves."

My own eyes threatened to overrun with tears, but I kept my face firm.

My mother, to her credit, held my gaze, her motherly determination a match for my own. But as we stared at each other, a silent agreement was struck. She knew that I wasn't going to be swayed, and I knew she wouldn't accept the threats I would have to put myself in front of, but we loved each other.

"You are too much like your father," she finally said, smiling.

I smiled back. "Thank you."

I joined my siblings outside, where Grace was gently petting Jill, and Gregory was going through her saddle bags.

"You find anything interesting?" I asked, startling Gregory who quickly pulled his hands out of the bag and hid something behind his back.

"Where'd you get all the cool stuff?" He asked, shifting himself so that I couldn't see whatever he held behind his back.

"A few different gifts," I said, catching a peek at my dimensional box behind his back. "But the box you are hiding behind your back was a very special gift from a special lady and I'll be needing it back."

I held out my hand expectantly and Gregory let out an exaggerated sigh, handing over the box over.

"What's it do?" He asked, kicking at the dirt with his shoes.

"Remember that time father brought a feast of tasty food and gave us each a small cherry pie?" I asked. They'd been so young, but it had occurred just months before father died, so I hoped that it might ignite the embers of his memory. I smiled when I saw his eyes light up.

"I thinks so," Gregory said, and I saw Grace nod her head as if she had no doubt and recalled the memory perfectly. "He played a game where he'd pull out funny items for us. You've told us before, and I think I've dreamt of it a few times since."

"Right," I said, barely having to look down on Gregory—he'd grown so tall recently. "The bag he used came from a dungeon and could store countless items inside and only grow slightly heavier. This," I held the box up for them both to see, "does the same thing, but it's a box instead of a bag."

"What's inside?" Grace asked, leaving Jill's side and admiring the beauty of the box.

"A few odds and ends," I answered, smiling at them both. "I've got something I need to tell you both and I will need you to be brave in the coming months."

"Okay," Gregory said, sounding suspicious. Grace remained quiet, but her attention was fully on me.

"I got the *Spark* and I'm going to be an adventurer like father was," I said simply.

"You are leaving?" Grace asked, speaking before Gregory could open his mouth. "Do you not like it here anymore?"

"What, Grace, no," I said, reaching down to grab her hand. "I love you both and I love spending time with you, but I have a responsibility to use the gifts I've been given."

"Who will look after mother and tend to the orchards?" Gregory asked, his tone all business. "And what will happen to Breanna if you aren't here to take care of her?"

Turning my attention to Gregory, I said, "The two of you are a team and I am trusting you both to watch over mother, the orchard, and Breanna. You are nearly the age I was when I had to take over father's responsibilities, but you both are far luckier than I was."

"Why do you say that?" Gregory asked, his brows scrunched and his face frowning. He was clearly not convinced.

"I didn't have a twin to help me figure things out. Between the two of you, I expect you will fare much better than I did. Besides, mother is better now and will help where she can. Part of my new life as an adventurer will help keep her well. But I can't do that unless I know you two are up to the task. So, what do you say? Can you tend to the farm while I'm away?" I fixed them both with a serious gaze and awaited their responses. Grace spoke first.

"I will miss you," she said, tears forming at the corners of her eyes. "But I can do it." Her face hardened over with determination.

"It'll be easy," Gregory said, lifting his chin haughtily. "We've got this, Gracie."

Satisfied that they would do their best to help mother out, I went to my room to pack what little belongings I had. I was in the middle of packing an extra pair of clothing when my mother knocked on the door frame. The door was open, so I smiled in her direction, and she entered.

"You know how proud I am of you, don't you?" She asked.

I smiled and nodded my head.

"After your father died and while I was still in the middle of dealing with his death, Warrick gave me something that I think you should have now," she said, reaching into her apron and pulling out a tarnished silver ring.

I reached out, and she placed it in my hand. It was a signet ring with the symbol of the Arcane Knight on its surface.

Slipping the ring onto my right-hand ring finger, it fit perfectly. I felt no different while wearing it and wondered if it had any magical properties. I didn't remember him wearing the ring, but now that I thought about it, I never saw him wear any jewelry, which would be uncommon for an adventurer. I decided he probably just took his magical items off when he was home.

"Did Warrick say what it did?" I finally asked, looking back up at my mother.

"No. Only that he'd found it when they were cleaning out their guildhall before they disbanded. He did mention that it was silver and held the symbol of Elkor's class, the Arcane Knight."

"Thank you," I said. "I'll keep it safe." I knew she understood what it meant to me to have a part of my father. Now I could carry a reminder of the responsibility I had, to do as he had done.

She pulled me into a hug and I closed my eyes, filing away the feeling of her love to be used in the darker days to come.

"I'm going to start working on dinner, but if you feel up to it, there's fruit to be picked and the barn could use some fresh hay spread out," My mother said, releasing me and heading back into the kitchen.

I went to work, picking fruit and cleaning the barn with Gregory and Grace at my side. I gave them pointers and suggestions as we worked. They would be fine, I decided. Everything was going to be okay.

CHAPTER 23
GONE SHOP'N

The town's magic shop stood out among the rest of the buildings in the square, being constructed of stonework, whereas the rest of the buildings were wood. Intricate designs ran up and down the front of the two stone pillars, each one built into the low archway at the face of the building.

There was a hitching post outside the shop, so I tied Jill off and made my way to the front door.

I'd thought about what it would be like to be a mayor of a town like Creeshaw during my ride into town. Looking up at the magic shop, I noted that it would be considered a Prime Construction, a tier above anything else in the city, which explained the stone construction.

Much about how buildings worked under an *Awoken* Mayor was lost to me, but I knew that it benefited from reduced taxes, better trade prices, and a certain amount of magical growth and protection for the building. This shop, for instance, had been around for at least twenty years and probably had most of its perks, buffs, and levels maxed under the Mayor of Creeshaw.

I walked under the shop sign, made of thick black oak with golden inlaid letters, 'Barton's Magic Shop'. It didn't have any symbols like most other establishments had, but you would be hard pressed to mistake this building for anything but a magic shop.

Two wide display windows opened to the street and displayed a variety of magical items. There were magical scrolls, books, rings, wands, armor, and several random nick-nacks that likely had special use cases.

I pulled open the door and felt a whoosh of magical energy that I had never noticed before being *Sparked*. The entire room held a thick measure of energy just vibrating all around. Whether this was from being a Prime Building or perhaps the amount of magically infused items the store held, I really didn't know.

"Welcome to Barton's Magic Shop," a familiar voice called out from across the room. Ismene stood behind a checkout counter and only looked a few moments later as I approached.

"Caldor!" Ismene squealed happily. "I heard you got into a bit of trouble while out hunting?"

"You can say that," I said, shrugging to hide my excitement. "Thank you, by the way. I heard you took time to check in with my siblings."

Ismene hurried around the counter and gave me a tight hug. "I'm glad you are okay. What happened?"

"Is Emory still in town?" I asked, releasing Ismene from the tight hug, a large grin on my face. "I have some news I want to share. Maybe we could grab a meal with Emory first?"

"Nah, he left," Ismene said, taking her place behind the counter again. "Said something about finding another dungeon group, but he had to travel a few days to get to them, so it probably isn't any of the close ones."

"Oh damn," I said. I scratched at my chin and looked at some rings that were behind a glass cabinet. "In that case, I need to buy a thing or two, and then afterwards maybe we can get dinner? There are a few secrets that I really want to discuss with you."

"Sure thing," Ismene said, waving me goodbye. When I didn't move and continued looking at the rings, considering a few other items, her face screwed up in confusion.

"Can I see this one?" I asked, still grinning.

"What do you need a Ring of the Bear for? Better yet, how are you going to afford it?" She asked, then her eyes went wide, and her head jerked forward. She scanned me and truly looked this time. First, she noticed the cloak, then the sword, and then lastly, my armor. "You *Sparked*!"

"I *Sparked*!" I screeched back, both of us jumping in excitement. "But it gets better. I think I know how to get you *Sparked* as well!"

Her face went pale, and she stopped jumping up and down. "Don't you dare tease me Caldor, or so help me I will bludgeon you to death."

"It's no joke," I said, raising my hands to forestall her. "I'll give you more details tonight, but take a deep breath Ismene, we are going to make you a *Sparked*!"

"You can't do that to me," she said. She was smiling, but at the same time, tears began to form in the corner of her eyes. In all the time that I had known her, she had never cried. Her emotions were something she kept a tight grip on, but now that wall seemed to be crumbling in the face of the one thing I knew she wanted as much as I did.

"It's true, Ismene, I promise," I said, moving over to put a hand on hers. She met my gaze, her eyes gleaming with determination.

"Fine," she said, moving her hand to squeeze mine. "Were you serious about buying a ring? I'm thinking I should close the store early, and Mr. Fawlkner isn't here, so we can go to the pub right after."

"Yeah, I was thinking it'd be nice to get a head start on things and buy a magic ring to increase my overall health."

"Well, we have a few choices, but they're pricey."

We spent the next thirty-minutes haggling over the price until I eventually bought a ring for a single gold that had a minor increase of Constitution, Strength, Concentration, and Intellect. She said it was so cheap because the more attributes that an item gave bonuses to, the less those bonuses tended to be. According to the little white card beside the item, this one provided only one attribute point per attribute listed. So, while a plus four attribute item would normally go for four times as much, they'd lowered the price because nobody wanted that spread on attributes. Especially the magic-related and physical-related attributes.

After buying the ring, I slipped it on and felt the magic take hold, strengthening me. Normally I'd have not put the ring on until I became a true *Awoken*, but I knew since I was *Sparked* I could benefit to a certain extent from the items.

"Here for a meal? Shall I send Rusty out to tend to your horse?" Merlin asked, his voice surprisingly fatherly and gentle.

"Yes, and yes, please do. I need a private room for my friend and me," I told him.

"All of our rooms are private, and I'm not sure I appreciate the insinuation," Merlin said, frowning at me.

"You misunderstand me. I need a private room to eat in,

Mer- the previous Merlin kept a private dining room off the back that patrons could pay a fee to use for a meal's length of time." I did my best to explain myself and watched the light of recognition flicker in his eyes.

"Oh yes, yes," Merlin said. It was his turn to go a slight shade of red, and he didn't disappoint. "I've been using that room as a private study of sorts, but I see that you are a man of good reputation—not an easy feat for someone not yet *Awoken*. Give me six and a half minutes to clear it, then return."

I thanked him as he turned around, and I disappeared into the back to wait for Ismene.

The sun was setting on the distant mountains, and with it came a chill in the air. I took a deep breath, my mind fumbling over the events of the week. It had only been a week, and barely that, I mused. How that could be possible, I honestly didn't know.

I thought about first hearing Alayna's scream echoing through the trees, it felt like it had been months. But it really wasn't all that surprising if I thought about it.

My life before all the adventure had begun was filled with orchard farming, family worries, and the rare escape to study with Warrick.

I needed to visit with Warrick. When traveling past his secret grove, I was tempted to see if he had come back, but something held me back. Not so deep down, I knew what.

I was all but certain now that Warrick was the reason I hadn't *Sparked* until recently. All the emotion and friendship that we shared threatened to melt away under the heat of my

229

anger and confusion. Taking a deep breath, I reminded myself that it wasn't, in fact, completely his fault.

I felt myself relax at the thought. I couldn't be angry at my father, nor could I pretend to understand his intentions behind keeping me from my power. While I contemplated the oddities of the events that led my life to this point, I was interrupted by the Pub's door swinging open.

"It has been nearly seven minutes," Merlin declared, his face screwed up in a frown. "Have you no sense of time?"

My face took on an expression of confusion, this Merlin was much stranger than the previous, but I found it amusing.

"Thank you, Merlin," I said, "I know the way back to the room. I'm waiting for someone, and I'll be right in."

"As you wish," Merlin said, giving me a gentle nod and letting the door swing closed behind him.

He was a bit of an odd duck, that man.

The steady trickle of foot traffic continued for another ten minutes. I watched as people headed to their various destinations, and my mind wandered again.

My days working at the family orchard, slaving away to make the smallest amount of coin to support my family, were over. The earnings of even a low-level adventurer were said to be substantial. Although the cost of being an adventurer was also said to be expensive.

That didn't bother me. I was going to live the life of an adventurer, fighting back the darkness as my father before me. I would be a hero, and I would provide for my family, just as my father had done...before he died.

Just as my mind began to contemplate the darker ends of the life I wanted; I was interrupted by a touch on my hand.

I looked up to see Ismene's dark purple eyes staring into my own. The dark thoughts washed away under her friendly gaze. I smiled and took her hand, squeezing it in appreciation.

"I got us a place to talk," I said, holding onto her hand and guiding her into the pub.

She didn't speak, but her eyes had taken on a sheen of determination that I recognized from the many times we'd discussed how both of us would be adventurers no matter what. I had relit that fire inside of her, giving her the possible means to make our shared dream a reality.

The room in the back wasn't nearly as well kept as it had been under the other Merlin's care. The large communal table had nearly every surface covered in stray papers, oddball objects, and to my utter surprise, a variety of weapons; from daggers with rune script on them that glowed a faint blue, to great axes that streamed eerie red mist inches from the metal's surface, despite not showing any signs of rune script on them.

In one corner was an edge that had been cleared from debris and two plates of steaming stew sat beside two large mugs of what I hoped would be his signature sweet ale.

"Whoa," Ismene said, echoing my own sense of shock at the state of the room. "Do you see the-" She began to ask, pointing towards one of the glowing weapons. Before she could finish, I answered back.

"Yeah," I said. "I see them too. Probably best we don't touch them, could be dangerous." I added, seeing Ismene take an unconscious step towards the side of the table with the enchanted items.

"Yes, uh, yes, of course," Ismene said, shaking her head as if pushing herself out of some temporary trance. "Let's eat. I'm starving."

Settling into place next to each other in front of the cleared section of the table, we began to eat. The stew was hearty, thick, and wonderfully delicious. We finished our meal in relative silence, both of us used to each other's company enough that words weren't needed to fill every gap of silence.

I caught her several times staring hard at the equipment I wore and smiled at her each time but said nothing. I knew how odd it was that I had continued to wear the armor and drake cloak, but they were by far the most comfortable clothes I owned.

In the relative heat of the day, the armor kept my body cool and comfortable. The cloak was heavy enough that I felt the heft around my shoulders, but wearing it energized me. Several times I had considered having all the items properly identified by an *Awakened* with a spell or ability to do so, but another greater part of me wanted to wait until I went through the *Awakening* ceremony to discover the attributes of the items myself.

I had been nursing my ale for several long minutes when Ismene finished her stew and looked at me expectantly. I smiled over at her, raising my eyebrows.

"Stop it, Caldor!" she exclaimed, hitting me playfully on the shoulder. "I've been patient. Now tell me everything!"

I told her everything.

I filled her in on what happened to me over the last week, leaving out a detail here or there concerning Alayna, the politics, and a few smaller details like being granted a keep and being made a Lord. It wasn't that I didn't want her to know, or anything like that. I just didn't want her to look at me differently or see me as anything other than what I was, her friend.

"It's that easy?" Ismene asked, her face screwed up in frustration. "So, if I can be around a monster when it dies, I get the essence and become *Sparked*? Do I have to be the one that does the killing, or will being close enough work?"

"It isn't that easy," a voice said, startling both of us. My hand *Sparked* with raw energy in response, my heart beginning to pound in my chest.

Merlin stood just behind us, his hand absently scratching his bearded chin.

"The point of using the private dining room," I said, looking up at the elderly man. "Is to have some privacy."

"Yes, yes, and I've provided that," Merlin said, waving his hand around the room. "I've blocked at least two separate attempts to scry on you and your conversation. Some pesky diviners don't understand the etiquette of peeking in on others' lives. I'd get an anti-scrying trinket if I were you." He suddenly tugged at his beard, raising his finger in the air as if something occurred to him. "I think I have just the thing!"

And just as fast as he appeared, he was gone. Ismene and I shared confused looks and I shrugged. He hadn't turned and walked away, he was there one second and the next he was gone. I felt no buzz of power that I was becoming accustomed to feeling when magic was performed around me. I heard no words of power being uttered; he had simply just gone.

An awkward silence hung in the air as I tried to decide if Ismene and I should continue our conversation or wait to see if Merlin appeared once more. After several long seconds, I turned back to Ismene, shrugging my shoulders again, and continued.

"As far as it was explained to me, it is just a matter of getting the essence," I said. Before I even finished speaking, I saw Merlin appear out of the corner of my eye, and I turned to him.

He opened his palm, holding it out to me, looking,. I saw he held a chalk white pair of wide rings. Upon closer inspection, I realized they weren't rings but earrings. From what I could see, it looked like they would clasp over the upper part of the ear lobe, each of them having a slight curve to go along with the natural shape of the ear.

I picked one up, the gentle pulse of mana barely perceivable. Holding it up to one of the many glowing daylight orbs that filled the room, I could barely make out the faintest of scratches on the surface. Running a finger down the length of the smooth white metal, I wondered at its construction.

"Masterwork Refined Mythril Ear Clasps," Merlin said, turning his palm over so both fell into my hand. "They create a barrier around you. You won't be able to scry others while you wear them though, something to remember. They give you a small increase in mana regeneration, but the complexity of the barrier took up nearly all available surface."

"How much," I asked, my face remaining as passive as I could under the circumstances. My life had changed so drastically lately, but if I was learning anything over the last week, it was that nothing came without strings attached.

"Nothing from me," Merlin said happily, "They weren't doing me any good anymore, and I have several sets lying about."

I blanched, and my passive face shifted to one of surprised horror. Everyone knew that Mythril was one of the finest metals due to its ability to so readily accept large amounts of mana, but Refined Mythril and in the form of a Masterwork item was something I'd only ever read about in some of the oldest texts.

Refining Mythril was, according to Warrick, a lost art. If he truly had several sets, then I had made up my mind, this had to be the Merlin that Warrick mentioned.

"Your name really is Merlin, isn't it?" I asked, wishing that I had asked Warrick more about the powerful Wizard that he had said made his power pale in comparison. "You are a powerful Wizard. Why are you running a pub in Creeshaw?"

I received only a gentle smile from the elderly man in response. He motioned to the earrings in my hand and said, "Well, put them on, and I'll tell you more about 'becoming *Sparked*,' as you two call it."

With a weary hesitation, I clasped the earrings on the top of each ear. Perhaps I was too trusting to do so, but there was a kindness in Merlin's bearing that made you want to trust him.

As soon as the final earring was clipped into place, I felt what could only be described as an expansion in my chest, quickly followed by a soft warmth forming around me. After a moment, I felt normal, adjusting to the new effects.

I noticed Ismene looking at the earrings with wide-eyed amazement, and I felt momentarily guilty. Before I could say anything to try and pacify her, Merlin spoke up.

"I'd offer you a pair," he said, "But from what I can see, you aren't ready to be *Awoken*. You're still out of balance but on the low side."

My concerned gaze snapped to Merlin and shifted to confusion.

"Low side?" I asked, my eyebrows raised questioningly.

"Oh, don't concern yourself about it just yet," Merlin said, his hand waving away my concern. "You wish to know the secrets to unlocking your *Spark*. It isn't as simple as the nobility would have you believe." He emphasized the words unlocking and *Spark* as if we were using some off terminology and not the exact phrasing everyone I'd ever spoken to, or read about, used.

"Yes, I do!" Ismene exclaimed, no longer keeping quiet.

"Most of what you heard is true," Merlin said, his hands waving about as he spoke and turning his gentle gaze to

Ismene. "People are like containers that can hold essence. Most of the world draws in too little essence, and when an individual is out of balance, their bodies begin to deteriorate, what you would call aging. However, a small number of the population, like Mr. Miles here, draw in much more essence naturally than is needed to sustain themselves. That is where the *Spark* comes from, like trapping lightning in a bottle not equipped to hold it, the energy lashes outward, threatening to shatter the vessel."

"That is pretty much what I was told," I said, not seeing any difference from the narrative that Alayna had given me yet.

"Yes, indeed, but what she failed to mention is that not all containers, as it were, are made equally," Merlin said, his gentle gaze falling back to Ismene as he spoke. "Most souls that have a naturally high draw are equipped with bodies hardy enough to endure the process, at least for a time."

"And those that don't," Ismene asked. By the frustrated look on her face, I could tell she was finishing his line of thought in her head just as I was doing.

"Have you ever seen a clay pitcher crack or shatter from an extreme temperature change?" Merlin asked, looking at each of us in turn.

We both nodded in the affirmative. Both Ismene and I had been just above what would be considered poor, and most of what we used was constructed of baked clay. The thinner constructions used for pitchers had a bad habit of shattering if you tried to transfer too hot water into a too cold container.

"If that's true, then why are so many nobles able to make their method work?" I asked.

"They aren't," Merlin said flatly. "They suffer the same risk of certain death that everyone who uses the method of flooding their body with essence takes. I know they tend to fill themselves full right before the *Awakening* process, but that doesn't fix their naturally low essence gathering. Making the path forward slow and difficult. If they were smart, they'd just train themselves until they could reach equilibrium naturally."

"What is equilibrium?" I asked, my academic interest overriding the implications for Ismene's chances of becoming *Sparked*.

"It is when your essence draws, and your expenditure is in true balance. Neither being too high or too low," Merlin said as if that explained everything. Seeing my blank stare, he elaborated. "Have you ever wondered what happens in an *Awakening* ceremony?"

"You get *Awakened* and gain access to the powers of Order," I answered, paraphrasing a passage I had read.

"Well yes it does have the added benefit of putting a layer of 'Order' over things, but that isn't what I meant."

"What do you mean," Ismene asked, leaning forward, completely drawn into the conversation.

"What I mean to say," Merlin said, clearing his throat. "Is that during the *Awakening* you are forced into balance or a state of equilibrium."

"If that is true, then how does someone reach equilibrium?" I asked, craning my neck. It had become increasingly uncomfortable craning my neck up toward Merlin. I turned all the way around in my seat, something Ismene had done minutes ago.

"By training themselves," Merlin said flatly, looking down at me with a critical frown. He continued after several long moments of my blank stare. "Very well, it varies and depends on what you lack. But in most cases, it takes learning mental control, physical control, and expanding your understanding of the threads that bind our world together."

"Oh, that's it? Sounds easy." My snark wasn't missed by Merlin, who huffed in my direction in response.

Ismene stood and looked up to Merlin. "How long does it take?" She asked, her eyes burning with the fire of determination.

"No more than three or four decades if you have a good teacher," Merlin said matter-of-factly, then eying Ismene, he added. "For you, I think you could get there in a matter of years. You are already so close and seem like the determined type."

Ismene deflated in front of Merlin, her eyes losing the fire under the weight of the time required. She turned towards me and asked, "Will you help me kill a monster and become *Sparked*?"

"You could die, even if we killed a monster," I said. Taking her hunting had been my plan from the moment I learned of the method of becoming *Sparked*, but the reality of the increased risk, gave me pause.

"You are *Sparked*," Ismene said, her voice dropping to barely above a whisper but filled with a sorrow that I understood. "You've had your greatest wish granted. Try to understand. Help me or don't help me, but I am going to find a monster and find a way to kill it."

"The easiest path forward," Merlin said, getting Ismene's attention. "Is not going to be the most rewarding. Heed my words or do not, I only offer what little wisdom I am able to give. I must attend to my other patrons, please leave eight coppers on the table when you leave."

Merlin left through the door this time, his robes billowing dramatically behind him as he disappeared from view.

I turned back to Ismene, silent tears rolled down her cheeks.

"Ismene," I said, pulling her into a tight hug. "I'll help you. Whatever it takes, I'll help you."

"Thank you," she whispered into my ear. Her breathing steadied, and she pulled back just enough so that she could look me in the eyes.

I sometimes forgot how beautiful she was. Many years of being her friend and a failed attempt at a relationship together had added a kind of blinder. But as she gazed at me and slowly began to close the distance between our lips, my heart raced.

I quickly pushed my head forward and gave her a gentle kiss on the cheek. It wouldn't be right to lead my friend along when I was beginning to get feelings for another.

"Thank you," her voice was velvety smooth, her words beaconing me closer, but I didn't lean forward, and her next words brought me back to reality. "You are a great friend."

"Uh yeah," I blinked several times, trying to clear my head and get the blood flowing in the right direction. "You...uh, you are too. I mean you are a good friend."

Her mood shifted as she scooted back on the bench and her eyes filled with determination. "Let's go kill a monster," she practically growled the words.

CHAPTER 24
HUNTING RATS OF UNUSUAL SIZE

"The key to killing a monster is preparation," I announced as we stood, preparing to leave.

"Oh, you've had one run in with a monster and now you're an expert?" Ismene asked, teasing.

"I don't think I'm an expert," I said, sighing. "But I've given this a lot of thought. I was determined to be an adventurer even if I didn't get my *Spark*. And the one rule I was planning on living by was, 'Always be prepared' because I wasn't going to have any spells or an enhanced body to fall back on. That's all changed now, but it applies to our situation."

"Okay, obviously I agree," Ismene said, pushing me playfully as we made it out on the street. "But what does that mean? Where are we going to find a monster and how will we prepare if we don't know beforehand what we are going to come across?"

"Let's start by looking at the notice board at the long house just north of town. I know it's only supposed to be for adventurers, but I've gone by a few times and I've seen quests to kill monsters there before," I said, a devious smile splitting my face.

"I've also just had an interesting idea. What if I pay to have an adventurer go with us? I mean it'd be nice if we could find Emory, but you said he left town, so why don't we just pay someone else to go with us."

"You have enough money to do that?" Ismene asked, her expression suspicious.

I let out a nervous laugh and decided that it was time I tell her a bit more than I had. "Well, there was a small part of the story I left out about becoming *Sparked*," I said, giving her a sheepish grin as I headed up the hill and out of the main part of town.

I relayed the rest, sparing no detail this time as the sun set on the horizon and the chill of night began to take root. Her expression as I told my full tale changed from confused to angry at parts to teasing, as I told her about Alayna and our blossoming relationship.

"You got yourself a girlfriend, a castle, and a knighthood?" Ismene asked, her question filled with sarcastic surprise. "Wonder what I'll get when I unlock my *Spark*?"

"Be made Queen of Newaliyn most likely," I shot back, and we both shared a deep hearty laugh.

The long house just outside of town looked like someone had taken a modest woodland cabin and made it twice the height of a barn and many times longer. But the same log house look covered the majority of the design. At its base and about three feet up was a solid stone foundation, and the roof was made of sturdy looking clay tiles, broken every ten feet or so by a chimney.

I'd never been inside, but if I had to guess I would say that several hundred people could stay in there at once. But I knew that the inside wasn't just sleeping areas, it was like a mini adventurer's hall inside, with shops, work stations for crafters, and of course many, many, beds.

It didn't take a lot of searching to find what we were looking for; a small group of adventurers were picking through posted notices on a ten-foot-long board. It was overflowing with requests, and each request had an area you could rip off to show you'd selected it. Pushing our way through I began to search the board.

I didn't know what magic ruled the board, if any, but as I studied it, several new items appeared and a few disappeared. A rotund bearded man must have caught my look of amazement and leaned down a bit to say, "First time getting a good look at a quest board, eh? They be wonderful works of magic. You see this side over here." He gestured to the far end away from me. "That is where local notices will appear. The middle here is where dungeon requests get gathered. And lastly these here are adventure guild-wide requests." He ran his hand down a bunch of requests in front of me. "You be wanting the local side of things I think?"

He posed it as a question with the way he spoke, so I nodded in the affirmative and made room for other adventurers while I checked out the local side. There was only a single person checking out this side of things, he wore dark robes and had pale white skin. My gut told me he was a magic user of some kind, but I really had no way to tell given my current skill sets.

I waved Ismene closer, she'd taken a step back, not willing to dive into the huddle of adventurers like I did. She approached and I told her knowingly, "These are the local listings, what we're looking for." I happened to spare a glance back over to the helpful bearded man and he winked in my direction, likely hearing me pass off his useful information as my own.

"So, what are we looking for?" Ismene asked, her finger running down one that requested two dozen red root plants. After giving it a quick read through I saw that it gave pretty detailed instructions on how to find them, but that wouldn't work for what we hoped to accomplish.

"Try and find any kill quests," I said, my eyes scanning away. "It should be something relatively low level if we can find one."

"Rat infestation south of here, close to dungeon 5812, or the Crimson Crusades Dungeon per its original naming," the dark cloaked boy said. And he was a boy I realized after hearing his voice. I peeked a bit under his hood and saw that he couldn't be more than my siblings' age, thirteen at the oldest.

While *Sparked* did tend to manifest around puberty, most were able to hold—or down right told to wait—until they reached adulthood at seventeen. He must be pretty powerful to have gotten permission to unlock his *Spark* so young. I was about to ask if he'd be willing to partner up for a small payment to take out these rats, when he spoke again.

"You're *Sparked*, she isn't, but you hope to have her unlocked," he spoke the words quieter than a whisper and I barely heard him, Ismene obviously hadn't. I looked around and none of the other adventurers seemed to have heard either. How many people knew this damned secret? Had Ismene and I been the only ones out of the know.

"How much to accompany us?" I asked, matching his whispered tone.

"I get to keep the tails and the venom sacs if any rats mutated," the boy said, then pausing, he added in normal volume. "My names Creed, Creed Volkroy."

I held out my hand and said, "Nice to meet you, Creed. My name is Caldor and this is my companion Ismene. We accept your terms."

Ismene seemed confused at the sudden change in the conversation as she'd missed much of what he'd said in a whisper but understood that we'd be hunting rats of unusual size after Creed pulled a token from the board. I examined the listing after seeing him grab a tag from it.

It held information about an infestation around the dungeon area to be exterminated. A reward of twenty copper per rat's tail returned, meaning it would take five tails just to get to a silver and I'd been willing to pay the kid a gold or more for his help. The listing was one of the more tattered ones, which meant that it had been there for a while.

"How do we know if the rats are still a problem?" I asked our new walking companion Creed, as we made it down the hill. Creed was a mysterious person, keeping his hood so far over his face that it was hard to make out much, unless he was looking up. Several times the young man had to lift the hood up and check that he was still traveling in the right direction.

"The dungeon is well used," Creed said, as if that explained everything.

"So, if there had been a change someone would have reported it," Ismene added in, her mind catching on quicker to his meaning than mine had.

"Aw gotcha," I said, turning from the road and to Merlin's Pub to get my horse Jill.

"The road is this way," Creed said, his head perking up and his very pale skin poking out as he tried to see where I was going.

"I'm getting my horse and I suggest you get yours as well," I said, indicating Creed. "Ismene you can ride with me. Jill is strong and if we keep it at a nice steady pace, we won't tire her out. How far is this dungeon?" I'd heard of the Crimson Crusades dungeon, but I only knew it was one of the dungeons that people visited in the area, not how far it actually was from Creeshaw.

"Right, but uhm I will call my mount after we leave town," Creed said, suddenly nervous. "I was given a summoned mount as part of one of my first-class spells."

Confused at why he wanted to wait until after we'd left town to show off his class mount, but not wanting to offend the young kid, I just nodded along and went to fetch Jill. Soon enough we were heading out of town, all of us on foot as I figured we could let Jill rest while we waited for our young pale friend to mount his own steed.

It took nearly an hour of steady walking before he finally agreed to summon his mount.

"Don't be afraid," he said for the fifth time. The conversation between the three of us had been limited and this being the most he'd said to us in a while.

"We aren't," Ismene said, then putting a hand on his shoulder, added. "You don't have to be so afraid. You're helping us out a bunch and we won't judge you."

She must be queuing into whatever the young caster was afraid of, because he relaxed a measure before speaking again.

"It's just...I am afraid. I'm only level four and my class makes people uncomfortable. I'm just a warlock-based class though, not a servant of Chaos! Warlocks are good people too," Creed said, his words losing steam as he spoke.

That explained a bit. Warlocks were a caster class, but also used as a general classification for several classes that had spells and abilities that the unlearned would categorize as darkness or evil leaning. But as it was a class under the system of the Ordu,

I didn't see the logic. Chaos Lords and their kind were outside the control of the Ordu therefore easily recognizable when put against a warlock who relied on the Ordu's system.

I met eyes with Ismene and knew that she had probably just gone through a similar train of thought. We nodded to each other, ready to give young Creed any support he needed when summoning his horse.

Creed lowered his hood, and we got a good look at him for the first time. He had straight black hair, but it was ashy as if he was much older than he appeared. His eyes were a blue so light that they appeared gray, and his skin wasn't just pale, it held a dusty quality to it. Creed noticed our stares and said, "My class did all this." He gestured to his face and hair. "My Da says he's still proud of me, but I don't know if I believe him after he had me leave House Nefrah and take our families oldest surname, that way no one could connect me to him. I've studied the area and tried to be nice, but no one wants to party with me because of my appearance and class." Creed was practically crying at this point and Ismene came to the rescue again, bringing him into a warm embrace.

After a few very awkward seconds of hugging and crying, all the while I pretended not to notice, they finally separated, and Creed pulled himself together enough to summon his mount. He held up a short sword—perhaps I was wrong about him being a caster—and spoke several words in a very guttural language that made my inside squirm to hear them.

Runic shapes appeared on his blade and a cloud of misty haze grew around him. A second later it cleared, and a terrifying skeletal horse appeared beside him. It was a strange mix of half dead and half alive, with frosted flesh open to the air in several parts. Its eyes glowed an eerie green and it spit blue fire from its mouth as Creed mounted it.

Jill was obviously upset and reared hard to be away from the undead horse.

"I'm a Death Knight," Creed said, his voice had an ethereal echo to it as he sat atop his mount.

"Aren't death knights servants of a Chaos Lord?" Ismene said, her smile wavering.

"No," I cut in, pulling myself atop Jill and calming her enough to walk beside the undead horse. "Death knights are a very rare and uncommon subclass of warlocks that have an obvious bad stigma. Why would you pick Death Knight as your class, Creed?" I asked, shaking my head.

"I am unable to speak of the class selection process with those who haven't been through it," Creed said, seeming surprised at his own words before recovering. "Right, I was about to break an oath. That would have sucked. Uhm, I picked what I was told would be best for my progression. And that is as much as I can say until you both get your *Sparks* unlocked. Are you still going to help me?"

I smiled over to Ismene who was finally approaching to sit behind me, before saying, "Under one condition. Why do you need to kill these rats?"

"Isn't it obvious," Creed said, sighing and shifting uneasily under the ethereal echo of his own voice. "I need the essence so I can reach level five and start dungeons, that is, if anyone will have me in their group." The ethereal voice sounded very depressing coming out of a sad young kid.

"We also need essence, so count us in good buddy," Ismene said, leaning over to pat his shoulders. "Shouldn't you have, like big scary armor, if you're a knight? And what kind of abilities do you have?" Ismene peppered him with questions as we continued down the road.

The trip took several hours, and I learned a good bit about Creed in that time. For one, his voice only became the odd ethereal sound after casting one of his spells or abilities, and only for a few minutes after. So soon enough, we were talking with plain old soft voiced Creed. He said his class had three main focuses, but only told us about the one he'd picked, endless frost he called it.

His spells and abilities focused on mid-range attacks and slowing of enemies, all while sucking a bit of their health and converting it into his own. In short, he was an off tank that had wonderful support abilities. I was playing around with the idea of asking him to join us in a dungeon run when we all got to the proper level, but Ismene beat me to it.

"You should be in a party with us," Ismene said, then checking my reaction continued. "We have a friend named Emory who is a main tank, and I know Caldor here will try and be like his dad, so a mix of range and upfront fighting like you, so if I am able to pick either a ranged or healing class, we'd have most of a group right there!"

"You'd do that?" Creed asked, seeming legitimately surprised. But then his expression fell, and he said, "There is no telling which classes you'll be offered, what if all four of us are stuck as mostly front-line fighters? We'd be at a severe disadvantage."

"I think it's a good plan," I said, supporting Ismene and giving Creed a reassuring smile.

The road we traveled had gone from nicely maintained right outside the village, to filled with potholes and missteps that slowed us considerably, but now it began to even out again. On all sides of us were massive pine trees, different than the black oaks I was used to, but they had a pleasant scent that I could get used to. We'd seen some wildlife, but nothing wanted to approach Creed, so everything, including a gray wolf, stayed clear.

The terrain had gained a hilly quality to it, not quite an uphill mountain, but enough that the horizon hid what was just ahead as we dipped and showed a vast distance when we crested the hills. Creed and Ismene talked quite a bit, she was taking a liking to him in a sort of little brother way I could tell, and I just listened while enjoying the views.

Creed gestured to a worn side path that led into the trees. "Dungeon's this way and the rats just a bit further," he said, leading his mount to the well compacted dirt path.

While traveling down this road we passed several adventuring teams of five, all coming from the dungeon and none heading toward it. The first group drew weapons when they saw Creed and I began to understand the discomfort he had to deal with daily. Between the three of us we were able to convince them he had chosen a warlock path and was not in fact a Chaos Lord. One of the group members commented that he'd seen other warlocks before and they had the same look about them, so they'd passed by without incident.

We walked on foot from there on out, Creed returning his summoned mount to wherever it came from between uses. With him just wearing his dark hood he looked much more like a general caster type, and we didn't have any more trouble with the next few groups.

The line of trees gave way to an opening filled with an array of tents with at least a few hundred people doing one thing or another. Some were lined up outside a nicer looking dark brown tent that turned out to be a merchant, purchasing dungeon loot, while others congregated in and around an expansive blue tent that had a cobble stone floor with tables and a bar set up inside.

As we marched through the sea of tents, I saw an organization to it. Smaller tents, most likely used for sleeping, were neatly set up in rows covering the southern and western sides, while the merchants had nicer looking tents to the east—which also happened to be the closest to the dungeon entrance— while the northern side was filled with a mess of different establishments. I saw a blacksmith, a few bars, a cobbler, and even a tailor.

It was like its own little town, but everyone used tents.

"You know why they use tents?" I asked, then clarified as Creed looked at me like he wasn't sure what I meant. "I know this dungeon has been here for some time, you think that at some point it would be worth just building actual structures."

"You don't know much about system buildings, do you?" Creed said, his expression hidden behind the cloak, but he hadn't sounded judgmental, despite his words.

"I guess not," I said, shrugging while my eyes went from one adventurer to another, admiring their armor and weapons.

"If you start making permanent structures you need a mayor to benefit from proxy levels, which even if you are an *Awoken* you will benefit from under a mayor or someone of higher administration title," Creed said, pointing to a path to the north he added. "Monster sightings were reported up this way."

"So, what does that mean?" Ismene asked, her brow furrowing. "No one wants to be a mayor of a dungeon town?"

"Dungeons don't last forever," Creed said, as if he was repeating information we should already know.

"They can," Ismene interjected. "But I know all about dungeons. If someone were to take the Core or destroy it, then the dungeon would fail. But other than that, it is very rare for a dungeon to fade by itself."

"You're right," Creed admitted. "But it really isn't all that uncommon for dungeons to have their Cores destroyed or taken by the highest-level adventurers. It is frowned upon and usually done in secret, but it happened very often in Nefrah. So much so, that we had more young dungeons than we had older ones, so it was quite common to have adventuring parties travel into the Southlands to challenge their dungeons."

"Even so, this dungeon has been here long enough that it seems like it would warrant a mayor and some proper buildings," I said, putting in my two coppers of thought.

"Establishing a settlement is a century long commitment," Creed said, his hood pulled back and his expression was one of deep confusion. "I forget how much system education nobles get that others don't. A settlement, like Creeshaw for instance, is established and over the years will have many mayors but those mayors work to improve the settlements level, and as long as it isn't disbanded for any reason it will continue to get system benefits that are greater and more useful as the years pass. So even if a dungeon lasts for a hundred years, eventually it will fall and then you will have a town in the middle of nowhere. Which funnily enough is how many towns and kingdoms were first started, but since there are so many high-level settlements now it is rare that someone decides to establish a new one. That is where caravan leaders come in handy."

"What is a caravan leader?" Ismene asked, and I was wondering the same thing. Even having been raised in and around the system and despite my father being an adventurer, it seemed that there was much I didn't know yet.

"It's a title that can be earned and grants you a caravan, benefits that are similar to settlement benefits but much more limited. Traditionally I think it was meant for migration and not to be used as we do now for dungeon areas, but the effects provide enough of a continuous buff and perks to those that gain proxy levels under it. It also helps that proxy levels under a caravan are some of the few in the system that can be transferred to any caravan leader," Creed said, he had really gotten into a rhythm and showed more enthusiasm about system facts around leading settlements and caravans than any other topic.

And just as much as he enjoyed speaking about it, I found it equally fascinating. Not enough that I'd consider the offer to become a mayor myself, like my mother would like, but still very fascinated. The system controlled almost every aspect of life, but even when you were someone with only proxy levels it seems like you don't ever fully understand what is going on behind the scenes.

"Can we circle back to when you said people from House Nefrah go into the southlands?" Ismene asked, her eyes a bit wide at the prospect.

I had to agree that it seemed odd to me as well. It was well known that the Southlands were home to the kingdoms of the goblins, orcs, and all manner of 'darker aligned' creatures. It was more of a human assigned alignment than something from the system, but everyone knew that the Southlanders were blood thirsty beings just a step up from being monsters themselves. Even in Variyn you had to be careful because tribes of Southlanders existed in small pockets throughout the human lands, but they tended to operate underground or in hard to find places, which made clearing them out difficult.

"Yeah, it's rather common among all the border houses and it benefits the kingdom as well," Creed said. "Because adventurers venture out in search of dungeons it thins the population of Southlanders that are likely to mass and attack the borders. It still happens, but much less so since our higher-level adventurers began to seek dungeons in the Southlands. Oh, looks like we are here."

I looked up and saw nothing, then looked at Creed, his vision glazed over and his hand swiping at something that only he could see. He must have some system notification that was telling him we've arrived.

We stood in between a cluster of pine trees, with high brush impeding our way forward. The sun was high in the sky, its rays lighting the floor around us, so we had plenty of time to search out the rats. Creed's robes were catching on the underbrush, so looking back and forth making sure we were alone, most likely, he slipped the robes over his head and off. One moment he was holding it and the next it was gone.

I looked at him with a raised eyebrow and he said, "Gift from my Da. It can hold a limited number of items." He lifted his hand up to show a signet ring with a wolf's head carved into its face.

A ring that acted as dimensional storage instead of a clunky box? I didn't want to be ungrateful towards Alayna's gift, but I instantly wanted a ring to store things inside of. Perhaps I could store my dimensional box inside a dimensional ring? I looked back up at Creed and noticed his armor for the first time, pulling my eyes from his ring.

He looked much more like a Death Knight now. His armor was simple and mostly plain, leather with several lines of thin metal plates. It had an aura surrounding it, perhaps a part of his class abilities. It was like a blue fog hung around his entire armor and the once vibrant browns had been muted to almost look gray. In total, he wore a leather banded chest plate, a tight fitting pair of leg plates—also hardened leather—, boots, and vambraces.

He raised his hood, he wore a hooded tunic beneath his armor, and gestured for us to take a step back. "I'm going to clear some brush. Keep an eye open for any burrows or rats running about."

Ismene and I stepped back, both of us with eager looks of excitement on our faces to see what he was going to do to clear the brush.

Creed pulled free his short sword from his scabbard. The blade was simple and not at all ornate, but the scabbard that had previously been hidden beneath his cloak, was crafted from beautifully polished black leather with silver trim, very ornate.

Creed took a passable swordsman stance and slashed outward with his blade. The sword took on the hazy blue fog, similar to his armor's aura, and as he swung, little runes danced over the surface. An arc of blue frost energy shot forward, cutting down the brush in a cone before him. He turned and smiled at us, we both giggled like school children at seeing his cool spell.

This continued on for several minutes until we sighted our first rat. To call it a rat was a bit of a misnomer. I'd more accurately call it a boar sized rat. It stood well above Creed's waistline as he rushed forward unafraid. The length of the damn thing nearly matched my height and it had to weigh several hundred pounds. I drew my sword, a bit longer than Creed's and readied myself for battle. Looking over to Ismene I saw she'd drawn an arrow from the bow I'd lent her, ready to take a shot if it presented itself. We were like our own little dungeon party!

Before Creed reached it, he sent out an icy blue sword arc of energy. It struck the rat in the face and it screeched in response. It showed two long sets of teeth on the top and bottom, they were the length of daggers and had the same pointed edge as one. I rushed forward to try and flank it, just as Creed got into place in front of it. The blue hazy fog around his armor solidified and suddenly he was wearing plate armor made of transparent ice, topped with a wicked looking spiked helmet.

"That's so badass," I mumbled just as I rounded the side of the rat. Creed struck out first, slashing the rat in the neck, but barely cutting into its skin. An arrow shot just left of me and slammed into the side of the rat, luckily it pierced its thick hide. I checked over my shoulder to see Ismene had also moved to flank the giant rat of unusual size.

I struck out with my sword, going for a slash I'd practiced hundreds of times from one of the books I'd read, but my blow glanced off, not even piercing the rat's hide. I nearly lost grip of the sword when my blade bounced back on me, but I righted myself to try again. Creed jumped backward four feet and cast his icy blade arc spell again, it must have a range requirement.

The rat took the attack full on in the face but seeing as Creed wasn't in its range to bite at anymore, its attention shifted to me. Turning its back toward me suddenly, I was thrown off my feet as it used its tail like a heavy whip against my legs. Pain lanced up my thigh and I felt my *Spark* flare up. Clenching my fist as the power grew in my arm, I thrust it forward just as it turned its face to me, its teeth flashing.

A blue bolt of cracking energy smashed into the rat's face and broke free one of its top teeth. Creed closed the gap by that point and a lucky arrow shot hit the rat right in the ear, pushing deep but not killing it. I made it just in time to see another cool ability from Creed.

He raised his sword and runes danced around the weapon like falling snowflakes in a storm. The next moment he sliced downward and penetrated deep into the rat's skull. It fell still, his final blow being enough to end its life. I felt a rush of something get pulled into me and I blinked several times before I realized it must be essence.

"That wasn't so bad," Creed said, breaking into a fit of nervous laughter. "You should have seen the Undead Ice mage I had to kill for my class, I beat on that thing for over ten minutes before it went down and if I hadn't paid to have a healer to go with me, I would never have taken it down."

My heart still thrummed in my chest, and I had to focus to force down the *Spark* that wanted to lash out. It took several long seconds, but I felt it begin to recede and I let myself relax. That had been exhilarating but I was surprised at how ineffective my sword turned out to be, it looked so sharp.

"Did you see my last arrow?" Ismene asked, excitedly. "I got it right in the ear!"

"Do you feel any different?" I asked, looking her over for any sign that she'd *Sparked*. "You feel any *Spark*ing or swelling of something inside?"

"Not yet, but I definitely felt a slight tingle when the rat died," Ismene said practically bouncing on her feet.

"That would be the essence," Creed said, he'd pulled out a large dagger from someplace and was struggling to cut the large tail free. I moved over to him and offered to help, which he accepted by stepping aside.

I swung down with my sword and to my relief—I was beginning to think I'd been given a dull sword—the blade cut straight through without any issue.

"I guess I need to work on my swordsmanship," I said, holding the blade tightly in my hands as Creed flipped the rat over and began to cut into its belly. "I practically lost my grip when I struck its hide."

"Monster hides, as a general rule, are much thicker than

anything you'd normally encounter in nature. In fact," Creed said as he struggled to cut the softer underbelly of the rat. "I'd be willing to bet that there is a spawn queen out here to be producing such strong rats."

That was something that interested me. I had read about spawn queens, basically monsters that had become the strongest version of themselves out in the wild and they begin to spawn offspring of equal potential. In fact, it was the most common way the wilderness got filled with monsters. There was also no way we were ready to take on even a rat spawn queen.

"We better be careful," Ismene said, looking a bit worried. "I doubt we are ready to take on something so powerful."

I was glad she verbalized it, I didn't want to come off like I wasn't willing to take on a challenge, but man, if my performance against this rat was any indication, it would not be a good idea. I stopped that train of thought right away. I'd taken down a freaking Chaos drake, even though it was a baby, it was still an accomplishment. Plus, there was the Boar.

"I think we could do it," I said, my chest rising in confidence. "As long as we have a plan and pay attention to possible weak spots, there is no reason we couldn't have ended this fight in seconds."

"He's right," Creed said, grunting as he struggled to get his sword free. "If I'd led with my Rune Strike, I might have been able to one shot it. Either way, we should be careful, I bet these things would mob us if given the chance."

Ismene nodded along, her determination returning with each word. She was raring to go again, I could tell. With everything decided we huddled together to come up with a plan before heading out to search for the rat queen.

CHAPTER 25
THAT'S A FAT RAT

O ur adventure became far less exciting and more methodical from that point on, we slew another three rats and even encountered a venomous one, which Creed said had mutated, so he harvested its venom sac. The large tails and now venom sac all disappeared into his handy storage ring, which was good because carrying those around would have been a pain in the ass considering their size.

We'd finally made a breakthrough on the last rat. Creed missed his Rune Strike, slicing a large section of the rat's side of the head, but not killing it. But instead of staying to fight, the rat turned and fled, so we tracked it and found it dead further into the trees. A stone's throw away from where it fell was a burrow with two rats standing guard outside. Creed stopped us before we came into view and told us that he was certain that would be the queen's burrow, he said he could feel it.

I tried reaching out with my own senses, but they just weren't as keen as someone who'd been fully *Awoken*. We needed to figure out a plan to deal with two at a time, since our

'One shot' method wouldn't work here. But before we got into that, I had to ask Ismene a question.

"How are you feeling?" I asked, checking her up and down. She didn't look any different and hadn't shown any signs of *Spark*ing. "Any feelings or signs of the *Spark* yet?"

"Not yet," Ismene said, sadly. "I keep feeling the smallest of rushes when we kill these rats, so something is definitely happening. I just don't know what I am supposed to feel."

"For me, it's like a build up inside and sometimes an intensity that is hard to describe," I said, trying and failing to give words to my feelings.

"I barely felt a tingle myself," Creed said, shrugging. "I didn't *Spark* naturally, and my father had a group of adventurers clear out an entire den of Dire Bears before I finally felt it. In House Nefrah, nobles are encouraged to *Spark* as early as they can, my Da believes that the younger you make the switch the more powerful you'll become."

"Let's hope a rat queen is enough to put you over the top," I said, crossing my fingers and giving her my best cheesy smile.

"Merlin seemed to think I was close," Ismene said, shrugging. "Honestly thought the first rat would do it for me."

"About the queen rat," Creed said, bringing us back into focus. "They tend to be larger versions of their offspring, but because it's probably actively spawning, it shouldn't be mobile. It will just be a matter of clearing any rats from around her before we sneak in and get the kill."

"Let's take it a step at a time," I said, peeking around the tree at the two rat guards. "How are we going to handle those two?"

"I'll take one and you two take the other?" Creed offered.

Ismene and I shared a look. We'd been all but useless since we'd devised the plan of Creed just smashing in their heads right from the start. I'd had a few opportunities to swing my sword around and Ismene had used another arrow, breaking it against the rat's skull and leaving us only seven intact.

"I think I can use my *Spark* to charge my sword," I said, considering my words carefully. "I just don't know if that will work. Using my *Spark* is a bit wild and I don't really have a handle on it if I'm being honest."

"I'll aim for its back leg and see if we can hobble it," Ismene said. "Then if we have to run away to stall for time we can."

"Good plan," I said, making Ismene beam with pride.

"I'm going to start things off with an Icy Slash," Creed said. "That way we can pull them away from the burrow entrance. We don't want to accidentally pull more mobs."

All being in agreement, we enacted our plan. Creed stepped out to where the rats could see him, surprisingly they didn't charge or seem to even notice him until he slashed his sword down, sending forth an arc of blue icy power at the left one. As soon as it was hit, both rats locked on target, rushing for Creed. Ismene acted next, scoring a perfectly aimed shot to the right one's back leg and slowing it considerably.

I rushed forward pulling deeply from my core and giving purpose to my *Spark*. Whatever I was doing had a few unexpected side effects. My speed nearly doubled as each stride I took shot me that much further, and my eyesight sharpened, I was able to see the rat in perfect gruesome detail. Trees whizzed past me as I held back my sword, ready to thrust using one of the many techniques I'd studied from a book.

Power began to travel down the length of my blade as I neared the rat and *Spark*s of blue energy appeared. The increased speed, and newness of using the technique in battle didn't work in my favor, I stumbled just as I reached my target. Luck was with me. My blade thrust into the shoulder of the rat, moving in easily and farther than I would have expected. I lost my grip on the blade and fell to the side as my momentum kept me going forward.

Painful scratches hit my arm, most of it being deflected by my armor, but some making it through. The rat ran over the top of me, and I rolled several times before making it back to my feet, my dagger out and ready. Ismene hadn't wasted any time, filling it with several more arrows, one of which must have gotten through its thick hide, because it had fallen and wasn't moving. I ran forward and stuck my dagger in its other eye, as I hadn't felt the release of essence yet. Just as I did so, it thrashed and then went still, releasing a final wheeze as it died.

Creed had finished his target off as well and cleaned his blade off with a length of cloth before sheathing it. I took a deep breath, relishing the moment and everything we were doing. I was hunting monsters; I was a freaking adventurer even before I became *Awoken*. It was a marvelous feeling and one that I could tell Ismene shared, though she had a measure of tenseness as she hadn't *Sparked* yet.

We took our time retrieving arrows and my sword, the sun still high enough in the sky that we would have a few more hours before worrying about losing the light. It took a good bit of hefting to get my sword free, it must have been wedged into a piece of bone. Without the power of my *Spark* filling the blade, it lost quite a bit of its cutting power. I did notice something cool after I got the blade free, all the grime and blood dripped off the blade within seconds, leaving it as clean as the day I received it. I'd have to see what kind of enchantment it had when I Awoke, because I'd love to put that on the armor too.

I was dirty from our several battles, a mix of blood, dirt, and even pinecone pieces stuck in odd places like the back of my shoulder. Ismene had tried her best to get it all, but several parts were wedged in there pretty good. They never talked about how dirty you get when monster hunting, and I could only imagine the long dungeon dives would be so much worse.

But dirt, blood, and all, I was brimming with self-confidence and practically giddy with excitement. I loved being an adventurer.

We approached the entrance to the burrow, a six-foot-wide opening in the dirt with three-foot-high mounds of fresh earth all around. Keeping to a low crawl, we slowly worked our way over the three-foot mounds of dirt and peered inside. It was dark, but not pitch black. The angle of the tunnel was gradual enough that the time of day and the angle of the sun considered, I could nearly make out the back of the cave and several things moving inside, but the details were sparse.

"I can see six rats and the queen," Creed whispered, his light blue eyes seeming to glow with power as he stared.

"Do you have some form of dark vision?" Ismene asked, beating me to the punch.

"Because I can't see shit," I added, squinting as hard as I could to make out a specific number of them.

"Yeah, it's a class passive ability," Creed said, crawling backwards away from the entrance.

We all moved about ten feet away where we could talk without alerting the rats.

"There is no version of this where we can kill six and the queen at the same time," I said, voicing the concern we were all feeling. "So, let's figure out how we tackle it. Any suggestions?"

"I wish I'd taken a crowd control spell to buy us time while we dealt with a portion of them," Creed said, biting his lower lip as he thought.

"You said the queen was likely to be immobile right?" Ismene said, rubbing her chin as she considered things.

"Spawning monsters makes the queens immobile or at least very slow, but that doesn't mean they won't be able to fight," I said, rehashing what I knew about monster spawns and queens.

"I've got six arrows left," Ismene said, counting what was left in her quiver. "What if someone got all the rats' attention and ran off, giving two of us time to finish off the queen?"

"That could work," I said, my mind racing to figure out the details. "I bet I could use my *Spark* to run a bit faster again, staying far enough ahead of the rats to be safe, but close enough that they'd think they had a chance at eating me. You have to be close to where the queen dies if you want the essence." I gestured to Ismene. "Do you think you can take the queen out by yourself?" I asked Creed.

"If we catch it while it's still spawning, I think so," Creed said. He seemed unsure and I really saw his age as he considered his abilities against the queens. Resolve hardened on his face, and he continued. "The queen was pretty fat and about three times the size of the ones we'd killed, but I bet one or two good Rune Strikes on her head and she's dead. Are you sure you'll be safe with the rats on your tail?"

"I don't see another way, so I'm going to have to be," I said, shrugging. "Just be as quick as you can because there is no telling how long they'll follow me for."

"Let's do this," Ismene said, an excited grin spreading across her face.

The sun was dipping closer to the horizon, but it worked to our advantage, shedding more light into the burrow. It would also be shining directly in my eyes as I ran, but it was the best direction for what I needed to do. I could see the area rise into a rocky hill and I hoped that with how thin the rats' legs were, that if I needed to climb atop a large rock for safety that I'd be able to do so. It wasn't a perfect plan but given what we had at our disposal it was the best we had.

I gripped a fist-sized stone and prepared to throw it down the hole. We had no way of knowing if all six would come out or maybe we'd get lucky and just one would investigate. If that were to happen, we planned to ambush it, giving it a quick death. With all the strength I could muster, but without tapping into my *Spark*, I threw the rock down the burrow. It hit something with a quiet 'thump' and a rat screeched.

I quickly stepped back far enough to see how many would be coming out while still giving myself space to run and kite the rats. Two rats, a bit smaller than what we'd been killing outside the burrow, appeared and I got ready to run if anymore came out. But our luck held, and the rats saw me and screeched again, charging forward. Ismene had orders to call out a bird caw if more came out after we committed to our attack, but she remained silent as I led the two through the trees to where Creed waited.

Just as I crossed a particularly large pine tree, Creed appeared and slashed downward taking the lead rat's head in a single strike. I knew by experience that he had to wait three seconds before he could do another Rune Strike, so I wasn't surprised when he leapt backwards and slashed out with his sword, sending an icy arc of damaging energy at the other rat.

Not wasting a single moment, I back tracked and thrust my sword forward. I was getting better with my attacks, real life experience helping to solidify the knowledge from books and years of self-guided training. My thrust was aimed true and pierced it right in the eye, sinking deep into its brain without the help of my *Spark*.

I let out a whoop of excitement just as I heard a 'caw caw' from Ismene.

"Hide, I'm going to get their attention and take them to the hill," I said, forcing my sword free and back into its scabbard. Then taking one last look at Creed I said, "Keep Ismene safe and kill that queen fast!"

He nodded, and I couldn't help but see a little bit of my twin siblings in him. As I rushed forward to see how many rats had surfaced, I pictured the twins getting their *Sparks* and worry wormed in my stomach. A part of me suddenly could understand why my father might want to keep me from being an adventurer. This was dangerous work with no guarantees of a long life, it would only take a single mistake or misstep to bring about my end. I pushed the distracting thoughts aside just as I hit the clearing around the burrow.

All remaining four rats had surfaced and roamed in the open grass around the burrow.

"Over here you fat ugly rats!" I yelled. Letting my *Spark* build, I threw out a ball of blue energy at the furthest one. It left a scorch mark and had the desired effect. All four zeroed in on me and began to scurry toward me, tails swishing in agitation. They moved faster than I'd expected but I was sure I'd be able to stay ahead of them even without my *Spark*, so I turned and ran.

As scary as it was, I made sure to let them gain some ground, putting only six feet between me and the lead rat. I did my best to control the amount my *Spark* increased my running speed, but it was hard and several times I unknowingly began to outstrip the rats, but so far, I'd kept all four's attention. Nearing the hill, I had to pump my legs as the incline began to become gradually steeper.

Hundreds of rocks of varying sizes covered the semi steep

hill, more than I'd thought there would be, and I began to lose ground as I weaved and jumped over them. I turned my head and could barely make out a rat behind me in my peripheral vision, but the obstacles were too great to give it my full attention. I tripped on a small rock, and it tumbled down breaking loose more rocks as it went.

I was lucky, a few of them hit the lead rat and must have disoriented it long enough for me to make it to my feet. However, I realized something, and a pit grew in my stomach. Only two rats still followed me up the semi-steep hill.

I had to get back to warn Creed and Ismene!

My mind went into overdrive thinking of what I could possibly do as I kept moving up the hillside. There was a good size rock ahead and it gave me an idea. Moving behind it I began to push, hoping to dislodge it and create a rockslide big enough to do some damage or distract the rats long enough that I could flank around them.

The boulder wouldn't budge, and I heard the rats drawing ever closer. Closing my eyes, I pictured the *Spark*ing core of my power inside of me and began to pull as much as I could stand into my muscles and hands. The rock began to move, slow at first, and eventually rolling free. It was remarkably spherical and each foot it moved it added more rocks to its fall until a veritable sea of rocks, all smaller than the first, shot down the hill.

I felt the first release of essence as the rocks began to settle at the bottom of the hill, but not the second. Drawing my sword, I surveyed the damage. There was a big pile of debris at the bottom of the hill, but no signs of either rat. Moving slow and careful as to not disturb any more rocks, I made it to the bottom. In between two of the larger rocks was a rat's face, it spat and hissed trying to free itself, but it was pinned pretty thoroughly. Ending its life quickly, I sprinted back to the burrow, hoping I'd make it back in time.

I didn't encounter any rats on the way back, but I must have been just behind them because I heard Ismene scream just as I reached the burrow entrance. My body went full protection mode hearing one of my closest friends in peril. My *Spark* buzzed around me, and I rushed inside to help. The first thing I saw was Creed holding a bloody arm, the ice armor having been broken away. The queen was a bloody mess and unmoving. One of the rats faced off against Creed while the other was atop Ismene, a new scream filling the burrow as it thrashed into her.

I could see she was holding an arrow and stabbing into the side of the rat, but it mauled with vicious animalistic rage. Holding out both my hands I let my *Spark* fly, a stream of blue flames hit the top of the rat, but it didn't stop or turn, so I cursed and plunged my hands down. To my surprise, my hands, glowing a faint blue, pierced straight through its hide. My rage grew and I began ripping chunks out of the rat, taking it apart piece by piece.

At some point I must have killed it because I heard Creed telling me to stop, that we needed to move the rat's body. Covered in blood and feeling empty from the sudden withdrawal of my *Spark*, I helped him push the rat off Ismene.

She was covered in blood and dirt, but her chest moved slowly up and down. She was still alive!

"I have a potion!" Creed said, pushing me aside as a red vial with motes of white appeared in his hand. He uncorked it and splashed some on a large gouge in her neck before tilting the rest down her throat.

I knew very little about healing potions, other than they were something every adventurer should have at least one of. Watching it work I made a mental note to get me a dozen or more. Her wound was closing, her skin slowly knitting itself back together. Then all at once she gasped and woke up coughing.

Her eyes went wide as she looked at me and she whooped for joy. "I'm *Sparked*!" She exclaimed, before promptly falling unconscious once more.

CHAPTER 26
HEALING UP

Despite her moment of clarity in which she announced herself *Sparked*, Ismene remained knocked out, but breathing hard. Creed's arm healed up with a few sips of a green potion that he called a 'regeneration' potion, I guess it healed slowly and while less effective during battle, increased the already high regenerative abilities of those who'd *Awoken*. Working together, we got Ismene back to where I'd tied Jill up on a tree at the edge of the area where we found rats. I felt a little guilty having left her there, but by the time I realized I should have stabled her we'd already found the first rat.

Jill took on the load after that, carrying Ismene to the small tent city outside the dungeon. After asking around a bit, we found a healer's tent and someone to look after her.

"Her body is in a form of essence shock," the old healer was saying, his grizzled face and sagging skin speaking to the years he probably spent as an adventurer. Now he owned a traveling healer's station to deal with more grievous dungeon wounded adventurers, he told us as much when we first stepped into his establishment, nearly refusing to treat a non-*Awoken*.

"What does that mean?" I asked, hoping that what Merlin had warned hadn't just come to pass. "Is she going to be alright?" I added.

"Well, you see now, she has too much essence floating around inside of her and at these levels I'd say she should have gone through the *Awakening* ceremony years ago," he said, rubbing his chin and regarding me with a keen eye. "Same goes to you boy, you are burning like a furnace that's ready to melt away the very stove meant to hold in the coal. A pair you make."

None of that answered my questions and I decided to just fix the older gentlemen with a stare, saying as much with my eyes.

"I can do a bit to help her," he said with a huff. "But it'll not come cheap. Give me two hours and I'll have her awake and on her feet."

I agreed to his demands and handed over all my gold coins with the promise of more, but he told me I'd given enough, even giving one of my gold coins back. I wanted to stay and wait outside the tent, but Creed had other ideas.

"Waiting won't help, let's get something to eat and drink. That potion and our mini-adventure really took it out of me," Creed said, yawning as if to add weight to his words.

We left to find a place to eat. I stayed quiet during the entire meal, but managed to eat a good bit, my body's hunger overriding any grief that tried to keep me empty. We'd finished our meal and began to drink; Creed didn't hold his ale very well and became louder as the minutes passed.

"I earned enough essence to make it to level five," Creed was saying, his words turning several heads as he was louder than the din of conversation that filled the busy tent. I smiled awkwardly at a few heavily armored adventurers and decided I better engage with Creed before he got any louder.

"I'm not so far away," I said, catching his eye. "You don't have to shout. That's good about your levels, I'm glad for you."

Creed leaned in and cupped his hand over his mouth before saying, "And she got her *Spark*. That means I finally have a chance at my own dungeon group!" His words started at a low raspy whisper and ended in practically a shout as he grew excited.

Using my hands, I motioned for him to keep it down, and he apologized, setting his drink to the side.

After several long minutes of silence, he spoke again.

"I'll have enough to reach level five, add at least one attribute on top of the level, and even have enough to purchase a new ability," Creed said, his voice only a measure above what would be considered normal, and low enough that it blended in with the general noise of the tent.

I was interested again, hearing about the many uses of essence. I had to admit that I hadn't studied the classes and the methods around leveling, which involved increasing an adventurer's overall strength and power. "You can increase attributes directly with essence?" I asked, focusing on the part that I knew the least about. I vaguely understood attributes, there were several defined categories that outlined the parts of an adventurer, like Strength being the person's overall ability to move and lift heavier objects. It went deeper than that I knew, but I didn't even know all the attributes, just that there were a few of them and each could be raised every time you leveled. Hearing that essence could accomplish the same thing I wondered why anyone would focus on leveling if you could just throw it all into attributes and be the stronger for it.

"Yeah, only a few per level though, otherwise it gets too

expensive," Creed said, settling into the stool and relaxing visibly.

"Too expensive?" I asked, my curiosity in full drive now.

"The cost of buying extra attributes rise with each purchase," Creed said, then added. "I've raised my attributes a good bit, stupidly as it kept me from getting to level 5 sooner. But that was when I was level 3, it has a sort of soft reset each time you level. The base amount required still goes up, but not nearly as much as when you buy multiple attributes at once. Most people agree that purchasing two per level is the best way to do it, but even that gets expensive down the line. If you aren't purchasing at least one additional attribute per level, you won't keep up with other adventurers of the same level. I've been shooting for three per level but stopped after level 3 because it just takes too much. The idea was I'll be a bit stronger than someone of equal level and when I get to a high enough level, I'll completely outstrip my peers, but now I'm not so sure. It's harder to get essence when you can't get into groups to take down more challenging monsters."

My mind reeled from this new information, but as the wheels began to turn in my head, a thought occurred to me. Had my father done something similar as Creed? He'd always been talked about and considered, from other perspectives at least, to be one of the strongest adventurers of his time, but he wasn't that old. I knew he was older than mother by a good bit, as once you reach a certain level you aged much slower, but there was no way he was that old. Perhaps he'd sunk more essence into raising his base power with attributes and when he reached higher levels it gave him an edge over others of like power.

I was grasping at straws at this point, but I filed the

thought away as something to explore when I'd *Awoken* and gained access to my attributes and levels.

The sun had all but set and a dark gloom settled over the tent city. By my guess it had been at least two hours, so I made up my mind to see how Ismene was doing.

"I'm going to go check on Ismene," I said to Creed, then decided this might be the time to part ways. "It was a pleasure to meet you and if you are planning to stay in the area, just talk to Merlin at Merlin's Pub, he can get a message to us after we've both been *Awoken* and we will get a group together."

Creed stood, shakily at first but he found his feet after a moment. "I'm going to try and find a group here but I will one hundred percent go talk to Merlin so we can run some dungeons together. I'm hoping I can get at least a run or two finished while I wait, just gotta find the right group," Creed said, looking nervously around the bar for prospective group mates.

He'd put on his black cloak again and I thought to tell him that people would likely think he was a mage if he didn't correct them but decided it would be best to let Creed figure things out on his own. Instead, I shook his hand, his grip was surprisingly firm for someone his age and had a coldness to it that wanted to suck away my body's heat. We parted with a farewell nod, and I went to seek out Ismene.

I found her standing just outside the healer's tent and rushed forward to see if she was okay.

"I'm feeling better," she said as she saw me hurrying over to her, probably with a worried expression on my face.

"The healer said as much?" I asked, peeking past the canvas tent flaps and into the dimly lit tent. There was no one in sight, so I didn't rush in asking for an immediate diagnosis.

"Yeah," Ismene said, stretching her neck to the side and

275

rubbing at it with her hand. "I've been up for nearly an hour, and he said he'd done all he could and that I'd better 'get to an *Awakening* ceremony post haste', like I'd do anything else." She mimicked the old man's voice pretty decently and I couldn't help from laughing, releasing a measure of nervous energy I'd been holding onto ever since she went out and didn't wake up.

"Good, good," I said, pulling her into a tight hug. "Are you feeling up to traveling? We can make it to Merlin's before it's too dark if we leave now."

"I think I'll manage," she said, smiling at me, but it didn't touch her eyes. She was obviously feeling whatever had happened to her and the bags under her eyes spoke of an exhaustion that wasn't likely to go away anytime soon.

"We can take it slow," I said, already guiding her to where I'd put Jill on a hitching post. "You can ride, and I'll walk beside you."

"I'd prefer if we both rode and made better time," she countered, a bit of her familiar firmness returning to her voice.

"Deal," I said, unhitching Jill and patting her on the back. She was a strong horse and I think between the enchanted horseshoes and whatever weight reducing enchantments were placed on her saddle, we'd be able to make decent time.

Into the night we galloped toward Creeshaw and a warm bed at Merlin's Pub.

CHAPTER 27
HOPE FALTERS

B y the time we trotted into town atop Jill, Ismene had all but released her grip on me and I was beginning to worry. The hour was late enough that only a few people walked around under the light of burning lanterns. A cool breeze brought with it the sweet smell of food and drinks from Merlin's pub. I rode all the way into the alley, only then getting off of Jill.

Ismene was barely conscious, and her face had gone red with white spots all over. Moving as swiftly and carefully as I could, I helped her down. She'd went limp and I had to support her full weight. She felt hot to the touch, her skin wet and clammy.

"I'll get you inside, Merlin will know what to do," I said, dropping all pretense of helping her walk and picking her up in my arms. We made the door in a few short seconds and the din of a dozen patrons quieted at once as we entered.

"Merlin, we need your help!" I called out, straining for my eyes to adjust to the light so I could find the elderly pub owner.

Several adventurers stood looking alarmed, but a moment later Merlin was there.

"Settle down everyone," he said, calming the crowd with a wave of his hands. "Follow me to the back and I will see what I can do to help. I'm no healer mind you, but I know what sort of trouble this is." He eyed me fiercely and I nearly took a step back, afraid of the sudden intensity and anger in his gaze.

He had kindly suggested to us earlier that we shouldn't do what we did, and we understood the risk, but if Ismene died now, I didn't know how I'd deal with myself. Even with his warning, we took the risk and now had to live with the consequences of our actions. And though I was worried about Ismene as I followed Merlin to the back room and set her atop the table for him to examine her, a part of my mind knew that she wouldn't have changed a thing.

The idea of becoming a *Sparked* and eventually an adventurer meant everything to us. We both had our individual reasons of course, me my dad and the sense of purpose and responsibility he instilled in me, and Ismene her own parents and the sacrifice they made, giving their lives to fight back the Chaos. There was probably more to why Ismene felt so strongly, but her secrets were her own and I was just trying to distract my mind from the reality of what was happening in front of me.

Ismene was shaking now, her entire body convulsing violently and foam coming out her mouth. Merlin worked with a speed and ease that I wouldn't have thought possible for someone his age. He chanted over her body, one hand held out over her while the other held open a book, his eyes flashing over the pages.

This continued for another five excruciating minutes before Merlin let out a heavy sigh and fell back into a chair.

Ismene had gone still, too still, and I rushed over to her side fearing the worst.

Her body was cold to the touch and her skin had taken on a gray sheen to it that seemed unnatural. In my confusion and anger I turned to Merlin.

"You've killed her!" I yelled, my rage building and *Sparks* of blue energy arcing off me. I couldn't believe it! I'd come here for help, and he'd killed her without doing a thing for her!

"I've expended a great deal of power and don't have the energy to deal with you right now," Merlin said, and with a simple wave of his hand I felt that familiar blockage that had been used against me before, rising up and separating me from my power. I fell to the ground in a heap from the sudden change and my chest exploded in pain.

My breathing came in ragged bursts, but whatever had been feeding my rage was subsiding and now a deep sorrowful despair began to fill the hole. I'd lost Ismene and it was my fault. How could I do this to her? All former justifications my head had tried to form shattered into pieces. It no longer mattered that I knew beyond a shadow of a doubt that given the chance again she would risk it. Nothing mattered in that moment other than the fact I'd lost a close friend.

I cried then, in a heap on the ground, curled up like a child, I let myself weep. It was only then that Merlin decided to pay me any mind again.

"Quiet yourself boy," Merlin said, his words no longer soft or gentle as they had been earlier that same day. "I've performed a damned miracle and you should be thanking me, not crying at my feet like a whipped dog."

A miracle? My sudden grief paused as my brain tried to come to terms with what he meant. Letting her die was definitely not a miracle. I used what little strength I had, my body still reeling from the sudden disconnection from my *Spark* and checked on Ismene once more. She was as cold and still as ever, then what had he meant? I decided I should ask him, struggling to get ahold of myself I stood.

Wiping away tears and feeling like a foolish child I said, "What miracle?"

"I've stabilized her core from ripping apart her body," Merlin said as if I should have already known. "She had maybe a few hours left before she would have died from the stress of it. Whoever you took her to had placed a few very impressive wards around her core and bought her the little time she had left, but it was like using your hand to stop the flow of a river, you aren't stopping much."

"She's ice cold and isn't breathing. What are we going to do now?" I asked, my grief suddenly replaced with a sliver of hope.

"We," Merlin emphasized the word, "don't do anything. I will take her someplace to *Awaken* her, but the only convergence of ley lines that I know of with enough essence gathered to accomplish the job is several hundred miles away, which is why I am trying to rest."

"You'll never get there in time, that's just too far," I said, the bit of hope I held onto remaining firm. Surely, he had a plan, some way to get there in time.

"Damnit boy I need a moment to gather my wits," Merlin said, standing up and pushing books aside until finding whatever one he was looking for. "Stand back so I can work."

Flipping through an ancient tome with words on the cover that I couldn't understand, Merlin found a page and began to chant. Ismene rose up from the table just as Merlin slashed down with his free hand and a rip in the air formed. I really couldn't call it anything but that, tattered edges of the space in front of Merlin swayed awkwardly and made my stomach feel like it was going to retch. I moved my eyes someplace else and as I was trying to do so, saw through the rip.

On the other side of the rip in the air was a dimly lit pillar of stone, while I recognized the stone as a Prime Mana Shrine, I couldn't make out where it was exactly. In the distance I could hear the crashing of waves and smell a waft of salty air. I looked away just in time to see Merlin with Ismene floating like a stiff board walking through the rip.

I caught a mumbled sentence from Merlin as he stepped through. "The things I do for Elkor's troublesome brat..." Whatever else he was saying was lost to me as the rip in the air closed and I was left alone in Merlin's pub.

Did that mean she'd be okay? Merlin hadn't really only said he bought her time, but now it seemed like she would become *Awakened* before me? I was fine with this, not at all feeling jealous, in fact my hope that she'd be alright swelled again until I decided to trust it.

"She will be alright," I announced to no one in particular.

There were a bunch of books spread out on the table, mixed with a few scrolls and even a few mismatched rings and baubles. I pulled up Merlin's chair and sat down. I didn't expect that they'd return soon, I knew a little bit about the *Awakening* process, enough to know that she'd need to unlock her class at the same Mana Shrine she used to *Awaken*. Which meant, assuming Merlin continued to help her, that they'd be gone a few days.

I was looking through a book that covered the history of an ancient civilization, it was written in an older dialect that I could technically read, but only one in every five sentences made any sense. The various usage of words and phrases had changed so much over the last thousand years that it was almost like a language of its own. Most everyone spoke what was called 'Common' tongue, but what 'Common' was had shifted enough that you might struggled to understand what some older elves said to you, or—at least I'd heard as much—could barely understand the Southlanders' version of common, which was mostly shortened to the point of barely being speech.

I gave up on the book around the same time I heard footsteps approaching the room. Pushing the book away and doing my best to appear like I hadn't just been snooping, I looked up just in time to see Merlin's Runeforged, or what'd he call it? A golem. It set a bowl of hearty stew in front of me, along with a small plate of butter and several large slices of thick warm bread.

"Thank you," I said, the words coming out as if I were asking a question. Was this food meant for me or had Merlin instructed food be brought here and I just happened to be where Merlin was when he ordered it? It only took a single whiff of the food to reach my nostrils before I decided that I didn't care. It had only been a handful of hours since I'd eaten with Creed, but my body yearned for more food, and I planned to oblige it.

I fished out a chunk of beef, warm and stringy, and placed it atop a warm piece of bread that I'd spread a thick portion of butter on and took a bite. Words cannot properly describe how wonderful it tasted, so I didn't try, instead, focusing in on the meal I devoured it within minutes. To my wonderful astonishment the Runeforged returned, replacing the meal with a cold ale and a slice of cherry pie.

He had to have meant this for me, I decided, because I was a huge fan of cherry pie. Cherries were not something that grew locally, having to be imported from the elven lands. A fact I only knew because my father would occasionally bring some back for my mother to bake up a pie. My younger self had all but demanded more cherry pie each time, but my father assured me it was a delicacy that couldn't be enjoyed very often due to the difficulty in obtaining the fruit.

He'd then regale me with a funny tale of how he'd had to do some odd puzzle and quest for an ancient elf to earn the right to buy cherries. As a kid I didn't realize what he'd been talking about, but now I recognized his tale for what it was, a story about a dungeon dive. Not all dungeons were infested with large varieties of monsters, some had very few and specialized in traps and puzzles, giving you a chance to earn powerful loot if you could solve increasingly difficult tasks.

I savored every bite of that cherry pie, thinking of my father as I ate. My emotions had gone for quite the trip today and after finishing my pie and downing the large mug of ale, I needed a place to sleep. Finding where Merlin kept the keys to the rooms above, I picked one out and left several silver. Surely, he wouldn't mind if I rented myself a room. I went up and passed out moments later atop the soft comforting embrace of the blanket.

CHAPTER 28
SIGN ON THE LINE

Morning came and I was up with the sun. It was surprising to me, but I wasn't sore, and I felt absolutely amazing. With a spring in my step, I walked down to the pub below and found that Merlin still hadn't returned. The Runeforged saw me and disappeared into the back, returning a few seconds later with a bowl of steaming mush and chilled milk. Some type of porridge no doubt, I dug in, enjoying the warm mushy quality of the food. The milk was a refreshing touch and I wondered how he'd gotten it so cold.

Finishing my meal, I waved goodbye to the Runeforged, it remained silent, and I headed on my way to say my goodbyes. I was three days away from my *Awakening* ceremony and it took most of two days to get back to the capital of Variyn.

I was sure that my mother was still doing well, and the twins were up to their everyday mischief. I was surprised to find all three of them up and out working, picking Kelt fruit.

"We're heading into town when we're done," mother said as I approached atop Jill.

"You selling the bushels to Phillip?" I asked, thinking the

greedy grocer might try and buy our supply for less because my mother wasn't up on the current prices.

"I am," she said, smiling happily as she worked. "I got him to commit to as many bushels as we could deliver for a silver and fifty copper each."

"What? He really went for that price?" I asked, shocked.

"I've got my fair share of proxy levels in bartering," mother said teasingly. "Honestly I think he just felt sorry for me and maybe worried that if he didn't give me a good price, I might pass my craziness to him." She grinned at me, and I felt my heart warm. It had been so long since she'd been herself that I'd almost forgot how dark humored she could be. I loved my mother and seeing her like this brought back memories of my parents together.

They'd been the perfect couple as far as I was concerned. My mother always joking and able to take the most serious of topics and poke fun at it. My father always so serious but gentle. He'd often scold my mother playfully that she ought not to be so crass about things, but I know he loved her for it. They shared the best and worst parts of each other, coming together to be something great.

"You got a much better deal than me," I said, deciding to emulate my father and give her a measure of seriousness. "Can I help you finish? I have just enough time before I need to go."

"I'd come to your *Awakening* if I could," she said suddenly, reaching out and taking my hand after I dismounted. "But these trees need tending and the elf said I shouldn't push myself too hard too fast. Probably shouldn't even be out here but I needed the fresh air and these little devils needed something to do." She reached over, letting my hand fall away, and tickled Grace on the side.

Grace giggled and jumped out of reach, loving every

moment of it. Seeing them together I had all the reassurance I needed that they'd be alright when I left.

"I know," I said, meeting her eyes and reassuring her that I didn't mind. "From what little I know I'll need to be able to go straight out and begin adventuring to gather essence and objects for my class and skills. But I promise to visit the first chance that I get. I will be safe, don't worry."

It was her turn to give me a reassuring look. "Mothers always worry, but I know you'll do your very best," she said.

We picked kelt fruit for the next half hour before I left, saying goodbye to each of them. It was hard, but a good kind of hard, knowing I'd be back eventually but as an adventurer with an unlocked Class.

The first day of my ride ended, Jill never tired or slowed, but I was growing saddle sore. I started a small campfire and spent most of the dark evening thinking of Ismene. My own path to becoming *Sparked* had been filled with fabulous prizes, a fair bit of pain, and a little bit of anguish, but poor Ismene had been a step from death just to get what I'd gotten by happenstance.

I slept under the stars that night and as I gazed up into them, I wished that I'd been able to convince Ismene to take Merlin up on his offer to change herself the slow way. Had she survived last night, I found myself wondering. My small flicker of hope was waning in the darkness of the night, but by morning with the feelings of freshness and newness, that hope blossomed, and I decided that 'yes' she had survived. She was probably on a grand quest right now, living the dream we'd always shared together.

It was with that hope in my heart that I reached my destination. I really wanted to travel straight to the keep and visit with Alayna. The few days we'd spent apart felt like weeks and it took all my willpower to keep myself from going to the keep. A larger, prouder part of myself decided that it would be best to just stay in an inn for the night and go to the *Awakening* ceremony by myself. Sure, House Variyn had a stake in my success now, but I was my own man as well and I needed this to be my path forward.

It was with those thoughts rolling around in my head that I found a place to stay for the night. It was called 'Hound's Perch' and had the oddest little carving of a dog perched on a branch with its paw up on its head as if giving a salute or guarding its eyes to see something. Going inside I was lucky, they said, to get the last room, saying that tomorrow's ceremony had brought quite a few people in from the surrounding villages and towns.

I'd never actually been to an *Awakening* Ceremony, so I didn't know that it was more of a public event. People from all around sat and drank together, some sharing stories of their sons and daughters being *Awoken*, a few proclaiming that they'd be going tomorrow themselves. Those last few got drinks bought for them by the keg full, but I gave no public proclamation. A few stray patrons asked if I was here for the ceremony, I just smiled and nodded that I was, but despite the armor I wore they didn't ask me any additional questions.

My emotions kept shifting about, my nerves and my worries getting in the way of any fun I could have, but I sat down among the crowds sipping at my drink late into the night.

Tomorrow everything would change for me, and I wanted to enjoy my last night before the change.

Despite the late hour that I went to bed, I rose with the sun. I made my way down to the common area and ordered food. They provided wonderful bacon, eggs, and a mix of cubed potatoes with onions and colorful peppers. I ate my fill but restrained myself when I thought to have seconds. It wouldn't do to go into the Ceremony with an engorged stomach.

I wasn't the only one up early, the three I recognized as the others being *Awakened* were also up with the sun and were wearing their best clothing, clean and pressed cottons and one even wore silk. I wore a loose cotton tunic myself and a pair of pants that needed a wash. My excitement threatened to overtake my good sense, as a good part of me just wanted to spring from the Inn and be the first to arrive.

I settled down enough to see things objectively, I need a bath and to change my clothing. Inquiring with a bar maiden I was told a tub could be filled for me downstairs in a room adjacent to the kitchens. I paid a silver coin, telling her to keep the rest, and went upstairs to pull out my fine dress attire that Lord Variyn had provided earlier in the week. The silk shirt was cool to the touch, and I ran my hand down its length.

There would be no hiding who I was when I wore these clothes and good thing too, because I didn't want to hide who I was destined to be. I just hoped that with all my special Arcane Knight embroidered items that I'd truly be able to pick the class I wanted. Having bundled up my clothing I found the room beside the kitchen and stripped down.

The bath was pleasant but not nearly as much as the one I'd had in the keep. The water, for one thing, didn't hold its temperature nearly as long as I'd have liked. But I bathed quickly enough to avoid the worst of it. Drying off with a towel they'd provided, I changed into my dress clothes, then in a last-minute change of plans, I also put my armor over the silk attire.

I'd worn it quite a bit, but it must have had a similar enchantment as the sword, though not as fast acting, because all the debris and filth from our rat hunt was gone the next day. Leaving fresh smelling and clean looking armor.

"You're looking like a fierce little warrior now aren't yah?" the older Innkeeper said, she had big rosy red cheeks and a pleasant smile.

"Thank you," I said, offering her an awkward smile in response.

"You ready to be *Awoken*?" She asked with a cunning smile crossing her face.

I thought to tell her I wasn't, keeping up the charade from the night before, but I just sighed and nodded my head.

"The other lads already left," she said. "Best get moving if you want to make it to the pre-registration."

"Pre-registration?" I asked, confused. What was pre-registration and why was I going to be late for it?

"Just outside the garden where they line you all up before you touch the big ole stone. The parade afterwards is what starts in the afternoon, but by then you've all been *Awoken*."

I barely heard the end of her sentence as I rushed towards the door. How hadn't I gotten all the damn facts? Did they think I'd be returning to the keep beforehand so they didn't need to fill me in, perhaps. Either way I rushed to the keep now. There was a garden just behind it where I knew the Prime Mana Shrine was located, the one that would *Awaken* me.

The city blurred around me as I ran as fast as I could safely do so through the streets. I reached the gates to find a really long line, maybe fifty people in all, on a side path going toward the back of the keep.

There were a pair of red heads at the end of the line who turned to look at me as I approached.

"Welcome to the back of the line," the man said, his red curly hair was shoulder length, but most of it had been pulled into a messy bun. His eyes were green and striking against his fiery hair. He had high cheekbones, kind of reminded me of an elf, but his ears were rounded.

"It's not so bad here. We'll get to see everyone else go through the process of *Awakening* so there'll be no surprises left for us!" the woman said, she had the same curly red hair as the man standing beside her, but she'd managed to tame it into a proper tightly set bun atop her head. She even added a strip of black silk, the ends of which fluttered in the breeze as I took in the sight of her. She shared the man's eyes, sparkling green. I noted that she had a long sword at her hip, in a plain white wood scabbard, it stuck out against the black and gray clothing they wore.

I didn't need to be told that they were related in some way, probably siblings I guessed.

"Yay for us," I said, laughing a bit at our misfortune. "Name's Caldor Miles, nice to meet you."

"I'm Fred," the man said, then pointing beside him he continued. "And this is Fran. We're twins."

"You should give him our entire life story as well, brother. He's probably eager to hear it," Fran said, smiling sarcastically at her twin.

"I could tell him if you think it'd help," Fred said, completely missing any sarcasm. "The line's long enough."

"Gods you are insufferable sometimes," Fran said, face palming. Then recovering herself she continued. "My brother is a bit overwhelmed by the sheer number of useless facts he's accumulated over the years. So don't mind him if he can't see his way into or out of a normal conversation."

They appeared to be a few years younger than me, but still

a few years older than most of the teenagers here—a few looking like they hadn't even reached seventeen.

"Are you implying that I've filled my head with knowledge and you in turn have not?" Fred asked, but he held no hint of sarcasm or playfulness, just a serious confused face.

Fran gave me a look that just said, 'See what I mean?' and I nodded, giving her a friendly smile in return.

Their antics continued for the better part of an hour as the line slowly moved forward. I learned that they'd both *Sparked* rather late in life, age nineteen, but that both of their parents were still active adventurers. Fred was hoping for a caster type class like his mother and Fran said she refused to accept anything short of a martial class that allowed her to use her father's sword in battle; he'd given her the same blade he'd used most of his life. I couldn't help but wonder what he used or how a sword lasted so long.

Weapons, even enchanted ones, had a shortened lifespan normally as killing dungeon monsters and monsters in general took a lot out of the weapons used by adventurers. We decided right there in the line together that we should try to do a dungeon run together at some point after our *Awakening*.

As we neared the front of the line we went around the bend and into the garden area that took up much of the back of the keep. A single round table had been set up outside and one at a time people went up, filling out paperwork.

"There's paperwork involved with becoming *Awoken*?" I asked, honestly surprised.

"Oh yes," Fred said, perking up. "For the last several centuries there have been meticulously kept records by the order of King Newaliyn."

"Looks like I'm up," Fran said, stepping in front of Fred and beginning her registration. Fred didn't seem to mind though; he'd produced a book from somewhere and had his nose deep into it.

I waited patiently until finally it was my turn, and I stepped forward.

"Welcome to the *Awakening* Ceremony, my name is Grendel, can I get your name please?" Grendel asked. He spoke quickly and to the point, having probably said the words hundreds of times before. He wore a simple shirt with a tight vest that held the House Variyn seal on it.

"Caldor Miles," I said. Grendel began to write down my name then paused and looked up at me.

"Caldor Miles, Knight of House Variyn and Lord of Blackridge?" Grendel asked, before I'd even answered he'd pulled out a new sheet, that had been set aside from the normal pile.

"Yeah, that's me," I said, kicking at the stone paved path the table had been set on.

"You could have come straight to the front," Grendel said, his smile never wavering. "But I bet all these soon to be adventurers are happy you didn't, good to stay humble. I've got all your information, but I wanted to check a few things with you."

"Alright," I said, peeking at the paper and seeing it was all filled out, but one space labeled 'Chosen Class'.

"You intend to try for the Arcane Knight classification?"

"I do."

"Your primary residence is set as Blackridge and a secondary is listed in Creeshaw?"

"That's right, I guess," I said, not sure if I'd consider my primary residence a keep I'd never seen yet, but could understand why they'd want to list it that way.

"Okay just sign here and that's all I need from you," Grendel said. "Follow the path behind me and place your hand on the Primary Mana Shrine when it's your turn. Good luck."

I signed on the line after reading the small bit above it just stating that I vowed that the information given was truthful. "Thank you," I said, taking a deep breath and walking around the table and towards my future.

CHAPTER 29
ONE TOUCH IS ALL IT TAKES

The Prime Mana Shrine came into view, half blocked by a crowd of people, but glowing like a powerful lighthouse during a storm. I was transfixed by the view, the light was a pulsing mix of whites and blues, but the pattern and rhythm of the pulse was so mesmerizing it almost made me forget what I was doing there.

Fred was approaching the Mana Shrine now, and as I watched, he placed his hand on its surface. The stone monolith let out a brief flash, brighter than the pulsing before, and he removed his hand, staggering backwards. His eyes seemed glazed over as he turned and joined the crowd watching the pulsing light show. It was my turn I realized, stepping through the crowd. I did as Fred had done, walking right up to it and placing my hand on the stone surface.

It was warm to the touch, and I felt a great pulling, like my mind was being forcibly ripped from my body.

I was in an alleyway, it looked vaguely like the one beside Merlin's pub, but there were no stables and deeper down I heard muffled cries for help. Without hesitating I rushed forward to investigate. As I stepped closer, the world shifted again and I was in an open town square standing shoulder to shoulder with several people as I saw ahead of me, on a raised platform, someone was bent down on a block, ready to be executed.

Without needing to think about it I knew this man had been accused of murder and other more heinous crimes. Something inside of me thought he should surely get what he deserved, that I wouldn't be bothered by this in the least. The scene shifted again, and I stood over a familiar man, the one who'd been about to be executed. I held a knife in my right hand and below me was the dead mutilated form of another man.

It was clear by the blood on the man before me and the dead body, that he'd been the one to do the horrid act. With barely a second thought I lunged forward, plunging my blade into his guts. The world shifted again, and I was back in the alley by 'not Merlin's pub'. Screams filled the alleyway and I ran forward to assist, but when I got there it was two men, one had been stabbed and coughed blood and the other had blood on his hands. His face was white with fear and stuttering words I couldn't make out.

A dagger appeared in my grip, and I felt the urge to act, but I was unsure.

"He killed me!" A voice I recognized called out from the ground. I looked again and it was Emory there. Rage flared inside of me that this man had killed my friend and I went to stab but stopped at the last moment. The figure standing over Emory had shifted as well, now my father stood over him, a grim expression on his face and a knuckle-white grip on his dagger.

My dagger fell from my hands and a flood of emotions ran through me at seeing my father, so alive, but in a position of having killed my friend. A part of me wanted to step forward and embrace him, but another part screamed at me that he had murdered Emory and justice demands he also pay a price. I steeled myself and stepped forward, raising my dagger.

"You will submit and be judged," I said the words, but what authority figure I had in mind I didn't know; the words just came to me.

My father's visage changed, and the world shifted to the lake we'd spent so much time at between his adventures. He didn't speak but I saw the love in his eyes, and it melted away any malice I'd begun to feel at seeing him in such a murderous position. He reached up and touched my face.

The scene shifted, this time more violently than before and I found myself in a library. Throngs of people filled many hundreds of tables, and a wizened old man approached me in oversized blue robes.

"You must help us solve the riddle!" He shouted at me, guiding me to a seat and placing a book in front of me as well as a slip of paper. The paper was written in a language I had never seen before. A sudden thought hit me that I'd find answers in the book, so I opened it and began to decipher the paper.

This continued for what felt like days, where I'd be given a task or shown a scene or thing then I'd react. At one point I was hit with hunger so painful that I knew if I didn't eat soon death would surely take me, and so I stole food. Then another, I was tempted with an item that was said to be able to return the dead to life but I instinctively knew that the only way I'd get to it was by stealing it.

I'd made a choice, deciding that it was worth trying to steal it to bring my father back. When in the act of stealing it, I was told that it already had a purpose of utter importance. A foreign king had died and if he were not revived it would plunge the world into a war so deadly that countless souls would die. Though it pained me, I left the item behind so that it could be used to prevent additional bloodshed.

I was challenged in every way possible, but finally after what felt like a month straight of grueling tests the world shifted, and I was in a vast dark room. There was a certain amount of illumination, and I could see several objects but no source of light. On a grand wooden table there were weapons and trinkets of every kind. Swords sat beside large tomes with ancient runes on their spines, daggers, wands, staffs, maces, and all manner of things.

I inspected many of them but felt drawn to a particular sword, set all the way at the end of the long table. It shone like brilliantly polished silver and had a walnut sized gem set into the pommel. I know the different types of rocks and gems, but this blue gem was cut in such a way that light appeared to be reflecting within it. Every square inch of the blade was covered in barely noticeable runic words, like finely cut scratches.

I reached out and grabbed the blade, raising it into the air and I felt a surge of warmth so great that my knees buckled a little.

"You sure you can bear the weight of such a choice?" A booming voice said, echoing all around me.

I pried my eyes from the fascinating blade and was surprised when the largest man I'd ever seen, stood bending over to regard me on the opposite side of the table. My first instinct was to fall into a defensive stance, but as soon as I moved to do so, the blade and the table it had once sat upon disappeared into a cloud of dust.

"Do not worry, I am but an arbiter fashioned by the ones

you call the Ordu. You can call me Arb," Arb said. "You needn't fear me, I am here to see that you begin your path on the right foot, so to speak."

"That sword," I said, my mind still yearning to hold it again. "Where did it go?"

"Your father was also drawn to that instrument," Arb said, his form began to shrink until he was only eight feet tall, and two chairs appeared. He took one and gestured I take the other.

"He was?" I asked, my eyes finally able to focus enough that I truly saw Arb. He was naked but didn't have any of the usual parts you'd expect to find. His body shone like newly polished steel and his eyes glowed an orange and red of ever-shifting molten rock. I should be terrified by his very visage, but I wasn't.

"Yes," Arb said simply, then continued. "But I will tell you what I told him." Arb shifted in his chair and scratched at a heavily bearded face—but as it was the beard of a stone sculpture and not individual strands of hair—his hand just ran over the outside surface of it.

He didn't continue to speak for several long moments, but I held my tongue waiting to see what information he had given my father.

"It is good to see patience in one so young," Arb said, chuckling. It sounded like metal bars clanging together. "You have been given the trials. The tools you saw laid out before you represented the path forward. Few are given the sheer volume of options provided to you, but only eleven before you have been offered the sword you rose into the air and your father was one such individual."

"I know you can't understand the gravity of that but let me tell you what it truly means to be what your father called an 'Arcane Knight'. It is worth noting that those who take up the

299

blade of the Ordu are able to give name to the path they will be seen by, which is why your father chose to be called an Arcane Knight, a classification that doesn't truly exist, but we will get to that later."

Arb leaned forward and peered into me with his fiery eyes, and I felt a shiver run up my spine. "That sword and its classification put as simply as I can, is Protector, Champion, and Judge of the Ordu. Those who walk down this path must keep to a code and oath requiring they keep the balance between Order and Chaos. Note that I haven't told you to seek out all Chaos and destroy it, because as your father learned, there is a balance to all things. Order cannot exist without Chaos. Do I make myself clear?"

"I think," I began to say but stopped myself. Did I understand what he meant? My father hadn't just been a normal adventurer or obtained a straightforward class as I'd expected. There was no Arcane Knight in the traditional sense. He was an instrument of the Ordu, the ancient ones, the creators of this world, or so I was taught.

The one thing I'd always wanted was within my grasp, to be as my father had been, an Arcane Knight. It didn't matter to me that it carried extra responsibility or that once more I'd found out my father had kept more secrets. Becoming an Arcane Knight was what I needed more than anything. A small voice inside my head scorned me at my mental declaration. It told me that following my father's path wouldn't bring him back or truly make us closer, but I pushed it away with a violent determination.

"I accept the weight of this responsibility," I said, standing as I spoke. "I will be an Arcane Knight as my father before me. I will stand in the path of Chaos and bring Order. The balance will be maintained, I swear it."

"You could be a great and powerful wizard," Arb said, standing as well. "The greatest in many ages I believe. Or if you walked the martial path there would be none that could oppose your blade. Strength beyond measure would be in your grasp. Many options have been laid before you and the one you are choosing will be the least of them."

Before I could respond to reinforce my commitment, he held up a hand to forestall me.

"The path of 'Champion of the Ordu' leaves your spells and abilities quite open, but you will be forced to pick two paths and focus your efforts there. Your father picked a specialty wizard classification Evoker and a specialty warrior classification Blade Master. Both are common enough classifications, but together you will be able to wield powerful magics and deadly martial attacks. But it will take you twice as long to master either path as you must keep both in balance as you learn. For each evoker spell you learn it must be paired with an ability gained in your blade master path."

"I understand," I said, seeing how it might be challenging but totally worth it. I knew for a fact my father had been able to use his Arcane Knight class to become one of the most powerful adventurers and I would do the same.

"Kneel and I will anoint you as an Arcane Knight, Defender of the Balance," Arb said. I did so and watched as the same runic blade I'd picked from the table appeared in Arb's hand. It was larger and more menacing in his grip, but I didn't fear what was coming. He brought the blade across my shoulders then pressed it lightly on my head. "Rise and begin your path toward being an Arcane Knight."

I felt a rush of energy fill me, beginning as a gentle warmth at first, but quickly transitioning to an intense heat. It became overwhelming but I stayed on my feet, eyes closed from the excruciating pain. And just as quickly as it came, it ended.

The sword had gone, but Arb was still there. "Let's get you adjusted to the system and its various functions," Arb said, a gentle smile on his face.

CHAPTER 30
SYSTEM ACTIVATE!

"You will become more acquainted through time and personal investigation of the system, but for now I want you to focus on the phrase, 'Stat Sheet', it's a shortened term but it'll work," Arb said.

I did as he requested, thinking about the phrase 'Stat Sheet'. As I did, a semitransparent sheet of information appeared before me.

Name: Caldor Miles | Classification: Arcane Knight (Locked) | Species: Human
Level: 0, 450 Essence to Lvl. 1 | Essence: 145,084 | Reputation: Rank 1, 0%
Health: 200 | Mana: 200 | Stamina: 180
Attribute: Value, Affinity
(Affinity Base values determine the amount of Essence required to raise Attributes. You have a Paragon attribute, meaning you are a Paragon. Paragons have reached peak affinity in one or more Attributes)

20, Paragon | Intellect: 20, Paragon | Endurance: 18, 81%
ragon | Concentration: 18, 89% | Strength: 17, 73%

. . .

I scanned it, not fully realizing how quantified the system really was until this point and let the information sink into me. There were several other tabs, but my brain was a bit on overload, so I left them be. As I focused on specific parts of the information, Health for instance, I instinctively knew what it was quantifying. For health it was straightforward, it was a number representation of my wellness, and ability to function. So, it wasn't as cut and dry as you reach zero and you die, it was more of a 'at full health' I am operating at my highest, well if I hit 'half health' I'll be injured to the point where my ability to defend myself might be impaired.

I quickly looked at each of the attributes in turn and got a clearer understanding of them.

Strength: This Attribute determines the amount of force your muscles can exert to any given task. The higher the value, the stronger you physically become.

Constitution: This Attribute determines your overall health and wellness. The higher the value, the more apt you are to deal with sickness and recover from wounds.

Endurance: This Attribute determines your body's ability to deal with physical hardships and push past normal limits.

Intellect: This attribute determines your overall ability to learn, remember facts, and bring to bear your mental force through the use of spells.

Concentration: This Attribute determines your ability to focus and regenerate your Mana after use.

Core: This Attribute determines the amount of Essence you can safely store within yourself. The affinity for this attribute differs from all the rest as it doesn't affect the value's output, but rather the rate at which essence can be pulled into yourself.

What did it mean to be a paragon I wondered? I understood that it basically meant that I was naturally better at whatever attribute I had reached Paragon with, but I wondered how common it was, and decided to ask Arb as much.

"Paragons of a single attribute are rare," Arb said. "But Paragons of three are once in a century."

"Has there ever been someone with a Paragon affinity for all attributes?" I asked, my academic side taking over.

"There have been three in the ten thousand years that the Ordu implemented system changes to account for affinities. It is extremely rare and in each case, they were individuals who shaped the very future of the lands around them, some for the better, one for the worst," Arb said.

"What can you tell me about them?" I asked, wondering if perhaps I knew of any from legend or stories.

Arb either didn't hear me or chose to speak over me. "You have a few pending quests, but I am locking them away until you've accomplished your Class Quests. Please go to 'Quest Log' and take a look at your quest," Arb said.

I focused on the words 'Quest Log' and the same transparent window appeared but on a new tab. I focused on the single quest I saw, and new information was revealed.

Unlocking your Class

You have come before the Arbiter of the Ordu and sought out the path of Order. Not all that come are worthy and you will be put to the test. Seek out an acceptable sacrifice and present it to the Arbiter.

Warning! The Arbiter has offered you a time sensitive quest. You have 168 hours to complete this quest or risk losing access to the system.

Objective: Search out a creature of both physical prowess and magical strength. [Acceptable Item List] Return with the item to the same Prime Mana Shrine. In addition, you must pick and learn two abilities, either spells or skills available to you.

Rewards: Unlock three Class Abilities. 1,000 Essence.

Accept or Decline?

Warning! If you decline, you forfeit the gift of the Ordu and any physical pain or resulting death will not be the fault of the Arbiter.

Not that I'd ever decline, but it didn't feel like there was much of a choice once you'd come this far. I sent the mental thought to 'accept' and the 'Accept or Decline' portion of the quest went away, and a timer began to count down, but I noticed it only went so far as one second before pausing.

"To aid you in your upcoming challenge a wise man would seek help if the task were too great, this is acceptable as long as the correct reagents are collected and returned within the time given. It is time to pick which abilities you'd like to learn. Special reagents are required as well as an amount of essence depending on the ability. Shall we start with your available Evoker Spells?" Arb asked, and I nodded quickly wanting to see what I could learn.

A new sheet appeared before me containing four spells with a name and a description.

Firebolt: For 20 Mana you can hurl a bolt of fire at a target within 150 feet. It does $(10 + 5x)$ points of potential damage, where x is caster's level. Cast time 1 second with a 2 second cooldown.

Light: For 5 Mana you can summon a globe of Light that you can direct for up to 20 feet around you. You can summon up to 5 at a time. Instant Cast with a 5 second cooldown.

Physical Resistance: For 50 Mana you can infuse your aura or the aura of another willing target with 10 percent resistance to physical harm. Lasts for 3 hours. Cast time 4 seconds with a 1 minute cooldown.

Blade Ward: For 50 Mana you can ward a blade's edge against damage and ensure a sharp edge. Increases base damage of weapon by $(1 + 1x)$ base damage, where x is caster's level. Cast time 4 seconds with a 1 minute cooldown.

I focused on each one and a cost and reagent cost appeared.

"I see that you have a reagent box on your person," Arb said, startling me from my intense focus. "I am able to pull any required items straight from there, so please pick which spell or spells you'd like to learn. But remember, you must pick and learn an equal amount of Blade Master skills."

"Can you show me the Blade Master skills?" I asked, deciding I needed to see both sides before making any decisions.

"Very well."

A new window appeared showing four available skills, so I took a long look at each.

Power Strike: For 20 Stamina you can infuse your strike, dealing double damage. Cooldown 4 Seconds.

Stamina Surge: Activate skill to completely restore Stamina over a period of 5 seconds. Cooldown 1 hour.

Preferred Weapon: For half of your total Stamina, you can make a weapon your 'Preferred Weapon' adding a permanent

(1+1x) to base damage, where x is caster's level. Only 1 weapon can be 'Preferred Weapon' at a time. Cooldown 1 day.

Hardy (Repeatable): (Passive) Increase your Health and Stamina by 50. This is a passive ability that can be taken multiple times, but not more than once per level. With each increased level the rarity of reagents and essence required go up.

Some definite useful skills and abilities there as well. The Hardy repeatable passive ability really called to me, as raising my Health and Stamina by 50 would be a full quarter increase! I had no idea what reagents I had, so I checked my essence amount, something I'd sort of glazed over. My head tilted to the side a bit and I wasn't sure I was seeing things right.

"Uhm...Arb, I have a question for you," I said, looking at the amount of essence and the amount required for these abilities, then over to the amount needed to level to 1. I had 145,084 essence and it took 450 to get to level 1, and 100 per spell or skill. I knew I could raise my attributes as well, so I checked the price on that.

It turned out that wasn't as cut and dry, but roughly it would cost close to three hundred to raise an attribute, and if what Creed had said ended up being true, it only got more expensive the more you raised them.

"What is your question?" Arb asked, probably frustrated at me for going silent as I reviewed the numbers.

"Am I reading this correctly? It says I have over a hundred thousand essence."

"You are correct, you have 145,084," Arb said, smiling down at me. "It is an incredible number to be sure. But with your Core Attribute being Paragon it is explainable. You should spend a good deal of that before we finish, your Core can only safely hold 200,000 essence at your current level and attribute of 20. I can't imagine why you waited so long or why you went out of your way to collect so much essence."

I was dumbstruck. I found myself wondering how high of a level could I reach with so much essence? But then a better thought occurred to me, how high could I raise my attributes with this much essence.

"Another question," I said, but didn't wait for Arb to prompt me. "Can you remove the spells and abilities I don't have reagents for and just show me the ones I can learn? Also, would you mind showing both lists together?"

"Very well," Arb said. "It is done."

My eyes flicked back to the list, and I was surprised to see all eight in a single row.

"I have reagents for all of these? Are there any that take the same that would prevent me from learning all eight?" I asked, thinking I knew why all eight had appeared.

"Physical Resistance and Blade Ward share a reagent and you only have one," Arb said, then continued. "As well as Stamina Surge and Hardy, each require the same and so only one can be chosen."

"Thank you, Arb," I said, my mind churning out what I thought would be the best combinations. I settled on the following Blade Master abilities, Power Strike, Preferred Weapon, and Hardy. My thought process was, first I would take all the skills I could, but I definitely saw more value in having a high base value for my wellness and ability to perform, then a quick recovery of my Stamina. I would need to learn it eventually as none of these first skills were something I wanted to be without.

As for the Evoker spells, that was a bit harder as I wanted the resistance and the increased weapons damage, both suited my path forward as an Arcane Knight. In the end I had to be practical and pick what I felt would help me survive longer, and a potential buff that could be applied to more than just myself was a key spell to have. I chose the Physical Resistance spell.

I mentally picked each, having to pick a spell and a skill before I could learn either. It was a package deal. With each spell and skill learned I felt knowledge injected into my brain, knowing instinctively how to do each of them.

"Our time is coming to an end," Arb said, just as the final pair solidified in my mind. "You have enough time to increase your level and any attributes you wish before I must end our connection."

I nodded, not even bothering to answer as I needed to act fast.

I focused on the level a bit more intensely wondering if there was a way to tell how much essence was needed per level and to my surprise a window appeared showing as much. It only showed the first twenty levels but after some quick mental math I saw that I'd be able to reach level 16 if I didn't purchase any attribute points.

"How many attribute points do I get per level?" I asked, knowing that it was a thing, but not knowing how many.

"Because your Core attribute is Paragon you will receive 3 per level, 1 more than is standard," Arb said.

I quickly thanked him and went back to work. Spending 286 Essence, the required amount to raise my Strength—which was currently my lowest attribute—I increased it by 1 to see how much more it would cost afterwards. To increase it by another one it now costs 429 essence. Checking my other attributes, I saw their values had also increased. As painful as it was to spend so much essence, I increased Strength two more times, paying 429 for the first one and 643 for the third. Then I raised my Concentration two times, to put all my attributes—except for Endurance—at an even 20. That cost me 843 and 1,264 essence respectively. For a grand total of 3,465 Essence or enough to have leveled myself to level 3 and half way to 4.

I'd purchased 5 attribute points for the same amount that I could have gotten 9. The thought was hard to swallow, but I just had to remind myself that the cost to level didn't increase past its set value as I raised my overall attributes, so I would still get those 9 and have more than the average adventurer. I could definitely see why two or three additional attributes were the norm. Creed could have hit level 5 much sooner if he hadn't been keeping up to the extra attributes per level.

Knowing time was short, I stopped my train of thought and threw in 450 essence into my level, reaching level 1. A golden wave of light pulsed from me, and I felt pure ecstasy radiate through my body. It was beyond anything I'd ever felt, and it took considerable effort not to immediately add another level to feel it again.

I saw that I had three attribute points to assign, so I did so, adding two into Endurance and one to my Core attribute, making them 20 and 21 respectively.

I was going to go for level 5, so I had to be quick with my picks. I didn't honestly know which attribute would benefit me the most, but if I was understanding things right, increasing my Core attribute any more would probably have no effect on my ability to adventure, but I would need to raise it at higher levels to be able to hold enough essence to increase my level or buy skills. As it sat now, I focused on my stat sheet and saw an Essence limit of 210,000. That was a problem I'd deal with down the line.

Looking over the cost to raise my attributes I saw that it had a soft reset to it, bringing the overall cost down now that

I'd entered into a new level. Though the base cost was a bit higher than it had been when I was still considered 'Level 0' so that was something to remember. I looked at the price to raise one of my Paragon attributes and was surprised at the base cost of 169 Essence. Checking against my Strength attribute, I saw that it came in at 286. Then I figured I might as well compare it against my Concentration which was a higher affinity than Strength, it came out as only 250. Less, but not as drastic as the Paragon attribute. A thought occurred to me, if Paragon attributes were so much less to increase, I should probably pay for non-paragon attributes first, since Creed said the base cost rose up with each level.

Using that train of thought I raised my Endurance to 25, for the cost of 3,531 essence. I had to move quickly; I could feel my time coming to an end. I paid 900 essence to level up and went to work raising my Strength to 25, paying 7,537 essence and adding 3 additional points that I'd gotten for leveling to bring it to 28. I paid 1350 essence to reach level 3 and set my eyes on Concentration, raising it up to 25 by paying 9,881 essence and topping it off with an additional three from the level up, bringing it to 28.

I paid 1,800 essence to reach level 4. Each new level shot off a golden ring out all around me and filled me with just a little less pleasure than the one before it. Deciding I couldn't focus on it, I cleared my head. First off, I added 3 spare points to Endurance bringing it, Concentration, and Strength all to 28 and set my sights on raising my Constitution. At base, it only cost 675 for the first one and a total of 5,540 to pay for 5! That was half of what it took to raise a non-paragon attribute the last level the same amount of times! I clenched my teeth deciding to go for it and brought my Constitution all the way up to 28, but those last 3 attributes cost me a whopping 7,854 essence, meaning just for attributes this level I'd spent 13,394 essence on 8 additional attributes.

Hurriedly I paid the 2,250 essence to reach level 5, spending 2 points of Strength, bringing it to 30 and 1 into Endurance, making it 29. Then I followed my original idea, just buying 5 attributes per level, regardless of their affinity. I added 5 attributes to Intellect, paying a total of 6,925 essence and bringing it to 25.

I took one final look at my sheet just as I felt myself transferring back to my body.

Name: Caldor Miles | Classification: Arcane Knight (Locked) | Species: Human
Level: 5, 5400 Essence to Lvl. 6 | Essence: 93,001 | Reputation: Rank 1, 0%
Health: 280 | Mana: 250 | Stamina: 290
Attribute: Value, Affinity
(Affinity Base values determine the amount of Essence required to raise Attributes. You have a Paragon attribute, meaning you are a Paragon. Paragons have reached peak affinity in one or more Attributes)
Constitution: 28, Paragon | Intellect: 25, Paragon | Endurance: 29, 81%
Core: 21, Paragon | Concentration: 28, 89% | Strength: 30, 73%

For whatever reason my attribute values didn't reflect any benefit my gear gave me, but I quickly guessed that it had to do with the out of body experience I was having with Arb. After all was said and done, I'd spent 52,083 essence. It was the last thought I had as sunlight flashed around me, and I was back in my body. I didn't just stagger backwards; my joints froze up and I fell back. I was fully conscious, but for three agonizing seconds I could feel my body adjust, twist, and shake as my new attribute values took hold. I was already well on my way to standing by the time the first person reached me, it was Fred, more of his red curls had come loose.

He scooped me under the arm and said, "You don't look so well."

"Of course, he doesn't," Fran cut in, reaching us. "By the smell of him he somehow passed multiple thresholds. How'd you get any attributes past 25 already?" She asked, leaning in at first but having to withdraw from the smell that just that moment hit me hard in my face, chasing away any remnant of the high passing multiple levels had given me.

"I need to get cleaned up," I said, breaking away and standing on my own power. "You two want to team up for our class quests?" I asked, turning back after I'd already taken a step away.

"With someone who already passed a threshold, hell yes we do," Fran said, and we made plans to meet after the parade. A parade I was going to be missing, as I needed to clean up.

As I made my way toward the keeps entrance, I checked my information and attributes, sure enough they'd risen to account for my gear. I couldn't work out which items gave what bonuses yet and determined that at the first available chance I would figure out how to identify my items.

CHAPTER 31
DINNER AND DESSERT DIVINE

It was surprisingly easy to get into the keep, the guards knew me by sight. It wasn't long before I'd found a special 'forever hot' bath and even a few servant girls to help scrub the stank from my body. I thought to protest the arrival of the servants but decided against it as their intense scrubbing was something I really needed. My skin was covered in a thick grimy paste and smelled even worse than it looked.

My clothing and armor were taken for cleaning, and my belongings set aside. I'd been soaking for close to an hour, the water staying wonderfully clean despite all the grime that was scrubbed from my flesh, when a servant boy I recognized as one from the kitchens poked his head in.

"I come with a message from Lady Variyn," he said, his fidgeting motions just as nervous as before.

"It was Jon, wasn't it?" I asked, repositioning some bubbles to cover my private bits.

"Yes, Lord," Jon bowed his head a little as he spoke.

"Quit with the formality. I'm just like you, remember?" I

asked, he had a letter in his hand, and he offered it to me. I took it and gave him a reassuring smile, but he still seemed nervous.

"Yes, of course, Lor- I mean sir, thank you, sir," Jon said, bowing his head as he nearly tripped over himself to leave the room.

An odd duck, that one. I unfolded the letter, it hadn't been sealed or anything, and read the contents.

Alayna wanted to meet me at a restaurant for lunch before I left, if I was okay with skipping the normal ceremony celebrations. I wasn't looking forward to any of that, so I would gladly blow it off for her. However, Jon had left so I had no way of giving a yes or no response.

Deciding that Alayna would know me enough to guess at my response I determined to find some clothing and be on my way. The steam running off the water felt amazing on my body, and it wasn't long after Jon's appearance that a servant girl returned with my armor and clothing cleaned and ready. Deciding it'd be best to have a lighter shirt and pants on under my armor I packed my nicer clothes and pulled out a clean pair of simple cloth attire.

My small pack held my items well enough, but soon I'd need to figure out my box of holding. Alayna would be the perfect person to ask about that, so I hurried from the keep and headed to the area in town that had held all those restaurants. I encountered the parade and the party that followed it as I walked, even seeing Fred and Fran having a good time.

Foradee Elama was a place Alayna had wanted to visit because they were said to have the best desserts and it only took me about twenty minutes to find it. The entrance was grand, but in a very non magical way. It had large stone pillars flanking the entrance and a door at least three times too big. There was a finely dressed man standing outside greeting guests as they entered.

I'd put my armor back on, which was fairly nice looking I thought, but the greeter held out a hand to forestall me.

"This establishment is by reservation only," he said, his tone implying I couldn't possibly have such a reservation. Which of course I didn't, but I imagined Alayna must have had one. I was about to say as much when I spotted Alayna wearing a beautiful black dress with golden embroidery, walking toward me from inside the establishment. She smiled when she saw me, and I decided to mess with the greeter.

"I hear you have the best desserts," I said, leaning forward as if I was about to tell him a secret. "Any chance I could just get a bite or two of your best?"

"I would think not," he said, staggering back as if I'd struck him. "I will summon the guards immed-"

"That won't be necessary," Alayna said, putting a pacifying hand on the greeter's shoulder. He turned, looking aghast but seeing Alayna he became a mix of fluttering apologies and sorry ma'ams. "He's with me." She added taking my hand and practically pulling me into the restaurant.

"Thanks for that," I said, a broad smile on my face.

"You're almost too much trouble," Alayna said, teasingly. "How's it feel to be..." Her eyes glazed over as she stopped to concentrate in my direction. "...Level 5 already? And from what my servants told me you've broken through some thresholds."

"Yeah," I said, my hand going behind my head to rub my neck. "I had a bit of extra essence and added a few more attributes than might be normal per level. Level 5 seemed like a good place to stop since my time with Arb was running out."

"Arb?" Alayna asked, her head shaking in disbelief. "You

mean the Arbiter? He let you call him Arb? You never cease to amaze me, Chaos Slayer."

I hadn't realized that the Arbiter hadn't let everyone call him Arb and it got my thoughts churning as to why he was so lax with me.

"I got the class I wanted," I said, deciding not to dwell on it. "I will be the same as my father, an Arcane Knight." I left out the extra bits, deciding I might tell her later, but something told me that my father had never revealed his secret calling, so I should probably follow in his footsteps.

"That's wonderful!" Alayna said, we finally reached our table, it was a single table set out on a balcony overlooking a grand garden. Alayna must have seen my surprise at the secluded venue and added, "I have a standing reservation and this table here is always made available to me."

"It's a great view," I said, not taking my eyes off her.

She blushed and we both sat down. "I take it you didn't have the reagents for your class quest?" She asked, a knowing look on her face.

"No, but I did learn a few spells and skills," I said, talking about them really gave me the urge to try them. It was such an odd feeling, knowing without a doubt that I could cast or use the spells and skills, but having never done so.

"For whatever reason, class quests always end up being something you have to go and get, kind of like a test of strength or something," Alayna said.

Just then a waiter in fine white and black dress clothing appeared. Alayna ordered for both of us, something I didn't mind as there were no menus that I'd seen, and I hadn't the slightest clue what I'd have ordered.

After the waiter left, filling two narrow and tall glasses with some kind of sparkling liquid, I turned to Alayna to ask her a question. "How do I use this box you gave me?"

I'm sure I looked odd carrying a small pack, but I ruffled through it until I found the box, setting it on the table.

"Oh, I thought you heard when...no matter, here let me show you," Alayna said. She indicated a small copper ring and said, "Turn this here and you'll see."

I took back the box and turned the small copper ring. What happened next was the first, but not the last, of the surprises of being an Adventurer. A voice, not even sure if I could call it a voice, but more of a feeling that included distinct words and phrases popped into my head. It was almost as if I could see them floating just beyond sight and it said the following.

Do you wish to infuse 10 Mana and soul bind 'Crafted Dimensional Box - Small' to yourself? Yes or No.

Following the same pattern that Arb had told me, I directed my thoughts into a response and got the following message.

You have soulbound 'Crafted Dimensional Box - Small' to yourself. Would you like to inspect the contents? Yes or No.

I figured I might as well take a look despite knowing what would be inside. This time a window I recognized opened, but with a new tab labeled 'Crafted Dimensional Box - Small'. Inside there were twenty-five small squares each filled with a small representation of the item inside. Eight slots were filled right now, the reagent box, a bedroll, some basic supplies took up a few slots, and the last three with potions, three red, three blue, and three yellow. I thought it was neat that items of the same kind, like the three red potions only took up a single slot and showed that three of them filled that slot.

I grabbed my bag and all the clunky items I'd brought and attached to my pack, determined to add them into the box. My memory stirred and I remembered Alayna opening the box to get it to work, so with my spare hand I tipped the box open and was greeted with another message.

Focus on the items you wish to store inside of 'Crafted Dimensional Box - Small'.

I followed the prompt and pictured the entire backpack going inside. One moment the weight was there on my arm and the next it was gone. I saw that the bag had only taken up a single slot, despite being filled with a multitude of items.

"This is just too cool!" I said, my love of all things magical made me practically giddy.

Our food hadn't come yet, and Alayna seemed content to let me play with my items, so I decided it was time to see if I could take a closer look at specific ones. It only took me half a minute and a bunch of random tries to figure out how to do it.

I was looking through my main system info and found a tab that showed me, an odd but accurate representation, wearing my armor and the ring I'd bought. Each filling a square slot, but I hadn't the slightest clue how to see the attribute benefits it gave me. I did note that my attributes were higher than when I'd been with Arb, the ring and armor were doing something.

Giving up, I decided it was time to ask Alayna, but in that same moment our food arrived, so I dug in instead.

"It's a pretty amazing feeling being *Awoken*, isn't it?" Alayna said between bites.

"Yes, it's everything I could have hoped for," I said, taking my first bite of food since my *Awakening*. It was like fireworks went off in my mouth. Flavors I couldn't have even imagined played across my tongue and I very nearly fell out of my chair.

Alayna had a fierce smile on her face, as if she was about to break out into giggles. "You passed your first constitution threshold! I knew it!" She exclaimed. "Do you know what that means? You've unlocked several decades of natural life at least. Just wait until you unlock your class and can pick out your level perks! If you wanted, I bet you could already pick the 'Long-Lived' perk because of your attributes. Normally someone doesn't unlock their first threshold until around level 15 because you don't want to unbalance your natural attributes too far early on. But I bet you didn't, did you?"

She'd just thrown a lot of information at me, but I was still dealing with the fact that food tasted more wonderful than anything I'd ever experienced. "I uhh..." With effort I brought my mind back to a functional state. "...Yeah, I raised all but my Core attribute over 25."

Another ripple of pleasure passed through me as I took another bite—it rivaled the elation I felt when leveling up. The food looked like some type of beef steak, and not even a large portion at that, but it was heavenly. As I floated through the new pleasure of eating food, something occurred to me.

"I'd started with most of my attributes at or around 20, is that normal?" I asked, wondering why everyone would take so long to raise their attributes past 25.

"You what?" Alayna said, leaning forward and dropping her fork. Her eyes narrowed on me as if she could see the truth of my words by staring. "I've never heard of anyone with a base attribute higher than 10, that is standard. How could you raise your attributes before gaining access to the system?"

I didn't know the answer to that, so I just shrugged and said, "I honestly don't have a clue, but I did notice that my affinities must have affected my attribute layout. All three of my paragon affinities were at 20 and the others matched up more or less to the percentages it showed beside them."

"You have THREE paragon affinities!" Alayna exclaimed,

she was beginning to look funny, her eyes going so wide I thought they'd fall out of her head. "My father was right to get you under his thumb..." Her voice turned to a whisper despite the two of us being very much alone. "You should keep your paragon attributes a secret. There is no telling how many people would want to attach strings to you if they got the opportunity."

"Why would anyone care so much, am I really that much different?" I asked, in my mind even with the extra cost I was willing to spend I didn't see a huge advantage I'd have over anyone else. I'd be as strong as someone of a higher level, but until I was a much higher level, what good would that be?

"How much do you know of King Newaliyn?" Alayna asked. I could tell she was trying to get me to understand something without her needing to say it, but I was no student of history and her words failed to guide me into whatever fact she hoped to lead me.

"As much as anyone I guess," I said, shrugging. "He's ruled for a few hundred years and his father ruled before him."

"Yes, but that's not what I mean," Alayna said, she let out an exaggerated sigh and I chuckled at the display. "King Newaliyn is one of the strongest adventurers this world has ever seen. While his father ruled, he defeated some of the greatest threats to come against the kingdom, including driving back the Southlanders so deep into the south and gaining much land in the name of his father."

"Okay," I said, trying to see where she was going with all this. "So, he was really strong, are you saying he had a paragon attribute and that's why he's so strong?"

"Yes," Alayna finally said, after staring at me for several long moments.

"It is well known that King Newaliyn and his father both

had Paragon attributes, though his father's remained a mystery into his death, his son—our current King—shared one of his Paragon attributes with many. One is Strength and he's shown a level of pure strength that no other adventurer has come close to in recorded history, but his other is unknown."

"And I have three, none of which are strength," I said, wondering how my Core, Constitution, and Intellect Paragon attributes would affect my progression. I knew that purely raising my Intellect for instance, wouldn't make me a genius or anything, but I would be able to remember a great deal better, learn new things swiftly, and increase the potency of my spells. I leaned in closer to Alayna, practically crawling over the table at this point and said, "Constitution, Intellect, and Core."

Her eyes widened as the realization of what I'd told her sunk in. "You shouldn't have told me. I put some runic scrying blocks in place but there is no telling how powerful the spells might be after we blocked them in the library." I pulled back the hair around my ears enough to show the ear clasps that Merlin had so freely given me.

"I think these will protect me," I said, amusement playing across my face at the expression she had while inspecting it.

"Those are Masterwork Refined Mythril Ear Clasps!" Alayna exclaimed. "Those are worth a fortune..." Her voice trailed off as she shook her head in disbelief.

"How did you know that?" I asked, realizing I hadn't gotten any skill or ability to allow me to see the name or properties of an item.

"I just used the Inspect skill, since our reputation is 'Friendly' I'm able to see as much as you can without any special spell," Alayna said, she spoke as if it were a simple thing that I should already know about.

"Where do I learn the Inspect skill?" I asked.

"Oh, you get it at level 1 as part of your basic skills. Just check your abilities list, there should be a place for your spells and skills. Above all of that is a bar that says, 'Basic Skills' you can expand it and see what you have access to," Alayna said.

I didn't even wait for her to finish, opening my menu up and going to the abilities tab. Sure enough, right at the top was a bar that said, 'Basic Skills' and when I opened it up I saw that I had three.

Inspect (0/1000) - You are able to inspect items, people, and monsters to gain a measure of information. This is a basic skill. The amount of information gathered depends on the level of the person using it as well as the level of the item, person, or monster being inspected.

Mana Sense (0/1000) - You are able to sense the latent Mana inside others. This is a basic skill. The range and intensity of the target you are able to sense depends on the person using it and those they are attempting to target.

Perception (0/1000) - You are able to perceive possible threats, hidden doors, and other things that might be out of place. This is a basic skill. The range and complexity of the target you attempt to discover will determine your success.

I'd discovered three new skills, but that didn't explain to me how I could use them. Before I had a chance to even try, I noticed another small expandable bar of skills called 'Basic Weapon Skills' and opened it up.

Unarmed Fighting (0/1000) - You are able to fight without a weapon and can leverage your attributes in battle. This is a basic skill that will do increased damage depending on the level of the person using it as well as the level of the target. Increased levels will increase base damage.

Swordsmanship (9/1000) - You are able to fight with a sword and can leverage your attributes in battle. This is a basic skill that will do increased damage depending on the level of the person using it as well as the level of the target. Increased levels will increase base damage.

My ability to use a sword had been quantified and it didn't look too impressive. Making a note to practice with my sword and see if my skill increased, I switched my focus back to trying to inspect things.

Changing tabs to the version of me with the small squares showing what I was wearing, I focused on the ear clasps and thought about the Inspect skill activating. Something different happened this time and I could feel the skill working. A small window appeared next to the ear clasps giving me the following information.

Masterwork Refined Mythril Ear Clasps

Creates a Psi Shield around the target, blocking all scrying, mental intrusions, and minor psychic attacks.

+10% Increased Mana Regeneration
Durability: *75/75*
Rarity: *Crafted*
Weight: *5 Grams*
Item Level: 90, Level Required to Use: 0, Crafted by: Merlin

The first thought to cross my mind was how Merlin had thought a flat ten percent increase to Mana Regeneration was small. I poked around my menus for a few seconds and found where my Mana Regeneration was listed. I could regenerate 28 mana per minute without the clasps and 31 per minute with them. That would shave an entire minute off how long it took me to reach full mana.

I took a quick count of what else I was wearing. My armor set, my sword, my drake cloak, the ring I'd bought from Ismene, and that was it, I double checked my menu tab to be sure, I had eleven items equipped, the earrings taking up a slot on each ear. I started with the armor, inspecting a single piece first, then realizing I could inspect the entire set, I did that instead.

Leather Banded Armor of the Owlbear Set

Set items (6/6)

Enchanted with 'Finer Things' enchantment.

Finer Things - This enchantment will keep the bearer cool, clean, and unburdened by the weight of the item or items.

+12 Strength (+2 Per set Item)

+12 Intellect (+2 Per set Item)

+15 Constitution Set bonus (Only applies when the entire set is equipped.)

Durability: *532/600*

Rarity: *Crafted*

Weight: *32 pounds (Weight Reduced to 1 tenth by Finer Things Enchantment)*

Item Level: 10, Level Required to Use: 0, Crafted by: Matthew Keely

The grateful feeling inside of me towards Alayna and her father rose significantly while I looked over the stats of the items. Taking another bite of my food I let the feeling of pleasure wash over me and inspected another item.

Cloak of Negation

+100 Health

+100 Mana

+100 Stamina

Chaos Negation: *This Cloak represents Chaos tamed by Order. As such any magical or physical Chaos based attacks will be negated upon contact with the Cloak. Effect can be triggered once every 10 minutes.*

Drake Hardiness: *This Cloak was crafted from the scales of an Elite Fire Monster and as such will provide resistance to heat-based attacks as well as a measure of physical-based attacks.*

Durability: 1,000/*1,000*

Rarity: *Crafted*

Weight: *1 pound*

Item Level: Unique, Level Required to Use: Unique, Crafted by: Micheal Eldar

Stunned once more I wondered what the sword would be, a legendary Ordu artifact maybe? Putting my silly thoughts aside I inspected the blade.

Enchanted Arming Sword +2

Enchanted with 'Well Maintained' Enchantment

Well Maintained - This enchantment will do the necessary task of maintaining your weapon, keeping it clean, sharpened, polished, and oiled.

8-12 Base Damage

+2 Strength

+2 Endurance

Durability: 100/*100*

Rarity: *Crafted*
Weight: *1.5 pounds*
Item Level: 4, Level Required to Use: 0, Crafted by: Sheena Mahry

While the sword was a bit of a letdown when compared to the others, I was happy to not only have a decent weapon, but the handy enchantment that would maintain the blade for me. My last item was something I knew the attributes of, or at least I'd been told what they'd be.

Silver Talos Ring

+1 Strength
+1 Constitution
+1 Intellect
+1 Concentration

Durability: *25/25*
Rarity: *Uncommon*
Weight: *5 grams*
Item Level: 8, Level Required to Use: 0, Dropped by: Crusader Dawn

It was as I'd expected, useful if only barely. Alayna must have caught on to what I was doing, because she left me alone to finish inspecting my items. I shot her a look of appreciation and quickly finished off my food, each bit sending waves of pleasure through me.

"I take it you found your basic skills?" Alayna said, finishing up her own food just in time for a waiter to appear with what I could only guess was dessert. Two large chocolate domes with liquid chocolate poured atop them were set in front of us. The waiter leaned over and sprinkled some white powder atop each of them before disappearing back to the kitchen.

"I did," I said, picking up a fork and poking the dessert. "I am a bit overwhelmed by the generosity your family has shown me. It's too much, but I don't think I could bring myself to return them."

This made Alayna blush for some reason, but she didn't speak again until after she'd taken a bite. Her shoulders slumped forward, and she let out an exaggerated sigh.

"That good?" I asked, trying a bite myself. If I thought the food gave me an overabundance of pleasure, this made the food seem bland in comparison. I didn't have words for the things I felt as the chocolate played notes in my mouth I'd never experienced before. Alayna had said something, but I was still savoring the bite so deeply that her words were lost on me, and she had to repeat herself.

"I'll take that as a yes, you are enjoying it," she said, her smile shifted, and her face went serious. She set aside her fork and spoke. "Part of the reason why my father did all the things he did for you, Caldor, was I asked him to. I saw the way you handled that drake without even being *Awoken* yet and I knew that you were going to be something special. I felt guilty about it when my father decided to make you a knight and a vassal, because those titles don't come without a great deal of responsibility, but I am glad things have worked out."

The sudden switch to serious discussion took me a moment to adjust, as the pleasure of the dessert still ate away at me. "I'm thankful, responsibility or not, this is the life I was meant to live, and I'll be so much better off because of the help you've provided," I said. I tried not to sound so rigid in my words, I was very grateful but expressing that properly wasn't something I was good at. The best I could do was live up to the gifts I'd been given and show that they weren't given wastefully.

CHAPTER 32
FINDING A MAP

We made pleasant conversation for the rest of our meal, and I tried several times to get her to agree to go on a dungeon run with me when I returned. She agreed to think about it, figuring she might be able to convince her father to let her go if she played the 'we need him as strong as possible' card since I was now one of his knights. We were walking outside the restaurant when something occurred to me.

"How will I know where to find the class quest item?" I asked, pulling up my quest and looking through the list of acceptable items. There were four total, Owlbear heart and Sea Serpent eyes, catching my attention, the other two referenced monsters I'd never heard of so they probably weren't local. Not that finding a sea serpent outside the elven coast would be possible, and that'd be a couple days journey.

"You need a map and then just focus on the quest objective," Alayna said, taking my hand in hers and pulling me off in what I thought was a random direction. It wasn't, we soon arrived at a dusty looking shop with many tomes and scrolls on display.

"What are we doing here?" I asked, but I had my guesses.

"This place sells maps," Alayna said. "You should pick one up and see if you can get a magical one that will interface with the system. They are a bit pricier, but totally worth it. Oh here, I was supposed to give you this, it's your first allotment of funds to help with the maintenance and repair of keep Blackridge."

Alayna pulled out a bag of gold, bigger than the small pouch she pulled it from, she must have a traditional bag of holding. I took the bag and let it slip into my dimensional box. It had one thousand gold!

"Is this normal?" I asked, thinking she might just be showering me with gifts that her father hadn't intended.

"It is for a new vassal," Alayna said, all business. "In fact, I think he is shortchanging you, but since you will have to adventure and grow stronger first I doubt you'll be hurting for gold soon. Each time you clear a full dungeon you can earn several hundred gold easily."

"And I can use this gold for anything?" I asked, looking around the map shop.

"It's yours, but I'd make sure to put some aside for wages and possible supplies you think you might need," Alayna said dutifully.

I stepped up to an elderly gentleman who was slowly hobbling in our direction and offered him an arm to help him walk. He did not look well enough to be walking without a cane.

"I'm fine, I'm fine," he said, in a voice so dusty and throaty that I likened it to a corpse trying to speak in my head. "Welcome to Mab's Maps and Exploring Guides. We have updated maps of the entire Western continent and even a few ancient maps of the Eastern side past the mountains, but those aren't good for much nowadays."

He droned on not even looking at me and turned to walk towards a counter in the back of the shop. I followed him, letting him know what I was interested in. "I am newly *Awoken* and would like to buy a magical map."

"Oh yes we have many such maps, as well as non-magical maps that lay out dungeon locations with notes on level requirements, loot expectations, and monster types, though those cost a pretty penny," the shopkeeper said.

"Any magical maps that have the dungeon info added and any additional information that you think might be helpful?" I asked, figuring I might as well get the best I could afford.

"Yes, let me see here." He pulled out six rolled up maps and set them out before me. "Each of these are updated with different bits of information, this one here..." He lifted a darker tan looking map tied into a purple ribbon. "...while this one here has monster migrations, this one has dungeon loot approximations, and this one here is said to tell you the most recent dungeon mobs." He pointed at one with a red ribbon.

"How much and can I buy multiple ones to get the additional information?" I asked, considering just buying the lot.

"I could part with each map for say..." He scratched at his chin and gave me a once over, paying particular mind to the cloak over my shoulder. "...500 gold each and that's a bargain!" He added, probably seeing the breath leave me at the price.

I couldn't justify paying for even one of those maps for that price. I had more gold than I'd ever come across before but still there were so many things out of my reach to be able to afford.

"That is a very inflated price," Alayna said, stepping up beside me.

"Nonsense! I go by the guidelines that Mab herself put

TIMOTHY MCGOWEN

forth," the shopkeeper said. "Besides, with that Gilfoy's Emporium opening up I've had to increase prices to make up for my lost customers."

"Perhaps we should check out Gilfoy's then," Alayna said, turning to me and taking my hand.

I was about to protest and just see if I could buy a normal map, when the shopkeeper let out a loud huff and spoke up.

"I've got an older outdated map that will work just fine if you want all the information for a quarter of the price," he said, his shoulders slumping in defeat. "Just be aware that you'll need to visit these dungeons to get the updated information. Not many care to do that kind of work for an old shopkeeper anymore."

"What's the price?" I asked, feeling the weight of the incoming price already.

"One hundred and twenty-five gold, and you are breaking me at that price."

We haggled for a bit, and I got him to sell it to me for one hundred gold, my Magical ring, and a promise to return and let him siphon some of the new information I collect after I visit a few dungeons. I hated to part from an item that increased my attributes, but I'd sold him on the idea of the ring after flat out denying him when he asked for a price on my cloak.

"It was a good deal," Alayna assured me as we left the shop.

The sun hit the highest point of the sky, meaning it was midday and I should go look for Fred and Fran before they decided to leave without me.

"Thank you," I said, pulling Alayna into a close embrace. "I really mean it. You-" I never got a chance to finish the sentence as she went up on her tippy toes and pulled me into a deep passionate kiss.

Everything had changed since I'd *Awoken*, and I was just

getting used to and feeling all the changes. One such change was the way I felt things. Her lips brushed against mine in such a stimulating way that I felt chills pushing down my spine. I had thought eating had improved, but this was no comparison. I pulled her closer, our bodies touching as I lost myself in the moment.

Too soon she broke away and we shared a dizzying and slightly awkward goodbye. I think she instructed me to be safe and I must have told her I would, but I was so caught up in the moment that I was halfway down the road toward Fred and Fran before my mind rebooted.

"I should have asked her to come with us," I mused, practically skipping down the road, and turning swiftly just to feel my body move. The Strength attribute was fantastic and one of my highest values currently. It allowed me strength but also a measure of agility or smooth muscle control.

This had been the best of days.

CHAPTER 33
FRED AND FRAN

I found Fred and Fran with the rest of the newly *Awoken* adventurers in a town square where many people still drank and partied. The adventurers were meant to leave soon, as the time limit imposed was for all class quests and waiting too long could be disastrous.

"Thought you might have changed your mind," Fran said, her tight bun had come apart a bit and stray curls bounced in front of her vibrant green eyes. Fred turned as she spoke, just noticing me. He had a drink in his hands and took a long pull on it before greeting me.

"Hey it's you!" He said, getting a bit louder than I thought was necessary.

"He can't hold his drink, but he'll work it off before too long," Fran said, pulling free a map and opening it to show me. "I have to collect a Dire Bear heart here..." She pointed to a spot to the west. "And Fred needs to collect a Fae heart here and if we have time, a fiery elemental core here. We didn't have any of the reagents needed for abilities, so any detours we can afford to do will help. Where are you headed?"

I pulled up my quest and pulled out my map. To my surprise when I opened the map, I got a message.

Do you wish to incorporate Mantan's Magical Map? Yes or No.

I sent the yes needed and the map dissolved in my hands. Before I had a chance to express my utter horror, Fred burped and said, "Hey you got a magical map? That's neat."

Focusing on the word 'map' my menu showed a new tab labeled map. It had several marks on it, but there was one in particular that I recognized. Not far from where Fran wanted to take down a Dire Bear, there was a tiny Owlbear symbol on the map.

"My class item is here," I said, pointing just a tiny bit more west than the dire bear's location. Our travels would take us outside of House Variyn lands, but as adventurers we were allowed to travel abroad, or so I had been taught.

"Even if each item takes a day to find, that leaves us three extra days," Fran said, her hand on her sword.

"You both have mounts?" I asked, the furthest distance was at least a day's ride from here.

"Nah we are going to run it," Fran said.

At first I thought she was joking, but she never smiled. When my confused look didn't change and she didn't elaborate I decided to ask.

"You are going to run?" I asked. "Will we make fast enough time?"

"Both Fred and I increased our endurance to twenty, so while we haven't passed the threshold, we will be able to run the speed of a normal horse in open ground," Fran said.

I wasn't sure how that could be, but she seemed confident in her explanation, so I let it go. My endurance was even higher so if they could do it so would I. It did mean I'd need to go pay for a week of stabling for Jill, or I could just bring her back to the keep. It wasn't like I'd been given her permanently or anything.

Deciding that would be best I told Fred and Fran I'd be right back and poked my head into an inn, catching the attention of a young boy. Paying him a silver I told him to fetch my horse and bring it to the House Variyn keep. He gladly accepted the coin and rushed off with my instructions. I trusted in the coin to keep him honest.

Returning to Fred and Fran I was disappointed to see a familiar face talking to them. It was Zander, Alayna's cousin. I got there just in time to hear Fred's answer.

"Oh yeah we should be able to find our stuff in time, and Caldor here just needs to grab an Owlbear's heart, so it won't be too hard for us to work together, why do you ask?" Fred said, slurping down another large gulp.

"I just know how difficult it can be to work with someone like Caldor," Zander said, a wicked smile appeared on his lips as Fred answered him and I felt a pit grow in my stomach.

"Hey Zander," I said, catching his attention. He didn't seem at all surprised to see me. "You get yourself knocked out in front of any monsters lately?" I didn't have too much ammunition against him, but what I did have worked just fine. His pale face went slightly red, and his lips became a line.

"You know every once and a while someone doesn't complete their class quest and you know what happens?" Zander asked, two goons appeared at his side, probably paid help.

"Why don't you enlighten me," I said, catching a look from Fran.

"They have their *Spark* ripped from their body. It feeds the

Mana Shrine and I hear it is incredibly painful," Zander said. "Be sure to let me know how it feels in a week?"

And with that he turned, taking two muscle bound goons with him. He was up to no good and I didn't need an increased Intellect attribute to tell me that. What were the chances he could stop me from completing my class quest. Even if he somehow managed to find and kill the Owlbears before me, there were other options that, while further away, were still doable in the time I was likely to have left.

Let him try, I thought, sending mental curses in his direction as he blended in with the crowd.

"Friend of yours," Fran said, her grip had tightened on her sword during the conversation, and I couldn't blame her.

"That was none other than Lord Variyn's brother's kid," I said, shaking my head. "I think he's mostly harmless, but he's got it out for me."

"You're mixed up with nobles?" Fran said, raising an eyebrow.

"You could say that," I said. We set out to leave and I filled them both in with a loose set of details regarding my appointment for House Variyn and implied that I saved Zander but embarrassed him as well. We'd made it a short distance outside the gate when Fran pulled us to a stop.

"Fred drink this," she said. "It'll clear your head so we can start running. You might want to strap that down." Fran pointed to the loose sack I kept my dimensional box in. I did one better, pulling my sword belt off and storing it inside the box, then tying the box with some twine tightly to my back. It was a bit awkward, but it wouldn't impede my movements as I ran. Eventually I'd want a belt or something fashioned to hold the box.

"I'm feeling quite well now sister, thank you," Fred said.

Instead of putting their weapons away, Fran pulled her sword free and Fred pulled out a swirling red and orange orb that sat nicely in his hand.

"What's that?" I asked, the swirls seemed to draw me in as I watched.

"It's a spell orb," Fred said. "It was my mother's before she retired. Currently it is keyed to a spell called 'Firebolt', she had to pick a spell that I could use with my reduced attributes. However, I think she was still able to use the level 2 version of it."

"And this," Fran said, swiping her sword out in front of her in a controlled and elegant swing. "Was my father's blade before he retired. It has a very rare durability enchantment that makes it nearly indestructible. He used it his entire career as an adventurer, just switching out the gem slots to increase its power." She indicated a line of cloudy white gems that were fixed into the backside of the sword's grip.

"So it must be pretty powerful?" I asked, admiring the curve of the blade but preferring double edged swords myself.

"Well," she said, her words faltering and Fred finishing for her.

"Those gems don't do anything but maintain the durability enchantment," Fred said. "Our father had to remove the powerful gems slotted in because it raised the blade's level requirement making it impossible to use.

"The level requirement really stops you from using it?" I asked, not knowing enough about magical gear or level requirements.

"Oh yeah," Fran said, finally finding her words. "It practically jumps out of your hand and will cut you for your trouble." She showed me her arm, she had a straight scar running the length of it. "From when I tried to use his sword when I thought I'd learned enough. I barely swung the weapon, and this happened."

"That's insane," I said, glad I'd been gifted with items that wouldn't kill me. "What if you get a sword from a dungeon or something, can you safely carry it around until you're strong enough to use it?"

"As long as you don't actively try and use it, then you are safe," Fred said, any slur from drinking had cleared away completely now.

"Before we go, do you guys mind if I test my abilities?" I asked. "I've got spells and skills I know how to use but haven't ever actually tried."

"You learned spells and skills already?" Fran said, her eyes going wide. "What class did you say you were again?"

"Arcane Knight," I said proudly. "It is a mix between evoker style casting and blade fighting. Did you guys tell me yours yet?"

"I'm a Blade Master," Fran said proudly, then added a little less enthusiastically. "Or at least that is the name of the class I'm going for."

"I chose Flame Born, a sorcerer specialization that my mother followed," Fred said, his manner of speaking was very academic, sounding as if he was just numbering off one or more facts from a book.

I recognized one of the classes, since I was walking basically the same path, just not fully as she would be.

"You any good with that sword?" I asked Fran as I searched the side of the road for a place to shoot off my spells, the path west we had taken had very few travelers.

"I've practiced since I was old enough to hold one and my father has been a great teacher. He always says that as a Blade

Master, he was one too, your technique with the sword is more important than any system skill or ability," Fran said.

"Have you read Holond DeMark's studies of blade forms?" I asked. It was my favorite of all the books on sword techniques and forms.

"She doesn't read," Fred said, then added. "By choice, not by inability to do so."

Fran glared in his direction. "You do enough reading for the both of us. I rely on good ole fashion blood and sweat. Everything I've learned has been from my father and believe me he is the best teacher you could ask for. He fought side by side with my mother in the Battle of Lynsteen Pass, staying alive when all those around them fell. They'd have some friends over, the ones that survived, and they'd tell grand stories of how the undead and Chaos monsters alike fell in a tornado of flame and steel."

Fran was obviously proud of what her parents had accomplished, but it was hard not feeling a gut punch from her words. Try as I might, I could tell she noticed and I turned away quickly to cast Firebolt into a patch of rocks and dirt.

It felt like heat bubbled through me and then just as fast as it came the heat was expelled in a narrow bolt of fire. It smashed into the rocks, throwing them aside, but the burst of fire was relatively weak, dissipating on contact.

I heard Fran say my name, trying to get my attention, but I didn't want her to see my face yet, as I struggled to keep water from gathering at the edges of my eyes. Instead, I cast Light, which was more like a gentle flickering feeling that ended with a small globe of light appearing. What the spell description hadn't said was that I was able to easily move the light with a casual thought. I moved it as fast as I could manage around me,

343

until it was a steady beam of light. I reached out, curious to see what would happen if I touched it while it moved so fast.

The light shattered upon contact, it felt like I'd put my hand into a gentle warm ray of sun. Finally, having recovered myself enough, I had one more spell to try.

"I have a spell that will make you physically resistant to damage for three hours," I said. "It would probably make sense to use it on all of us."

I searched my head for the knowledge to cast it and started the process. This was the longest cast of all. Where Firebolt had taken no more than a second and the Light spell even less, it took a good four seconds to cast 'Physical Resistance'. But when it finally went off, I felt a weight settle over me like a thin net covering my entire body.

"I'm sorry, Caldor," Fran said, forcing me to look at her. "You lost someone at the Battle of Lysteen pass, didn't you?"

I gave her a curt nod, pushing my head aside as I felt making eye contact would just bring up emotions I'd rather not go into at the start of my adventure.

"Who was it?" Fred asked, he seemed genuinely curious, and Fran slugged him in the arm for asking.

"It's okay," I said. "It's just been an emotional day for me, I can talk about it. My father was Elkor Miles, also an Arcane Knight. He died fighting the lich, but not before he killed it." My words came out proud, and I was, but a part of me wanted to say more. Say that he'd left his family, choosing to fight against evil instead. Even now, walking the path he'd walked, I couldn't help but feel a bit of resentment for him. My emotions toward my father were anything but cut and dry, but I supposed even those with living parents experienced that.

"Elkor Miles?" Fred said, sounding less academic and more surprised than I'd ever heard him. "My parents talked about him all the time! They said that even from where they fought, they could see him battling against wave after wave of Chaos monsters."

"My mother said he summoned up a fireball that not even she'd have the power to create. He obliterated that lich and as soon as he did, the waves of monsters either fell dead or fled. Your father is the reason ours made it out alive," Fran said, a look of respect and astonishment on her face.

"Father said they'd all but given up on the idea of escaping, they'd been cut off from the rest of the adventurers fighting as the lines surged and the others fled backwards. They fought back-to-back pushing themselves farther than they thought possible," Fred spoke in a reverent hushed tone. Then he and Fran did something I found a bit embarrassing.

They took a knee before me and Fran spoke, "We vow to fight beside you and answer the call to battle, should you sound it. For the lives of our parents our bond was sealed by the blood of yours."

I was about to ask them to please stand when a system message spoke into my mind.

Fred and Fran Esel have offered you their oath of companionship for the service your father rendered to their parents. They will come to fight at your side when you call. Your mission will be their mission should you just ask.

You have gained 2 new Companions.

Reputation with Fred and Fran Esel increased from 'Friendly' to 'Honored'.

General Reputation has increased. Your deeds have been heard of by a select few. The more you do the more well-known you will become.

Beside the notifications that spoke into my mind I felt a connection with the two of them begin to grow. Not knowing what would be considered a proper response, I thanked them and bid them to please stand. After a few awkward seconds, I buffed them both and we prepared to leave.

"I need to do one final thing before we go," I said, remembering my Preferred Weapon skill. I felt it take effect and it was like I knew my weapon that much more. Its balance and weight, the potential damage output, all of it was plain for me to see. Unfortunately, I also just consumed half of my Stamina, which felt like someone had suddenly pulled the wind from my chest. I recovered enough to tell them I was ready, and we were off.

I hadn't been much of a runner before, but I was now. Even with my Stamina recovering, I outpaced both of them and had to rein it in a bit so they could keep pace. This wasn't like normal running either, our strides bounded us six or more feet as we cut down the open road. After nearly an hour of straight running, we took a break to rest for a few minutes, which was good because my stamina was getting pretty low having started at nearly half gone.

There hadn't been any opportunity to talk during our run, any words we tried to exchange were lost to the wind. So I took the chance to speak with them, long enough time had gone by that all our emotions had a chance to settle.

"What you both did back there," I said, meeting each of their eyes so they knew I was serious. "You don't have to honor that oath; I release you of it fully. We just met and I can't ask you to put yourself in who knows how much danger to come to my aid if I need you, because if you don't break your oath and I need your help I will call on you."

They nodded along as I spoke and to my surprise it was Fred who spoke first. "I will not break my oath and I meant the words that my sister spoke for both of us. We may not know you, but we know what your father did not only for our parents, but for countless adventurers that day. I will hold true to my oath."

"So will I, so shut up about it," Fran said, laughing as she reached out and punched me in the arm. Though playful it was surprisingly strong, showing me that she could indeed use that sword to its fullest effect.

"Okay fine," I said, throwing my hands up in mock defeat. "I give up, I'll be your friend." That got a chuckle from both of them, and we spent the next ten minutes joking back and forth as our stamina refilled.

CHAPTER 34
MAGICAL MAPS

W e ran for several more hours, the sun beginning to fall down behind the horizon, taking breaks as needed. As we cut off of the main road and toward our first target, the Fae monsters, I decided to take a look at my stats and see where it all stood now.

Name: Caldor Miles | Classification: Arcane Knight(Locked) | Species: Human

    Level: 5, 5400 Essence to Lvl. 6 | Essence: 93,001 | Reputation: Rank 2, 6%

    Health: 580/580 | Mana: 470/470 | Stamina: 295/460

    Health Regeneration: 43 Per Minute | Mana Regeneration: 41 Per Minute | Stamina Regeneration: 31 Per Minute

    Constitution: 43 | Intellect: 37 | Endurance: 31

    Core: 21 | Concentration: 28 | Strength: 44

. . .

That was neat, I thought to myself between strides. My sheet had streamlined a bit after I thought how nice it would be to have the regeneration on the main page instead of the page with weapon damage, defense, and other readouts. The books I'd read hadn't mentioned much about the flexibility of the system and how it seemed like it was adjusting small bits of things for a single adventurer.

It was probably foolhardy, but I really wanted to get my 'Core' attribute past the first threshold of 25 to match the rest of mine, so next time we stopped, I paid the required essence, 11,877 to push it to 25. I figured that buying attributes would only get more expensive as I leveled so I might as well. To my surprise it took my essence leaving me only 81,124, but the attributes didn't go up.

"I think I broke something," I said, only half joking to Fran. Despite Fred being the more academically inclined, I found myself relating more with Fran and her carefree way of carrying herself.

Fran gave me a look that said, 'what do you expect me to do about it' and Fred spoke up.

"You broke a limp?" Fred said, looking down at my feet and seeing that I was standing just fine. "With our new health regeneration, it will take several hours for a fracture to heal, less if it's a clean break. This will most definitely set us back."

"I didn't mean," I started to say and then just laughed deciding I needed to be very literal with Fred. "I added essence into my Core attribute, and it didn't go up."

"Oh even I know the answer to that riddle," Fran said, poking me oddly with her finger. "You can only solidify essence while in contact with a Shrine."

"How did I not know that?" I asked, more to myself than anyone else. My studies had been based around monsters and magic, but in all that I read I guess I never paid much mind to the parts that talked about after being *Awoken*, as it always seemed so far away.

"Does your magical map show any Shrines nearby?" Fred asked, finally understanding what I meant.

I decided to check, not really having the chance to explore my map and its features up to this point. Focusing on 'map' I brought it up. There were a multitude of marks on the map, and I found that if I focused on which ones I wanted to see, the icons would be filtered away. So thinking about Mana Shrines, I saw an overlay of little shrines with a few larger ones mixed in.

"If we head East for ten minutes we will hit a Mana Shrine," I said, pointing in the direction the map indicated.

Once they'd fully recovered their Stamina, mine still sat around half, we were off again. I explored the map as we ran. The map had a darker haze to it for places I'd not traveled yet, but I could still see the locations well enough. All of the places I'd been, like my entire life, were slightly lighter or darker depending on how long ago I visited the area. It gave me a measure of sadness to see my father and my favorite lake spot had turned a light gray.

I saw where my town was, Creeshaw, far to the south from our current location. Then I traced my path I'd taken during my boar hunt, twisting and turning all the while headed toward Royal hunting grounds. It was on the edge between Blackwood and Shadowcrest forests. There was a small icon with a rock and door symbol that I deciphered as meaning it was a dungeon over the area where I'd killed the boar.

Focusing on the icon I was given additional information.

Wildheart Dungeon

Type: Nature
Floors: 5
Monster Levels: 13-19
Notes: The dungeon used a variety of woodland creatures for the first three floors but starting on floor 4 there began to be elemental spirits and golems. Final boss, an Amalgamation of several woodland creatures, fairly difficult considering the ease at which I cleared the rest of the dungeon. -Michael Moth

I wondered if the information updated without me having to go past the initial dungeon rest area that I'd been able to enter or if this was all manually entered like the 'Notes' section from someone named Michael Moth. The more I thought about it, I bet it was a combination of both, where the type, floors, and levels would be filled in as I defeated them and dove deeper into the dungeon and the notes were obviously manually entered.

Focusing on the notes section I saw a small window open, and I knew instinctively that I could pour my thoughts into it, the message being transcribed. I added the following note.

As a Sparked and not Awakened yet I was able to enter into the rest area, but not gain access to any of the floors. -Caldor Miles

I wasn't sure if being able to enter before becoming a full-fledged adventurer was normal or if my information would be considered useful, but I left it regardless. Zooming out I looked at the full extent in which the map covered. It was obviously out of date on the size and layout of the Houses, because there was still a 'House Gilfoy'. I tried to remember how long ago Alayna had said they'd lost their House status, but I'd only been half paying attention to the impromptu history lesson.

The Southlands were oddly shaped as well. I wasn't a

student of topography, I'd seen a map of the kingdom here and there, but each one I'd seen showed the Southlands to start at the Paugmook, a large river that was a mile or more across in places. Its name was orcish in nature, but it had changed and evolved over the years, settling on a word that meant nothing in both languages, Paugmook.

I noticed that even the name of the mighty Paugmook wasn't the same on this map. It was labeled as Spaugcrook and the 'Southlands' were given a name too, Sathergorgan. I knew that 'Southlands' was more of a Human name we'd given it, but I wondered why or who had updated this map with the names used by the Orcs, goblins, and other races that lived down south. With a thought, I added the new name of the river, but left the old name as an abbreviation. No point in losing out on old names.

Looking closer I saw that entire cities were labeled in the Sathergorgan, or Southlands. Some even went so far as to say which race and tribe occupied the areas. As I looked at each one, the names were difficult for me to pronounce or understand as they'd sound not much more than nonsense in my language, I saw one that even listed major trade items. Apparently, the city Gfhordylft had access to a mythril mine.

Not that I expected to ever need to go into the Southlands, it was useful information that might be worth something to the right person. The elven lands were the darkest of grays and very few pockets of civilization had been filled in, the same was true for the northern Beastkin lands. It didn't even have a name for their territory, just labeled 'Beastkin Territory'. It wasn't even gray, instead everything north of the mountain range was black. Must be completely unexplored.

That wasn't as surprising, as even I had heard of the suspicious nature of Beastkin toward outsiders. The few beastkin I'd come across seemed friendly enough though, but I could count on one hand how many I'd met. Moving the map over a bit I tried to see the Eastlands, a place of unending mystery and campfire stories.

It was all black, unexplored. The dwarves of Lynsteen were the only ones who had regularly interacted with the savage Easterners and so little was known about them to common folk such as myself. No adventurer that I'd asked had ever even been able to tell me what races lived on the eastern side of the continent. I'd read a very old book of Warrick's once that spoke of magic veins beneath the surface called Ley Lines, and how the writer of this particular book had been a part of an expedition into the Eastlands to create towers that would siphon off some of the latent power that lived beneath the surface.

He'd briefly mentioned 'wild people' who were without Order and lived lives of Chaos. But the book had been about Ley Lines specifically and that was the only mention, other than they were driven out shortly after arriving. And when I'd asked Warrick about the Eastern lands he told me that he knew little of them, and what he knew wasn't worth sharing.

I did remember that the particular book on Ley Lines was ancient, probably a thousand years old if I was remembering the date right. Perhaps what everyone said was true. That it was a land of Chaos where dragons, drakes, and wurms roamed free. I remembered a story Emory had told me one of the few days where we'd gone out with Ismene to go 'hunting' when in fact we'd just messed around out in the woods, drinking and having a good time.

Emory said that an old man had come through town and told him a story about Knights clad in armor as black as night, that roamed the Easternlands recruiting disobedient young men into their army of darkness, to be soldiers of Chaos. There had been more to the story, but that was the gist of it. We laughed and joked about the old man trying to scare us straight at the time, but it did make me wonder.

At the very edge of the map, I saw what looked like a land mass, just off the black filled coast of the East side of the continent. I moved the map over and found an island just a quarter the size of House Variyn lands. And on it was a city just labeled, Camelot and around it, forming a sort of triangle, were three dungeons. There was little info, not even a name for them, but the Dungeon Levels section was filled out for all three. They read, 64-71, 82-89, 110-120, starting with the western one and going to the north and eastern respectively.

Even the 64-71 leveled dungeon made my eyes go wide. I did a quick search on my map and found that the highest-level dungeon listed was 59-62. That was the kind of dungeon run my father and his group would be hard pressed to get through, much less any other dungeon groups. It had to do with how essence gains changed the higher your level went, this I knew from my studies.

If I remember right somewhere in the level fifty range, essence required to increase to the next level became much harder to achieve. I realized as I pondered over these things that I had never known my father or Warrick's exact levels. I'd asked them both at times, but it had been when I was younger and both came up with ways to distract me without answering.

Just the fact that it took so much essence to make it past the mid-level 50s, solidified in my mind the importance of buying the extra attributes. The idea of someone, let alone a group of people, getting to levels ranging from 110-120 was mind boggling to me.

One day I would be strong enough to dive those dungeons, I promised myself, staring at the location intently.

I had been running on mostly auto pilot for the last ten minutes and I saw Fred and Fran stopping, so I slowed down as well. Ahead of us was a stone pillar, maybe half the size of the one I'd touched earlier in the day to *Awaken*. It had the same glowing runes, but they glowed far less brightly.

Reaching out I pressed my hand against it and received a message in my mind.

You have uncommitted essence placements. Would you like to commit them? Yes or No.

Sending the 'yes' I felt something begin to stir inside of me. It was slow at first, but then it became more intense. I was on my knees struggling to breathe the next moment. I felt a cracking and then suddenly I knew my core was condensing itself, what exactly that meant I didn't understand, but the knowledge came just before a small pulse of energy shot out from within me traveling in all directions.

"You passed your core threshold," Fred said. "My parents said we should wait to do that until we'd reached at least level 30."

I stood, panting hard from the intense experience. Fran had rushed forward to help me stand, but I was already feeling back to normal, and better yet, didn't stink or have grime on me.

"Why is that?" I asked, stretching out my muscles. I felt more solid, but it was hard to say why. My strength attribute hadn't been affected, or my constitution, or endurance, the three attributes that dealt with my body.

"Don't mind him," Fran said. "He takes everything our parents say as rules to be followed. Basically, they told us to focus on attributes that would make us stronger and save our Core attribute for when we'd grown as adventurers. As to the why? I honestly don't know."

I checked my essence limit now; it was 250,000 and I

thought I could guess why they'd given that advice. I bet that their parents were around the 40-50 level mark and had barely enough room to hold the essence required to level further. And from what Fran and Fred said, they are retiring now, so it would be wasteful for them to have spent more on an attribute that only benefits those wanting to push the limits of leveling.

I would reach the highest levels and be stronger than those I find there due to my strategy of purchasing more attributes per level.

CHAPTER 35
THAT WAS UNEXPECTED

I t was getting late and harder to see as we weaved through trees and brush. Just when I was getting ready to signal them that we should slow down our pace or stop all together for the night, something big rushed out of a line of thick brush and slammed into me. As I flew through the air, smashing hard into a tree, I felt a more subtle bit of words come into my head. It was so much lighter than any of the other system notifications that I could have missed it if I hadn't been seeing stars and trying to work out what hit me.

You've taken 44 Blunt Damage (Critical Strike)!

Shaking my head my vision cleared enough to see what had hit me like a runaway wagon. My eyes had cleared but I still wasn't familiar with whatever was attacking. It looked like a bear mixed with overly large claws and a narrowed face, but the coloring was all wrong. It had beady red eyes and faced off against Fred and Fran, claws swiping wildly.

I used Inspect and got a bit of information.

Giant Badger, Level 4

It wasn't much but at least I knew what to call it. Unfortunately, I'd let the buffs fall off and hadn't reapplied them, but now wasn't the time. Fran was like a wraith with her movements and sword strikes. Weaving in and out, slashing and stabbing.

Meanwhile, Fred stood a ways off with his fiery orb held high. A Firebolt, larger than mine had been, flew out of his free hand, striking the Giant Badger full in the face. It staggered backwards and Fran got a bloody strike against its exposed belly. I needed to get in there before I missed the entire fight!

As I ran, I cast Firebolt, putting it on cooldown. My bolt hit it on the shoulder, glancing off and leaving a small scorch mark. I came in giving Fran a wide berth as she swung her sword in artful and deadly strikes. The badger was laser focused on Fran and I was able to successfully flank it. Using my Power Strike skill, I raised my blade and felt my muscles take an extra portion of my Stamina to increase the attack's damage. With massive force my blade came down and I cut one of the badger's legs clean off.

Blood sprayed out as it's leg fell free and the giant badger made a noise that could only be described as a scream. It took on a red aura suddenly and moved faster than it had before, striking down with its good leg at Fran. It didn't look like she'd get her guard up in time, so I dove forward letting loose another Firebolt as it came off cooldown and getting to Fran just as the claw came down.

We tumbled together, luckily not cutting each other as we fell out of the path of its strike. Looking up while we hurriedly tried to stand, we saw the giant badger gunning for us. Just as it would have reached us, teeth baring, a Firebolt from Fred caught it full on in the face. Fran and I both acted, instantly stabbing forward together into the stunned badger and ending the fight.

It fell backwards, throwing up dust as it landed.

"Everyone alright?" I asked, looking over Fran and seeing that the only blood on her appeared to have come from when I tackled her, seeing as I had been half covered by the spouts of blood. "Oops, I got you a bit messy there."

Fran started to laugh and to my surprise Fred joined in, soon all three of us were laughing with some mix of hysteria and relief.

"We did it!" Fran said getting control of herself. "We killed our first monster. Our parents would be so excited for us!" She had the biggest smile on her face, and I couldn't help but feel excited for them.

This had been my sixth or seventh monster killed, but my first as an official adventurer and definitely harder to kill than a rat.

"How much essence did you get for that?" Fred asked Fran, his gaze looking far, most likely looking at his menus.

"I got 84 Essence, how 'bout you?" Fran asked back.

"Only 81, I told you having a few percent extra in your Core affinity mattered," Fred said, frowning.

Fran turned to me and smiled. "My Core affinity was two percent above his and he hasn't been able to stop complaining about it."

"That two percent will increase the gap in our progression as we get to higher levels," Fred said, back to his usual academic way of speaking. He turned to me and asked, "Will you share the essence amount you received?"

I checked my total and saw that it had definitely gone up at 81,354, but it took a bit of searching to find where it would tell me the exact amount. As it turned out, there was a specific tab on my menu that showed me all the mental whisperings I'd been getting. I saw how much exact quantified damage I'd done to the Giant Badger and how much essence I'd received from its death.

Doing a double take I almost didn't tell them the truth as it was vastly different from their portion, but I knew I could trust them, despite having only just met them it felt like we were fast friends.

"Don't be mad," I said prefacing my answer. "It says I received 230 Essence."

"What?" Both of them asked at the same time, neither hiding their shock.

Fran broke from the shock first and fixed me with a critical stare. "Can I make a suggestion?"

"Sure, go ahead," I said, wiping some blood off my armor as it slowly worked to expel the filth through magic.

"Lie next time," Fran said, her eyes hard. "I know, even without being as book smart as my nerd brother, that getting that much essence means you are a Paragon. It makes sense now why Lord Variyn wanted you under his direct authority. I bet he knew or at least guessed that you had a paragon attribute."

"Paragons are beings of legend and folklore," Fred said. He spoke with barely contained excitement. "I bet your father was a paragon too! That would explain how he was so powerful."

"You really think people are going to care?" I asked, neither confirming nor denying their accusations of my paragon status.

"They will," Fran said. "If they find out. Which they won't hear from us, right Fred." Fran elbowed her lanky brother in the ribs, he flinched back before agreeing he wouldn't.

"Well, I appreciate you keeping my secret and I guess I'll be careful to not reveal details in the future," I said, then added. "I had no idea I was going to get so much more essence than everyone else." After a bit of a pause while the rest of the muck and blood cleaned itself off of me, I cleared my throat. "So should we see if the monster core is intact?"

It took some looking, but we found it attached to the badger's spine, and it was cracked, meaning the essence was lost. We decided to let me keep the cracked core, and Fran would get the next one, then Fred. But all bets were off if we found an intact one, we decided on basing it off the merit that we showed during the actual battle.

Even cracked Cores, which were rare to find on monsters lower than level 5, were valuable. The dust was used in almost all *Awoken* professions, but most importantly it was used in the creation of new enchantments. I figured I'd be able to sell it for a pretty good amount when we made it back into town.

"I'm planning on taking the Alchemist profession when I hit level 10," Fran said, staring down at the bloody mess that was the badger. I'd gone elbow deep to find the core and other reagents, we'd decided that since my armor had the self-cleaning enchantment it only made sense.

"Okay," I said, pushing more blood off my newly wet hands. I felt like she was going to tell me something that involved diving back into the huge nasty corpse.

"And I won't know for sure until I've taken the profession, but I think there are a few parts that would be useful," Fran said, giving me her best 'dive back in' smile. "I'll split any earnings from things I make or let you have half of the raw materials if you grab them?"

"Tell me what to get," I said, letting out an overly exaggerated sigh and kneeling back into the puddle of guts.

It took another half an hour before we'd collected all the parts that she felt were possibly valuable, which included things like the claws, eyes, a few organs, and some of the more delicate bones. I'd agreed to hold the items in my dimensional box as

Fran and Fred didn't have anything that would preserve the items. The sun had all but set by that point and we decided it was time to make camp, but there was no way we were going to do it within a few miles of the corpse. It was bound to draw in more predators.

Jogging lightly and at a medium speed, we headed out towards a crop of mountains, whose name eluded me, and I had grown too tired to check. It was because of this tired state, that all three of us obviously felt, that we didn't see the traps ahead.

CHAPTER 36
EXPLOSION IN THE NIGHT

I t was a tripwire and I felt it brush against my leg, nearly tripping me, before the world around me became a flash of red and orange. I heard screams and shouts of pain, just as the ground around me gave out and I was plunged into darkness.

Getting knocked unconscious was beginning to be 'my thing' I thought as my head vibrated with pain. We'd run into something that sent me flying and while I was sure that I'd taken a lot of damage, I felt fine now, even my headache cleared moments after I woke up. Checking my menus, I saw that my Health was 510 out of 580 and slowly ticking upward at a rate of one point every second and a half. At this rate I'd be at full health in just under two minutes.

A muffled groan caught my attention from mere feet away, but it was pitch black around me so I couldn't make anything out. I cast my Light spell, which took a few tries as my hands kept bumping into something and throwing off the cast. Finally, I managed to do it and the light revealed a mess of roots, dirt and rocks. I was buried up to my stomach in dirt, but it was loose enough that I felt I'd be able to pull myself free without too much issue.

Just to my left lay Fran, her eyes shut tight from pain and her entire body laid out on several large rocks, and her legs covered in dirt. We were in a pocket of space under a tree, was my best guess by the absolute tangle of roots all around.

"Are you alright?" I asked Fran, but she just continued to groan in pain, not hearing me.

With a bit of work, I slowly made my way over to her and carefully pushed the dirt off her legs. She screamed as I accidentally touched one and I saw her shoot up suddenly fully awake and scream again, as doing so moved her legs.

"What in the absolute hell," Fran said, panting hard, sweat pouring down her face.

"Your legs look pretty badly broken," I said. I'd uncovered enough of them to see that her left leg was pushed off in an awkward angle and her right ankle was twisted unnaturally.

"You have to," Fran began to say but she stopped the pain becoming too much for her. After several minutes she tried again. "Put them straight otherwise they won't heal right."

I used my Inspect skill on her, wanting to see if I could tell how bad things were and got a little information.

Fran Esel, Level 2, 29/150 Health, 100/100 Mana, 40/200 Stamina

I reached into my Dimensional box and pulled free all three of my health potions. "I want you to take one first and then I will set your legs, then take another one. Otherwise, I'm not sure you will survive me moving your legs back into place."

Fran just nodded her head and drank the potion. Inspecting her again I saw her health was slowly rising until it stopped at 82/150, so wasting no more time I went to work. After each movement I checked her health and had to give her a second one to keep her above 50 health, but eventually I set her legs enough that they'd heal correctly. She took the final potion, because moving her legs had caused a bleed effect that was slowly killing her, and the potion stopped it.

But that left me without any more potions and no idea how injured Fred might be or where he'd gone off to.

"It was goblins," Fran coughed, the dusty air getting to her. "I saw some just before the explosion. The hell are they doing this far from the Southlands?"

"How long do you think it'll take for your bones to heal?" I asked, wishing I knew more about the healing process.

"Thanks to those potions I think I've got a few hours before I can walk on them, but that bleed effect is still active, just slowed down. My status says I'll suffer 10 points of damage a minute for six hours or until fully healed. Luckily my natural regeneration is at 15, so I'll survive, just be very slow to heal until it's done. You have to find Fred and help him. There is a plant that will increase healing if you can find it," Fran said, her voice weak. I could see she was healing very slowly, but it might not be fast enough if anything else happened. She explained to me what the plant looked like, and I promised to return to her with some if I could and that I'd find her brother, but first I had to shore up our little hole.

Focusing on the area atop Fran, I moved dirt and twisted roots around with relative ease until I was sure it wouldn't come crashing down on her, then I worked my way up and out. It took longer than I expected and for a moment I was nearly covered on all sides from the dirt but using the roots I pulled myself up and out of the ground. Behind me I felt a hole just big enough for me to slip in or out of. I knew my light spell wouldn't last long after I'd left, and I told Fran as much, so she would have to deal with being alone and in the dark for however long it took me to find Fred.

The tree whose roots we'd found ourselves under was a massive oak, that had a chunk blown out of it and was tilted in a slight angle, but still standing. I made some marks with my sword to be sure I found the right place again and worked around under the light of the moon to look for signs of Fred. There weren't any, but I did find the signs of a large group walking through the area. Broken brush and a multitude of tracks.

Crouched down as I was with my nose to the dirt, I was sure of a few things. First, these small footprints would be the goblins, they were smaller statured creatures, but tended to travel in large groups to make up for it. Secondly, in the middle of all these tracks and leading off into the darkness was a distinct marking that could easily be dragging marks. I think the goblins took Fred with them and I was going to have to get him back.

Following the tracks in the near blackness of the half-moon meant I had to backtrack several times, and it was during one of the many times I'd lost their trail that I heard a rumbling ahead. Moving as slowly as I could I peeked over the bushes to see what was sleeping in a large divot on the side of a mountain cliff.

Whatever it was, it was at least four feet long and just as tall. It looked like an armored beetle with a mouth far too big and dozens of short legs. At first, I had assumed it was sleeping, making a sort of gurgling noise, but now I saw that it was spitting out some kind of liquid onto the rock and slowly munching away at it. I used my Inspect skill and my jaw dropped open.

Baby Rock Eater, Level 19, 940/940

As slow as I could, I began to take steps backwards to get away from the 'Baby' before its mother showed up. This Baby Rock Eater would be enough to kill our entire party several times over. Despite having less than twice my health, it had armor that would make damaging it extremely difficult and a mouth that could nearly swallow me whole. After I'd gotten out of earshot of it, I studied the tracks, finding where I'd lost my way.

The coolness in the air spoke of the growing late hour and I began to worry that perhaps I wouldn't be able to find the goblins. It was a moment later when I heard the far-off sound of drums beating. Following the sound, I began to see large bonfires through the trees and heard the occasional scream of pain. It was hard to tell who was screaming, but I had a good guess.

Still a distance from the camp I heard something moving through the brush, and I slipped behind a tree just in time to see two goblins, a patrol I guessed, walking in my direction. It didn't appear they'd seen me, but I'd gotten a good look at them.

The goblins were short, maybe half my height on average, and had a larger head than would be normal for a human. Tipped ears like an elf, but wider at the bottom and most looked nicked or had bites taken out of them. These two carried rusted daggers, but despite the worn look of their equipment, the blades' edges gleamed sharply in the moonlight. Neither had anything I would consider armor, wearing tattered mismatched clothing and leather chest plates that didn't even appear to be boiled.

I was content to let them pass me by when I shifted my foot and a dry stick cracked beneath my weight. Those big ears they had weren't just for show, and both of them stopped abruptly, turning to my hiding place. I slipped my head back behind the tree and readied myself for an attack. There were two of them, but I needed to deal with them quickly.

I wasted no time and began to cast Firebolt, revealing myself just as it finished.

The goblins were close, so close in fact that my Firebolt spell exploded—relatively quietly luckily—so close to its face that I singed my fingertips. But I wasn't done, just as the other goblin tried to call out, I activated my Power Strike ability directly into its bulbous head, splitting it down the middle. What felt like the hundredth time, my chest was covered in blood from the spraying remains.

When I was sure no other goblins had heard and would come running, I pulled the remains into cover. It wasn't a perfect place to hide the bodies, but I was counting on the goblins to be true to the descriptions I'd heard of them; lazy inefficient fighters who probably wouldn't even bother to use scouts if it weren't one of their most common available classes. My knowledge was limited of course, because goblins, while foul and angry little things, weren't classified as monsters. In fact, they were the opposite, they were beings that the Ordu extended the ability to gain a class.

Careful to keep to the thicker brush and doing my best to leave no trace of my passing, I neared the goblins' camp. There were patrols, but they were so close to the borders of the makeshift camp that they would be all but useless. So only twenty feet from the edge of the camp I lay on my stomach searching for any signs of Fred.

The goblins here looked much the same as the scouts I'd dispatched. I did note that all of them carried short swords with daggers in their belts, rusty but sharp. All but a few had mismatched armor, the rest were fairly well-armored.

Why or how goblins had gotten this far from the South-lands was beyond me, but this looked to be an entire camp of their adventurers, because each of them had levels.

Using Inspect on a few goblins I learned that most were between level 2 and level 6, with health pools not over 200. There were a few exceptions, a single larger goblin with deep gray skin instead of the usual forest green, he'd been called a 'Deep Dwelling Goblin' and his name was D'uhk. He was level 9 and had a health of 310 and a mana pool of 150. But I wasn't positive that I'd identified them all, as many tents were obviously occupied.

Fred was nowhere to be seen. It wasn't until he screamed again, that I figured out that he was in a tent toward the center, and I could barely make out him begging for them to stop over the laughter of the goblins. I began doing a count and came up with forty-six, but I might have counted a few twice. Either way, I would be hard pressed to deal with all of them.

I thought about what my father would do. He was always a very straightforward person who dealt with threats, I imagined, the same way. If I followed his lead, as I tried to do in most things and as I had by walking the Arcane Knight path, I should rush in using my spells and sword to fight for Fred's freedom. However, as heroic as it seemed, I just couldn't picture my father doing something so foolhardy if he had only what I had to work with.

Instead, I allowed myself a chance to think how I should handle things. My father had taught me to be a critical thinker, so maybe I was underselling him, and he would have come up with a clever plan as well. Whichever it was, I had the inklings of a very dangerous plan begin to form in my mind.

CHAPTER 37
FOLLOW THE LIGHTS

M y light spell would work at the distance of twenty feet and after that it shattered away into a dusting of *Spark*les. I'd moved out of sight of the goblin encampment and tested this several times. However, if I placed it just on the edge of that range and moved, it would move with me as if tethered to me. My plan was simple and extremely dangerous. I was going to use my light spell to get the Baby Rock Eater's attention and run like hell toward the goblin encampment.

If all went to plan, it would be a simple matter of getting it into range and letting it wreak havoc on the goblins. During the commotion I would split into the camp and free Fred. And hopefully we could get away before the Rock Eater killed all the goblins and us.

A voice in my head told me that it wouldn't be so easy, that I wasn't skilled enough to sneak past so many goblins or strong enough to fight my way in. This offered a happy medium ground with much risk, but much reward as well. With so many goblins dying from the giant beetle looking monster I imagined we'd collect a fair bit of essence as well, again if we stayed just close enough before escaping. My better sense told me that staying even a second later than I needed was probably suicide.

But I had to balance risk with reward if I wanted to become a powerful adventurer. I said a silent prayer to Vanir, a god and religion I didn't practice, and hoping that where there was one 'Baby Rock Eater' there wouldn't be more.

It didn't take long for me to find my way back, and soon I was ready to cast the Light spell. So why was I hesitating? Fred had been captured and is being tortured, I told myself. Now is not the time to rethink what is probably a bad plan. It will work, it will work, I repeated in my head as I cast the Light spell just feet from the large 'baby'.

At first, it didn't react, and I waited an entire three seconds before moving the light in a quick zipping pattern back and forth. This caught its attention and faster than I would have thought, it lashed out. My light globe went up in a spray of *Spark*les. I immediately cast another, a bit further away and this time it saw it.

The cliff face was nearly a ninety-degree angle with the rock eater consuming rocks about ten feet up. Which meant I was barely in brush cover, and seeing how fast the thing could move, I sprinted away, hoping to hell that this thing followed. I didn't have to turn to confirm that it was indeed following as I could hear smaller trees and brush being trampled as it moved.

I spared a glance behind me anyways and increased my speed. Now that it was moving, it looked less like a beetle and more like a cross between a boar, a beetle, and a spider. The bulk was less stiff than a beetle's exoskeleton, shifting as it ran, but it had large overlapping sections of plated armor that would be difficult to get through. It made a 'fffhhtt fffhht' sound as it moved.

The legs were a different matter altogether. What I'd at first assumed were small stubby beetle-like legs must have been retracted, because at full run they came out like thick spider legs, armored like the body and pointed at the end, kicking up rock and dust as it moved. During my brief moment of insanity where I'd slowed down enough to glance behind me, it retracted its legs an entire foot to avoid a large branch but lost no speed while doing so.

The Light spell zipped and weaved as I cut a path through the thick trees at the base of the mountain. It was because of the light that I was able to finally get a good look at the color and face of the monster.

The armor plates were blacker than the night with a mirrored sheen to them, while the occasional patch of skin on the back that appeared between the plates and several open areas around the face were a dull gray and had the textured look of boiled leather. Its face was another matter altogether. Four eyes, black beady things with no irises, stared directly into the light and its jaw slammed forward occasionally as it took a bite at the light.

It almost seemed angry, making a gurgling, keening noise after each attempt to snuff out the light. I wish I knew more about this monster, but in my many readings of dungeon monsters and free roaming ones, I'd never encountered anything quite like this 'Rock Eater' as the system labeled it. I once read about a 'Rock Gopher' that instead of burrowing around in soft earth and eating plants and roots, burrowed deep into mountains and consumed valuable ores. According to the book I'd read on them, the Dwarves had hunted them to extinction.

The Baby Rock Eater, whatever its diet might be, had not been hunted to extinction and while I was happy to have the chance to use it in my crazy plan, a part of me wished it had been. I was distracting myself from thinking about the mouth and the dripping yellow substance that oozed all around the large flat teeth.

The mouth had opened twice now, I'd stolen another glance, and each time I hadn't seen any sharp teeth, which to me meant it probably didn't normally eat meat, or it had other ways to do with eating flesh that didn't require sharp teeth. I'm sure the yellow substance that hissed loudly as it fell on dirt and stone, would accomplish that feat just fine.

The tongue however was odd. It looked like the source of the yellow substance; large oozing pustules covered the tongue in the sticky substance. It was fat, flat, and wide enough that it sat perfectly inside its mouth.

I stumbled after taking yet another look, it was gaining on the light and me, slowing to right myself during my run was all it needed to catch the light in its maw. Cursing I tried to cast another Light spell while moving but struggled to get the hand movements right and realized with a measure of dread that the Baby Rock Eater was still running forward, it was chasing me!

It became more apparent as it crashed through some brush, having a sudden burst of speed and nearly biting me. A fleck of the yellow mouth acid got on my arm as I ran, it hissed and pocked my armor. Thinking fast I slammed my arm painfully against a tree as I passed it, successfully wiping enough off that the only sign that it had been there was a few pocked holes no bigger than my fingertip.

Shit, shit, shit. This wasn't what I wanted to happen.

The fires of the goblin encampment loomed over the horizon, and I began to alter my plan. I picked up my speed just as the Baby Rock Eater did that odd keening noise. But unlike the times before, this time I heard it echo in the distance. Oh no, that wasn't an echo, that was something answering the call.

Things would be substantially worse if it was doing what I thought it might be doing. If this was a baby, then it was probably crying for its mother...

I picked up my pace again, increasing my speed as I began to hear crashing in the distance and a rumble of earth beneath my feet.

A goblin appeared just in front of me, dagger drawn as I neared the camp. They must be scouting out further than I realized before. It faced off thinking that perhaps I'd stop to fight him, but instead I shot past him like a speeding arrow. I had to risk a look behind and immediately regretted it. The Baby Rock Eater crashed through some trees behind me and without stopping scooped up the goblin in its jaw.

The yellow acid substance instantly went to work, and the goblin screams were silenced a moment later when the maw closed around it, chewing it up easily. I ran by three more goblins and a cry of alarm could be heard as they tried to rally together against whatever threat had entered their camp. An arrow zipped past me, going very wide, as I beelined toward the middle of the camp. By sheer dumb luck I'd not been injured and as I stopped outside the tent in the middle I saw why.

There were at least fifty or more goblins and they'd surrounded the 'Baby Rock Eater' stabbing and shouting. For their credit they were doing a decent job of occupying it for me, but one by one they were getting eaten or stabbed by the long spider-like legs. A flash of purple light slammed into the monster, throwing it back slightly. That was followed up almost immediately by a familiar flash of orange and red from a Firebolt spell.

I followed the line of the spell and saw a taller than normal pale-green skinned goblin wielding a staff with a glowing purple stone at its tip. He wore mostly ragged and ripped black robes, but appeared to be rather strong, as he threw another bolt of purple energy from his staff and a section of the armor shattered in the front of the monster. That had the bonus effect of killing the closest goblin, but they were as ravenous as the monster, stabbing and slashing into the exposed flesh.

Suddenly I didn't feel so great about my plan, I needed to hurry. Pushing through the tent, I had to stop and hold my ears as the keening of the monster hit a new height of painful volume. It was because I dipped my head in sudden pain, that the strike from the goblin that laid in wait for me missed.

Right in front of me stood D'uhk the gray skinned goblin, if he could even be called a goblin. He was as tall as me, I realized, and I dove to the side to avoid another strike, managing to pull my sword free as I did so. Wasting no time to use the distance I'd created, I launched a Firebolt for his face. He swiped downward and an arc of black energy shot forward meeting my Firebolt halfway.

The resulting impact blew outward, and I took a few points of damage.

Because it only took a moment, I used the Inspect skill to remind myself what I was dealing with.

Deep Dwelling Goblin: D'uhk, Level 9, Health 295/310, Mana 115/150

His attack had been some kind of spell, the mana drain confirmed it. But why couldn't I see his Stamina? Now wasn't the time for questions I chided myself as the Goblin slashed downward and I caught his blade with my own, glancing it to the right. In the momentary opening my block had created I thrust forward while activating Power Strike.

My muscles bulged and my stamina was depleted as I thrust

forward unnaturally fast. To my utter surprise, I saw the goblin's own muscles seem to grow slightly and he twisted out of the way of my thrust. He had a dodge ability! I swung wildly, trying and failing to follow any known fighting pattern that I'd studied. It was untrained and unbalanced striking, but however amateur my strikes looked, my strength put enough power into them that when I finally did score a hit, it cut the goblin open wide.

He yelled and fell to a knee.

"D'uhk surrenders," he said, then coughed up a little blood. "Take weapon, human wins." He threw his sword in front of him and without thinking I reached down to grab his rusted longsword.

"He's got a dagger!" Fred yelled from the dim light of the back end of the tent, but I was too slow.

A sharp pain in between the edge of my chest plate and left arm seared into me. I jerked up, further causing myself pain and looked to see the hilt of a dagger poking out of my shoulder. I ripped it free and felt blood stain my under clothing and warm my skin. My anger flared and with gritted teeth I cast Firebolt on the goblin just as it began to rise with his sword. Whether from the close distance or where I hit him atop the head, my attack went critical, and I put a smoking hole straight into D'uhk's skull.

I felt his essence travel into me, and I knew he was dead.

CHAPTER 38
MOMMY'S HERE

"You alright?" I asked Fred, his robes were torn, and his arms, chest, and face were bloody.

"I look worse than I feel," Fred said, his left eye swollen nearly closed. "They actually healed me a few times, so I didn't die while they questioned me. They have a caster that took my mother's Fiery Orb, we have to get it back!"

"I don't know if there will be time right now, we still need to find some healing herbs to get back to your sister and hope that she is alright," I said, cutting the ropes that were tying the makeshift cage closed. A sudden explosion rocked the tent and made the ground shutter.

It was followed by goblins screaming and another explosion.

"They had several goblin engineers," Fred said, meeting my eyes. "What are they fighting?"

"By the sounds and feel of it, nothing we want a part of," I said, realizing that the mother must have made an appearance. "I lured something called a Baby Rock Eater and I think the mother found her baby."

I stopped to check a chest that was unlocked and open, finding Fran and Fred's packs. I was ready to toss them both inside my inventory for safekeeping when Fred whispered back to me at the tent's exit.

"I have a potion and so does Fran inside our packs. I still have 85 health so one potion should be sufficient," Fred whispered. I dug into one of the bags and found it, tossing it lightly to Fred as the sounds of battle grew louder.

"The fight is moving this way," I said, throwing the bags into my dimensional storage. "We need to run now!"

"I agree," Fred said, his eyes slowly pushing itself back to normal. "But it is wonderful to get all this free essence. More so for you I'd assume."

It wasn't as noticeable as when the gray goblin had fallen but I felt it too, small trickles of essence filling me as goblins died.

"At this rate, there can't be many left," I said, now playing with the idea of staying around to gather all the essence we could, but how far was too far to collect some, because we definitely didn't want to be around to fight the mother Rock Eater.

Just then, a larger rush of essence hit me and I had to blink rapidly from the sudden rush. I moved to the edge of the tent to see what was happening with the battle. It wasn't what I'd thought after all. The mother hadn't been the only one to arrive, there were two eight foot tall 'Adult Rock Eaters' each level 40.

I was amazed that there were still a dozen goblins left, including the caster. Though it didn't look like they'd last long, the Baby Rock Eater had fallen and its parents didn't seem to be happy about that, both of them had a red glowing aura that meant they were using some kind of enraged ability.

I watched with morbid curiosity as the fight continued. The goblins that remained were each level 18 I realized, inspecting them, and the caster was level 20! They were skilled fighters, each of them, but they faced impossible odds. Two fighter types, wielding what would be a long sword to me and looked like it might as well be a spear in their hands, activated skills. Their blades turned a slight greenish color, before they launched forward striking at the left Rock Eater's face.

One attack slammed on target but hit one of the large face plates guarding the softer flesh beneath. His sword broke clean in half, and he was thrown to the side, only to be stabbed through the chest a moment later by the Rock Eater's spear-like legs. The second attacker aimed too low, and the Rock Eater simply opened its mouth spraying out yellow gunk all over him.

His screams were silenced a moment later as it landed in the Rock Eater's mouth. This didn't deter the other goblin fighters, they leapt, rolled, and slashed. I was surprised to notice that one of the Rock Eaters had already lost a significant chunk of health, but then I saw why. The caster was chanting a spell and though it was hard to see there was a faint grayish smoke connecting the most injured one to the caster. Some kind of draining spell maybe? Whatever the effects of the spell, it seemed to be working.

Another two goblins fell, and their front line was reduced to eight. Two parts of me were at war then, one wanted to get the hell out of there because it was the smart thing to do and the other wanted to run into battle thinking that perhaps I could turn the tide. My smarter side won out.

"We need to be smart," I said, grabbing Fred's arm. "We will return after the goblins are finished and see about recovering your Fiery Orb."

"Right, I agree with your assessment," Fred said, his face almost completely healed now. Together we hurried off into the night, taking a wide roundabout way to get back to the fallen tree. We heard a few distant keening roars, but they were far behind us.

I had an odd feeling of guilt when thinking about the monsters. I'd lured their baby to its death, but it was a monster I told myself. If I'd not dealt with it, what was the chance some innocent bystander would have found their death in its acid maw? Yeah, I'd done what needed to be done, but that didn't make the knot in my stomach go away.

CHAPTER 39
BLOODY ROOTS

We approached the tree from a different direction than I'd left, which is why I found the herb in a patch of moonlight, not more than half a quarter of a mile from Fran. It was a thick stemmed plant that she'd called Felistia or something close to that, and it required a very careful hand to extract the roots that had the healing properties.

Digging several inches away from the purple stem and careful not to disturb the plant's leaves, per Fran's instruction. After I'd gone down a hand's span into the soft earth, I dug inward with the tips of my fingers, moving slowly and stopping if I felt any roots. Luck was with me, and I only grazed one root, digging under it a bit more I got the plant out of the ground. Then I went to work, gently breaking the half a dozen roots off right where the purple ended, and the ruby colored rest of the length began. It was a slow process, but soon I had at least ten workable lengths of root.

Fran would have to do the rest, as she hadn't told me what else to do with them, other than return them to her. So, with a single remaining potion and the roots I'd collected stored away in my dimensional box, we finished our journey.

I bid Fred to stay above ground, leaving him with a Light globe, and I wormed my way back through the hole and summoned another Light. Fran was sleeping and her head was hot to the touch when I arrived. Pushing on her shoulder to gently rouse her didn't do the trick, so I pulled out the potion and poured it into her mouth, tilting her head back as I did so.

She woke up a second later coughing and I checked to make sure her Health had risen. It had.

"Here are the roots," I said, her skin was pale and clammy, but I could see a bit of her color returning.

She shifted, which moved her leg, and she groaned in pain. "Fred?" She asked, the words were scratchy and dry. Pulling my water canteen from my storage I gave her a drink.

"He's fine, but I have some bad news," I said, fixing her with my best serious face. "He got several hundred essence, so now you're behind."

Fran's face went from concerned to annoyed and she punched me in the arm. I figured it was a good sign of improving health and let it slide, despite how much it had stung.

"You and Fred are a pair of asses," Fran said, her voice clear after drinking some water. "Give me two of those roots, my bones are pretty much healed I think, it's just this bleed effect and a new condition called Blood Rot. I'm pretty sure something was biting at my backside and now I've got a fever and have been slowly losing more Health while I sat here. No idea how long I've been out, but if you hadn't returned soon, I don't want to think about what you'd have found."

Another good reason we didn't stay to see what other

essence we might have gotten, I said in my head, scolding myself for even entertaining the thought.

"We got here as fast as we could," I said, handing her several of the ruby colored roots.

She just nodded at my words and took the roots. She carefully peeled back the outer skin, revealing a much deeper red flesh. "These are one of several reagents that can be used in creating Health potions. And if I can get the skin off and remove these knots it should help me heal back to full health." She pulled a knife from her boot and began to cut into the root to remove clear squishy sacks from the center. In all, she pulled out half a dozen from just one.

The root was stringy and cut open in many places by the time she was done. She put the entire thing into her mouth and began chewing it. It was a significant bite, and she coughed a few times, red juice running down her mouth, but she didn't spit it out. After a good five minutes of chewing and swallowing she spit out the remains of the stringy root. It had lost much of its red color, now barely a light pink and Fran's face was stained red around the mouth.

"That's a good look on you," I said, gesturing around her mouth.

"Worth every drip," Fran said, smacking her lips. "I think that did it for my legs and it cured the bleeding effects as well. In fact, I think I might be able to stand." She took my outstretched hand and only groaned a little during the effort.

"You feel steady?" I asked, before letting her hand go.

"Yeah, I'm fine, my muscles are sore and stiff, but my bones feel solid," Fran said, releasing my grip and stretching as best she could in the tight confines. "Let's 'leaf' this place behind."

"What, oh ha that's funny," I said, understanding a

moment later. The root had done the trick, although her humor needed work, but I wasn't sure that could be fixed with any potion I'd heard of.

CHAPTER 40
DEATH, GUTS, AND LOOT

We decided it was going to be worth it to check out the goblin camp, and we didn't want to wait until morning to do it. There was always the chance more goblins would arrive, perhaps they were out scouting, or this could be a smaller advanced party meant to lead the way of a larger group. I was speculating but Fred and Fran agreed that I had a valid point, even if after suggesting them I felt they weren't so much.

It was well into the night, if not close to morning by the time we began approaching the goblin encampment. Fires still burned, but they were no longer the controlled look of bonfires, but some brush and even a few tents had been set alight. If anyone else was in the area, like additional goblins, they would surely see this and come to investigate. My weapon felt heavy in my hand as we cut through the trees enough to see the carnage.

You could see where most of the fighting went down, near the edge we were entering a small mound of goblin bodies piled against the dead 'Baby Rock Eater'. Where the two bigger Rock Eaters had fought against the final wave of goblins and the caster goblin with the purple staff, the ground was scorched black. At least half a dozen bodies burnt into crispy versions of themselves.

"Goblin BBQ anyone?" I asked, Fran laughed nervously, and Fred just gave me a look. Sure, it wasn't the funniest thing I'd ever said, but I was in a bit of shock from the sheer amount of blood, guts, and gore that had resulted from the battle. Searching around further back I found the place the goblin caster fell.

His body was half melted away, on stubs where his legs had once been. Based on the location of the large gashes in the ground, which I was pretty sure had to be the footsteps of the adult Rock Eaters, they hadn't gotten very close to the caster. I deduced that they'd spit some of their nasty acid saliva from a distance, totally eating away the poor fellow.

Staying clear of the yellow stuff, though it no longer appeared to be eating away at him, I searched his corpse. He had a black over the shoulder bag, but most of the contents had been destroyed by the acid spit. I was able to salvage two red gems that had been carved into the likeness of a crude sun and crescent moon. When I inspected them, I got some basic information.

Carved Ruby Gemstones (2) - Prepped for Mana Storage (0/250)

They weren't much bigger than walnuts, but they could hold 250 mana each, which could come in handy. I kept searching, finding a staff a few feet away and a spherical orange and red swirling orb.

"Fred, I found your Fiery Orb!" I shouted across the battlefield. Fred wasn't rifling through bodies, instead nudging the one Fran was searching with his toe. He wasn't the type to get his hands dirty.

Fred turned and quickly made his way over. I handed off the Orb and held onto the staff.

"Thank you so much," Fred said. He was holding the orb close to his chest like an infant child. "I don't know what I would have done if I lost this."

I gave him a reassuring smile and switched my focus to the staff. Inspecting it, I got its information.

Staff of Concentration
1 Spell Gem Slot

Current Spelled Gem: Shadow Bolt

Shadow Bolt: Throw a bolt of condensed Shadow energy at a target. This spell has the chance to give the target shadow burn, inflicting half the base damage over sixty seconds. (Once every 8 seconds the user can activate the Shadow Bolt spell at half its 120 Mana base cost.)

3-8 Base Damage

+5 Concentration

Durability: *43/90*

Rarity: *Rare*

Weight: *3.5 pounds*

Item Level: 12, Level Required to Use: 5, Dropped by: Arcane Mistress

What dungeon had a mob named Arcane Mistress, was my first thought after reading the description but I didn't dwell on it. I aimed somewhere clear of Fred and Fran, letting loose a Shadow Bolt. The feeling was different from casting Firebolt, the heat and knowing instinctively how to cast it. When casting through the staff it just felt like a portion of my mana was sucked into it and poof, like magic, the attack appeared.

The rest of the camp yielded even less useful loot. The warrior type I'd killed in the tent had a basic long sword that was so low in durability that it would be useless soon. He had a ring that increased strength by 1 and I gave that to Fran in exchange for keeping the staff. I wasn't sure what occasion I'd have to use it, but Fran really wanted the ring and insisted that we split the loot up evenly. I'd tried to tell her that the staff was probably worth a bit more than a simple magic ring, but decided to just give in.

Fran worked with Fred to identify what parts of the monster might be useful and we split the reagents equally. A monster core was discovered, but it was broken, and Fran took her turn to claim it.

We found a chest with mostly ruined items, low durability and no magical properties, except for a single belt. Named the 'Belt of Keen Sight' and gave a buff to your perception. I hadn't found where 'perception' was quantified in the system menus, but I'm sure I'd find it eventually. Fred took the belt and Fran joked that he could use it because it was hard for him to see past his own nose, whatever that meant.

I did learn something cool about my Dimensional box though. We found a very large crate filled with random armor, swords, and daggers—none of them very well made or good quality. When I jokingly tried to fit the crate that was twice my height and as wide as I was tall into my storage, to my surprise it went in just fine, taking exactly one slot. Taking the crate out again we filled it with anything, and I mean anything that wasn't bolted down and looked valuable.

There was definitely going to be a need in my life for several large crates in the future. Both Fred and Fran were feeling much better after we set off and away from the blood and gore. I'd given them back their backpacks and now had several free spots in my storage. It would be nice to have something a bit easier to carry, the box stayed mostly in place as we ran, but occasionally it jumped annoyingly against me. We searched for a safe place to get a few hours of sleep.

We'd been going for nearly a day without sleep now, Fred and Fran were losing speed with every mile we covered.

"I'm losing Stamina at twice the rate as normal," Fran said, our pace slow enough that we could speak.

"Me too," Fred added.

"Let's make camp," I said, pulling to a stop. "I'll take first watch." I didn't know if it was because my Endurance was past its first threshold or what, but my Stamina losses continued at their usual pace. Sure, I was tired, but not nearly as tired as I should be for being awake this long.

"Good idea, I guess any spot will do for a quick nap," Fran said, rolling out her bed roll and laying in it within seconds of us stopping. Fred was a bit slower but laid his out beside hers and they were sleeping within moments.

The chill of the morning still bit at my exposed flesh, so I decided it'd be worth it to build a fire. I didn't roam far, not wanting to leave them unguarded, and soon I had a small fire roaring away. I would let them sleep for a few hours and then I'd get a couple myself. But until then I needed something to occupy my time.

I pulled my backpack from my storage and found the two gems I'd gathered from the goblin caster. They were light, almost oddly so, and the morning chill soon transferred to them, sapping what little warmth they'd held onto. According to my Inspect skill, these gems could hold mana, but how did I add it? I tried doing what I'd done to interact with the system, sending actions in the form of thoughts, but it did nothing.

It took nearly an hour for me to work anything out. I stared into the sun gem and from within it, I got the barest of feelings that it had once held mana. I took that feeling and compared it against the moving and shifting I felt when casting Firebolt and more recently the sucking feeling I'd felt when casting Shadow Bolt. There was the barest of commonalities between the two and using the spell, knowledge injected into my mind, and I began to understand.

The common element in the two castings were me paying Mana from within myself to power the spells. So, I began to search within myself, stirring up the same feelings and doing my best to focus on how to do more with it. That was when I felt that I could direct my mana if I focused hard enough. It was similar to the feeling I had when moving my *Spark* around.

The only difference being that my *Spark* wasn't quite the same since I'd been *Awoken*. I tried to do as I had done before, moving around my core energy or mana I now realized, but it was much more rigid than it had been before. Using the gem as a goal to reach, I pulled and coerced the mana up and out of my core, down my right arm and into my hand. It worked; I felt the mana get pulled into the gem a tiny bit at a time.

Had I done it correctly? I wasn't sure, but this method seemed a bit difficult to be what everyone else was using. I made a mental note to ask Fred and see what he knew on the subject. While I waited for them to get their rest, I filled both gems with Mana, taking it slowly so I was never below half myself. My mana regeneration while not in direct combat, worked pretty quickly at 31 mana per minute, so in the matter of an hour or so I'd regained the expended mana.

After I'd done all that could be done, I was left alone with my thoughts. This was only day one of being an adventurer and already I'd done so much. It had been one quick thing after another with very little chance to reflect on my actions. Killing the baby monster bothered me less the more I thought about it. What started to bother me now was why it didn't bother me that I'd been instrumental in the deaths of forty or more goblins.

Try as I might, which to be honest I really didn't, I couldn't feel bad about their deaths. They'd acted against my friends and I, probably assumed they'd killed us and took Fred to torture him for information. The Southlanders weren't technically evil, but everyone knew they were much more prone to the darker arts of magic and cruelty. They lived very different lives and were raised to be ruthless, so why should I feel bad if I gave them what they expected.

If it came down to being us or them, I'd pick us every time.

My thoughts brought me to what Fred had said about them wanting information from him. I would need to ask him what they wanted to know. We weren't in House Variyn lands anymore, but intel regarding an invading force might help save lives if I found the right person to tell. Wishing again I'd done even the slightest research into the history and current ruling Lords, I tried to remember what I knew about our western neighboring House.

It was embarrassing, but I had to check my map to make sure I was remembering the House lands we'd traveled into. It was House Blalor, one of the smaller Houses, and what little I could recall about them had to do with their primary export, iron. Though small overall, Blalor had extensive iron mines and rarely had to worry about border wars with their three neighboring houses because of the wealth they earned by trading almost exclusively with the elves.

The only reason I knew any of this had to do with a time Warrick had angrily declared House Blalor fools for expanding their mines deeper into the mountains, saying they were likely to stir up trouble for the kingdom with the Beastkin nations. Nothing had come of it, or at least nothing I'd heard about. Instead, Blalor maintained its borders, similar to how House Variyn did, through trade contracts.

Though from what Warrick had said, House Blalor had the finances to hire an army big enough to take over half of Newaliyn, which he'd only mentioned because he thought it might not be enough to deal with the Beastkin.

It made me smile to think of Warrick. Despite the betrayal of my trust, I still cared deeply for him and couldn't wait to tell him that I'd become an Arcane Knight like my father. Maybe after I finished with my quest and had my class unlocked completely, I'd ride down to visit Creeshaw. I'd just left but it wouldn't hurt to find out if Ismene had made it through everything okay. Plus, I could check out Warrick's tower and give him the good news, if he was back.

Ismene would be okay, I told myself. Ismene, Emory, and I had all had our greatest desire answered. Though Emory didn't know it yet, unless he'd come through Creeshaw and heard the news. It would be a day to remember when we finally all got back together and did a dungeon run. Maybe they'd be willing to help me establish Blackridge keep, despite what condition it was in now.

If Zander had been telling the truth, it wasn't much more than ruins, but even the ruins of an established keep would have benefits. I didn't know what they'd be, but I understood the basics of established territories, lands, and strongholds. I'm sure with it unoccupied, despite being on the northeastern border between House Variyn and House Attra, there were benefits lost.

I just hoped that dungeons paid a lot better than killing goblins, we'd split less than a hundred gold between the three of us after looting every corpse and turning out every tent.

I was lost in such thoughts when I heard movement to my right. It was Fran, wiggling herself out of her bedroll. She smiled at me, and I returned the gesture.

In a quiet whisper she said, "I'll take watch for a bit. I'm feeling loads better and I want Fred to get his sleep, he's had a rough day."

"I can still hear his screams in my head sometimes," I said, frowning at the thought. "It's good that they thought they could get information from him."

"It was good they tortured him?" Fran asked, her voice rising above a whisper and her eyes narrowing.

"Yeah," I said, ignoring her hurt gaze. "Because if they didn't, I bet they'd have just killed him and taken his stuff. He seems like a strong guy, he'll pull through."

"I guess," Fran said, looking at her brother with concern.

"I'm going to try to get an hour or two of sleep, but don't let us go for much longer. We have a lot to do still, and time is counting down," I said, pulling out my own bedroll and placing it a bit closer to the fire.

I was out within a minute or two, it was possible that I was more tired than I'd thought.

My dreams were filled with blood, guts and fire. Goblins begging for their lives and me mercifully cutting or blowing them up with fire spells to reach something in the distance. I never got through the sea of angry goblins, instead I just heard screams echoing far off. It wasn't until I woke up with sweat on my brow and my breathing labored that I understood what was happening. I'd been having a nightmare about trying to save Fred, for whatever reason my mind chose that nightmarish scene as the best way to cope.

I slipped back to sleep seconds later and this time it was dreamless and still.

CHAPTER 41
HUNTING FOR FAE HEARTS

We slept well into the late hours of the morning, but soon enough we went on our way. Following the foot of the mountain we moved ever closer to our destination. With a slow trudge into the afternoon came a pleasant heat. It wasn't like the heat in the forest just a week ago that made me wish for the colder months, no, it was a gentle heat with the occasional cool breeze.

I was probably imagining it, but I swear I could smell the faint scent of salt from the sea well beyond. That wasn't likely though, as we were at least a day or two journey from the coast. The Elven nations had the entire western coast, save a bit down south, as their land. It was said they were talented fishermen and boat captains.

I couldn't remember if I'd ever seen the sea, lakes were more my speed, and as we jogged carefully over the rocky terrain a part of me wished for a trip out to a lake. Just me, my fishing pole, and the fish. But I could do that anytime, this was the adventure I'd dreamt about my entire life. Snapping myself back to the present, I got Fred's attention and we stopped for a quick rest. I insisted that they let me Cast my Physical Resistance buff on them, so we waited on the cooldown until all three of us were ready.

"This terrain is harder to pass through than I thought," Fred said as soon as we'd stopped. "It'll take another hour before we reach the place my quest indicated."

"We'll make it with plenty of time," I said. I wanted to find an opening to ask about the questions before I forgot, but I didn't know where to start. "How are you feeling?" I asked, settling on the lame straightforward method.

"I'm doing well," Fred said, his eyes glazed over for a moment—something I was beginning to recognize as a sign someone was looking at system information. "My Stamina is depleting at a normal rate again. I will be raising it, along with my Intellect, when I level. Could you check and tell me where the closest shrine is located?"

"Uh yeah, sure," I said, doing a quick check on the map I saw one about two hours west in the general direction we would be heading. I told him as much and then decided I better just go for it. "Can you tell me what the goblins were asking you about?" I asked, giving a weak excuse for a smile when I saw him flinch from my question.

"That...uhm...I mean sure, I can talk about it. I'm fine," Fred said, more to himself than to me. I gave him the time he needed to get in the right headspace.

Between the three of us Fred had gotten the worst end of things, with Fran a close second. I'd been fortunate that I'd passed my thresholds and my body was a good bit sturdier than Fran's, otherwise we'd both been stuck in a hole with no hope of escape.

"Take your time," I said, putting a hand on his shoulder. "I think any information could be important, maybe a clue to why goblins are this far out of the Southlands."

"They really didn't ask me much," Fred began to say, stopping to take a deep breath before continuing. "They wanted to know if I was alone, I lied at first saying it was just me, but it didn't take long before..."

Fred's breathing grew ragged, and he had to stop.

"Is this really necessary?" Fran asked, her disposition toward me hardening.

"I think it's important," I assured her. It didn't do much to take the angry glare off her face, but she nodded, and Fred did his best to continue.

"I told them I was out here with you both. Then I told them all about you and my sister, but they didn't really seem interested in any of that," Fred said, gaining control of his breathing and launching into it. "They asked a few questions about how many champions, I think they meant adventurers, did 'this land' have. They got angry when I wasn't sure and even more angry when I asked if they meant all of Newaliyn or just House Blalor."

"Did they not even know where they were?" I asked, confused.

"It didn't seem like it," Fred said, he had calmed to his more stoic tone of voice again. "They hurt me a lot after that until the one you killed came to talk to me, he was actually sort of nice."

"Nice? How so?"

"Well, he gave me water and asked how long I'd been a champion," Fred said. "I told him, and he seemed sympathetic, despite his limited ability to speak common. He did say something that stuck out to me. He asked if our chiefs fought dragons, or at least I think that's what he said. I passed out not long afterwards."

"He probably meant the House Lords," I reasoned. "But what was this bit about dragons? Why would he want to know if anyone was fighting dragons?"

"Maybe the Chaos Beasts are a problem in the Southlands too," Fran said, in a halfhearted joking tone. But I latched onto that thought and ran with it.

"What if they are?" I asked. "And maybe the goblins were looking for someplace else to go. I have it from a reliable source that the southern border is pretty well defended though, so how the hell did they get so far north?"

"If you'd left one alive, we could have asked," Fred offered.

I flinched slightly at that, still dealing with my part in the battle and the death wrought. Fred had no ill intent and he had to have known that I only took the lives necessary to save his own. If it hadn't been for the two adult Rock Eaters though, we'd probably be fleeing the remnants of the goblins. Not a thought I wanted to entertain between the caster and whichever goblin had made those explosives.

"I think everything worked out fine," Fran said, her annoyed look fading into a pleasant relaxed one.

"I agree," I said. "There is a mana shrine an hour past the Fae area we're headed to, so anyone that wants to level up or assign attributes can do so then. Let's get moving."

I'd studied a wide variety of monster types and Fae were ones I had knowledge on, though limited. The kind of monsters I'd read about were mostly tricksters, like pixies or stealthy ambushers, like the Dark Dryads. Fred told us that we'd be looking for a Fae 'fire sprite', a type I'd not really read about, so it was anyone's guess which role it would take.

The trees thickened as we left the base of the mountain

range and followed a stream, drawing ever closer to the indicated area. The light from the sun was slowly disappearing, the overgrowth so thick that it was blotting out any light. We traveled for another ten minutes before slowing to a walk.

"Any complaints if we walk from here on out and I cast my Light spell?" I asked, and when I got none, I cast my Light spell.

The globe of light struggled to illuminate more than a few feet out, so I waited for my cooldown and cast another one, but it didn't help. It was around that time I felt something tingling against my mind. It only took a second for me to realize what.

"This entire area is infused with mana," I said, drawing my sword. "Keep your eyes moving and call out anything you see."

"You think a monster is casting a spell or something?" Fran asked, in her calm manner that she kept most of the time. She drew her sword as she spoke, the curved blade making the slightest of scratching sounds as it was pulled free.

"I do," I said, pivoting on my feet to look behind us. I saw nothing, that was my main problem. Outside a three-foot ring around my lights nothing was visible now, not even the trees or underbrush.

Fred was the last to react, pulling his Fiery Orb free. I was surprised to see that the orb's red and orange coloring let off a faint glow that penetrated the sheen of darkness, outlining trees and brush around us.

It was because of this that I saw a quick movement to the left, but whatever it might have been was lost to sight before I could even consider trying to cast Firebolt. We continued on like this for nearly a minute, I checked my map a few times and we were moving closer to the destination it indicated. If it weren't for the stream we were following, it was doubtful we could have stayed on course.

A sharp and sudden pain erupted from behind my knee. I slashed downward as fast as I could, but it was gone before I could move my eyes to see what it had been.

"I saw it," Fred said, his face looking back and forth as if trying to find where it went.

"Well, what was it?" I asked, reaching down and feeling a small bit of blood on my leg. It had stabbed me right between my armor gap. I checked my health and I'd only lost 14 points, so I'd be fine. What worried me was how fast it had moved.

"It looked like a stick man with long fingers and twigs for hair," Fred said, he had a look on his face that said, 'what kind of monster looks like that'.

I agreed with his expression, what monster indeed.

"There!" Fran yelled, a sudden whoosh as her blade reacted to whatever she'd seen. I felt another sharp pain in the same exact spot, and my knee gave out momentarily.

I saw a two-foot-tall stick man, his form made of old looking twigs and his fingers like elongated knives, staring right into my face. It reared back its fingers, dripping already with my blood, and aimed right for my throat. Before I was able to bring my sword to bear, Fran's came down, splitting the thing into two pieces.

"Nice save," I said, getting to my feet and limping forward. The last hit had given me twice as much damage and made the area extremely sore. "What is it?"

"My Inspect skill calls it a Shade Slasher and it was level 2," Fred said, leaning over the dead thing.

"Get ready," I said. Realizing that if this 'Shade Slasher' had caused the darkness there were probably more, because it was still dark.

Three more appeared, moving with incredible speed and disappearing from sight a moment later. It was only when attacking that they seemed to slow down. I slashed downward, killing one just as it tried to hamstring Fred. Another exploded in flames as Fred let loose his Firebolt spell. I readied a Firebolt spell as well, realizing that I could do the 'cast' and hold it for a few seconds before it faded away.

At least twenty of the Shade Slashers later and the darkness flickered away, leaving us in a shaded grove. There wasn't much sunlight, but enough to see by, the previous darkness having been an effect of the monsters.

The stream ended ahead, pooling in a wonderfully strange pond. There were orange lights, dozens of them, inside the water, moving and shifting just under the surface.

"It says we are here," Fred announced.

Fae were tricky creatures, and I had a good guess where we'd find the 'Fire Sprites'. To confirm, I used Inspect and my suspicions were confirmed.

Fire Sprite, Level 4, 50/50 Health

"Those are what you are looking for," I said, looking at Fred and seeing he understood as well. "This is for your class quest, so I'd be ready for a decent fight. The random one I Inspected only had 50 health, so hit them fast and maybe we can kill the swarm before things get out of hand."

"Good plan," Fran said, gripping tightly to her sword and spreading out.

The pond was maybe five feet across from edge to edge and by the looks of it not very deep. We gave each other enough space to fight and when everyone was ready, I nodded to Fred to start the fight.

He stepped forward, the Fiery Orb blazing against the shadows, and stuck his toe into the pool of water. I was about to tell him that getting into the water wasn't the right way to start the fight—not that I knew what the right way would be but that didn't seem right—when several orange burning lights shot out of the surface of the water.

They were hard to see at first, they buzzed and moved around erratically. But I got a good enough look just as one flicked past me, nearly singeing my nose. I saw pointed ears and an angled face. They were tiny little elf looking people with wings made of fire. The one that had flown across my face had also been very naked. Her tiny form had breasts that could almost be comical given their size. Like two round balls nearly as big as its head.

Then another swished by my face and I learned that they were not all female, and the enlarged parts didn't just apply to breasts.

"They haven't attacked yet, should we?" Fred asked, he sounded unsure, and I could tell why. The monsters were oddly human-like, well they had pointy ears, so I guess it was easier to say that they are elf-like, but regardless they didn't look like any monster I'd killed yet and it gave me pause as well.

Fran on the other hand didn't seem to hold our same hesitation. She lashed forward with her sword, striking one that was just about to fly past her face.

Nothing happened. Or at least nothing happened to the sprite she struck out against; it kept flying forward as if a blade hadn't just passed straight through it. Fred let off a Firebolt just as the erratic swarm began to move closer to us, their speed and sound increasing. This time something did happen.

A large group of sprites shot together and took the Firebolt straight on, exploding outward in a *Spark* of flame. However, they didn't fall to the ground dead, no, their wings seemed to expand noticeably, and they dove at Fred. I shot forward, swiping downward with my sword in hopes that I'd get them to scatter, but my blade had no effect and they continued on course, striking into Fred.

"Ouch, shit, aww that hurts!" Fred yelled, I Inspected him, and he'd only taken a dozen damage, probably one or two per sprite that struck him. So, while painful, their attacks were weak.

"My sword isn't working," Fran said, swiping at another one.

"Neither is mine," I said, charging a Firebolt spell and shooting it at a sprite. Again, several dove into it and blew outward, growing in size. "Firebolt's no good either." I added as if we already didn't have proof of its ineffectiveness.

Half a dozen large, winged sprites smashed into me, it was as if they could pass straight through me, and it hurt. I took a single point of damage each, but I felt burnt in the places they'd touched, and it left me aching.

"What do we do?" Fred asked, he was getting pelted every few seconds by sprites now, and his wild swiping with his hand wasn't having any effect.

What did I know about the Fae? I asked myself, struggling to concentrate on the knowledge somewhere in my head while an occasional sprite hit me, doing minimal damage but causing me sharp pains. Weakness...what weakness do Fae have? Nothing came to mind. I thought perhaps the water would put them out but they'd come out of water so that was a bust.

"Should we retreat?" Fran asked, already taking a step backward. "They aren't doing much damage but it's going to add up."

"I need the heart," Fred said, pleading. "Why can't we just kill one!" His voice turned harsh, something I hadn't heard from him before, and he cast another Firebolt.

I didn't have time to yell at him to stop, the casting

through his Orb was much faster than my own. He screamed in pain and frustration a second later as another dozen pelted through him. His health had dropped to just a hair above one hundred, and I had an idea.

Quickly letting my blade fall to the ground, I opened my hand and pulled the staff from my dimensional storage. Taking aim at the center-most cluster, I shot off a Shadow Bolt, and three sprites screeched an ear-splitting cry, nearly causing me to drop the staff so that I could cover my ears, but I held onto it. Quickly inspecting one of them before I lost them in the swarm, I saw that it was below half health.

"The staff works but—" My words were cut off as all of the fire sprites formed up and flew straight through me. I took fifty damage all at once and they were circling again. The staff had a cooldown of 8 seconds and there was no way I'd do enough damage before these things killed me.

"Let's run," Fran called out. She grabbed ahold of a reluctant Fred and pulled him back the way we came.

We instantly ran into an issue though. The opening in the trees had shut. Where they had once been several feet across, they were now growing within inches of each other and created a solid barrier around the spring.

"We're going to die here," Fred said, his voice losing the anger from before and was filled with the eerie calm of accepting one's death.

"No, we aren't," I said, scrunching my forehead in an attempt to loosen any thoughts or ideas that might be hiding below the surface. Then like a sudden rock smashing a giant rat to bits, it struck me.

A passage in a book I'd read only a year after my father died, when I was first getting deep into studying monsters.

Fae are unique in that many of their kind only live partially in our realm, which makes them very difficult to kill. Iron is a sure way to combat all Fae, spirit or otherwise. It acts as a disruption to their dual nature, sometimes killing them outright.

"Does anyone have iron!" I yelled just as I lost another fifty health, bringing me below 500. I was lucky that I had such a large pool of health already, but Fran and Fred didn't have that luxury, so I needed to act fast.

"The end of my sheath has an iron cap," Fran said, showing me the end of her sheath.

Fred shook his head that he did not, swatting at any approaching sprite.

"Iron will hurt them, drop your sword and get to swinging!" I yelled, rolling to the side just in time to avoid another fifty damage. Where would I find more iron? Then the realization hit me. I'd inspected a few of the goblin's weapons and at least two of them had been made of iron, a fact I only knew because they'd been called 'Iron Dagger' or 'Iron Sword'.

"The goblins had some iron weapons; make room I'm bringing out the entire crate!" I yelled accessing my Dimensional box and selecting the large crate of weapons and armor. In doing so, I left myself open to another strike, taking more damage.

Fred wasn't doing so good, and I did the only thing I could. Pulling out some of the prepared healing roots I sprinted over to him and shoved it into his mouth. Small as the damage was, he'd been taking a consistent beating, a few sprites targeted him even while the swarm attacked me. His health began to slowly tick upward, so I rushed back to the weapons crate.

Ahead of me Fran danced amidst angry sprites, half of her swings hitting their mark, but the half that didn't was costing her health. She was doing better than Fred though, so I instead turned my focus on finding iron. The crate was open, and I pulled aside armor pieces inspecting each weapon for the name 'Iron' until finally I found one. It was a rusty iron short sword, but it would do for what we needed.

"Fran, catch," I said, tossing the sword low. It clattered at her feet, and she scooped it up. Each swing caught one or two at a time and they instantly burst into a fiery lightshow of flame.

Back to my search, the swarm hit me with another fifty damage, and I turned, letting loose another Shadow Bolt, then tossed the staff away. Anything I could do to keep their attention focused on me was worth it, because Fred and Fran's health was just too low.

I located a pair of iron daggers and threw them to Fred. He had a look like 'what am I supposed to do with these' but he soon figured it out. That's the thing about being in a desperate life or death situation, you either figure stuff out or you die. I am glad that Fred chose the former.

Finally, I found another iron sword, this one a bit longer than the short sword that Fran was using to explode the sprites by the handfuls. It was my turn to go to work. The swarm had gathered to deliver another fifty damage to me, but I was ready.

I used Power Strike right down the center as they rushed me. At least a dozen erupted into flame at once, disturbing them enough that they parted and did no damage to me. It was just a matter of cleaning up now, we worked efficiently and deadly, killing them two and three at a time.

The final dozen no longer tried to attack us, just fleeing back to the water.

"Don't let them regroup," I said, heading to the water's edge. "There is no telling how many more might be hiding."

My heart thumped and adrenaline coursed through me,

urging me forward. Fred and Fran advanced with me, our new weapons held at the ready.

The water began to ripple as if someone had dropped a stone into it and the orange lights of the Fire Sprites disappeared. I made it to the edge and looked down into the pond, but it was black as the night sky now, but without the benefits of the moon and stars to light it.

Then all of a sudden, the tip of a human sized head emerged, followed closely behind by the rest of the body. A naked female form appeared, she had black hair with strands of green weaved in it and eyes that glowed with a purple light. She stood a head shorter than me but had a lean lithe quality to her. Her face and bearing were that of a confused child, her head turned slightly to the side as she regarded us. I used my Inspect skill on her.

Fae Elf.

It didn't give me a level, health, or mana figure on her, just Fae Elf. This was concerning for several reasons, but the one that bothered me the most was the fact that I'd used Inspect on the Adult Rock Eaters, getting their level and health, so either she could shield herself from my skill or she was much stronger than two level 40 Rock Eaters.

"Be careful," I said, stepping back and holding the iron out in front of me. "I'm not seeing her level, so there is no telling how strong she is."

Fred and Fran took my words to heart, stepping back and raising the iron between her and us like a shield.

"Why do you kill my children?" the Fae Elf asked. "You have taken so many of their precious lights from my garden."

I looked to Fran who just shrugged, then turned to Fred but he was already answering by the time I regarded him.

"I seek a heart of a Flame Sprite to give to the Arbiter," he said, with a note of formality.

"The Arbiter?" she said slowly as if tasting the words. "I know of such a being; you are seeking the approval of the sky makers. What kind of Hero would you be?"

"Me? Uhh, well I don't know if I'd call myself a hero," Fred stammered his response back, I think the lady's nakedness was too much for Fred, so I stepped in.

"We will be the Heroes that we need to be," I said, doing my best to keep my eyes on her eyes and no place else. "I will do as my father did and protect those who need it, and drive back Chaos wherever I find it."

"Yeah," Fran said, cutting in. "Me too."

I'm sure if this Fae elf was looking for a specific answer, we'd definitely not hit it, as she raised an eyebrow in my direction and spoke.

"What do you know of Chaos," she said, stepping out of the water and moving toward me. Her words weren't harsh as you'd expect, more curious, and I felt a great innocence from her. I lowered my iron sword and let her walk right up to me, close enough to reach out and touch.

"I know that there is a balance," I said, the Arbiter's words ringing through my head. "And I will help maintain it."

"Will you?" she said, her head moved in close and for a second I thought she was going to kiss me, instead she sniffed deeply right in front of my face. "You smell of Chaos. Be sure what master you serve, for we are all servants in the end. Know yourself or risk losing who you are..." She turned then and pointed delicate fingers at each of us. "...that is a warning that each of you should follow. Take the remains you wish and leave my grove."

She turned, her soft delicate features extending to her backside as well as the front and I found myself momentarily entranced. I didn't need to look over to Fred to know he was under a similar magic spell, but not the magic we both loved to study, this was the magic of hormones. As quick as she'd come, she was gone, slipping back into the water and out of sight.

"Well, that was..." I was at a loss for how to finish the sentence I'd started to speak.

"It certainly was," Fred said, his eyes still staring longingly at the pool of water.

"Are we going to try and find a heart or are you two giving up being adventurers and want to be Fae women chasers now?" Fran said, her voice held a sharp edge to it, but when I looked over to her, I could see it was mostly jest.

It turns out that killing Flame Sprites the way we did turned them into balls of ash, so we were lucky that I'd killed at least two with the staff's spell, otherwise Fred would be out of luck. He found that the item called "Heart of a Flame Sprite" was in fact a tiny red stone, he collected both of them. Fran had us collect their wings and some of their dust remains as reagents.

CHAPTER 42
CLIFFS OF FIRE

"That was a pretty good haul of experience," Fran said, our next destination wasn't far, and we'd decided to take it at a slow jog so we could discuss things.

"At this rate I'll be able to hit level 5 and begin dungeons by the time my class is unlocked," Fred said, his academic tone returning. The ogling, drooling way of speaking he'd adopted when under the spell of the female elves' femininity was all but gone.

"I'm already level 5," I said, I hadn't meant to sound like I was bragging but wished I hadn't said it the moment I had.

"That explains how you took so many hits," Fran said, shaking her head and smiling at me. "I bet your Paragon stat is your Core attribute, right? You probably started with more essence than we've collected this entire trip."

"I have enough," I said, wishing we'd change the subject. My entire experience coming into being an adventurer had been filled with fortune and I didn't want to let slip that I'd probably be able to hit level 10 by the time we finished.

What would Emory say when he found out that I would be

415

either his same level or close to it around the same time I tell him that I'd become an adventurer. He had been out challenging dungeons for nearly a year without getting to level 10 and I started with enough raw essence to hit 10 right away if I wasn't trying to inflate my attributes even further.

"What are your plans after you finish your class quest?" I asked, trying to change the subject.

"Our parents want to run through a dungeon with us," Fran said. "They know a healer and want to teach us the ropes personally. All their training up to this point hasn't been practical so I think they're just excited to see what we can do."

"Well, if you ever want to do a dungeon run together just let me know," I said, though I wasn't sure how that'd work as my level kept shooting up higher and normally you wanted to run dungeons with someone within 5 to 10 levels of each other. A fact I'm sure they were aware of or at least they would be very soon when they ran a dungeon with their parents. At the higher levels they would take a substantial amount of essence from the lower leveled adventurers.

"We would be honored," Fred said, inclining his head.

"You keep getting essence so fast I'm not sure how much help we'd be," Fran said, swinging her arm out as we ran and punching me playfully.

"I think there will be plenty of chances in our future to grow stronger together," I said, returning the playful punch with a punch of my own. Fran veered and had to kind of spin herself to avoid hitting a tree. "Oops sorry. Still trying to get used to my own strength."

We reached the Cliffs of Fire not long after and what laid out before us was a majestic sight. Three types of elementals battled at the top of a large plateau and all its adjacent spires, reaching up to the skyline tops like a spear.

"How do we do this without them mobbing us all at once?" I asked, from a distance, it appeared they were clumped very close together.

"Let's get closer and see what we are dealing with," Fred said, his gaze passing over the many hundred elementals.

So we did, traveling carefully we approached a pathway that snaked up the side of the mountain toward the plateau, soon getting close enough that we could see several elementals up close. The fire elementals were like large balls of flame with no legs but two large arm like appendages made entirely of flickering fire. The Air elementals would be hard to see if it weren't for the red dirt that most of them passed over, showing their entire bodies to be five-foot wind funnels. The rock elementals were simply larger boulders with legs, arms, and heads made of smaller rocks attached to a middle boulder.

"Let's steer clear of the rock elementals if we can," I said, one about a hundred feet away slammed and crashed against a fire elemental, killing it before it took much damage at all. Where the fire elemental died was a black sphere with red and orange lettering on the surface. What it said or even what the symbols looked like was impossible to tell from this distance and we didn't dare approach the rock elemental without a sure way to deal with it.

"There," Fred said suddenly. "A fire elemental is alone and if we circle around, we can catch it by surprise."

"It won't be immune to fire-based attacks, but very resistant," I said, recalling what I knew about elemental monsters. "If we aim for its most middle section, we can damage its core and that'll take out the monster."

"What about melee attacks?" Fran asked, eyeing her sword and most likely remembering how ineffective it had been against the Flame Sprites.

"Melee strikes will do damage, but not much," Fred explained, giving Fran a reassuring nod. "Their form is maintained by their magic and since elementals are creatures of pure elemental magic, you damage their form, you deplete it and if their magic is completely depleted, they die."

"Whoa, spot on Fred," I said, clapping my hands together in mock applause. Now that he said it, I remembered reading something to the same effect, but I hadn't known he was this knowledgeable about monsters.

"Yeah, he reads everything he can about magic," Fran said. "So, if elementals are 'magic monsters' then he's probably read about them."

"I've read about them," Fred said, interrupting his sister. "Because elemental cores are a common reagent in Enchanting, the profession I will be taking once I hit level 10."

"That makes sense," I said, before quieting them with my hand motions. We were approaching the Fire Elemental and needed to focus up.

Fred and I hit it first, each using our items that had spells keyed to them to hit the fire elemental before it saw us. It flared when hit, not making a sound per se, but the fire crackled dangerously in response to our attack. The ground below where it floated became black scorched earth and it raised a limb toward Fred.

"Move!" I cried out, and he jumped to the side just in time to miss the jet of flame that spouted forth, scorching where he stood only moments ago.

Fran was there with her sword a moment later, swinging with expert practiced slashes. The fire elemental seemed to shrink back from the attacks, and I felt a buildup of mana from my mana sense skill.

"Get back!" I yelled, Fran reacted with expert grace,

bounding back just as the fire elemental let out a blast of fire all around it. The attack had a limited range, and she was lucky enough to not get burned too badly. As it was, she had been hurt a bit and was clutching at her left arm, smoke trailing lazily up from where her clothing had caught aflame.

I ran in with the staff, swinging it for all it was worth at the fire elemental while my companions pulled themselves together. After my third strike, I jumped gracefully back and cast Firebolt, there was a safe minimum distance and it exploded on impact, so I didn't want to be too close. The fire elemental barely seemed to notice that attack.

The staff came off cooldown and I let loose another Shadow Bolt, making the elemental swell inward in a fiery rage. I threw the staff aside, pulling my blade free from my side and jumping forward to use my Power Strike skill. It came down in a deadly arc. Fran was there a moment later, her strikes weaving together and showing off her skill with the blade. The fire elemental held out both arms and I sensed a buildup of mana.

"Watch out," I said, keeping my eyes on the fire elemental but backpedaling and watching to see what it would do.

It was good I'd moved back, and I was happy to see Fran not far behind me, because the fire elemental began to spin, and flames shot free from its arms. Soon it was a tornado of flame, sucking everything in toward it.

"It's getting close to death," Fred yelled over the growing roar of the fire. "Let's hit it one more time!"

I nodded my head that I was ready and held out my hand to cast Firebolt. At the same time Fred let his attack fly, with my slightly smaller one hurtling after his. Our combined attacks hit the swirling fire elemental and caused it to explode outward in a flare of light. My eyes went white, and I shielded them from the intense light, only to find a smoldering core seconds later when I uncovered them.

That had been a quick, but intense fight. Fran took a seat to my left and pulled out some red roots to chew on.

"It got you pretty good?" I asked, seeing her sleeve had been charred significantly.

"Nothing that won't heal," Fran said, nursing her arm.

I didn't envy her the pain she was likely feeling. I'd been burnt a few times in my life, once fairly bad when I was younger when a pot of boiling soup had overturned. But luckily my father not only knew some basic heal spells, something I had learned Evokers had access to on a limited scope, but he had special burn potions that anyone could benefit from, *Awakened* or not.

The pain had lasted only six hours, give or take a few, but it had been relentless. The increased healing and straight health regeneration that *Awakened* had would do wonders on her burnt arm though, plus the roots could speed things even further.

"The core is cracked," Fred said, calling over from where he stood examining the leftovers of the fire elemental. "We need to kill another one."

And so we did, in fact it took all day until we found an elemental core that hadn't been cracked. A few times things got a bit tricky, but after killing 15 fire elementals, 3 air elementals, and 1 rock elemental, he finally got one that hadn't been broken. And on top of that, we got three monster cores, different from the elemental cores Fred needed, that we split evenly.

We found a place to camp and rested the evening away while discussing the essence gains we'd gotten from so many kills. Next on our list of things to kill was Fran's class item, a

Dire Bear's heart. The area indicated on the map wasn't terribly far, maybe a few hours journey. We planned on getting an early start so that we could make it to our final destination and wrap up our class quests by killing an owl bear for me.

"Halfway done," I said to Fran. Fred had snoozed off already, happy that he had not only gotten his class item but also the reagent for a powerful fire spell.

"Yeah, sorry this side quest took so long," Fran said, shaking her head at her brother. "We wouldn't have been able to afford the reagents for his fireball spell without just getting it out here in the wild. Elemental cores are extremely expensive. But between all the broken ones and broken monster cores I think I'll be able to afford a few skills finally."

"It's crazy," I said, summoning my reagent box from my dimensional storage. "I have no idea how expensive some of these reagent items are, but I bet I could sell this box for a pretty penny. I won't of course, I need as many skills and spells as I can get."

"You are going to have to work twice as hard to keep up," Fran said. "Being a split physical and magical fighter means you have two paths to walk. I could show you a few things about the sword if you want. I can tell you've studied some, but I'd be willing to help you."

"Yes please," I said, not hesitating a second. Proper training from someone like her, someone who has studied alongside their father for as long as she had, would be invaluable.

I felt a pang of regret for the lost opportunity as I thought about how my father could have helped train me in the ways of both magic and sword fighting. Why had he tried to hide this gift from me instead of embracing what I was and teaching me how best to handle the things I'd encounter? As much as I tried to stay angry at him, I couldn't. I knew my father and he never did anything without reason. I just wished I knew what that reason was, and I prayed silently to the gods of Vanir, that it wasn't what I thought. Perhaps my father didn't' think I was worthy of the power, maybe he saw something in me that I hadn't learned to recognize myself.

Fran promised to help me for a short time in the morning and then an extended period of time if we finished up early enough with our class quests. We chatted a bit more before laying down to sleep. She took first watch and promised to wake me in a few hours. I got very little sleep, my mind stuck on the awful thought that perhaps my father was right, and I shouldn't have taken this path. In the end I was able to overcome the bout of depression that came with my dreary thoughts and came to my own conclusion.

I was worthy as anyone and nothing, not even my father's own efforts, would stop me from being as he was, an Arcane Knight.

CHAPTER 43
CHAOS WURM

The early morning dew wet my bare feet as I went to the water's edge for a quick bath. We would be leaving soon to seek out a Dire Bear, but I convinced Fred and Fran that I needed to get some of the grime off me before we continued. It was nice having armor that cleaned itself, and because my Dimensional box held a good number of items without the worry of the immense weight, I had several outfits to cycle through. None of that mattered if I didn't keep myself clean.

A shiver ran up my spine as my toe dipped into the water and I wondered if it would be possible to set a self-cleaning enchantment on myself. Making a note to ask Fred about that later, I clenched my teeth and dove into the freezing water. While I scrubbed off the dirt and muck that had built up over the last couple days, I let my mind wander.

It was truly a whirlwind of emotional and physical change being an adventurer. One moment I'm a step away from death, the next I spend all day killing elementals and not once did I fear for my life. A small part of me remembered fondly the steady and boring life of orchard farming with a measure of longing. I squashed that stray feeling and felt guilty for having it.

This had been my one great desire and just because things got a bit rough, did not mean I needed to start daydreaming about a boring life back home. Dangerous and scary were preferable over boring and meaningless. My mind set on the matter, I finished my scrubbing and checked my system menus. My stats hadn't changed but I'd gained several thousand more essence, and doing some quick and loose math I determined I would be ready to hit level 10 easily when we returned. I'd probably have enough for some new spells and skills as well, though there was no telling what the reagents required would be.

We moved swiftly at the edge of the mountain for about an hour before we changed course and headed deeper into the forest. It was a peaceful morning and the exertion felt good. My muscles and endurance were truly something different now that I'd raised my attributes. I could see Fran and Fred flagging and signaled that we should take a break.

As we stopped a sound echoed through the trees. It was a screeching roar that was followed by an answering yell that was less animalistic. Now that I'd stopped, I could hear the clang of battle not far off.

"Let's check it out," I said, and Fred and Fran fell into step behind me. We moved slow and carefully as there was no telling what we'd be poking our head into.

We moved through a thick cluster of pine trees, the scent pleasant on my nose. Though we moved slow, our steps were audible due to dried pine needles. When finally, we made it through the trees and brush, I was startled by what I saw.

A clearing roughly fifty feet wide had been created by several large pines cracked at the base of their trunks. And on one of the wood spiked trunks was a dead and bloody body of a man. But that didn't hold my attention for more than a moment as there was much to see. There was another four people, at least I thought they were people, one was clearly a beastkin bear, standing eight feet tall and three fourths as thick.

Squared off against them was a massive snake with black scales and a narrow face. When I tried to inspect it, I got nothing, not even a name.

"That's a Chaos Wurm!" Fred said, falling to his ass in surprise.

It made sense, I decided, the scales were draconian, a sure sign of a Chaos creature, and the face looked similar to a few depictions I'd seen in a book. The party of four weren't doing so great, as we watched the Chaos Wurm shot forward and snatched a caster from their ranks, leaving half his body behind as it gulped down the rest.

"What do we do?" Fran asked, she seemed even less eager to run out and help than her brother had been.

"I have to try and help," I said, the words as hollow as they felt. What would I be able to do? I had to think, what could I do to help?

The air around the wurm shimmered and it reared its head back. I thought for sure it was about to snatch up another one of their members, the party must have thought the same because they rolled or dropped down to avoid the strike. However, it didn't come, or at least not in the way they expected. Fire shot forth from the wurm's maw and fully engulfed another of the fighters, leaving two members left.

The large beastkin let rip a roar so powerful that I got shivers, even from this distance. Still rooted in place I watched his body shift, and he became a giant bear. His paws slashed forward and managed to knock free several scales. He might have a chance after all, if only we could keep it occupied.

"This is what we're going to do," I said, pulling the staff free and handing it to Fran. "Spread out wide and one after another we will hit it with our ranged spells. If we can even distract it a little, we might give them a chance to either kill it or escape with their lives. Move, let's go!"

And so we did, spreading out as fast as we could. We stayed on the more elevated area, the clearing where they fought was in a slight angle and downhill from where we'd arrived. It took only half a minute to get into place, but in that time, the remaining two hadn't been idle. A thin framed figure, an elf I thought, waved its hands wildly as if casting some complex spell. Then as I watched in awe a giant bird appeared slashing out at the large Wurm.

I couldn't see any damage being done, but it was distracting it well enough to buy the giant bear time to deliver several powerful strikes, one of which opened a large gash just below the head. I picked that moment to cast my firebolt. It flew through the air and sizzled against the open wound.

The Wurm reared back, and its form shimmered, another fire attack. I needed my attack to do more! The fire was directed at the large bird and the oddest thing happened when the fire struck it. It was like an image drawn in sand being blown away by the fierce attack. The slim elf appeared below the bird where he'd been before, his shoulders sagging. I realized what had been happening then, he'd summoned some kind of illusion.

He was at it again, his arms twirling and his voice rising

above the din of battle into a powerful chant. Then a moment later chains surrounded the Wurm, shooting up and out of the dirt. Surprisingly enough these didn't appear to be illusions or if they were, the Wurm didn't know, because it struggled and couldn't free itself.

A Shadow bolt and another Firebolt shot at the Wurm from opposite directions, causing the Wurm some visible pain. The bear hadn't stopped its attack either, slashing and biting the Chaos monster.

My spell came off cooldown just as the chains shattered and the elf fell backwards, passing out. The Wurm reared back and was surely going to deliver a deadly strike on the fallen elf. I began casting Firebolt, but I needed something more! I felt the strands of mana feeding the spell and focused on the feelings I'd had when I was just controlling my *Spark*, then forced more mana into the spell. Not in the way the spell required, but just jamming more into it.

I thought the spell failed at first, but instead, my arms ignited in flame and I screamed in pain. Holding my hands out I finished the spell. About a dozen Firebolts, three times their normal size, shot off directly at the Chaos Wurm. Each one hit with ear deafening booms, jostling the Wurm backwards and away from the elf.

I didn't see what happened next as I hit the ground rolling and screaming in pain. My arms were burning but something inside had been set aflame as well. I felt the push on my mind as notifications from the system were fed into my mind, but I ignored it, moving frantically to put out the flames. A haze of black smoke obscured my vision and for several long moments all I could think was I'd killed myself. It wasn't a pleasant few seconds, but it was only a few seconds.

After which my arms, while burnt badly, weren't still

aflame and I could see what had happened once more. I looked up, too tired suddenly to move much, and saw that the Chaos Wurm was missing its head. They'd done it.

I didn't lose consciousness, but I did lay there on the ground refusing to get up as each movement just caused me more pain. Burns were no joke and I'd just been retaught that lesson.

"Drink," a gruff deep voice said. A gray and black-haired hand tilted a potion into my mouth, and I accepted it sucking down the contents. Immediately I felt relief, like a cool blanket covering me, spreading over my entire form. Looking up I saw the beastkin standing over me, Fran and Fred on either side of him looking down at me.

"You saved Grugssir and he save you," the bearkin whose name I assumed must be Grugssir said. "We even, same same now. But you must tell Grug name of spell used to topple foe, it is good spell but hurts to use."

"Firebolt," I said, coughing to clear my throat. It was sore and my phlegm was black from the smoke I'd breathed in.

"That was your Firebolt spell?" Fred asked, his voice almost squeaking in surprise. "How'd you make it do that? That is not the way a Firebolt spell behaves."

I just shook my head, pulling myself up straight. The pain was barely there already, and I wondered what potency that health potion was that Grug had given me. I also felt even more tired than I had been after getting burnt. Healing had that effect sometimes, I knew. When your body is forced to heal great amounts of damage you feel a compounded effect equal to the damage healed. Whatever I'd healed it was way more than just the burns, I'd messed up something inside of me.

It wasn't time to check my system notifications yet, but I made a note to check them out the first chance I got.

Grug was one of three survivors, the burnt one had somehow survived being turned into a piece of charcoal. We agreed to help them harvest the scales and any other reagent items from the Wurm, each of us getting an equal share. After which we started a large bondfire and burnt the Chaos Wurm. The elf, who introduced himself as Adathin Valamin, said it was necessary unless we wanted to attract more such monsters.

I sat on a fallen log next to the slowly recovering woman. I didn't know what race she was and thought it would be too rude to ask while half her skin was still healing from terrible burns. The healed skin had a light ruby color to it, but it was smooth like human or elf skin. She had two horns on her forehead that swept back into her shoulder length red hair. And then there was her tail, as long as her legs but tapered to a thin point. It swished back and forth behind her.

"My name is Bethgrok, but please just call me Beth," Beth said, catching me staring at her. "I'll be good to go in another half hour or so." She had a very pleasantly warm voice.

"How did you survive that?" I asked, still dumbfounded at her recovering.

"I'm Delvish, we have an insanely high resistance to fire, despite how badly charred I became," Beth said, flicking a piece of black char from her arm. "I've never encountered flame hot enough to char my skin, our people will sometimes walk through fire as a way to cleanse ourselves, but that thing's fire was hot enough that it turned some of the forest ground to glass."

"That's insane," I said, shaking my head. "I managed to burn myself up a good bit without the help of a Chaos beast."

"Chaos beast?" Beth said, tasting the word with her strange accent. "My people have long lived within the borders of the elven nations, and I've only heard rumors of such creatures. Is it true what they say?"

"Probably, but what exactly do you mean?" I asked, the idea that someone had only heard of Chaos beasts and not had their entire childhood filled with stories and lore on them over campfires seemed strange to me.

"That they operate outside the rules of Order?" Beth asked, picking another small piece of char off her red skin.

"Well yeah," I said. "Order and Chaos. One side fights against the other."

"But where do they come from?" Beth asked, leaning forward and putting her head just a foot from mine. "I hear the mountains to the East hold entire peoples born of Chaos and disorder."

All of what she was saying rang true with the lore and facts I'd been told, but she made it sound so mysterious and mystical with her accent, that it drew me in.

"Wherever they are from," I said, leaning a few inches away from her. She smelt heavily of burnt flesh and I'd had enough of that smell to last me a while. "I hope they go back there. I mean what even brings them to this side?"

"Grugssir knows lands to the east. Not mysterious as companion Beth makes seem. Fertile lands, weak peoples, land ripe for taking," Grug's voice trailed off at the end as if speaking to himself.

"I've heard of the wild magics they wield in the east," Adathin chimed in, sitting across from me. Just as he sat, his hands swirled and twisted sand like substance blowing through his fingers.

A silhouetted figure stood beside a great black dragon. The sand shifted and showed a scene of the figure summoning a great ball of red and black energy. It launched its attack, and it was like the ball was coming for me, I flinched back just as the entire thing faded to nothing.

"Adathin enjoys tricks," Grug said, shaking his head as he laughed boisterously.

"They are minor illusions to give form to the thoughts and rumors I've heard," Adathin said. He grabbed a stick and poked the fire, causing sparks to spring up. As they did, he waved his hand, catching them and giving them form.

He depicted a large powerful figure standing tall with smaller forms gathered all around. "The Ordu were masters of Power, and it is because of them that we haven't all fallen under the weight of the Chaos." Adathin's voice took on a song like quality as he spoke. "Order and Chaos, two forces meant to be in opposition for all time. But what happens when one gains an upper hand over the other? Who wins when the balance is disrupted?"

He looked to me as he asked his final questions, but I had no answer to give him. So I shook my head and let the images he created play across my imagination.

Order and Chaos. Two forces that ruled our world and perhaps many more unknown lands. My mind yearned to have the answers to the mysteries I'd encountered. So I made an oath to myself, a secret oath, but an oath nonetheless. I would search out the mysteries of the world, find out what was behind the Chaos and the Ordu. But most important of all, I would grow stronger so that nothing could stand in my way of discovering the mysteries of this world and perhaps many beyond it.

They were heavy oaths to bind myself to, but I knew what direction to travel now, I wouldn't just grow stronger, I'd make myself a being of such great power so that no mystery could hide itself from me. The first mystery that needed solving was what the hell I'd done during that battle against the Chaos wurm. So I took a look at my system messages, looking for answers.

Unknown ability activated...processing...ability quantified.

New Ability Learned, Aura Manipulation. This is not an ability normally quantified, please visit a Prime Mana Shrine for readjustment.

Aura Manipulation, You can manipulate your aura to attack, defend, and increase the amount of Mana that can be infused into spell forms. (System does not advise use of this ability until an Arbiter can make readjustments.)

That was odd. I read it all again to make sure I was understanding it correctly and sure enough it was as plain as day, I'd somehow learned an ability outside of a Mana Shrine. As far as I knew, that was not supposed to be possible. Surrounded by relative strangers and Fred and Fran, I didn't feel comfortable sharing my discovery, so I spent the next bit just staring into the fire while everyone else talked.

CHAPTER 44
DIRE BEAR

I t wasn't long before everyone felt rested and ready to travel. Saying goodbye to Grug, Beth, and Adathin and promising to run a dungeon together later—they were all around level 20, but that didn't seem to bother them—we traveled west looking for a Dire Bear.

"Pretty strong group," Fran said. We slowed our pace while we searched for any signs of Dire Bears. "It's a shame they lost two of their party members to kill that Wurm. It gave off a fair bit of essence though. Did they explain why no one searched for a core?"

"Even if it had one it would be best to let it burn," I said, my eyes scanning the tree line for any moving shapes. "Lord Variyn made it seem like Chaos monsters could infect normal monsters and maybe even people. What if the monster cores acted the same? I wouldn't want to be responsible for what happens if it corrupted an enchantment or something."

"What of the essence it released?" Fred asked, his robes flapped in the wind as we jogged. "Could it be that we are infected by contact?"

"I don't feel infected," I said. "And this is the second Chaos monster I've been close to when it died.

"Don't worry Fred," Fran said, a sly smile creeping across her face. "I'll be sure to beat any corruption out of you if you get infected."

Fred's expression was one of annoyed fear and I decided that Fran had probably taken the opportunity to whoop her brother in the past.

"Not amusing," Fred said, curtly.

An ear-splitting roar echoed through the trees, and I fell grasping for my ears. Rolling as I hit the ground, I saw that Fran and Fred had hit the dirt too. Whatever that was had given me 30 points of damage and my ears tingled. The world around me had gone silent and I feared I might have lost my ability to hear. Stumbling as I rushed to make it back to my feet, I turned to Fran.

"I don't think I can hear!" I yelled. I heard the barest whisper of my words, but Fran and Fred didn't. Fran looked at me, nodding her head and pointing at her ears. They had blood dripping down the side of her face, and she was blinking rapidly.

Looking around the now still forest I saw in the distance towards the base of the mountain, dust and dirt being kicked up. I caught Fred and Fran's attention, signaling them to follow me as I headed in that direction. Whatever damage had been done to my ears healed enough that I began to hear the sounds of battle, but not the kind from humanoids fighting, no this sounded as if great beasts tore and ripped at each other.

Animalistic cries of pain and anger filled my healing ears. Fran and Fred still seemed deafened, as they showed no sign of the fear that filled my chest as we approached.

"What do I hear ahead, it sounds like wet cats going at it,"

Fran said, she was practically yelling, and I swiftly turned, motioning that she should remain silent.

There was no telling what had caused the damage to our ears, but I was beginning to guess at what laid ahead. Fran had described it as wet cats fighting, but I had heard the roar of an angry bear before and this sounded similar but amplified several fold.

I thought of the time my father and I had been hunting, a large scarred brown bear charged into our camp. My father hadn't even bothered to use a spell or draw his sword, instead meeting the beast claw against fist. It only took seconds for the bear to realize it was outmatched and it fled. When I'd asked my father why he hadn't killed it, I could still hear his words after all this time.

"Not all that attacks me deserves to die."

He didn't seem concerned at all that it had made off with some of the rabbit meat that had been cooking over the fire, just doing enough to scare it away. My father was like that, wise beyond his years and I couldn't help but think that he wouldn't think it wise what I was doing now. I had to see what was happening and maybe figure out what monster was strong enough to deafen us from nearly a mile away.

My ears were close to functioning normally again, but while they healed, I felt like my nose was working overdrive. Dozens of scents filtered through as we walked. The earthy smell of the forest floor, mixed with the sharp scents of different herbs. And distantly I could have sworn I smelt blood and something else that was familiar. It came to me, what the other scent was, as soon as we came to the edge of the tree line and saw what awaited us.

Muffled gasps sounded behind me, but Fred and Fran kept their surprise in check enough not to give away our location.

The tree line ended some hundred feet from a large cave opening and just inside of it is where the battle raged. We were in Dire Bear territory alright.

Elite Dire Bear, Level 61

Adult Dire Bear, Level 39

Dire Bear, Level 25

Dire Bear, Level 22

Dire Bear Cub, Level 10

Five bears of varying size were fighting a thin black dragon.

My attempts to inspect the dragon, who was only about the size of the 'Dire Bear' and dwarfed by the size of the Adult and Elite Dire Bear, each of which were nearly the size of a small cottage, failed to register anything. But based off the wounds and distressed look of the Elite Dire Bear, things weren't going well for them.

The bears were black, with touches of white here and there, except for the Elite. The Elite had streaks of black on a mostly silver fur. What was more, it had an extra row of sharp teeth in its mouth and while I watched, it tried to take a bite from the black dragon, but it hit nothing but air. One moment the dragon was right where it would have been bitten into two and the next, in a puff of black smoke, it was several feet away.

In response to the attack the dragon slashed out and left a red line on the Elite Dire Bear's face. It roared and my ears tingled. It wasn't the same thing that had damaged my ears, but it wasn't pleasant to hear either. This wasn't the kind of group we needed to encounter on our search to take down a Dire Bear, even the Baby Dire Bear would likely have been a challenge for us if these bears were any indication.

The battle continued while we watched, all five of the Bears working together failed to do much more than superficial damage to the dragon. I looked at Fred and Fran, but both had gazes locked on the fight. Perhaps the dragon would kill the Dire Bears and leave a heart for us to harvest? Because there was no way in all the hells that we stood even a passing chance against these foes.

Between the sound of battle, I figured we were okay to talk if we whispered.

"I think we are close enough to get essence from any kills, do you think it's worth the risk of sticking around?" I asked in a hushed whisper.

Fran looked at me wide-eyed, any previous humor long fled from her face. "Are you insane? We should turn around and run, putting as much distance between us as we can."

"My sister is right," Fred said, not taking his eyes from the battle. "Monsters of this level have ways of sensing prey, there is no telling how safe we'd been even this far off."

"But we need a Dire Bear heart for Fran," I said, my mind protesting against staying as well, but I wanted that essence. A mighty roar rang out and a rush of essence filled me, making me jerk in surprise.

Looking back to the battle I saw what had caused it. The Adult Dire Bear had gone down, the long sharp claws of the dragon, separating the head from its body. The roar was from the Elite, it took on a golden glow and struck out so swiftly that it scored a bloody strike on the dragon. A sound like fingernails on a chalkboard made me cover my ears.

This battle was far from over and it looked like the Elite had more tricks up its sleeve. Its right claw rose up in the air and its nails lengthened into six-foot spear like edges. In that same moment, as the dragon went in to try and bite at the Elite, it slashed at the neck. The same nails on a chalkboard sound rang out, but the dragon slammed into the ground in a heap a moment later. The Elite wasted no time, closing its mighty maw around the dragon's neck.

No essence followed but it was clear what direction the battle was taking.

"We need to leave and fast," I said, crawling backwards. "Fran, lead us to another location that has Dire Bears, this one is not going to work for us."

Without a word we crawled backward, eventually making it to our feet and turning to run. It took another six hours of full speed traveling in a southwestern direction before we entered a location that Fran assured us was also marked as a place she could hunt Dire Bears.

We rested, as the sun was beginning to set, and we needed to replenish our stamina after the hard nonstop run we'd just done.

Still out of breath, but not nearly as wheezy as the pair of them, I spoke. "Chaos monsters are getting out of hand. Did you see the blow that dragon took, and it still wasn't dead!"

"That...wasn't...a...dragon...," Fred said, panting out each word while he struggled to get his breath back. It was amazing what our new bodies could do, but they'd likely pushed themselves too hard and would need another hour at least to get back what they'd lost.

I didn't respond, instead waiting for Fred to catch his breath and elaborate. After a solid five minutes of waiting, he cleared his throat and began.

"It only had two legs and a pair of wings," Fred said as if that explained it, continuing when I gave him a deadpan stare. "Wyverns have two legs and a pair of wings, while Dragons have four legs and a pair of wings. From what I've studied dragons are much larger and muscled than the wyvern."

"A Wyvern," I said, tasting the word. I'd heard it before, but my area of study hadn't been Chaos monsters specifically, so in all I knew very little compared to anyone that had spent any amount of time studying them directly.

"I got just over seven thousand essence from that Adult Dire Bear dying," Fran said, her gaze was distant as she looked over her notifications.

If she got that much, how much had I got? I checked and my jaw dropped when I saw the amount. I'd received 21,060 essence from that thing dying. That was more than when the Wurm had been killed, which makes sense because that Wurm was nowhere as strong as even that Adult Dire Bear had been at level 39. My essence gains during this trek with Fred and Fran were getting a bit ridiculous, but I wasn't about to start complaining.

"I'm still ahead of you in essence, thanks to those dirty goblins and Caldor's quick thinking," Fred said, looking at Fran with his nose lifted in the air.

"For now," Fran said teasingly, reaching out and poking her brother in the side. He squirmed aside, not impressed.

"We are going to need to be extra careful," I said, seeing as everyone seemed to have at least caught their breath. "I always thought of bears as solitary creatures, but if we run into a pack like that we're done for."

"A circular search pattern, if started large enough, should provide the best coverage in our search," Fred said, standing and straightening his ruffled robes.

"I think we should just run here and there and see what we find," Fran said, smiling pointedly at Fred, who let out a frustrated huff of air in response to his sister. "What do you think?" Fran asked, and Fred nodded, also wanting to hear my input.

I didn't really want to get in the middle of their squabbles, but I wasn't about to waste time either.

"Circular pattern makes the most sense to me," I said, shrugging at Fran and her upset frowning response. "Time is ticking away and if we follow an ever-closing pattern we can always pick it up in the morning to continue our search."

"I doubt bears are going to sit and wait for you to find them," Fran said, still frowning in my direction.

"That's true," I said, returning her frown with a smile. "But if we come across any tracks, I can track one. I'm just not sure how well I can do that in the dark."

"Fine," Fran said, standing and folding her arms. "But I need another twenty minutes at least for my stamina. Let's eat something while we wait."

We enjoyed a meal of dried meat and kelt fruit, which had the bonus of speeding our stamina recovery. There were several times throughout our short journey when kelt fruit would have been wise to eat, but I'd failed to suggest it each time. I had half a dozen more and told myself I'd remember to use it next time we needed it.

Our circular pattern of searching yielded no results that night and so we awoke early the next morning, eager to continue our search. It only took an hour before I lucked upon some fresh tracks, and another to find the Dire Bear it belonged to.

Dire Bear, Level 12, Health 652/944

It was nursing an injured leg, part of why it had been so easy to track. We were careful to approach it downwind and as such remained undetected in the brush. No words needed to pass between us as we readied to attack, we discussed last night the best way to take one down and even with an injured leg it was going to be a difficult kill.

I ran out first, getting its attention with a Firebolt spell right into its injured leg. It let out a mighty roar and seemed to forget the pain of its leg as it lurched at me, moving swiftly. Fred let loose his attack when it was roughly six feet away, hitting it right in the side of the head. The blow must have stunned it, because it lost its footing and fell, its body sliding toward me.

Fran appeared a second later striking downward at the same time I arrived using my Power Strike skill. The Dire Bear was injured but far from out of the fight. My blow left a nasty gash on its forehead, but something I didn't realize was that bear skulls were thick and not the best place to aim for when going for a killing blow. Fran's attack had a bit more luck, she struck the injured leg, rendering it nearly useless.

The bear swiped out, falling as much as standing. It didn't seem able to put any weight on the leg and stood its ground, as best it was able, waiting for us to get close enough to strike.

The rest of the fight was uneventful, and I even felt a bit sorry for the monster of a bear. Fran focused on striking from behind, Fred and I circling it while we cast Firebolt as it came off cooldown. Finally with a weak roar the Dire Bear fell and moved no more.

"Bear with me," Fran said, her usual smile back. "But I feel a bit bad for this guy. He couldn't stand up to us with that broken leg."

Fred face palmed and I let out an exaggerated sigh.

"Jokes aside," I started to say, and Fran interrupted me.

"I never agreed to that!" She exclaimed, poking the bear with the tip of her sword.

I continued on, trying to finish my thought before I lost it. "Anyways, I was trying to say that I feel bad too, but we should hurry and get what we can from it before whatever broke its leg decides to come for a visit."

"Let's just hope it has a heart," Fran said, her grin widening. "I mean what are the chances we found the only Dire Bear without a heart."

"That logic doesn't track, sis," Fred said, looking perplexed.

I didn't add what I was thinking, instead let them poke fun at each other like they always did while Fran went to work to harvest the heart. The heart was where it should be and completely intact. What wasn't intact was the monster core, so we split it, letting it go to the next person in line. The dust alone from some of the higher leveled mobs we'd gotten would ensure we'd be set for supplies going into our first dungeon runs.

Fran went to work harvesting reagents, like teeth and claws, while I worked on field dressing the giant bear. It wasn't a perfect process, but Fran assured me that the meat from a Dire Bear was worth the effort, saying if prepared correctly it even had the ability to buff certain attributes. She couldn't say exactly how the preparation worked or what attributes it would buff, but I didn't care as it would be worth keeping either way.

I had several spots still open inside my Dimensional box so after draining it of its blood and removing its thick hide I did something I thought was rather clever. I put the entire rest of the Dire Bear's carcass into my storage, and it only took up one slot. Unfortunately, I'd already done the messy job of taking its pelt off so that took another spot. If my understanding of how dimensional storage worked was correct, then both items would stay preserved until I could either sell them or get them to someone who could properly prepare them for me.

I gave Fred and Fran a few gold coins each for their portion and a promise to pay more when I figured out the worth of it.

They tried to refuse, saying that I could just keep the meat, but I was insistent.

After the messy work of field dressing a bear was complete, I used my map to find a stream where I could wash myself.

With Fran's help I got my armor off; it was self-cleaning but the clothing beneath it definitely wasn't. We were far enough away from where the wyvern had attacked that we no longer heard the roars of battle, but I doubted it had continued for this long regardless. There was nothing but the still gentle hum of life all around the stream.

Birds chirped, other smaller vermin could be heard rustling around in the bushes, it wasn't very different from home, and I soaked in the sense of it all. My breath came in quick rasps as I entered the chill water, but I kept going until I adjusted to it. It was cold but felt so refreshing. Scrubbing at my shirt I got loose the grime and blood, before taking the shirt off completely, throwing it to the edge of the water on a low hanging tree branch.

Next came the pants, Fran made a show of turning away, both her and Fred sat with their feet in the water. They'd insisted they didn't need a bath yet and I didn't want to upset them by telling them about my opinion on the matter. It wasn't that they were overly smelly, but there was a certain musk that came with exertion and long hours of running. Fred had a bottle of something and splashed it on his neck.

"What's that?" I asked. Before he could answer I put my head under the water to clean my hair and came back up, the cold bringing a temporary chatter to my teeth.

Fred looked at me with a flat stare before finally answering as I ran my hands through my hair to squeeze the water free.

"Scented cleansing water," Fred said. "It's one of my

father's creations. He took Alchemy for his profession and creates many wonderful tonics, potions, and cleansers."

Fran cut in to add her two bits. "It's why we don't need to freeze our asses off in the water with you. I'd have offered you some, but we only have so much until we visit our parents."

I'd have to give them a good sniff after I got out, because that almost sounded too good to be true. The water was chilly but there was a therapeutic feeling to it all that I wouldn't want to trade for a few spritz of a magical cleaning potion.

Looking through my map I saw that there was only a single place where I could find what I needed, and it was only about two or three hours away. Owl Bear hearts would be equally as tricky to get as the Dire Bear heart had been and we couldn't bet on finding a wounded Owl Bear. The next closest area—in the elven coast where I'd need to get a Sea Serpent's horn—was two or three days away on foot, but maybe only a day or two on horseback. Enough time if I'd traveled alone to get my class quest item, but Fred and Fran had been invaluable, and I was glad that I'd stuck with them.

"It's early enough that we should be able to get your Owl Bear heart today and make it back to the Prime Mana Shrine either really late tonight, or early the next day. How many days has it been so far?" Fran asked, splashing her feet in the water and leaning back comfortably.

"Today is day four, so after today we have three whole days before the deadline runs up," I said cheerfully. My mood was light and happy. We'd just about finished, and I'd have time to spare. I was going to insist we travel through the night and get back so I could sleep on a comfortable soft bed. It wasn't so bad sleeping out here under the stars, and my body was much sturdier than any other time I'd done it before, but there was a certain comfort that came with having four walls around you to keep you safe. I decided I liked both, just not all the time for either.

"I'm going to use all my collected broken monster core dust to buy reagents and learn enough spells to be useful," Fred said, his voice a bit more deadpan than usual.

Before I could tell him that he'd been plenty useful Fran cut in laughing as she spoke.

"Can't wait to hear all about your new spells," she said, turning to look at him. "Caldor and I are getting tired of carrying your lazy butt through so many difficult fights when all you can offer is vital intel."

Fred was about to quip back at his sister, I could see it on his face, but he paused hearing what she'd actually said. "Thank you, sis. I endeavor to provide quality intelligence when I can."

I did the wise thing and said nothing. They were a strange pair, Fran teased Fred every chance she got, but I knew they cared for each other. Fred was very literal and often missed his sister's sarcasm, while Fran just seemed to want to have a good time and make almost everything into some kind of joke. I liked them both and hoped that we'd find a chance to dungeon dive in the future.

I finished my bath, switched into a fresh pair of clothes and as a team we sprinted toward the horizon to defeat our final class challenge.

CHAPTER 45
OWL BEARS

It didn't take long to reach the area designated by the quest. The trees here had a blue tint to the bark and even in the bright noonday sun, mushrooms gave off a faint glow, growing beneath the shade of the trees. The leaves that littered the ground were a faded blueberry color, whereas the ones on the trees were vibrant deep purple.

There was a sense of mana permeating much of the area as we traveled deeper into the woods. Even the chirping of birds had an almost ethereal echo to them, while there was a distinct lack of critters rustling through the bushes. A warm orange grass grew over most of the ground, tall stalks that reached nearly my waist. With the gentle flow of the mushrooms and the tall orange grass stocks, it was like wading through a shadowy fire.

"Do we want to do the circle pattern again?" I asked, my eyes taking in the majesty of the area.

"I vote we roam and see what we find," Fran said. "We have the time to kill. We might as well enjoy this place." Her eyes followed a bunny that appeared, fleeing for its burrow no doubt. It was an interesting type that I hadn't encountered before and wasn't able to get an inspect off before it was out of view.

The bunny had a horn on its head with a golden pattern snaking through the white fur. I could have sworn that as it shot forward it left behind a trail of tinkling golden sparkles.

"This particular wooded area isn't very large, either method should be effective," Fred said, surprising me. I'd grown so used to their bickering and challenging that I was sure they'd disagree on the way forward.

"Very well," I said, clasping my hands. "Let's just go this way." I pointed in the direction the bunny had gone and we started our trek. What we found made my heart sink and my anger rise.

It took less than an hour and we came upon a large cave opening littered with corpses. It looked like there had been at least a dozen owl bears here, but by the stink of them, they'd been killed at least a day ago, probably more.

The cave where we discovered them had a faint glowing blue rock, almost like a dungeon, and when we went inside we found what must have been the 'Queen' version of the owl bear, bloated and several times bigger than the rest. It had been killed as well and it only took minutes for me to confirm that they'd been stripped of all useful reagents, including their hearts.

"Who would do this?" I asked, my own suspicions beginning to form.

"Don't lose your head over it," Fran said, kicking at a headless owl bear. She gave me a weak smile and mouthed 'sorry'.

"We can keep searching. The likelihood that these were the only owl bears in the area is rather low," Fred said, he was crouched over one of the corpses slowly shaking his head.

I checked my map; we were in the direct center of the area highlighted by the map and something told me that we would find no living owl bears here. Was this deliberate? How could it be, who knew that I needed Owl Bear hearts? Shit.

"Zander did this," I said, my voice barely rising above a whisper. "I don't know how but he was the only one that knew. He must hate me more than I thought. How in the hells am I going to get another class item in time?"

"The white-haired guy?" Fran said, then suddenly her eyes went wide. "Is that why he was asking all those questions, oh gods Caldor it's our fault. Let's keep searching and I bet we find an owl bear like Fred said."

"Fine," I said, my teeth clenching as I spoke. I wasn't mad at them, but I was furious. If this stopped me from becoming an Arcane Knight, then I would end Zander. I didn't know how I'd do it or if I could, but I'd find a way.

We spent the rest of the day and several hours into the night before admitting defeat. Day four was over and I only had three days until I failed my class quest. If that happened, I'd be stripped of my power and if I understood the Arbiter's insinuations correctly, I'd likely die from the experience.

My emotions were a wildfire inside of me and I'd snapped at both Fred and Fran several times during our search. I hated how I was acting but it was so damn hard to accept what was happening. I'd spent all this time helping them get their items, even getting a stupid spell reagent for Fred and now I'm just royally screwed. I made up my mind, pushing my anger and pain aside as best I could.

"I'm returning to the city and getting my horse," I said, my words felt hollow, but I managed to not inject any of the pain or anger I was feeling into them. "I'll run all night and if I'm lucky I can catch a barge downstream into elven territory and be there by midday tomorrow. With a bit of extra luck, I'll find a sea serpent, kill it, take its horn, and be back in time. It's going to be close, and I can't have anything slowing me down."

There were a few long seconds of silence while Fred and Fran exchanged glances.

"We can't leave you to do it by yourself," Fran said, stepping up to me and putting her hands on my shoulders while staring into my eyes. "You've helped us do the impossible, without you we wouldn't have survived this, you can't ask us to stand aside now."

"He's right," Fred said, nudging a stone free from the dirt with his foot and keeping his head bowed. "We don't have the stamina he does or will have when he levels up at the Prime Mana Shrine. You do plan on leveling again don't you?"

I nodded that I did.

"See, sis," Fred said. "Even if we leveled to 5, we won't be able to go as long or hard as he can. We owe you a great debt."

"And we will pay it back someday," Fran said, finishing her brother's thought. "We won't be able to keep up even now, so run like the wind, but promise me you won't fail. You have to succeed." Fran became uncharacteristically solemn in her speech, and I thought I saw a tear forming in her eyes, but she averted her face before I could be sure.

"I promise," I said, my anger shifting into determination. My sadness becoming hope.

"If we see that Zander fellow again," Fred said, he held up his hand and shot out a Firebolt into the ground with a loud thump. "We will have words."

I thanked them both, giving them as many of their items as they could carry and promising to return any other in my dimensional storage when I got back. Then I was off, running at a speed and pace that they wouldn't have been able to match.

When my stamina grew low, I slowed and ate kelt fruit, pushing my body to its very limits.

Along my path I encountered no monsters, but I did happen upon a lesser mana shrine and used it to pour essence into improving myself. I made the hard decision to go with only 3 additional attributes per level, as doing the 5 raised the cost way beyond what seemed reasonable. But together I was able to increase my attributes by 3 plus the 3 I got from leveling. It cost me a total of 83,138 essence to raise my Endurance, Strength, Constitution, and Intellect and get to level 9.

I also had the reagents now to pick up Blade Ward and Stamina Surge, which I did. There were more spells available now but at first glance nothing looked exceptionally powerful, and I'd wasted enough time, so I finished up and pushed my even more enhanced body forward to the capital city of Variyn.

My new skill, Stamina Surge, was a life saver, helping me push my body past what I'd normally be able to do without rest. The sun rose over the horizon just as I approached the city, my body screaming at me to stop, but I refused to submit, activating Stamina Surge just as it went off cooldown. A rush of energy infused me, and I felt level-headed once more.

It was the start of day five and I had no time to waste. While jogging through the streets to pick up my horse Jill, I stopped into an alchemy shop and traded a few gold and some reagents for two more health potions, figuring I'd need them before my time was up. A part of me wanted to track down Alayna and enlist her service on the last leg of my quest, but I wasn't sure she'd be able to give me the one thing I desperately needed, time.

I got Jill without issue and soon we were headed on the western road, headed for the border into House Blalor and the town of Strethfore. It was a larger town that I hoped had a boat or barge I could take downstream to the elven city of Calenrah. My plan was simple, get to the elven city by nightfall and search throughout the night for a sea serpent to kill. Then immediately get back on Jill and ride her to her limits to arrive at the Prime Mana Shrine in time.

If I'm able to gain passage on a river boat of some kind it would shorten my trip by a day's travel at least, but getting back in time would be a challenge even on a swift horse like Jill. The air whipped violently around me as Jill practically flew down the road, each of her steps defying my doubt in her that she'd be too slow. I'd thought I was able to ride her fast before, but my new stronger body let her cut loose like never before.

It wasn't long into the early afternoon when we made it to the town of Strethfore. Jill was slick with sweat and breathing fiercely, but she seemed alright. My rear end on the other hand wasn't feeling all too great and I was sure that I'd taken a measure of damage from my ride, despite my health still registering as full.

"Please see to my horse, she needs food and rest," I said to a stable boy outside a larger drinking establishment, handing him several silver as I did.

"Oh 'es sir I'll be right to task for you," the burly young lad said. He had a strange way of speaking but it hardly registered as I entered the establishment and went straight for the bar.

"Looking right ragged adventurer," a stout weather worn faced man said. "Welcome to da Leaky Barge, I'm Leak, what I do fer you?"

"I need a drink, a meal, and the fastest and soonest way downstream to the Calenrah," I said, my words coming rushed and terse.

Leak appeared confused for a moment, as if my quick words were hard for him to understand, but after a moment he nodded his head and called out to a person named Cray to bring a lunch special. Leak poured me a mug of sour ale and set it beside me.

"I dink you came to da right place for each of dose dings," Leak said while I struggled to catch his meaning past his odd accent. "I 'appen to be sending a barge of ore and wood as far as Gelerfold, dat be only a half day's ride from Calenrah. Dere be enough room fer you and a steed if you 'ave one."

"How much and how soon does it leave?" I asked, digging into a plate of dirty rice and fish. It was seasoned well and my new ability to enjoy every note of taste and flavor reverberated through me as I savored each bite. They served enough to fill my belly with a single plate, and I washed down the remnants with more sour ale.

"Five gold 'll do it and she already left," Leak said, using his finger to pick some food out of his teeth. "The first few hours be slow, but if you take this..." He took out a slip of paper and scribbled a note on it. "...and deliver it ter the barge master in Waifer h'll let'cha on. Hurry you'll catch 'er before she hits the swifts."

I paid the five gold without a thought and checked my map, finding the town Waifer down the river probably an hour or two walk, with Jill I'd make it there in no time at all. I took the note, giving it a quick glance.

'Passage fer one -Leak'

I was taking a risk trusting this guy I'd just met, but I didn't have time to argue so I found Jill, she was just finishing up a nice meal of simple apples and a small pile of untouched hay in front of her. The stable boy was brushing her down as I approached.

"Time to go," I said, as much to Jill as the stable boy.

"Watered and fed," the stable boy said, I tossed him

another silver coin for his trouble, and he quickly finished brushing her out before I mounted.

"Thank you," I said, leading Jill back to the road. "Just one more small leg and you get some rest." I leaned forward speaking into Jill's ears. She neighed in response and I knew she was ready to go. Deciding I'd better be careful, I gave her a slice of kelt fruit, my last piece, and hoped it worked well for horses as it did for adventurers.

The road west curved alongside the river, but not too close, as the banks were heavily wooded and at times difficult to see. Our travels, as I'd expected, were short though. We passed through two towns before reaching Waifer, an even smaller town than Creeshaw. The largest building in town was built right up to the river and a contraption connected it to the other side, where another building lay.

The river narrowed at this point, maybe only a hundred feet wide here, and I quickly realized as I approached that the contraption I was seeing was some kind of gate. It opened letting a medium sized sailboat through, large billowing white sails flapping in the wind. Behind the sailboat were at least a dozen other crafts of different designs, most wide and flat vessels with ores coming out the side like legs of a spider.

Skirting the side of the building I approached a well-dressed man yelling orders to several sweating and worn looking men. There was a set of docks running the length of the building on the edge of the river and he stood atop the docks.

"What business do you have here, adventurer?" The well-dressed man spoke, his voice was very proper and he sounded well educated.

"I've come to board a vessel. Leak from Strethfore sent me with this note to give to you," I said, leaning down to hand him the note. I didn't know if it was truly meant for him as I hadn't asked any questions, just taking it and running but he seemed like a good bet.

"We are not a boarding station, and that damned Leak knows it. His barge is third from the front. Pay me ten gold and I'll have it brought to the edge so you and your horse can board," the man said curtly. I was about to protest, but I was desperate and very much doubted I'd have another way down the river without Leak's barge.

So, biting back several foul comments and remarks I'd love to tell the man, I paid him ten gold and went where he motioned waiting to board the barge.

I wasn't well versed in what a barge was meant to be, and so I was surprised when a sixty-foot-long craft that was only about twenty-feet-wide moved closer to the docks. It wasn't the largest or the smallest craft, but it didn't look particularly speedy either.

The flat deck was barely a man's height above the water and two men stood on each side of the vessel with long oars that they used to push the barge closer to the docks so I could board. The ship was made of a black wood that had been polished to a shine in places, but weather or time had worn it down more than not. There was no sail and large barrels filled one side while the other was loaded down with long black barked trees, running just short the length of the vessel.

I honestly didn't see where Jill and I would be able to stand, much less sleep.

"Why yer pulling me 'ere," a weather skinned man with a large scar running down his left cheek called out as he neared. I was about to answer when the unnamed well-spoken man did so from just behind me. I jumped in my saddle, not realizing he was so close.

"Leak found you a passenger, throw your gangplank and be quick about it."

"That slimy son of a b-" The scar faced man's words were lost to the sound of yelling from behind me. I turned to see the well-spoken man had moved a ways down already and shouted at a set of workers loading goods to a smaller barge some several hundred feet away.

"Don't mind my cranky uncle," a feminine voice said from the direction of the barge. The sun had reached enough of an angle to mask the person in a silhouette as they neared the shore and a heavy gangplank slapped down in front of me. "Name's Sarah, come on up."

I squinted my eyes up into the silhouetted shape and finally details emerged. A curly red-haired woman, her hair up into a messy bun, stood atop the gangplank. I urged Jill forward and realized I'd mistaken her for a man from a distance, but I couldn't make that mistake now. She had dark weathered skin, the kind you got from endless hours under the sun, with a flurry of freckles covering all exposed skin.

Striking green eyes gave me a once over as I approached, and I felt my face redden slightly. Her blouse was loose and her bosom exposed more than I was used to from the fashion back home. It wasn't as if she was exposing herself, I just wasn't used to seeing so much skin. I realized I was staring and my face reddened even more.

"Man of many words," Sarah said, chuckling. "You're an adventurer by the looks of you. What grand adventure awaits you at the end of this ride I wonder?"

"My class quest," I said, letting the words out before I had a chance to think about whether or not I wanted to share anything about myself. She had kind eyes and a caring smile though, so I found it hard not to be forthwith. "I'm a Caldor, uh I mean Caldor, Caldor Miles."

"Well met 'a Caldor'," Sarah said teasingly. "There is a bit of space in the back of the barge next to my roost, let's get your sweet little lady settled in." She rubbed at Jill's ears affectionately and Jill leaned into it, letting her take her reins without protest.

Turns out there was a space big enough for me to stand, and even an area laid out with hay where Jill promptly laid down to rest.

"This vessel is named, Silwhar," Sarah announced. She was at her post again, using a large oar to push us back into line. "This will be her thirty-fourth time down the swifts. Do you know what to expect?"

"Honestly? I don't," I said, shrugging. "I'm from a town called Creeshaw in House Variyn. So I've little experience with all things House Blalor."

"The swifts are something special that the elves had a hand in some thousand years ago," Sarah said, her eyes straight forward and watchful as she helped direct the craft. "It takes less than a single day for a craft to make it down and into elven lands, but a week or more to get back. I won't spoil the fun of your first ride, but before we make it past the gate, you'll need to secure yourself and that lovely horse of yours. The first hour is pretty rough waters and you wouldn't be the first lost to the swifts if you fell overboard, adventurer or not."

I looked around for some way to attach myself to the ship and saw that each side of the ship had great ropes lashed to thick metal rings on the inner edge. Most were being used to tie down cargo, but there was one on each side that I figured could be used to tie myself and Jill. It was harder than it looked, and more than once I saw Sarah grinning down at us, before quickly averting her eyes back to the path ahead of us.

I managed to get us both attached in one manner or another just as Sarah called out.

"Entering the swifts in ten, nine, eight..." With each count her voice grew more excited and a bit wild. I looked up just as she reached three and saw that she'd pulled the tie on her hair, letting it blow behind her in the wind. "...One!"

The entire barge lurched and I was thrown back and into the raised area where Sarah stood. I saw that she was tied down in several places, her feet had been lifted from the deck, but she landed lightly without a care. Her gaze was locked forward and she had a grin so wide I thought it'd split her face.

She whooped in glee as we lurched again, the entire barge was traveling at an unnatural angle, and I heard the cords that held the cargo down creak in protest. The air whistled and I felt my lunch threaten to come up, but I managed to keep it down. I wanted to call out to Sarah and ask if this was normal, but I could barely hear her as she whooped and hollered, so I figured my voice wouldn't carry much further.

Despite my better sense, I left Jill's side to peer over the edge. Jill for her credit seemed content enough to slide about here and there without ever rising. I couldn't say how fast we were traveling, but the speed didn't seem safe.

Reaching the edge of the barge I looked ahead and to the side. Trees whizzed by faster than I'd ever seen, much faster than Jill and I traveled at full gallop. The water to the side and ahead was white and frothy, but I saw no stones or obstacles in our path. This insane mode of transportation continued for another hour and then we slowed to a normal speed.

"It'll be at least half an hour to get through this gate," Sarah said, releasing her tie-downs and jumping down beside me. "There are six gates in total, they slow down the trip more than anything, but it's necessary. Can't have crafts smashing into each other."

"That was insane," I said. Finding my voice and untying myself. Jill stood as well, likely wanting to stretch her legs a bit. "With that kind of speed, ships must be smashed to bits the moment they hit anything."

"Which is why we have gates," Sarah said, smiling.

"What if you were to hit the shore or a rock or something?" I asked, I must be missing something, she seemed way too comfortable about such a dangerous mode of transportation.

"I've never heard of such a thing happening," Sarah said, still seeming completely at ease. "I told you; the elves built these swifts long ago and whatever enchantments they used keep things working without issue. The old magic they say."

"Old magic?" I was interested now. "Are you talking about Ordu enchantments?" It was said that the Ordu enchanted the Mana Shrines so long ago that only one moon filled the sky at the time. Ordu enchantments were things of legend.

"Old river legends really, but how else do you explain it?" Sarah asked, shrugging as if the answer wasn't very important to her.

I however was very interested. "What else can you tell me about the old river legends?" I asked, stepping maybe a bit too close to her.

She winked at me and said, "Unless you mean to kiss me, I'd wager you should take a step or two back."

"Sorry," I said, smiling meekly back at her. She just laughed and rolled her eyes.

"There isn't much more to it honestly," Sarah said, leaning back on the five-foot stand at the end of the boat that she stood while guiding the craft. "Just that elves long ago enchanted the riverbed to speed up transport of water and goods from further east. Some sailors will fill your head with nonsense that it used to travel both ways, but that if it ever did it was before the time of any alive, so it's likely just a tall tale."

"Has anyone tried to look for enchantments or check for any markings?" I asked, going to the edge of the barge and looking down into the clear still water. I saw nothing, but this section wasn't likely considered part of the swifts. The water in the swifts was white and frothy so I was unlikely to get a peek while we moved either.

"How do you expect they would do that?" Sarah asked, poking me with a teasing finger.

I just shrugged, admittedly I hadn't the slightest, but I bet Warrick knew a way to detect magic. My mind itched at a thought, and it finally occurred to me. Perhaps if I focused, I could use one of my basic skills to find out more. Between Inspect, Mana Sense, and Perception, there had to be a way to glean some sense of things.

"How long have you been working on the barge?" I asked, changing the subject.

"You mean how old am I?" Sarah said, sticking out her breasts and fluttering her eyes. Her obvious teasing made me blush, I wasn't used to such open flirtations.

"I was genuinely curious," I said, keeping my gaze locked on her sparkling green eyes.

"I bet you were," Sarah said, her smile was infectious, and I found myself smiling back. "I've been with plenty of adventurers over the years and I wouldn't mind adding another. You have someplace to be at the end of this trip? I'll even let you buy me dinner first."

My eyes widened in surprise a bit. It was one thing to be mockingly flirtatious, but Sarah was straight up proposing sex and that was surprising. Life as an adventurer was turning out to be all sorts of exciting. I couldn't help but look her over once more and I felt blood rushing to places other than my face.

Sighing I said, "I sort of have a thing going with someone back home. I'm flattered though."

"Flattered, eh? Well, if you change your mind let me know, it can get cold down the swifts and I'm always up for a good warming up session," Sarah said, winking at me again before going back to her post on the raised platform and taking hold of her oar. She had a powerful grip to hold so tightly to that length of wood.

We entered back into the swifts not long after and I got ready to try and detect any form of magic that I could.

The rush and speed at which we traveled wasn't nearly as fast as the first leg of the journey. A part of me wished I'd thought to check what I could feel where the swifts moved the fastest, but alas I hadn't. Going to the edge I focused on the water and used my Inspect skill.

Nothing happened.

Trying again I really focused, trying to imagine runes or something beyond. But again, the skill didn't activate. I spent the next five minutes trying any and every way I could imagine, coming up with nothing. Finally, I decided to move into my next basic skill, Perception.

I hadn't really had a chance to use the skill as it seemed to operate in a passive manner, not something I could just trigger. Perception worked off of my senses, sounds, sight, hearing, etc so I closed my eyes and focused on what I could hear first.

Water rushed all around the barge, occasionally splashing up and wetting my face. I heard nothing out of the ordinary. I hadn't been around much rushing water in my time, but it sounded basically like that, a rush of fast water. With my eyes still closed I focused on what I could feel.

Cool wind brushed against my face and other than the occasional spray of water nothing new occurred to me. Smell turned up nothing, fresh clean water mixed with the scent of pine trees. I wasn't about to taste the barge, but I let my mouth hang open and catch a few sprays of water. I was surprised by a tinge of bitterness in the water, and I opened my eyes to be sure it was water I had caught in my mouth.

Sure enough, when another spray of white splashed upward the taste of it had the very faint tinge of bitter mixed in. What did that mean? I filed it away in my head and moved onto the next sense. Sight.

I started with the swift's edge. The edge of the banks where the water traveled in such a swift fashion was raised to cup the crafts within it, not a natural shore as I'd assumed. Other than that, sight provided me no new insights. Although, I made a note to check out an area of the swift while not on a barge or craft. Perhaps the runes would be inlay on the edge? But if that were the case surely more would be known about the swifts and how they are maintained.

Who was to say more wasn't known. I was taking the flirtatious Sarah's words as the last word on the subject. I would need to do some research of my own and see what I could turn up. There was one final sense that I could try that would be likely more informative than the rest, Mana Sense.

Mana Sense worked in a way opposite than what I wanted to do here though, as it said in the description it was meant to sense mana within others. But I couldn't see why it wouldn't apply to spell forms or enchantments. They carry mana and should be open to being sensed.

I held tight to the edge of the barge, checking that I was

tied firmly to the craft before starting. Reaching out I let the water sting me as it rushed by and I focused with all my mind. I'd sensed others before, so I knew how to start the process, but this felt different. As if I was trying to get the skill to do something it wasn't meant to do.

This went on for the entire duration of this section of the swifts, and only once did I think maybe just maybe I'd felt something. There truly was no telling what I'd felt the more I thought about it. It was just as likely that my lunch was protesting again, than it was I'd sensed any magical constructs or enchantments.

I knew what I was doing though. Not in the senses department but distracting myself during the journey. I was worried I wouldn't have enough time, but I couldn't let myself think that way, so I filled the time with experiments and mindless chatter with Sarah between swifts. Eventually the sky darkened, and the last swift ended.

"This town is called Gucklog or something, most humans just call it 'Endsville' because this is the end of the line for us. See that river bend there? It's a slow and gentle ride back after we unload, but that's the path we'll take. We'll be gone by afternoon tomorrow. You sure you don't want to get a drink, I promise not to jump your bones if you want, but it could be fun."

I smiled, truly flattered. "Thanks Sarah, and you were fine company, but I'm in a terrible hurry."

She smiled back at me and then surprised me by pulling me into a hug and whispering in my ear. "Be safe out there."

I muttered a surprised thanks and helped her throw the gangplank down, before grabbing Jill who was well rested and eager to move on.

I was feeling the lack of sleep, but so far, my body held

strong. Only half a day's travel away I'd find the seaside city of Calenrah. In the night of the fifth day I rode into the early morning of the sixth, leaving behind the curvy road and making a beeline for the city. The land was mostly flat and easy to pass, road or not. I'd later learn why the road curved and bent as it did, and I'd regret taking the shortcut.

CHAPTER 46
AMBUSH OFF THE ROAD

The familiar black barked oaks I was used to seeing in Variyn and now Blalor were replaced with white barked trees with vibrant red and orange leaves. They looked similar enough that I called them white oaks in my head, but the color of the leaves reminded me that the seasons were getting close to changing or perhaps the changes happened sooner closer to the coast, I didn't know.

The flat mostly open plains lands were firm enough that Jill was able to really push herself, only having to slow when the trees became too thick. Several times during our gallop I thought I'd saw figures moving in the trees, but when we neared them, it was always nothing or just some small woodlands animals. The half a day's travel must have been if you stayed on the road, because before too long I could smell the salty aroma of the coast.

I was checking my map and confirming that we were less than a half an hour at our current pace from the coast, so I didn't see the grouping of figures that blocked our pathway forward. Jill did however, and instead of slowing or turning aside, she attempted to leap over them just as I caught sight of tooth and claw.

She made it over, but during our leap I was thrown from the saddle, and she cried out in a way that put shivers down my spine.

"Jill! No, no, no," I said, groaning from the sudden loss of health points when I struck the ground. My stamina was at about half, as it drained even when riding atop Jill at a fast gallop. Activating Stamina Surge I felt my head even out and I pulled my sword free, ready to fight for our lives.

What I found both sickened me to the point of needing to look away and enraged me beyond measure. Jill hadn't made it over the figures in one piece. Her back left leg had been cut entirely free from her body and she was screaming as she bled to death twenty feet from where I stood. Before I could think what to do next, one of the silhouetted figures jumped atop her, growling and biting. Her screams ended and I knew she'd died because I felt a small trickle of essence release from her.

Oh Jill, what the fuck had I led you into? You poor elegant horse. My anger bubbled over, and I couldn't help myself, I let loose a terrible scream of pain and rage. Casting Firebolt, I fired at the thing that ate at Jill's corpse.

It yelped in pain and scurried back to the other six figures. As one, they howled and the clouds shifted, both moons filling the area with light. Six dog headed humanoid figures stood in tribal cloth, one even wearing some basic looking leather armor. I used Inspect on the armored one.

Gnoll Fighter, Level 9, Health 495/495

I didn't have time to inspect any others as the one I'd inspected produced a spear from his back and threw it at me. It was almost as if he moved in slow motion, I turned my shoulder enough so that the attack glanced off, barely marking up my armor. My Firebolt spell came off cooldown, so I sent him back my own attack, striking him in the face with a Firebolt.

In the next moment, all six began to circle me and the fight was on. I hadn't noticed how tall they were until they began to close in on me, their shortest warrior easily a foot taller than me, however, they looked lean almost starved with only the Fighter I'd inspected having any kind of bulk.

I lunged forward at the closest one, the smallest of the bunch, and activated Power Strike. My thrust caught him under the chin and the power behind my skill drove my blade into its brain, killing it instantly. However, its kin weren't idle, I felt two sets of claws wrack down my back, one of the claws finding an opening and searing my flesh with fresh pain.

I spun violently, blasting the attacking Gnoll directly in the face with my Firebolt spell and singeing my hand in the process. But it worked to multiply its effectiveness, the Gnoll falling backwards and yelping in pain. Without checking, I could feel where my health stood at 550 out of 630. Most of that damage had been from my fall but even with those two down my odds weren't great.

As if the universe wanted to affirm that idea in my head, I felt my back flash in unimaginable pain as something sharp cut through my armor. I felt my legs go heavy and I fell forward. For a scary few seconds, I laid still, unable to move my legs, but just as the Gnoll fighter approached, turning me over to deliver a killing blow to my face with his bloody spear, my legs tingled and I could move them again.

I didn't wait for the death blow, I could sense my health had plunged beneath half, but I had no time to pull a health potion out. I kicked out hard against the fighter's knees and was rewarded with a satisfying crack. Despite the injury I gave it, the Gnoll was strong, and stabbed downward as he fell to the side. His attack hit me in the arm, but my armor protected me.

I cast Firebolt at him as he fell, causing him to yelp more. The remaining three Gnolls jumped atop me, slashing at my face and head. My helmet protected the top of my head, but my cheeks were soon bleeding from multiple deep scratches. I managed to slash my sword down on one of the attacker's legs, despite the length of my sword, and it rolled off me to tend to its half cut off limb.

With just two seven-foot tall Gnolls on me and the rage of seeing my horse die, I had the upper hand. With my extra attributes each level, I was easily as strong as someone 5 to 7 levels higher, and it showed. With a grunt of frustration, I used one free arm to throw the two-hundred-pound Gnoll completely clear of me, while with my other hand I touched my dimensional storage box and called free the iron dagger we'd used against the Fae.

Letting my sword fall free I used one arm to hold the Gnoll atop me and the other to stab it repeatedly and viciously in the back until it went still. With blood flowing down my face, chest, and arms I stood and let out another scream of rage, looking for my next target. The one I'd thrown aside was up on its feet and pulling the fighter away from the battle, while the one that I'd cut its leg nearly clean off lay still, most likely bled out.

"Get back here!" I yelled, dashing forward. The world swam a bit as my own blood loss and injuries were nowhere near healed. The Gnoll stopped dragging the unconscious fighter and turned to run. "No, you don't." I muttered and threw my dagger at it.

Now I wasn't a knife thrower by any means, and I'd never practiced the skill, but what I did have was a strength attribute score of 49 because of my gear and that meant something. The dagger hit the Gnoll in the back, handle first, and it fell forward from the sudden force. I summoned a rusty iron sword as I ran, my fingers touching the side of the dimensional box. Before it made it to its feet, I activated Power Strike and firmly planted the iron sword deep into its brain.

The fight was over, but I was still angry. The half-conscious Gnoll fighter died with a swift strike along his neck, my rage pushing me to strike his dead corpse several more times before I went to Jill's side.

I knelt down next to Jill, my breath coming in ragged heaves. She'd been a good horse, a swift steed that never complained. I took several minutes while I calmed down to think of her. She'd deserved better and because of my foolishness to shave a few hours off our trip I'd gotten her killed. A small voice in my head tried to say that she was only a horse, and it didn't matter in the long run, but I squashed it, knowing better.

I'd worked with Breanna the donkey for long enough to know that beast of burden or not, they had feelings and deserved a proper sendoff. So, I cried over her corpse and sent out my thoughts to the beyond that if there be a life after this one, Jill should have a place there. Whether my words were heard or not, I will never know, but I did all that I could think of to give her a suitable farewell.

I had three spaces left in my dimensional storage left, so I did something I found a bit crude, but I didn't like the idea of leaving her out to rot. I pulled her into a slot in my storage, saddle and all.

Today I lost a companion and quite possibly my only hope of returning in time to become an Arcane Knight. I pictured my father as I had many times, in his full armor and sword at his waist, ready to take on any challenge. Oh, how I yearned to get the chance to do as he had done. I thought of Fred and Fran, both able to turn their class quests in already. I thought about how they'd spoken of my father's actions, or how they'd said I'd saved them from the Fae.

I had so much more to do before everything came to an end. And I decided right there that somehow, beyond hope and reason, I would get back in time. To do that though, I needed to find and kill a sea serpent. I left the Gnolls to lay where they'd fallen, none of their items were worth taking, not even the spear or shoddy armor. A part of me wondered if sentient beings had cores that could be collected as well, but I didn't have the time to explore their corpses looking for one.

My body ached and my health slowly ticked upward from 200. I had a debuff called 'Spinal Damage' but it ended a few minutes after the battle, taking with it the tingling I'd felt in my legs. It was amazing what the body could heal as an adventurer. I was certain that passing my thresholds had been the only thing that kept me from dying in that fight. Fred and Fran, having passed no thresholds, were still basically the same as they had been, with the bonus of increased regeneration and a bit more health, but I was something different.

That attack into my back should have left me a cripple, but instead it stunned me for several seconds. What were the next thresholds going to bring and what attribute value would pass me over my second threshold? There were plenty of questions I needed to answer, but I was just delaying a painful run back, so I quieted my mind and began to run.

CHAPTER 47
SEA SERPENT HUNTING

The morning sun was out in full force by the time I reached the walls surrounding Calenrah. My stamina was no longer filling properly, and I'd used my Stamina Surge to get myself to the gate and I imagined that I'd not last much longer if I didn't at least sit to rest. It was because of these distractions that I didn't truly get a good look at the massive wall or the guards in polished white armor that stood at the threshold.

This early in the morning I was the only one approaching and the gate was not open. I did see a smaller door, just to the left of the gate that was swung open and headed in that direction.

"Halt," a voice rang out and I looked up to see that I was about to run directly into an armored elf. "What business do you have in Calenrah?"

"Sea serpent," I said, pointing vaguely in the direction of the seashore beyond the walls of the city.

"I have a long memory and it doesn't include you, Caldor

Miles. You are an adventurer, but you must earn passage to enter our lands."

I looked up at the voice ready to plead, but I was so worn thin from exhaustion that the best I could do was shake my head. Focusing, I stood tall and prepared to try and march past the guard, when suddenly a stern female voice sounded from behind the pair of guards.

"He has Queen Elsena's blessing upon him, Neldan. And surely you can recall his surname. Would you bar passage to the heir of the great protector of Order, Elkor the Arcane Knight? Can you not see that he too is trying to follow the steps of his father, I can sense his pending class, can't you? Or have you grown lax in your duties," A powerful female voice practically thundered the words and the elf, Neldan I assumed, shrunk back from me as if struck.

"My apologies mistress Havan, the surname of even honored guests sometimes eludes me. It is by first name and face that my memory excels, I meant no harm," he bowed, not to me, but to a stunningly beautiful elven woman wearing a flowing white gown.

Her gaze shifted from Neldan, stern and sharp, to me, softening at the sight. Her voice became gentle as well. "I see that you have traveled far, and I can sense that you have little time before your trials come to an end. Allow me to heal you and rest your eyes for a time. I will ensure that you are woken within two hours so that your journey may continue."

I was about to protest, but she raised her hand and a soft warm light emanated from it. My drowsiness took on a new level and before I knew what was happening, I slipped off into a deep sleep.

"Wake now."

My eyes snapped open, and I scrambled to a sitting position, looking around. I felt refreshed, renewed, and ready to go. Though I had been extremely tired I remembered everything that had happened in clear detail. I was in a small room, sparsely decorated with an odd abundance of plants growing up the walls and on the floor. Standing just to the side of the simple bed I lay on was the one Neldan had called Mistress Havan.

"I don't have time for this," I said, getting to my feet. At the foot of the bed were my belongings. My dimensional box in a loose sack, my sword, and my helmet. I strapped my dimensional box in place, buckled my sword in place and put my helmet on. All the while, the stunningly beautiful elf, with her golden eyes and her dark brown curls framing her face, watched with an amused look.

"Where did you start your journey? By the feet of a swift horse, you can return to the western Prime Mana Shrine if you complete your task by nightfall." Her words were like honey, sweet and gentle.

"In House Variyn, the capital city," I said, the gravity of failure threatening to overtake me. I steadied my breath and remembered my vow. I will figure out a way.

"If you leave now, you might be able to make it in time, we have swift mounts that could be provided by the grace of the Queen, but I fear I acted in error. I believe I stole from you the time needed to retrieve your trial reagent; may I ask what you seek?"

"Sea Serpent's horn," I said, my steady breath the only thing keeping me sane.

"We elves tend not to horde reagents of what your kind call monsters, but I can direct you to where you will find such creatures. If you finish your task, seek me at the palace. I will speak with those I can, perhaps we have a champion with means to travel such a distance in the time you've remaining," Mistress Havan's words were so caring and filled with genuine sorrow for me that it brought on a measure of sadness.

"Thank you," I said, my hope renewing. "I will retrieve the item and seek you out in hopes that my journey hasn't been in vain."

Mistress Havan led me from the room, which ended up being an attached section of the wall probably meant for sleeping guards or such. She indicated that if I skirted the outside of the wall, I'd find an area with several outlets that reached into the sea, those ends are where I'll be likely to find a Sea Serpent. She also mentioned that I would find several small boats and that I was welcome to use any of them if I had the skill, with the promise that I'd return them afterward.

I took the hope she gave and traveled outside the walls of the city, heading for the indicated area.

There was a pathway right along the bottom of the wall that I followed, otherwise I'd have to go down a steep embankment and find my way in the thick white oaks that so thoroughly covered the ground outside the seaside city. I was fully aware now and able to admire the majesty of the elven craftsmanship.

The walls stood a staggering forty or fifty feet high, it made me dizzy to look up at them being so close to the base. Every ten feet or so the stone wall was broken by a tower that stuck slightly out and emblazoned with golden leaf and vine work. The stone was marble with a light blue color traced throughout. It had the barest seams—though I was sure it was only visible because of my improved sight. In fact, if I didn't have the increased senses and sight that came with my elven blessing and increased attributes, I was sure I'd see it as a single slab of marble.

The salty air blew in from the sea and I took a deep breath of it. If anything could settle my nerves, this wonderfully cool and salty smell could do it. I could almost forget the anxiety of how tentative my situation was while jogging down the length of the wall. Whatever Mistress Havan had done for me, I was rested enough that my stamina was depleting like normal, and I didn't feel the least bit tired.

The wall curved so slightly that it was hard to tell it had any curve at all from so close, but eventually I traveled enough that I couldn't see the great gate that I'd started my journey in front of. Up ahead, the path continued until it reached the water's edge. The wall stopped there, going into the water and circling around what must be the docks of the city. That would be useful if there were any naval battles or boats wanting to harass them.

I knew so little about boats and ships, only that there were some great big ships that used to travel to distant lands in the time of the Ordu, now the best we had—or so I'd heard during pub gossip—were meant only to travel the length of the coast and down rivers.

I had a clear view of the sea now and I could follow the coast on both sides for as far as I could see. The city of Calenrah was inside a gulf with elven lands to the north and south. It wasn't their capital, I knew that much, and I wondered at the grandeur their capital city must hold if a seaside port city was so well and intricately defended.

A black bird cawed from the branch of a nearby tree, I'd been seeing them on occasion now, but this was the first time I really stopped to study it. I looked at it and wondered, not for the first time, why I'd seen so many of its kind. It had a large black beak, feathers black as night with a purple sheen on them as it fidgeted. It cawed at me again, even going so far as to make a nudging motion with its head in my direction.

"What do you want?" I asked it, speaking to one of them for the first time since I'd started to see them. "I'm busy trying to kill a sea serpent. So, unless you have a way to fly me back to the capital city of House Variyn you should bug off."

To my surprise the bird nodded as if to say it did. I was thinking that it was either a crow or a raven, but I didn't know enough about birds to make the distinction. Whichever kind of bird it was our conversation ended as it cawed again and flew off away from the coast.

"Safe journeys," I said to the fleeing bird. "I hope you get to where you need to in time, because I'm not sure I will."

Checking my map, I saw that the suggested area to look and where Mistress Havan had sent me were one and the same. There was a small area on the other side of the city that was indicated, but it was nothing compared to the large area I found myself in.

To start things off, I determined I should walk the length of the seashore and see what I came across. Of course, I hadn't given very much thought to how I'd kill a sea serpent. There was always that ability I'd gotten, Aura Manipulation. I hadn't thought to try and use it against the Gnolls, but perhaps it would be effective against the Sea Serpents. Memories of the damage it had inflicted against me when I supercharged my Firebolt spell ran through my mind, and I quickly dismissed the idea. I'd do what the system suggested and wait to see what the Arbiter had to say about the ability, unless it was the last thing I had.

The afternoon sun beat down on me as I searched, but beyond several white and annoying birds cawing in the distance, my time was uneventful. Deciding I must take my search further out in the waters, I made my way towards the city walls again. There had been several small docks built outside the wall with a few people coming and going.

As I approached, I saw that there were three boats and half a dozen people talking and going about their business. All of them were elves, but they wore casual attire, not the flowing robes of Mistress Havan or the intricate armor of the guardsman Neldan. One such casually attired individual saw me coming and lifted an arm in greeting.

"Well met adventurer, my name is Turon," he said, lowering his hand and peering at me with deep blue eyes. "Have you come to learn perhaps? I am a decent teacher if you wish to catch a fish, or perhaps you'd care to learn the intricate ways of weaving nets, then Pelmore would be the one to help you."

I tilted my head in confusion from the polite offerings and couldn't help comparing it against what I thought a human would do if a stranger, adventurer or not, approached them while they were at work. The elves were truly a blessed and kind people.

"I seek a sea serpent, have you seen any?" I asked, raising my own hand in greeting.

"You wish to kill one?" One of the other elves asked, clearly not a fan of the idea.

"Settle Pelmore, I can see you, Caldor Miles, blessed of our Queen," Turon said, smiling in a fatherly way. His face looked no older than mine, but his eyes told a different story. His eyes gave me the impression of countless years lived and I could only wonder at what he'd seen. "He is doing the will of the Arbiter. You haven't much time remaining on your trial, but I am afraid none of us will be of much use to you. This is indeed a place where the horned sea serpents roam, but their numbers have been greatly reduced from past seasons and we have seen none. They will travel further out in times of greater hunger, perhaps you can take a boat out, some bait and this old harpoon. I can provide you with that small help."

"I'd be grateful and I'm sorry I've offended you Pelmore," I said, looking to the green haired elf with the shortest ears of them all. I heard a rumor once that an elves' ears could be used to tell how long they'd lived. If that were true, then Pelmore was young and Turon was older than even Mistress Havan.

"I do not need your apologies, continue your path, human," Pelmore said. His words came out even and emotionless. Turon shook his head, and I thought I heard him mutter something about the follies of youth, but he cleared his throat soon after and directed me to a small paddle boat.

"Am I right in assuming you haven't learned how to sail?" Turon asked and I nodded. "Then this paddle boat will meet your needs. Be wise and don't travel out too far, the gulf is filled with more than sea serpents and some sea serpents are older and stronger than you'd like to encounter. Be wise and continue your path." Turon bowed his head respectively and the phrase 'continue your path' sounded far less insulting coming out of his lips than it had Pelmore's. He handed over a bag of fish parts, an old—but not rusty—harpoon, and waved kindly as I departed.

The docks we stood on were made of wood, likely taken from the white barked oaks that surrounded the city, as it had the same gray-white look to them and so did the boat. I waved farewell to the elves, getting a few waves and head nods in return. A paddle boat was something I could handle, I decided. There had been many seasons when I'd been out on the water with my father, but nothing so vast as the sea that spread out before me.

Getting into the boat I pushed off and took the oars in my hands. Having been a while since I'd rowed, I impressed myself at the speed I achieved with very little effort. I rowed harder, wanting to test my top speed and worried for a moment that my increased strength would split the time worn wood of the oars, but they neither creaked nor bowed, staying strong under the pressure I exerted.

Hopefully now that I was out in the water and with a harpoon and bait to boot, I'd get somewhere. Slowing the boat to a stop I grabbed a few pieces of the raw fish and threw it into the water. The harpoon had a rope on the end, and I tied it off inside the metal loop at the front of the boat to ensure I didn't lose my catch if I got in a good strike.

The water was choppy as the wind blew in from the north, but no matter how many times I moved and how much bait I threw out, no sea serpent appeared. The sun began to set on the 6th day of my class trial and what little hope I had, started to diminish.

Day or night I refused to stop searching. I ran out of bait hours before, but I decided that my Light spell could be just as useful of a lure. It gathered the attention of many fish, but again no sea serpent appeared. I'd been all over the marked area on my map with zero success. I ate a meal of dried meat and cursed my rotten luck.

"How is it that I can be so damned unlucky!" I screamed into the open waters. My words did nothing to sweeten my mood.

Though it was dark, the moons provided enough light to see by for miles all around. It was because of the brightness of the moons that night that I noticed a large black form dart across the night sky. Had that been a dragon? But no, its body had been the wrong shape, the only commonality in the silhouettes was the wings. Dangerous predators must be out hunting now that the hour grows late.

That didn't dissuade me, but it did give me an idea. That flying monster, whatever it had been, flew in the direction I needed to go. The last place I had left to check. In the light of the moons, I paddled toward the other side of the city and to the small spot indicated on my map to also have sea serpents.

It took another hour, and the moons were slowly making their arcs through the night sky when I finally approached the spot. Just as it came into view, I heard a powerful screech that was answered by an even louder hiss. I saw two forms engaged in a fierce battle. A crack of white light illuminated the area around them and the flying silhouette from before screeched and fell to the ground in front of the other form.

I cast Inspect on both as I rowed like a madman toward the shore, close but not too close to where the battle raged.

Black Griffin, Level 11, Health 871/1050

Adult Sea Serpent, Level 21, Health 1350/1750

Why had a level 11 griffin picked a fight with such a strong Sea Serpent? It didn't matter though, because I needed to kill that Sea Serpent. Throwing caution to the wind, I rowed the boat right to the edge of the coast where they fought. The griffin was a swift and deadly opponent, having regained its feet and striking and slashing at the sea serpent, rending dozens of health away from every hit it took. But if things continued as they were the outcome was clear, the sea serpent would win.

Just before reaching the shore, I untied the harpoon and sprinted onto land. They were fighting on a slightly raised section of the coast and the sheer size of this 'Adult Sea Serpent' was daunting. Its wide head was nearly as wide as I was tall.

Several rows of horns lined its head like tiny needles, but in truth each one was likely the size of my forearm.

What I was doing was extremely stupid and I knew this, but I needed one of those damned horns! There was likely zero chance I'd survive a fight between a griffin and a sea serpent, so I had to show the griffin that I was friend and not foe.

I watched the griffin fight as I approached, getting my Firebolt ready. It was jet black everywhere except a line of feathers on its wings that stood out golden against the rest. Even its powerful front claws and deadly beak was a solid black. Griffins were said to be extremely intelligent creatures, ancient mounts of the Ordu, but I didn't know how much of that was folklore or truth.

But I had to use the knowledge I had if I was going to get through this in one piece. I took out the goblin staff, keeping my sword sheathed and made ready. The moment I was looking for presented itself, the sea serpent lunged in to bite at the griffin and would have likely ended the battle, but I was there shooting out a Firebolt and Shadow Bolt within moments of each other.

The combined attacks smashed into the bulbous head and caused it enough damage for it to pause mid strike. It hissed in my direction and spit a dark fluid at me. I jumped out of the way, whatever it was sizzled against the rock where I'd stood only moments ago. I looked up just in time to see the griffin scratch free one of the sea serpent's eyes.

"Hell yes! Get that slimy bastard!" I shouted excitedly as I stood and held the staff at the ready. I fired another Firebolt from a distance waiting for the long cooldown on the Shadow Bolt to come off. I wasn't quite ready to run into the reach of the sea serpent, deciding as wounded as it was the griffin was still the better choice for that.

The griffin slashed and retreated as I watched. Then it did something that gave me hope. A red glow surrounded it and it looked at me, giving me a quick nod of its head as if acknowledging my help. The aura, whatever the ability was, made the griffin faster and now it seemed certain that the sea serpent would fall.

I cast out Shadow Bolt quickly followed by Firebolt, but they did little if anything but annoy the sea serpent. Dodging forward I narrowly avoided another spray of the acid that ate away at the rock. Turning around I saw it had created a five-foot-wide gap covered in acid. Though I was sure I could jump over it I didn't want to risk it and put myself too far from the battle to help, so I did something stupid.

I tossed down the staff and pulled free my sword. The battle was coming to an end one way or another, the griffin and the sea serpent had less than 250 health left. As I stepped forward, the unthinkable happened. The speeding flight of the griffin came to an end as the serpent managed to clasp its mighty jaw around it. The griffin screeched a terrible cry as the remainder of its health began to tick away. I rushed forward to the edge of the shore just as the sea serpent decided to back away and drag the griffin into a watery death.

Committed to my course of action I leapt from the edge activating Power Strike as I dove downward after the sea serpent. Just before its bulbous head broke the water my sword slammed into it. The weight and momentum alone from my reckless downward dive would have been enough to at least injure the sea serpent, but with my damage being doubled by my skill I felt my sword sink deep and a rush of released essence as it was killed instantly.

What I didn't think about was the dozens of forearm length horns that now impaled me from my neck down to my groin. The pain must have been intense, but my body had decided that enough was enough and within moments of sustaining the likely deadly wounds I passed out.

I wish I could say that it was a fierce determination to live or strength of will that woke me up just minutes later, but neither would be true. I woke up because pain decided it was a good time to return and I was going to have to feel every last drop of it before the end. And it was surely the end.

Though I could feel I was somehow laying on solid ground, my feet floated at the water's edge. As soon as I'd decided that death was surely the only thing my future held, I remembered the two potions I'd picked up. Looking around I took in my surroundings; my dimensional box had come loose and was just out of arm's reach. Next to it was the black griffin, barely breathing with wounds covering it from head to claw. My mind worked to fill in the blanks.

The griffin must have gotten free and somehow pulled me off of the sea serpent and onto the shore! I felt a great sense of appreciation wash over me and I decided that one potion would be good enough to get me off death's door. I crawled toward the griffin, which I'm pretty sure caused me more damage and brought me closer to death. Every painful inch I moved closer to my dimensional box and closer to living another day.

Finally, after what felt like a century of pain, I reached the box and pulled free the first potion. The griffin heaved and went still.

No, no, no! I got one working hand to get the cork off and dumped the potion down its throat. It couldn't die now, not after it saved me!

"You can do it," I said, my voice cracked and hoarse. "I was so close!"

The potion was empty, and I couldn't see any movement from the griffin. Tears welled up in my eyes as I realized I must have been too slow. Pulling out a potion for myself I struggled to get the cork off. My hand, wet with blood and sweat, dropped the potion. There were two fist sized rocks between the griffin and me and of course it smashed against the largest of the two, spilling out its contents.

"I'm dead," I said, as if verbalizing my thoughts would show me a way out. No, no, I refuse, I decided. "Hell no!" I screamed.

I dug my hand into the ground and pushed closer to the rock. Then I began to lick it, getting the tiniest amount of the potion into my body. The glass shards cut at my tongue, but I was past pain at this point and kept going. When I was finished, I scooped up the dirt and sucked any fluid I could out of it. At this point I was so close to death that the coughing fit that followed sent me back into unconsciousness. My body was stronger than a normal human now, but everything had its limits.

CHAPTER 48
AN UNLIKELY ALLY

I awoke to a warm blanket and something nuzzling at my neck. It took a few groggy moments for my mind to adjust to the fact that I was still alive, but as it did, several things occurred to me at once.

The first, was that I was not actually lying covered by a blanket, but in fact it was the griffin's wings. The second, was the griffin was very much alive and nuzzling my neck affectionately. And lastly, I worked out that if I was indeed still alive then I had a place I needed to be.

Struggling against the stiffness I felt running throughout my body I managed to get on my knees. That's when the coughing started. Violent and painful coughs that I was sure caused me several points of damage. Curious about my health and wellbeing I checked my status to see where I stood. It didn't look good, I was at 89 health and had several debuffs, one of which was halving my regeneration for another 12 hours.

Getting all the way to my feet as the coughing subsided, I looked down at my severely damaged armor. That would require some expert repair work. I took in the sight around me, the griffin was back on its feet and looked perfectly fine. It would seem his experience with the potion was far better than mine. As if to show off how well it was feeling it unfurled its wings and screeched in my direction.

It wasn't the angry sound I'd heard it make against the Sea Serpent, but rather a softer tone. Then it did something odd, it knelt in my direction, lowering its head.

"What's this all about?" I asked it, not expecting an answer but it rose its head and met my eyes again. Then deliberately bowed and lowered its shoulder. I slowly approached; my hand held out in front of me. When I was close enough to touch it, I scratched it behind the ears and felt it press into my touch. A mental system message pushed its way into my groggy mind.

You have bonded with a Female Black Griffin. This noble creature will fight at your side and do your bidding. In order to keep the bond strong, you must care for the griffin's needs.

"Whoa," I said, feeling a change come over me. It was like I could feel the surface level emotions coming off the griffin. I knew she was grateful for my help and that she felt deeply that a debt was owed. "You don't owe me anything, in fact, it's the other way around." I got the distinct impression that she understood my words and more so that she still felt strongly about hers.

"Very well," I said, remembering my sword and class reagents suddenly. "But I need to find a few things and then we can work out what to do next."

The sky above me was dimming and passing into the evening. Several orange, purple, and red colors played at the horizon. Had I already missed my time? When last I could recall, it was night and passing into the morning of the last day.

I stilled my thoughts realizing that I had less than a few

hours before my time was up. One thing at a time I told myself, though I admit my emotions were a bit of a wreck at this point. Luck was with me regarding my class reagents, the sea serpent had washed ashore, my sword still firmly planted into its head. I retrieved all my items and used my sword to hack off every single horn on the sea serpent's head.

If Fran were here, she could have told me which items would work as reagents, but I had neither the time nor know how myself. Several minutes had passed and the sky was already darkening to full night. Did I even have time to get to the elven city? And if I did, what was my hope? That perhaps they had a wizard or caster with powerful teleportation magic? I knew of two wizards who had such magic myself, Warrick and Merlin, but I was certain that it wasn't common magic.

Another screech sounded behind me, startling me from my slow thoughts.

"What's wrong girl?" I asked, feeling her emotions pressing on me. I got the impression that she wanted to help, but I didn't see how?

The griffin opened her wings wide and flapped them, blowing dirt and dust in my direction. Again, I felt an urgent need from her to help me.

"Oh," I said, suddenly realizing what she meant. "Are you saying that you could fly me? Can you handle my weight, and how fast can you go?"

I was already walking up to her working out the best way to climb up. I had little options left to me and this seemed as good as any. She did that bowing thing again and I stepped on her lowered shoulder, pushing myself into a sitting position behind her wings, while my hands held tightly to her neck. She was bigger than me, but not that much bigger than Jill had been if you didn't count her wings.

"I'm all set," I said, stroking her head to get my point across. A part of me couldn't believe I was about to fly on the back of a griffin. They were legendary creatures and said to be as old as the dragons, but they'd always served the cause of the Ordu. I was riding an Ordu mount!

I felt her mind rub against mine, she needed to know where to go. I focused on the area on the map and hoped that the impressions could be shared both ways. It looked like I was in luck because she screeched, her head shaking back and forth. She dug at the ground before kicking off into the air.

I lurched suddenly, holding tighter as we lifted off the ground. This was almost like riding the swifts, I decided, just no harness to tie me down. Once we'd gone high into the air where the city looked small enough that I could scoop it up with my hand, we shot forward and I found I had to hold handfuls of feathers to keep myself from slipping.

I decided there and then that this would work much better if I had a saddle, but the speed we traveled was hard to believe. Every few minutes she'd bank either left or right and I'd get a good look at the ground zipping by below us. Checking my map, I saw that after only twenty minutes or so we'd traveled past the place Sarah had called 'Endsville' and were speeding toward Waifer.

I tried to do some distance math or basic speed versus how far we moved on the map and determined I didn't have the slightest clue how to work it out but I could tell it was going to be a close call. Hopefully I'd be able to smash down right in the keep's garden and finish off my class quest. Because otherwise, things would be tricky. Checking my quest, I saw how much time I had left.

4 Hours 42 Minutes 12 Seconds.

I focused on sending the information to the griffin and felt her wings beat faster in response. Then she did something that nearly made me lose my hold. She began to fold her wings in and dive like a speeding fireball and then transition into a powerfully fast glide. She repeated this many times and I realized that it was making us go just a smidge faster.

Her wings and her body grew hot beneath me as we moved. I wondered at the limits of her stamina, but she never slowed and waned in her efforts to get me back to the keep. It was like when her mind had been set to the task it would be impossible to pull her from it.

"Stubborn girl," I said, hugging her tight and sending her my grateful thoughts.

Time was waning and I began to worry just as we passed over Strethfore. We'd traveled just as fast as the swifts it seemed, but she didn't have to stop for thirty minutes to an hour several times like the barges had. We were going to make it and with a bit of time to spare!

As if triggered by my excited thought, disaster struck. The black griffin traveled swift and hard, but suddenly there was a roar and powerful screech that nearly deafened me. It was a sound I recognized, but it was still further off than it had been before.

I sent a worried thought to the griffin, sharing the image of the lean dragon that we'd encountered days before and did my best to impart a sense of danger. No sooner did the griffin send back feelings of calm did a burst of fire spurt past us. She screeched loudly in response, and we veered hard to the left. I could hear the heavy beating of leathery wings, but in the darkness of the night I saw nothing—both moons provided little light this night because of the heavy cloud cover.

I happened to be looking to the left as we banked right and saw the skinny dragon just as it let loose another stream of fire.

Even from this distance I could see it was heavily scarred and wounded, even its wings seemed to have to work twice as hard to keep it in the air. Its wings were a mess of tattered leathery flesh. For a second I thought to tell the griffin to attack, thinking we might be able to get the upper hand on this thing and collect its hide for armor or something.

But no, we had a place to be, and I didn't want to put her at risk. The dragon seemed to already be falling behind, slow inch by slow inch, so I urged the griffin to bank low and lose it just above the tree line of the black oaks. She took my command and followed it by diving straight down only straightening out right above the trees. It worked; the dragon let loose another ear-splitting screech but it was even further now than it had been before.

Before long, not a sound could be heard from the flying menace. The walls of House Variyn's capital city slipped into view and not a moment too soon. I had less than an hour, so we'd need to go straight to the keep.

"Fly high and descend quickly so we don't get shot out of the air," I said, trying to express that what we were about to do was risky at best. She sent me a strange emotion in response. It was almost as if she was saying 'They'd have to catch me first'. Outflying the dragon had given her an over inflated sense of her abilities, though she was probably right, she wouldn't be an easy target. It was sweet how proud she was of herself. I sent my own thoughts of pride and thanks to her in response.

We rose high, much higher than necessary before we were right over the keep. Then we dove, we dove so straight downward that my feet and legs lifted off of her back and I was holding on for dear life to her feathers. Then much later than I thought necessary she put her wings as wide as they'd go and we slammed to the ground, sort of drifting as we landed, kicking up a large cloud of dust.

There were voices crying in alarm and several swords unsheathing, but I didn't have time to deal with that, so I sent a quick message to the griffin to stay close to me and that I'd be right back.

Stepping forward just as the dirt cloud cleared, I touched the Prime Mana Shrine with less than a minute to spare. As before, I felt my mind pulled someplace and the Arbiter stood in his overly large form, looking down at a pocket watch and making a tsking noise with his mouth.

"You cut that really close, Arcane Knight," Arb said.

Congratulations! You are an Arcane Knight.

CHAPTER 49
ARCANE KNIGHT

I felt, more than read, several additional notifications, but they were all related to things I could deal with later. The Arbiter cleared his throat to get my attention, so I looked up. All feelings of weakness and pain had faded as if I'd left it behind with my body.

"You are now an Arcane Knight, Defender of the Balance and as such I have a quest for you," Arb said, then suddenly a quest prompt appeared before me, and I read it.

Restore The Balance Part 1

As a Defender of the Balance, it falls onto your shoulders to investigate and restore the planet's equilibrium. To do this you must first understand why it is out of balance. Seek knowledge and understanding anywhere you may find it.

Objective*: Discover what has unbalanced the forces of Order & Chaos.*

Rewards*: 100,000 Essence, New Class Ability 'Restoring Light'*

Restoring Light: A spell that can be used to remove Chaos

corruption and heal a target for 255 Health over 10 seconds. This spell has a cooldown of 5 seconds and a cast time of 3 seconds.

Accept or Decline?

Warning! *If you decline, you risk further upsetting the balance of Order & Chaos.*

I read the quest twice before accepting it. There was no clue that I could find in the quest text that would help me figure out what was upsetting the balance, but I would work out a way, somehow. I did a quick look at my map to see if the quest had any specific marking or area like my class quest had, but what I saw instead was several small markings—the symbol for Chaos, two rings cracked in five places—in each place I'd encountered Chaos monsters. That would definitely be useful, I could share the information with Lord Variyn to help with the hunt of Chaos monsters.

"I've accepted the quest," I said, Arb nodded knowingly. "But can I ask a few questions about it?"

"I'd love to do your job for you," Arb said, winking. "But our time is coming to an end, and I need to look over your new class abilities and available perks. Since you've completed your class trials there are a number of new ones available to you."

I huffed in annoyance but pulled up my system notifications to see what I'd learned.

There were three new abilities: Blade Bond, Arcane Armor, and Light Blade. I focused on the first one, which appeared to be an ability that required no Mana or Stamina. Then I looked at each in turn.

Blade Bond: You can bond a single weapon. A Bonded Blade can be stored in the ethereal plane and summoned and dismissed with a thought. Furthermore, Bonded Weapons cannot be destroyed, doing so will cause the weapon to shift back into the ethereal plane and be restored to the state it was in at the time of bonding. *Any weapon modifications require you to re-bond your chosen weapon. There is no cost and cast time for this ability. This ability cannot be upgraded and has no further tiers.*

Arcane Armor: You can summon a suit of magical armor built from arcane constructs. At rank 1 this spell provides a chest piece, helmet, and pauldrons. Each piece provides equal protection from physical damage and magical damage. The armor exists several inches above the caster's skin and as such normal armor can be worn beneath it. The look of the armor can be adjusted by focusing on the form you wish for it to take. There is a 100 mana Cost and a cast time of 5 seconds. This spell is ranked 1, increased ranks will provide better and more thorough protection.

Light Blade: This spell lets you form a sword of light in your hand which can be used to make attacks. If the caster is already wielding a Blade, then it provides additional benefits for the weapon. At rank 1 this spell provides +3 to base damage, 40 Light damage per strike, and provides an adjustable light that can be used to see by. Additionally at rank 1 the caster can send the effect outward, sending a slash of damaging light at a target dealing 75 Light damage. There is a 10 Mana Cost and a cast time of 1 second. This spell is ranked 1, increasing ranks will provide better and more thorough protection.

I felt the descriptions were pretty straightforward, plus as I read them the knowledge implanted on how to use them rushed to the forefront of my mind, so there was very little I didn't know about the casting or use of the class abilities.

Shifting my attention to my menus I saw that there was indeed a new tab labeled Perks, something Alayna had mentioned once before, so I dove in looking through them.

At my current level I had two available and if I was reading the system messages right, I'd receive a new one every five levels. The first one must have come as a bonus, because I was only level 9 so maybe level 1 counted and every 5 levels. Either way I dug into the list.

There were a few that raised combat potency, like Toughness that increased your strength attribute modifier from a 1 to 1 scale into a 1 to 1.25 scale, essentially making greater use of each attribute point. It took some looking, there were literally hundreds of perks, but I found one for each Attribute except the Core Attribute.

I also happened upon the 'Long Lived' perk, there were five variations of it, each requiring the previous perk before you could take the next. It extended your natural age and beauty— whatever it meant by beauty seemed to be rather subjective— by tenfold at its highest or just doubling it at the lowest.

Alayna had taken the perk, at least the first version of it, and passed her first threshold so her natural lifespan had already extended into the two or three hundreds of years. For my first pick I added 'Long Lived' and accepted the prompt as it came. I didn't feel much of a change but being separated from my body as I felt probably accounted for that.

Several other perks called to me, there was one that increased the 'spring' in your joints, making you react faster, jump higher, and land easier called 'Rubber Joints'. I didn't know what Rubber meant, but I felt like I'd heard the word someplace before. But as alluring as they all were, I knew what Perks I needed to take until I'd at least taken all the base versions of them.

I found the Toughness Perk again and selected it. Using the mental selection process, I also tagged the other attribute increasing perks so I could find them easier next time. With so much effort going into getting extra attributes it would be silly of me not to take the perks to increase the value of them.

I did a final check, happy with my decisions, and let the menus close.

"I have no questions about my class abilities or perks, but can you tell me where I should go to find out about Chaos monsters? Give me something," I pleaded, but Arb was already shaking his head.

"I've given you more than I ought to," Arb said. "Besides, I am not all knowing, though I keep some secrets I do not have the answers you seek. Return to any Prime Mana Shrine to update your quest and be safe out there, Defender."

"Oh, and one final thing," Arb said, seeming to remember something. "That pesky ability you gave yourself, Aura Manipulation, I'm taking that away. When you are stronger, I'll give you a chance to learn it again, but don't worry, I'll give you an ability equally worth it. It's called Essence Infusion, it allows you to do something similar to your Aura Manipulation, but with a more stable energy."

Essence Infusion: You can take a portion of your essence and use it to enhance spells, objects, or skills. When used on an object, the amount said object can hold depends on the structure and durability. Spells and skills can take an essence amount equal to the cost of their Mana or Stamina expenditure to add an additional modifier when calculating damage. If used on a non-damaging spell or skill, results will vary.

As Arb finished speaking, the dark and empty room began to fade to white and suddenly I found myself back in my body. The sudden return of pain and my low health caught me off guard. I fell to a knee and the world spun. An insistent nudge from the black griffin helped me recover. I stood and looked out, just as before it appeared only moments had passed, the dust just beginning to settle.

Several adventurers, by the looks of them, had pulled

weapons and looked pretty surprised to see me and the griffin arrive.

"Sorry 'bout that," I said, smiling as I saw two faces I recognized.

Fred and Fran rushed forward, pushing some confused looking warriors and wizards aside.

"I was just telling Fred that short of falling from the sky you'd never make it in time," Fran said, laughing as she spoke. "Didn't expect you'd actually fall straight out of the sky and on the back of a griffin to boot!"

"Griffins are noble and powerful creatures. They only align themselves, or so legend says, with people that have great destinies ahead of them. How'd you find it?" Fred asked, quoting from a book I was pretty certain.

"Do either of you have a potion?" I asked, my body was beginning to feel too heavy for my legs.

Fran had purchased half a dozen from the items she sold it turned out and she gladly let me drink one of the more potent ones. It helped to negate the remaining debuffs I had suffered, and my health regeneration could finally do its job, healing me up.

"You look like hell," Fran said, we were still in the garden but sitting toward the back while the griffin kept watch dutifully.

"Yeah, I feel like it too," I said, even with the steady increase in my health the last week had worn me thin. What I needed was a good couple of days to rest. "I see you made it back in time. Tell me about your classes, did you get any spells or skills?" I asked.

Fran went first shushing her brother as he tried to launch into the spells he'd learned.

"I'm a Blade Master now and check out what I can do,"

Fran said. She held out her hand and the sword she'd gotten from her father appeared. Then just as quick, it disappeared. "Isn't that cool! My other class ability was a passive that increases my blade's cutting ability for a few extra stamina per swing. Beside that, I had reagents enough for a few more skills, but they were all pretty basic. One increased my health, another gives me a boost of speed, and the last one doubles my weapon attack's damage for a stamina cost."

It was interesting to see that we'd gotten similar abilities, but it was to be expected as one of my paths was the Blade Master as well.

"Someone needs to tell the monster you are going to fight to just run away, you are going to be a killing machine," I said, Fran smiled wide at that, and I could tell she thought so too.

"Okay Fred, you're up," Fran said, punching her brother lightly in the arm. "Bore us with all the flashy spells you learned."

"I'm a Flame Born now and as such all my spells will be fire based," Fred said matter-of-factly. "My favorite spell is Fireball, and it is channelable for a greater cost to do greater damage. I also learned Firebolt, though the Orbs version is stronger than the one I am able to cast currently. My first class ability is something called 'Heat Sphere' which provides protection against magical attacks and damages anyone who gets too close with intense heat. My second class ability is a passive called 'Hot One' that makes me one-hundred percent immune to fire damage and heat while simultaneously making my attacks stronger and less resistant to other sources of fire resistance. Look at this."

Fred held his palm out and put his forearm over it. His palm ignited, forming a ball of fire several inches above it. Though his forearm was directly in the path of the fire it neither burned nor smoked. It was as if the flames melted around his arm and his clothing without being able to actually touch it.

"Show off," Fran said, rolling her eyes. "He was always a pyro, so none of this is surprising."

"I was not," Fred said, his face flushing red. It was good to know both of them were doing well.

"I'm not sure what I'm going to do with this griffin, but we've bonded, and I get the sense she doesn't want to just leave me," I said, sending grateful and loving feelings toward her. She preened her neck in response and let off a low screech of pleasure. "But I really need to go get a drink and sleep for the next week. Do you guys have time to get a drink before you leave back to your parents?"

"Do we ever!" Fran said, standing straight and practically dragging me by the arm out of the garden.

"If you bonded it, then it should be free to come and go as it pleases," Fred said, knowingly. "I've read about a mental connection where you can 'call' it when you are in need. Though I'd suggest getting a bonding stone and a saddle made for her."

"Bonding stone?" I asked, stopping Fran before we'd gotten too far from the black griffin. She'd begun to walk after us, and I could feel she had every intention of coming along.

"It allows you to solidify your bond and make the creature you've chosen a summonable creature. For a griffin it would basically make it immortal, as long as the stone stayed intact, and you can only break a summoning stone by killing the user who enacted the bond," Fred said, scratching at his chin as he spoke and examining the griffin.

"How long do griffins live? Would I be shortening her lifespan so that she was more convenient for my uses?" I asked, shooting the questions off rapid fire. I'd barely asked the question when I realized I had the answer to its age in my head.

Griffins are noble creatures who only breed every sixty to eighty years. That combined with their lifespan of only two-hundred years, mean they are extremely rare to find out in the wild.

"I don't know the lifespan of a griffin, but as an adventurer and assuming you don't die in a dungeon of course, I'd wager your lifespan will far outstrip its own," Fred said nodding along with his own words as if agreeing that what he was sharing was in fact true.

From what little I'd learned about the ever-extending life-span of adventurers I decided that maybe I would be doing her a favor after all. Doing the best I could do to relay my thoughts to her, I got free of Fran and walked up to the black griffin.

She matched my gaze and I realized for the first time that her eyes were golden and not yellow as I'd thought. Her iris focused on me, and I got the impression that she was thinking over my proposal. I sent comforting thoughts to her, trying as best as I could to get her to understand that it would be a big change and she could live a long life or die when I did, having lived not much of a life at all.

The intelligence that looked back at me in that gaze would have been unnerving if not for the love I saw behind the look. Something resolved inside of her, and I felt her give her consent. She bowed her head and then I got the impression that she was hungry. Pulling out some of the bear meat I fed her several large portions while those in the garden looked on in awe.

I wondered if she had a name suddenly, as I wanted to call her something. 'Grif' was out of the question, she needed something feminine but also powerful. At a loss for options, I posed several random names that came to mind, hoping she'd have a better idea of what she should be called.

I sent her Goldy, Blacky, Midnight, and Gale. She didn't care for any of them. Goldenwing, Deloras, Seph, nope not a single name worked for her. She was a fast and fierce flier, what would encapsulate all those qualities? My mind ran over old legends and stories, searching for a name that would fit.

I vaguely recalled the story of a powerful Ordu who rode a griffin into battle, they'd been named Ares or something close to that. I couldn't remember if the griffin had been named that or the rider, but what I did recall was they were the bane of their opponents. A swift bringer of destruction and victory for their side. That seemed to fit well enough, so I posed it to her.

She preened at the name and the description I sent with it.

"Alright girl," I said, petting her head. "You will be called Ares."

"Isn't that the name of the Ordu champion that caused the downfall of his entire army," Fran said, overhearing my conversation with Ares. "Also," she added, "Ares isn't a girl's name."

"It is now," I said, hugging Ares's head and sending her a quick message.

Go be free for a while; I need rest and will call when I can.

I focused on the feeling of passing thoughts between us so that I would know how to summon her later on and felt I had a good grasp of it.

She understood and screeched into the air while I took a step back to give her room. With her powerful legs she shot up into the air and a moment later I felt her move off toward the east.

A mousy looking woman approached us and pointed at me.

"Could I get your name, class and level please?" I didn't

recognize her, but with the clipboard she held at her chest and the House Variyn attire she wore, I could guess at her purpose. I told her the information she needed, and she gave me a small token.

"This will grant you access to Adventurer Guild resources and vendors. Normally you'd be required to pay guild dues and taxes, but as a member of the House Variyn nobility, being a Knight and Vassal, you are exempt. Have a wonderful day and thank you for joining the Adventurer's Guild."

Fred and Fran showed me theirs as well, each of them were small coins that when inspected were listed as 'Soul-Bound' items. They provided no attribute buff and did nothing that I could discern. On one side was the symbol of order, two equally thick lines in the circle, and on the other side was the same, but broken by five cracks. If I had to guess by the weight they were made of simple iron, but I wasn't someone with any kind of know how in the ways of metal.

"Let's go get that drink," I said, using Fran to support my tired body while the last points of health replenished. By the time we found a pub, a good-sized place where many other adventurers awaited inside, drinking and eating, it was nearly morning. That didn't seem to matter though so we approached ready to enjoy ourselves. I used Stamina Surge, topping myself off so I'd be able to stay awake long enough to get piss faced drunk.

The night wore on into the morning and I was surprised to find Grug, Adathin, and Beth in attendance. We spoke of many things but ended on the promise they'd made to run a dungeon with me. I told them I knew of a healer that would be the perfect fit and we agreed to tackle a dungeon in a week's time.

CHAPTER 50
NEW ABILITIES AND A PROFESSION

I slept well into the night of the next day but found I couldn't sleep any longer. My body was healed and raring to go. The room I'd slept in was a simple affair with a heavy chest at the foot of the bed, a rosewood dresser stained with a light varnish to bring out the color, and a bed just big enough for me.

My armor was in disrepair, and had only a dozen points of durability left, so I stripped it off, having slept in it the night before, and put on a comfortable set of simple clothing. A tan tunic shirt with draw strings at the tip, soft leather pants, and a durable pair of black boots. There was a reflective piece of polished metal in the room, and I used it to look at myself.

I'd grown much more solid and filled out in the shoulders than I remembered. My wavy brown hair was growing longer than I was used to, falling over my eyes in loose curls now that I wasn't wearing my helmet to keep it back. The dark circles and stress lines from the previous night had faded, leaving my face looking fresh and young. I rummaged through my pack and found a silk vest I'd been given at some point, putting it on over the tunic. It did the trick, making me look less ordinary. It was all topped off by my sword belt and dimensional storage box hanging in a loose sack attached to my belt.

I looked into my sparkling blue eyes and nodded to myself.

"So much has happened to us," I said, speaking in a hushed enough tone so no one could overhear and think I was crazy. "But we are doing it, really doing it. We are officially an Arcane Knight with an epic quest to complete and friends to rely on. Heck, we bonded with a griffin, that's worth something all by itself. Sure, we aren't exactly like our father, but we have to learn to walk our own path. We got this."

It helped to affirm my thoughts verbally, even if it left me feeling a bit wacky. So much had happened in just a matter of weeks and I had countless years ahead of me if I survived. That was the key right there, how to survive long enough to matter. With the politics, the Chaos threat, and random monster encounters I'd had all trying to end my life I'd be lucky to make it to my next birthday, not to mention my hundredth or two-hundredth.

I pulled free my sword and began the bonding process. It entailed a deep meditative state, something that would be difficult without privacy. As I focused, I felt myself become more familiar with the blade. Images flashed through my head of its creation and of the monsters I'd used it to kill. The sword had a memory of sorts and I needed to align our goals. When finally, the process was complete I felt like I could retrace every swing and thrust I'd ever made with the sword. I knew this blade more than I knew the back of my hand. With that knowledge came the ability to call it forth at the mere thought. I had bonded my blade.

My stomach rumbled, reminding me that I was definitely still mortal and needed sustenance. I left my room, taking all my belongings with me, and found some breakfast. I had plans for today, not the least of which was finding Alayna and telling her all that had happened. Then I'd have to convince her to join me for a dungeon dive with level 18 to 22 adventurers, all while I was just level 9. I changed my plans then, deciding I needed to level up a bit first and tier up my abilities as well as get some new ones.

When I got to the Prime Mana Shrine the first thing I noticed was that it didn't have the bright glow from before, instead just giving a faint bit of light. I walked up to it, no one else was currently in the area but I had run into a few guards on my way back here, none of them stopped me.

Pressing my hand to the surface I didn't get the pulling I'd felt the other times, instead it was like using a non-Prime Mana Shrine. I could summon up a window with available spells, skills, and confirm amounts of essence to add to levels or attributes.

I had 105,069 Essence to spend so I started with looking at what abilities I had available. There was a surprisingly long list, and I dove first into the spells. There was a good bit of utility spells, like one that summoned a small measure of drinking water, another that would purify water or food, and even a spell to dispose of waste, but I wasn't looking for any of those. I picked out three potentially useful offensive spells and read deeper into what they could do.

Fireball: For X amount of Mana, where X is equal to the amount of Mana you channel into the spell, you can summon a fireball that grows in size the more Mana it is fed. The spell has a base range of 150 feet but decreases based on size and caster strength attribute. It does 1 point of fire damage per 1 point of Mana Infused into the spell. Cast time depends on amount of

Mana infused, starting at a base of 1 second per 50 mana infused.

Lightning Strike: For 95 Mana you can call down a single Lightning Strike on a target within 100 Feet. It does 155 points of damage and has a 30% chance to stun the target for 3 seconds. Instant Cast with an 8 second cooldown. Must maintain visible contact to cast this spell.

Arcane Missile: For 50 Mana you can send out three missiles of arcane energy. It does 40 damage per missile and can be directed at up to 3 targets. Cast time 2 seconds with a 4 second cooldown. This spell will not miss unless actively intercepted or blocked by the target.

Each of them were spells I wanted in my arsenal, but I didn't know how many skills were available to balance out my requirements to learn one of each from my pathways. Right before I was going to switch over to skills, I saw a spell that I knew I had to have and would have saved me so much trouble in the last seven days.

Lesser Heal: For 100 Mana you can send a surge of healing light into a willing target. It heals for 150 Health or causes equal damage to an undead target. Cast time is 6 seconds with a 30 second cooldown.

It wasn't offensive in the least, unless I encountered something undead, but even then, with a long cast time and an even longer cooldown it wasn't particularly useful in combat. That wasn't why I wanted it. If I could heal a large chunk, even every half minute, that would give me an edge that I didn't have last week. Getting practically giddy at this point, I went looking for useful skills that I had reagents for, and I wanted.

I found more than the four I needed but wouldn't have the reagents for all.

Swift Strike: For 65 Stamina you can add a burst of speed to your weapon, either moving it to block or feign your opponent or to increase the power behind a strike. If used to Strike an opponent, Swift Strike increases the likelihood of a critical strike.

Damage Proficiency: Pick either Crushing, Piercing, or Slashing damage and your proficiency will be increased, adding an additional +5 to damage output.

Force Wave: For 50 Stamina you can project a wave of force from your weapon's edge. It does base weapon damage as slashing damage at the target. Cooldown 8 Seconds.

Hardy II (Learning this overrides previous Hardy I): (Passive) Increase your Health and Stamina by 100. This is a passive ability that can be taken multiple times, but not more than once per level. With each increased level the rarity of reagents and essence required go up.

I noticed that I could increase my Power Strike skill to Power Strike II but I didn't have the right reagent, so I'd have to wait. Eventually I'd be able to upgrade my spells and skills but for now I was focusing on gathering a large arsenal of spells and skills. With that in mind, I picked Lightning Strike and Lesser Heal, using the reagents I needed for the other two, Arcane Missile and Fireball.

Then I chose Swift Strike and Hardy II, because you could always use more health and stamina. That left me with several spells and skills to choose from later when I'd purchased the right reagents. It cost twice as much to upgrade Hardy II as it had to learn any individual spell or skill. That left me just over 100,000 essence to work with, so I increased my level as far as I could.

Unfortunately, because of the ever-increasing costs of leveling and purchasing attributes, I had to spend 97,309 essence just to reach level 12. I did so, bringing my Constitution base up by 6. Next, I brought my Intellect up by 6. And lastly, I raised my Core attribute from 25 to 31, because I wanted to future proof myself as much as I could.

All that said and done, I was left with only 3,260 Essence and 17,550 required to reach level 13. Doing some quick math, I figured I was at least as powerful as someone near level 20, though I couldn't be certain. They'd definitely have more battle knowhow and possibly access to stronger spells, but I was confident in my abilities.

Before I removed my hand off the Mana Shrine, I realized a new tab had appeared and was blinking.

Choose your Class Profession!

That's right! I had gotten past level 10 and unlocked my ability to choose a profession. The list was ridiculously long but I found that I could filter through if I thought about what kind of profession I was looking for. The trouble was, I really didn't know what profession I wanted yet and it didn't seem wise to rush into it. I looked anyways and found several that I could see myself doing, a few of which were Jewel Inscriptionist, Jewelcrafter, or just plain old Inscriptionist.

I really wasn't big on jewels and rings, but I'd been thinking about the ones I'd gathered from the goblins and how effective it would be to have a bunch of gems filled with mana. I was also intrigued by the monster cores and their ability to hold essence. But neither of these interests or curiosities were enough to make me commit to such a big decision without researching it out first. So, I let my hand fall off the stone.

"That was quick," a familiar voice said behind me. I turned and saw Alayna, wearing her 'I'm going to sneak outside the keep' outfit. "I was worried for you when you didn't show up on the 7th day." She bit her lip as I approached, opening her arms wide and we embraced.

"It's been a wild week for me," I said, taking in the feel and smell of her. She had the same floral perfume that I remembered from before and she was warm to the touch.

I filled her in over dinner, we decided to eat at the place we had before with the large helpings, as I'd told her I was hungry again, despite having just finished breakfast. She'd informed me that interacting with the Shrine took a portion of you with it, often requiring you to drink and eat when leveling or adjusting attributes.

"You rode back here on a griffin, and you bonded it?" Alayna asked, her eyes wide in disbelief. "You are pulling my leg, aren't you?"

"I'm really not," I said, taking another bite of the seared chicken breast. The seasonings were divine, and the ale was the perfect mix of sweet with bitter undertones.

"You hit level 12," Alayna said, smiling slyly. I hadn't told her, but I was sure she'd just used her Inspect skill. "What profession did you choose?"

"I haven't yet," I admitted, eating a scoop of mashed potatoes. Then washing it down with more ale I continued. "I think I am leaning toward gems or inscribing, but I'm not really sure."

"I can vouch for inscribing related professions, it opens up a unique ability to infuse mana that comes in handy for all sorts of enchantments, spells, and such," Alayna said, she was picking at her food but not eating nearly as much as I had, my plate was half eaten and hers barely a quarter.

"Infuse Mana?" I asked, the words making me think of the ability that the Arbiter had given me. I hadn't gone into the details about that with Alayna, but now I thought I should. "I got an ability called, Essence Infusion that says I can infuse objects, spells, and skills with essence, is it like that but with Mana?"

Alayna looked at me with a very perplexed look on her face. Then dropping her fork, she leaned forward to say, "Did you say Essence Infusion? Like you could infuse a gem with Essence like a monster core?"

"I guess," I said, shrugging and wondering why she'd gotten so quiet. "I honestly haven't tried it so I couldn't tell you."

"Do you know how rare intact monster cores are?" She asked and I could tell she was trying to lead me somewhere, so I played along.

"Pretty rare," I said.

"And do you know why?" She asked.

"Because they crack so easily when monsters die." I knew that much at least, but where was she going with this.

"And if you put essence inside a gem, like the kind a skilled Jewelcrafter or Gem Inscriptionist could create. You'd have a way to store or even gather essence!" Alayna whispered so loud it might as well have been normal speech.

"Okay?" I asked, why was this important. There had to be thousands of people able to do it, making gems and adding essence.

"I've never heard of a single person able to transfer essence around, Caldor," Alayna said, staring deep into my eyes. "This could change everything! You are going to be rich and change the face of our entire nation's economy." She'd gone back to the quiet whisper and looked around the restaurant as if someone might hear us and attack.

"Wait, wait, wait," I said, letting the information process. If I'd just been given a never before seen ability to basically create monster cores or at least gems with essence inside of them, how did that change anything? I'd still need to go out personally and collect the essence and that took time, plus if I gave away all my own essence, that would just cripple my growth. Alayna seemed to be able to see where my thoughts had gone so she elaborated more.

"Did you know that there have been break throughs in all kinds of inscribing that allows for the collection of mana by imparting the ability to slowly collect mana into gems and certain complex enchantments, basically drawing it in?" Alayna had dropped all precepts of secrecy now and was speaking rather loudly as she grew more excited.

"That seems like it'd be so much more useful than what I can do," I said, nodding along.

"Well imagine if you took that knowledge and applied it to creating self-collecting monster cores. It's theorized that most of the essence from dungeons and slain monsters is lost. That's because each creature is a total value of its collected essence and our ability to pull in essence is limited by our Core affinity. Even with a..." she paused looking around. "...paragon, you don't pull in all the potential essence. But what if you could?"

"That sounds great and all," I said, rubbing at my temples. "But other than helping me grow stronger faster, what good does it accomplish? Why would I share this knowledge with anyone?" I was all for helping people, but I didn't want this to become just another way nobles could grow more powerful over normal folk.

"The highest level of enchantments, constructs, and spells require something purer than mana; they require the very thing that gives life or at least maintains it, they require essence. But sorry don't let my excitement over the subject determine your path forward. Just know that a profession like Gem Inscriptionist would give you the best way to leverage your new ability. With enough discoveries we could be well on our way to rediscovering the advancements that ancient texts speak of during the time of the Ordu. Could you imagine?"

I could imagine. I'd read both amazing and terrifying legends about what the Ordu could do. I didn't say it aloud, but I decided right then and there that I had picked my profession after all, and it was going to be Gem Inscriptionist. I would leverage the ability to make gems and inscribe specific instructions until I unlocked a way to gather even more essence.

We finished off dinner and we parted ways as I needed to do some shopping before I turned in, but we said we'd meet for a late-night snack later that same day. My head was spinning with ideas, but to accomplish anything I needed to do a few things first.

I had my armor repaired; the services were offered at Gilfoy's Emporium. They told me that I could return the next day to pick it up and I agreed. Next, I sold off all the reagents that I couldn't directly use, swelling my small pile of gold a good bit. Then went the meat and hides. Before leaving I purchased a Jewelcrafting and an Inscriptionist set of basic tools, they sold them as large chests stuffed full of items. Lastly, and most expensive, I purchased several dozen raw gems of varying types, a dozen cut clear quartz and other cheaper gems, and a dozen finer gems: from rubies to diamonds.

After doing all that, I tended to a task I wasn't looking forward to at all. I went to the keep and found Elandel, Lord Variyn's Master of Physicians.

"I don't know how best to say this, so I'm just going to come out and say it," I said, standing on the opposite side of her desk in what I'd been told was her office. "Jill, the horse you loaned me, she died during an attack on my way to accomplish my class quest. I made a stupid mistake and it cost her life.

How can I make this right?" I struggled to keep my eyes clear, remembering the faithful horse and how she'd died.

"Oh dear," Elandel said. "What of her remains, did you put her to rest properly?"

"I still have them," I said, indicating my dimensional box. "I couldn't stand the idea of leaving her out to rot and I didn't have the time or knowhow to properly put her to rest."

"Bless you Chaos Slayer, for coming to me with this," Elandel said, she seemed on the verge of tears as well. "Come with me and we will inform the stable master. He won't be happy, he's been asking after Jill ever since you left, she was a favorite of his."

I followed after her, ready to take whatever words the stable master might have for me. The stables were well taken care of, and several younger stable boys worked at brushing and tending to some of the horses. A grizzled old man was working at changing a horse's shoes and Elandel called out to him as we approached.

"Howard, I come bearing sad news."

"Hmm what's that then?" Howard said, not looking up from his work.

"Caldor, would you inform him of the fate of Jill," Elandel said.

Howard looked up then, his face weathered with time and all color gone from his hair from age. He had a face full of lines, but there was strength in those hands as he worked.

"Jill was faithful to the end, doing her best to get me to where I was going. I tried to take a short cut and we were ambushed by Gnolls. She didn't make it, I'm so sorry," I said, Howard stared into my eyes the entire time and though his facial expression didn't change or falter, I saw a bit of the light leave his eyes.

"Good horse that was," Howard said, returning to his work. "You buried her deep?" He asked looking up, the reflective sheen of tears filling his grizzled old eyes. "Good horse like that don't need wild things chewing on her."

"He's brought her back to be put to rest properly," Elandel said, gesturing towards my dimensional box.

Howard let the foot of the horse he was working with fall to the ground, and he got up from the stool he'd been using. "Let's be about it then," he said and Elandel and I followed behind him. He walked us just outside the gardens, by a fruit tree. "She always liked them apples. Lay her out here and I'll get the shovel."

"Can you get two?" I asked, Howard caught my eye and nodded in the affirmative.

Elandel excused herself, promising to return to say words over the horse after we'd put her to rest in the ground.

Howard returned with a pair of shovels, and we wordlessly went to work. We shared no banter or conversation. Instead, next to the corpse of the fallen Jill still as fresh as the day she'd died, we dug down deep. I didn't tire and kept a steady grueling pace, but Howard never fell behind working as hard or harder than me. I could tell this was part of how he said goodbye and so we worked hard, digging plenty deep so that Jill could rest undisturbed.

Howard left after we'd made it a man and a half deep, returning with a rope. Together we lowered her remains into the hole and Elandel, without us having to go fetch her, returned in time to speak over her grave.

What words she spoke I couldn't really say as it wasn't in Common tongue, but they were beautiful and song-like. She ended her words with her hands held out and a white light poured into the grave.

"From the Wyrd she came, to the Wyrd she returns," Elandel said, pulling Howard into a warm embrace.

"I'll finish here, go," Howard said and so I left, not wanting to deprive him of his chance to grieve alone. To some I'm sure Jill was 'just a horse' but to Howard it felt like losing a child, for he never had any children of his own, Elandel told me all this as we left, and I couldn't help but curse my rashness that had resulted in her death.

CHAPTER 51
SIDE QUEST

I slept in the keep that night, meeting with Alayna and having an exciting night that ended in us cuddling on a long sofa in the library. I bumped into Galt on the way back to my room, but he said nothing, just gave me the stink eye as I passed by him. The morning came too quickly.

Rays of sunlight were falling across my face, despite the fact that I'd closed the shutters the night before. As I woke up enough to look around the room, I was startled to find an overweight bald man standing at the foot of my bed.

"Good morning, Non," I said, glad I'd decided to go to sleep with some clothes on after all. "Have you brought me breakfast, or you just here to startle me?"

"I meant no harm, but I have an urgent task for you that cannot wait," Non said, stepping up to the side of the bed that I'd just pulled myself into a sitting position on. "I must request that you deliver a message to Merlin. And no not the cook, but the elderly fellow you met in Creeshaw that acts as the current owner of 'Merlin's Pub'. It is urgent and I have been led to believe that you have access to a griffin. There is no faster mount in all of Newaliyn."

"Uh I actually had some plans for today, but now that you mention it, I'm overdue to visit my family. Sure, I'll deliver your message," I said, holding my hand out. Non looked at me suspiciously before depositing a thick envelope into my hand.

"It is urgent, please leave at your earliest convenience and return in time to give an account to Lord Variyn on the state of the Chaos threat," Non said, raising a brow as he spoke.

In other words, he wanted me to get the hell up and be about it. So much for breakfast, I thought as I dressed in a pair of common pants and shirt while slipping on a long coat I'd picked up. Without my armor I imagined I'd be cold, as even with it I had felt the chill of traveling fast and high up in the sky.

I focused on Ares, sending her my thoughts and urging her to meet me in the gardens. The keep was like a maze, but I'd discovered a door not far from my room that led out to the gardens and the shrine last night when I picked up my 'Gem Inscriptionist' profession.

Far away and fast approaching I felt Ares get ever closer. At Gilfoy's Emporium I'd picked up a Companion Stone and a saddle that I hoped would fit her, but they said they could refit it based on her size if I brought her by later. Either way, Ares landed just in front of me as I made it to the gardens and startled a pair of guards patrolling the area.

"It's fine," I reassured them, recognizing one of them from the card games I'd played with Mick.

The elegant black feathers with the strip of gold on her wings looked much more majestic in the bright light of the morning. Ares regarded me and I sent her my thoughts on her beauty. She screeched agreeably back to me as if saying, 'of course I am'.

"I've got the stone I told you about," I said, pulling the hefty black stone from my storage. It was roughly the size of my head and had tiny inscriptions covering most of the surface. The nice lady working there gave me instructions on how to activate it. All I had to do was touch it to a willing bonded creature and let it take the required mana from inside me.

Ares straightened and tilted her head, examining the rock. I could feel a measure of concern from her, but she stood tall trusting in me. The bond was something special, it felt like I'd known her for years when in fact it had been less than a few days. I could sense she was hungry, and I'd purchased a few dead rabbits for her, the clerk assured me it was a preferred meal for griffins.

Throwing out one of the rabbits with my free hand, Ares caught it mid-flight and gobbled it down. I fed her another two, holding half a dozen in reserve. She was fed and happy, so now was going to be as good a time as any. Stepping forward I held the stone with two hands and pressed it against her.

Do you wish to transfer Black Griffin into Companion Stone? Yes or No.

I sent out the mental affirmative and felt a small rush as a little bit of mana was taken from me. There was no magical flash of light or *Spark*s or really anything. One moment Ares was there and the next she was gone. I looked down frantically at the stone thinking I'd somehow messed it up but when I did, I saw it had changed.

The black stone had taken on the shape of a sleeping black griffin with a golden strip of feathers on its wings.

"Ares?" I whispered under my breath and as I did, I felt her feelings touch mine. She was safe and wanted to know if I needed her. I sent back a gentle request that she return and just like that the stone was gone and in its place was Ares.

She preened and shook her head and spread her wings, as if testing that everything still worked. I felt the gentle press on my mind that I'd gotten a system notification and checked it. It was informing me that I now had access to an animal companion menu. Pulling up my own I saw that a new tab had appeared.

It laid out her information similar to my own, she'd even gone from level 11 to match my own level at 12. I could see her health, mana, and stamina, as well as her personal attributes. It was odd to me that she had the same layout as I did, a part of me thought maybe she was different enough that she wouldn't have need of things like Concentration or Core attributes, but they were there just the same as mine. The same attribute names, but not the same values, her build much more favored Strength and Endurance.

"I have another present for you," I said, stroking her head gently. I pulled out the saddle and she kept her wings out for me while I worked to get it attached correctly. It took a bit of work, but I not only got it on her, it looked like it was a good fit.

The saddle was made of Dire Bull leather and had been polished to a pleasant shine. I even paid extra to have the saddle enchanted so I wouldn't need to worry about the general upkeep of the leather. It was similar to the enchantment used on my armor to keep things clean and maintained.

"How does that fit," I said, finding the spot she liked to be scratched at and going to town. "Does that feel good, you deserve it, you are a good girl." I got a humorous expression from her; she thought the way I was talking just then was funny.

"It's okay if you find me funny," I said, pulling myself up into the saddle. "I'm not as goofy as Fran, but I can definitely sound funny from time to time."

We lifted into the air, and I sent our direction to Ares, but told her to keep the pace nice and even so that I could sight see a bit. Even going at a slower pace than the night before, we made it to Creeshaw in record time.

I enjoyed my time watching the tops of the trees zip by and small towns and villages looking like no more than little gatherings of dots that I could scoop up with my hands. We set down right in front of Merlin's Pub, several surprised adventurers crying out in alarm.

With dust billowing from her mighty wings beating from our landing, I slipped off the saddle. My coat whipped behind me and went still as Ares folded in her wings. I sent Ares to the stables with a thought of the location and that she could expect a metal man to tend to her. She screeched willfully at me but followed my suggestion.

It was still early morning, our flight having taken just over an hour, and the sun was warm against the back of my neck. Two adventurers were standing outside, a leather clad woman and an iron armored man. They spoke in excited whispers not hiding their fingers and eyes pointed in my direction. It was an odd feeling being on the other side of that excitement. I'd once been the one unable to control my speculations or excitement at the sight of adventurers and now I was the target of such excitement and from adventurers themselves.

I decided to lean into it. "Good morning," I said as I approached. "A good day to fly, isn't it?"

"How did you tame a griffin? They are supposed to be legendary beasts!" The leather clad woman asked, her eyes wide in excitement.

Of course, it was Ares they were impressed with, but that didn't bother me. I still felt extremely epic. "You kn-"

I was cut off as the other adventurer, the armored one, spoke up, speaking in an annoyed drawl. "He's only two levels higher than us. He must be some spoiled noble's son that had it handed to him."

His words stung more than I cared to admit, and I found myself reacting with anger in my voice. "I'm not a damned noble! I'm from this very town and worked as an orchard farmer most of my life." I didn't know what I was thinking but I surprised myself when I noticed I'd summoned my blade into my hand. There had been no spell or words exchanged, as the skill didn't require it, the blade just answered to my intentions.

This alone startled the iron clad warrior enough that he tripped and fell on his ass. The leather clad blonde girl was quicker on her feet, and I felt the cold touch of steel nick the skin on my neck.

"Not so fast," she said, the sweetness gone from her voice. "You'll dismiss that weapon and let Craig get back up or I'll end you before you can bring that sword down, high level or not you won't get far without a throat."

"Easy," I said, a growl of anger still in my voice. I dismissed my sword and it returned to my scabbard to wherever it laid in wait for me to call it back. I was so tempted to use Swift Strike to knock her blade aside with my sword, but I'd little practice with the skill and figured I'd be just as likely to cut my head off as I would be to deflect her blade.

This Craig character had stirred up an anger I hadn't known slumbered below the surface, and I'd need to do better to control myself. It wouldn't always be lower leveled adventurers I'd encounter if I kept it up. But damn if it wasn't just so annoying to have someone assume just because you had a run of good fortune that it must have been given to you by a doting noble family.

The blade moved away from my neck, and I had a very morbid thought. After all I'd been through and the crazy amount of injuries I'd survived, I was fairly certain that even if she tried as hard as she might that blade of hers wouldn't have done fatal damage. She might have a skill, I reminded myself, that could increase the deadly potential several fold, but there really was no telling.

"Sorry," the female voice said, all the sweetness and awe returning to her voice. "I've gotten pretty attached to my tanky poo Craig and well, you know how difficult it is to find a proper tank, I'm sure. Gotta keep them alive long enough to get things done."

I didn't really know that it was hard to find people to fill the role of tank, or a person who tried to keep the attention of the monsters during a fight. In fact between Emory, Creed, and Grug, the beastkin, I'd met three people that I felt could fill the tank role just fine.

"I'm sorry," I said, holding up my hands defensively. "The ability to summon my sword is a bit tricky and I hadn't actually meant to bring it forth. But you are pretty handy with that dagger, if you ever find yourself in need of a midrange damage dealer, I'd love to run a dungeon with you."

"We'll pass," Craig said before the woman clad in leather could answer. "Come on Dolores, I'm not hungry anymore."

Dolores gave me a 'sorry bout that' smile and followed Craig in the direction of the Adventurer's Hall. I'd only been trying to be polite, figuring it never hurts to try and mend bridges before outright burning them, but now I really wanted to tell Craig where he could stick it. I didn't, showing a measure of control instead. I pushed the thick oak door open and entered Merlin's Pub.

"It was you that brought that majestic creature to my stables," Merlin said as I entered. There was a group of four others sitting at tables and chatting idly, but none of them looked up. It was busier than it was most mornings, but none of that really occurred to me as I practically ran to the bar toward the back that Merlin tended.

"Is she okay?" I asked, holding my breath while I waited for the answer.

"Is who okay?" Merlin asked, tilting his head in confusion. "There are a great many 'shes' in this world and others. You are going to have to be more specific."

"Ismene dammit, stop playing with me old man!" I shouted, this turned the heads of everyone in the pub. "Sorry, just please tell me she is okay."

"Oh her," Merlin said as if just now realizing who I meant. "I don't know her state of being at this moment, but when I last laid eyes on her, she was in fine condition. She left with a fellow by the name of...what was it again... Emote...Emor...Emory, yes that was it, Emory. He was a low-level fellow and she seemed to know him. Not a good mix if you ask me, a Sentinel and a Scout. You really want to be sure to get a diverse number of damage types in a proper group. They'll both be doing plain old physical damage, useful most times, but when it's not, it's not. You following this?"

I heard every word, but I'd gotten stuck on the part where he mentioned Ismene's class, she was a scout! That was a type of stealthy ranged class that was fairly common, but she'd gotten a class! I could barely contain my excitement and I nearly turned right there and went looking for the pair. Just as I turned, I remembered why I'd been sent here, and I pulled loose the letter.

"I've got a message for you from Non of House Variyn," I said, pulling myself back to task. Merlin was wearing his usual blue robes with stars and clouds on them, but suddenly they shifted and the clouds darkened.

"What does that sneaky little piece of goblin dung want?" Merlin asked, readjusting his conical hat on his head so that it pressed closer to his brows. It made him look a bit angrier, but almost in a silly way, not at all frightening.

I handed over the thick letter on yellowing parchment. Merlin snatched it free of my held-out hand and made a show of ripping it open. There were at least half a dozen pages inside and his eyes ran over it all. Several scoffs and harrumphs later and he was finished.

Merlin's eyes, sparkling blue and ancient, studied me for a long few seconds. It was getting to the point of being awkward when he finally broke the gaze and shook his head.

"Tell that old fool that I'd not return for all the gold in a dozen worlds. This land and its people will get along just fine. Stupid royalty and their stupid squabbles," Merlin said, his robes now had a few streaks of yellow that were likely meant to be lightning. But after taking a few slow and steady breaths his robes returned to their light blue with yellow stars and white clouds.

"Did you want to write that down or just have me tell him?" I asked. I couldn't help but smile at the oddness that was Merlin.

"Verbal is fine, I haven't the inclination to waste my time writing him a scolding note. Children these days just want to take, take, take," Merlin said. The last bit had been under his breath, but I heard it fine.

For a moment I wondered at what he meant. Was he referring to me as a child or did he mean Non? Whichever it was neither of us were the age that someone would consider a child, but perhaps he meant the statement more literal. Could Non be Merlin's child? No, no they both appeared to be fairly old so that didn't fit at all. But how could I really know? Aging slowed as you passed thresholds, with even the first threshold in Constitution bringing you a hundred or more years. There were also the aging related Perks that increased your natural life up to five-fold if taken enough.

"I'll deliver your message," I said, deciding it was best not to ask any further details, lest I be lectured about some random fact. Merlin really was an odd fellow. "Do you know where Ismene and Emory went?"

"Hmm, oh yes Ismene hadn't yet reached her fifth level and Emory took her to that blasted Adventurers Hall to find something to do," Merlin said, picking up a clean mug and polishing it with a rag I hadn't seen him holding only moments before. He did odd things like that, showing off what must be magic without any signs of actually doing magic. "Haven't seen them since." Merlin added when I just stared at him for several seconds.

"Thanks," I said. I had to make a conscious effort to stop wondering about the oddity that was Merlin and get on to other matters. "I have a griffin in your stables, could you feed and care for it while I search for my friends?"

"Can I keep any shavings or feathers she leaves behind from the grooming?" Merlin asked, raising a single eyebrow and leaning forward.

"Sure, I mean, I guess. What good are they to you?" I asked.

"Powerful reagents, griffin feathers and nails. So are their eyes, but I doubt she'd be willing to give up an eye without a fuss," Merlin said, now seeming to just be talking to himself.

"Maybe I will take Ares with me," I began to say but Merlin cut me off.

"No, no, I speak in jest of course she will be safe with me. There is no one more qualified than me to care for a griffin and you can quote me on that," Merlin said, shooing me away with his hands.

"One last thing," I said as my stomach growled. "Can I get a quick bite to eat."

My quick bite to eat ended up being a large, delicious plate of bacon, eggs, fried potatoes, and cut kelt fruit. I learned from Merlin as I ate that my mother had sold him the kelt fruit directly. Apparently, she'd been going directly to businesses and offering to sell them the overstock of kelt fruit at base price, price cutting the merchant we normally dealt with. I wasn't keen on the idea of upsetting the merchants we would sometimes buy goods from, but I trusted that my mother knew what she was doing.

It wasn't long after that I found myself outside the Adventurers Hall. This would be my first time inside this place, and I felt a sense of apprehension as I pushed open the thin oak swinging doors.

"Guild coin," a voice to the left rang out and I looked to see who had spoken.

The immediate room I found myself in was expansive, with fifteen-foot ceilings, large draperies hanging on the wall next to monster trophies. I recognized a few, but most I didn't. There was an expansive rug made from the fur and head of a dire bear nearly as large as the Elite I'd come across. It had black hair though and sat just feet away from a massive stone fireplace directly ahead from where I'd entered. To my right there were a dozen tables, most of them filled by one or two adventurers drinking and eating, and on the far wall a bar with a man tending it.

To my left was a desk with an older woman leaning forward and giving me the stink eye. Behind her was a boxed off area with a door, but no roof from what I could tell, just two walls separating that space from the rest of the large entryway. Toward the back on both sides were doors leading to other places within the long house.

"Have you got mud in your ears? I said, Guild Coin!" The lady practically shrieked at me.

I pulled my pack free from my dimensional storage and went digging inside of it for the coin I'd gotten a few nights back. Finding it toward the bottom I fished it out and presented it.

She snatched it from my hand and set it down on a crystal-clear square, peering at it with a critical gaze.

"Welcome to Adventurers Hall number 69 in the Variyn district. My name is Gloria, do you have any new levels to declare?" Gloria asked. She had thick spectacles making her eyes seem larger than they were, and gray curly locks held firm in a bun atop her head. Several of the curls had gotten loose despite her effort. Her face was a mess of lines from the passing years and by the look of her she could rival Merlin in age, however her eyes lacked the ancient quality that Merlin's gave off.

"I'm level 12 now, is that what you mean?" I asked, not wanting to stoke the fire of this elderly lady's temper again.

"Give me a moment to update it here. There we are. I see you are exempt from the taxes due, so I won't bother you with questions about what loot you acquired to get those 3 new levels. Have a fine day," Gloria said. She smiled but it didn't touch her eyes.

"I'm actually looking for someone, would you be able to help me find them?" I asked, giving her a smile of my own but trying my damnedest to make it appear genuine.

"Names?" Gloria said, her smile fading much faster than it'd taken her to plaster it on.

"Ismene Gadar and Emory Faldel."

"Please stand by while I check," Gloria said, her finger dragging against the clear crystal. I couldn't see anything from where I stood, and I wondered what she was looking at. "Both checked in very early this morning and are likely still sleeping. They were assigned rooms in the D section, numbers 9 and 10. That way." Gloria pointed at the door to the left and I muttered a quick thank you, zipping away to find my friends.

Going through the door I was met by a long hallway; it looked as if it ran the length of the building. There were doors numbered from 1 to 10 with a letter next to it starting with A. I passed through the A's all the way to the D's, until I stood just outside doors D9 and D10. She hadn't said which was in which room so I did what any reasonable friend would do, I knocked on both of them at the same time.

I heard groaning from inside the left room but no footsteps. However, in the room on the right came a voice I recognized.

"According to guild rules I get this room for a full day before I need to check out, so get lost!" Emory shouted from inside the room.

I was tempted to pretend to be housekeeping or something to have a bit of fun at his expense, but my excitement superseded my funny bone.

"Emory Faldel you great bastard," I said, cupping my hands against his door to hopefully amplify my voice.

"Caldor!" A voice from the other room followed by a quick thud of steps followed, bringing Ismene and Emory to the door around the same moment.

Emory spoke first, but Ismene didn't wait for words, pulling me into a tight hug and kissing my cheek.

"She'd told me you'd become an adventurer, but seeing is believing! Look at you! You freaking turd, you did it!" Emory said, pulling me into a hug the moment Ismene released me.

"We did it," I said, looking at each of them. "We really did it! We're adventurers!"

We walked together while I filled Emory in on the short version of what had happened to me. Ismene had told him only the smallest bit of information, deciding it would be best for me to explain. I waited to tell them about my class trial, as I wanted to hear about Ismene's journey first.

We took up the last free table in the little pub area inside the Adventurers Hall and ordered a round of drinks.

"So you're an Arcane Knight like your father and basically a freaking noble as well?" Emory said, slapping his knee. "You don't do anything in half measures."

"I guess not," I said, savoring the amazing feeling of being around my two closest friends and all of us having our dreams come true as adventurers. "Ismene fill me in, what happened after Merlin took you through that portal?"

"I barely remember anything up to the point of touching the Prime Mana Shrine, but after touching it I met a woman who called herself Arbiter, but you know how that all goes. I had limited options for a class, just three actually, so I picked the one I thought would fit best in our group, a ranged damage dealer."

"What other options did it give you?" I asked, my curiosity getting the better of me.

"Well, there was a Fighter, which is I guess like a basic armor wearing class that most advanced martial classes are based off of. And then the one I nearly took, but couldn't picture myself doing, so I dropped it. It was simply called Monk. A front-line fighter that can't wear armor or wield weapons, relying purely on your body, like fist and kicks I guess. But what drew me to it was the promise of higher levels being able to use a special form of mana to do minor healing or strengthening yourself. But I couldn't get over the idea of not wearing any traditional armor or not using weapons, so I took Scout."

I reached across the table and put my hand on hers, squeezing it. "You are going to be the best damned Scout there's ever been," I said, my smile so wide it hurt.

"Oh, and at level 10 I can tame a medium sized animal to fight at my side or do things for me. Or at least that's what the Arbiter told me, she was very encouraging but said my path forward would be hard if I didn't surround myself with the right people. I assured her I knew just the people to watch my back," Ismene said, winking at me and taking a long pull from her drink.

"She's gotten like a thousand times better with the bow," Emory said, slapping her shoulder. "We cleared out a small pack of kobolds and she'd taken two of them out before I even made it to the front line. One of them straight through the eye!"

"It's my class ability 'Eagle Eye' I can activate it for five seconds at a time with a short thirty second cooldown. While it's active it's like everyone is moving slow and it's so easy to hit what I'm aiming for!" Ismene said, barely containing her excitement.

The other adventurers looked at us with side eyes, but we didn't care because this was literally the best possible outcome for our lives. No one was going to spoil that for us.

"Almost got her enough experience to do a dungeon," Emory said, sighing. "Her and I both gather essence so damned slow that I swear it takes us twice as long as anyone else to get enough."

"That's true," Ismene said, a quirky look on her face. "The Arbiter warned me that it was going to be that way, my affinity for my core is only fourteen percent. She even offered to allow me to not become *Awoken*, releasing my stored essence. Obviously, I told her as politely as I could to stuff it and let me pick a class. She seemed to understand, though, and instead offered me advice, saying I should do as many dungeons as possible as they are more essence rich than hunting monsters out in the wild."

"That is crazy," I said. "Before my class quest started, and I became so distracted with trying to stay alive, I really worried that something had happened to you. My better sense won out; I knew you'd make it!"

"Class quests are hard for sure, but why were you so worried about Ismene specifically?" Emory said, throwing a few pretzels into his mouth from the small bowl on the table.

Ismene kicked my leg from underneath the table and I stuttered the words I'd been about to say, falling quiet.

"Didn't I tell you I was feeling a bit ill before *Awakening*? That's why Merlin took me to a remote Prime Mana Shrine, I could have sworn I told you Emory," Ismene said, a fake smile on her face. Emory knew us well enough to tell she was hiding something, but for whatever reason he let it go and I changed the subject, making a note in my head to ask Ismene why she'd kept the truth from Emory.

"Tell me about your class quest," I said, grabbing a few hard pretzels myself. "If it was anything like mine, I'm sure you have a great tale to share."

"It was actually pretty quick, but a few interesting things did happen," Ismene said. "Merlin was with me, and my quest instructed me to collect the heart of a Skral Leopard. I'd never heard of such a thing, but Merlin said he knew just the place. He even gave me a map that worked with the system, and it showed me where to go, but here is the odd part. It wasn't on our continent, we were on some distant isle to the north-east, he called it 'Avalon' and from the map he'd given me I saw only a single city or settlement and it was labeled 'Camelot'."

"I have a map that shows that island too, but it didn't have a name on mine," I said, pulling up my map and labeling the island. "I also have information on three dungeons there and the levels of the mobs were ridiculously high!"

"Wait, you both have magical maps and I'm over here like a fool using this thing?" Emory pulled out a thin tube and pulled free a map. "I'd heard you can integrate magically created maps into your interface, but that must have cost hundreds of gold. You two are the luckiest sons of bitches I've met."

We both just smiled our cheesiest grins and Ismene continued her tale.

"So anyways, he opened another portal, this one took us across the island to a jungle like area and before I could even unleash an arrow it was over. Merlin killed the spotted cat, though how he saw it was beyond me. Until he hit it with a blueish bolt of energy, I had been looking in that exact spot and saw nothing. I got a good bit of essence from the kill so it must have been fairly strong. And then he opened a new portal, and I completed my class quest."

"Really?" I asked, dumbfounded. "Meanwhile I turned mine in with seconds to spare and almost failed it."

Emory nearly lost the drink he was gulping down and said, "You get an entire week! What were you doing the whole time, drinking and fooling around with all those noble girls? Couldn't pull yourself away long enough to do a quick quest?"

"As if," I said, laughing. "I grouped with a few other people, and we just happened to be close to their class quest items first. By the time we got to mine, some jackass had cleared out all the Owl Bears and taken the hearts I needed."

"What'd you do, how long did you have at that point?" Ismene said, leaning forward and squeezing my hand.

"Is there someplace private we can talk, and I'll fill you in on everything," I said, looking around the room. No one was overtly listening in, but I wanted to tell them about my affinities and swear them to secrecy, something I wouldn't be able to do in public.

"I bet Merlin would let us use his back room again?" Ismene said, standing.

We agreed and made our way out into the bright early afternoon sun. There was a cool breeze, the dew of the morning still cool on the wind. Emory still had his mismatched armor and I inspected him to see if he'd made it to level 10 or not.

Emory Faldel, Level 10

"You made it to level 10," I said, slapping him playfully on his back. He lurched forward and nearly lost his footing.

"And what level are you, damn man you nearly bowled me over," Emory said, staring at me critically. "Level 12! What in the absolute fuckery is this!"

I smiled weakly. "I'll tell you all about it when we get into the quiet room," I promised, both Ismene and Emory picked up their pace now and soon, with Merlin's permission, we were in his room and under the protection of his scrying defensive spells.

I left out as few details as I could, the bit with the Arbiter and my role as an agent of balance or whatever being the main thing. I went over meeting with Fred and Fran, how we killed loads of monsters and encountered stronger ones than we should have. Explained about the goblins and nearly being blown to hell. Then got to where the Owl Bears had all been killed when Emory cut in.

"That bastard you mentioned, Zander, was it? I'd like to have some time alone with his face. He sounds like an absolute asshat."

"An asshat, like one you'd wear on your head?" Ismene asked, snickering like a young child. I couldn't help it and I laughed as well at the thought of an 'ass hat'.

The next part of my story got them to quiet down as I explained the Gnolls and my horse Jill getting killed. Then explaining the fight, all that I could remember, with the Sea Serpent and the help of the griffin, Emory's eyes got wide.

"You didn't!" He was practically shouting.

"I did," I said, bouncing a bit in my seat. "I bonded a freaking Griffin and her name is Ares."

"Your luck or fortune or whatever you want to call it is unreal," Emory said, shaking his head. "On one turn some asshat just about ruins your chance at being an adventurer and possibly killing you in the process, then on the other hand you tame a freaking griffin! Like a real life straight from legend griffin!"

"He's right," Ismene said. I couldn't get a read on her

mood as her expression kept shifting. "You are beyond lucky, it's almost hard to believe."

"I mean, if you think it is hard to believe, try living it," I said, chuckling. "It's just a story now and a memory I can look back on, but dammit it was hard as hell and more painful than anything I'd ever experienced."

Ismene's expression shifted to one I knew all too well, the caring and concern of a good friend.

"We're glad you made it through it in one piece, because if you'd had died, I would have killed you," Ismene said, chuckling.

"Yeah, yeah," I said. "I'm not done yet, let me finish."

I continued telling them the rest of what had happened to me but leaving out the bit about being able to infuse essence. There was no point in getting them excited if I wasn't able to pull it off. They would be the most, in my mind, to benefit from my discovery. Imagine if they could carry around a few gems that collected larger portions of essence and increased their ability to level and gain attributes to a normal or even higher level. It would be life changing. Which is why I decided it would be just as life shattering for me to tell them now and later inform them that I couldn't actually figure it out.

"I need to get to level 5," Ismene said, putting her head in her hands and yelling into them. "I'm doing as Merlin instructed, adding at least 1 more attribute per level, but if I ignored level 4s extra attribute I'm only like 950 essence away from getting to level 5."

I cringed at that but hid the reaction by pretending to stretch. She was only purchasing a single attribute point per level! That would make her even weaker than what is normally accepted as standard. It wouldn't be so bad at first but the higher we got in levels the bigger the gap we'd have. I had no choice. I had to tell her about my potential discovery and urge her to do as many attributes per level as she could once she hit level 5.

"I've got one more thing I need to tell you both," I said. They saw the serious expression on my face and quieted down.

I told them about my ability and what Alayna had said about it. Then shared with them that I'd picked the Gem Inscriptionist profession and planned, very soon, to take as much time as I needed to begin learning what I could about making gems that would suck in essence instead of mana.

Emory and Ismene just looked at me, their jaws hanging open a bit and unable to voice a response.

"But there is no guarantee that I can figure this out," I said, trying to temper their reactions.

"You have to," Emory said, as he began looking back and forth at the exit and around the room as if he expected someone to barge in. "You could literally change the world. Bringing one of those inside a dungeon and you could just sit inside doing nothing."

"What do you mean?" I asked, confused.

"Dungeons have a large amount of ambient essence that your body slowly gathers as you fight through it, but it's so little that it's almost not worth mentioning. But imagine if you could pull harder and collect hundreds instead of tens. Just being in a dungeon would be worthwhile and finishing it could be life changing. If the large release of essence you get at the end of a completed dungeon was magnified, oh man you have to figure this out!"

"I'll do my best," I said. "You two can be my testing dummies, I'll make overly large gaudy jewelry for you to wear into battle."

Ismene laughed the hardest and said as she caught her

breath. "And I'd wear the hell out of them! You could give me a ring the size of a walnut and I'd gladly punch monsters in the face with it."

"Have you thought about the money you'll get?" Emory asked, then something occurred to him. "Also, you really shouldn't tell anyone and obviously we'll keep quiet about this and the Paragon thing, which by the way, how the fuck did you not *Spark* until a few weeks ago with an affinity that high? Like damn, man."

I just smiled and thanked him for being willing to keep my promises. I didn't have the heart to tell either of them about my father or Warrick. The two people I had been closer to than even Emory and Ismene and they'd betrayed me. But I didn't want to dwell on it, having already come to terms with it, so I just smiled and laughed with my friends.

We were at it for another hour until Merlin came in and asked if we'd finished as he had work to do, so we left. After introducing them to Ares I told them I planned on going to visit my family before heading back to the capital city, as Non had told me I needed to give an account of the Chaos monsters I'd encountered. They said they understood, and we agreed to meet back here in two weeks, which was how long Emory guessed it would take to find monsters enough for Ismene to gain 2 attributes and finally level to 5. They collected essence so slow that it was painful to even consider.

The flight to my house ended abruptly as I flew over Warrick's tower, or what had been his tower. I circled above a large pile of stone ruins, it looked like the structure had exploded, destroying trees all around it and burning away the field of mint around it. I landed and searched through the rubble, there were no signs of Warrick or even his belongings. It was all stone, just piled up and thrown about.

Where was Warrick and was he okay? New worries flooded me as I considered what this meant. I stayed for longer than I probably should have, but no matter how many stones I pushed aside or lifted free there was always just more stone. Not a single book or trophy or scrap of carpet could be found. Could that be a good sign? I didn't know how the magic for Warrick's tower worked, but maybe this meant he'd just moved it, and the stone was what had been left behind? I didn't think that was likely and if it was why had he destroyed the trees and flung rock so far from the center of his tower?

No, something was going on, but I had no clue as to what it could be.

The visit with my family was nice and we shared a meal together before I left back to Variyn. My siblings looked like they'd grown, and my mother explained to me her new business ventures, selling directly to the source for a price that Philip—despite what he'd told her—refused to sell at.

The flight passed far too quickly, my mind heavy with thoughts of Warrick. After landing in the keep's gardens, a favorite place for Ares it would seem, I fed her and she shifted back to the stone carving, where I tucked her away safely. Before I went to visit the nobles, I wanted to pick up my armor and change into my formal attire.

I wasn't looking forward to seeing Zander but imagined he'd probably be in attendance. I'd have to make sure my sword was nice and sharp.

CHAPTER 52
NOBLE REPORTING

D ressed in my best and armed with my sword and a new dagger—I'd had too many occasions where one would have come in handy—I approached the door to the great hall, where I'd been led to believe I'd be having dinner with Lord Variyn and giving a report on matters. What I didn't expect was another large party that ended in a dinner. Alayna wasn't present, she'd told me that her father had requested her tend to some urgent business elsewhere that afternoon before leaving, but she hadn't said where.

As before, I was announced and ushered into the room. I admired the awe-inspiring layout of the room, with its carved pillars and elegant draperies. But more than anything I really wanted to be left alone to pursue my profession and see if what I wanted would be possible. I drank and ate, keeping as far from Zander as I could. He wore the same overly ornate white armor and talked with a few others his age.

Several times during the dinner party people approached me and presented questions about Chaos monsters or other affairs to do with the kingdom that I didn't have the slightest way to answer, such as 'Did I know if Lord Variyn was open to new spice trade contracts. I didn't and I took a page from Non's book and remained closed lipped about the events surrounding the Chaos monsters. If they were meant to know it, then they could hear when I gave my announcement.

The night dragged and I was caught several times staring forward as I examined my menus. My profession menu for instance was filled with about two dozen crafting recipes, all of which were given without me having to spend any essence or anything. Alayna had told me to get books on recipes and general knowledge around my profession, as that was—according to her—the best way to increase your profession level and known recipes. Professions were unique in that leveling them didn't require essence or the need to visit a Mana Shrine. In fact, the closest parallel I could draw was proxy levels, which oddly enough I could still check and see within my menus.

The same well-dressed man that had announced everyone as they entered now spoke above the noise of conversation.

"Lord Variyn invites all those who have not been invited to stay for dessert to please depart now."

I looked around, thinking this would be a good time to escape and not have to give my report after all when the Lord's brother called out to me.

"Where are you going off in a hurry?" he asked, his cheeks red from drinking heavily. "You and my son are the guests of honor, come sit over here."

Begrudgingly I stood and made my way toward that end of the table. Lord Variyn and his wife, as they had before, sat on a high table at the end of the long one where everyone else sat. Across from Bren, Lord Variyn's brother, sat Zander. I was surprised to see he didn't have his normal self-satisfied look on his face, he seemed a bit nervous, his eyes darting here and there as people left. Perhaps he wasn't looking forward to the public speaking either.

When everyone had left there were just over a dozen present, including Lord Variyn and his wife. Lord Variyn stood and gestured in front of himself, saying, "Caldor and Zander please come stand before me and give a report. I wish to know what progress has been made against the incursion of Chaos into my lands."

Bren chuckled drunkenly behind me, but what he found so funny I couldn't tell. I wondered how much of what I'd told Alayna about my run-ins with Chaos monsters had made it to her father's ears, but figured I best just tell them all that I could remember.

I followed Zander's lead to a space in front of the Lord and Lady, standing some ten feet from them.

"Who wishes to go first," Lord Variyn said, his eyes passing over both of us.

"He does," Zander said, tilting his head towards me. I repressed a nervous laugh. What, did he think I was afraid to report what I'd encountered? That little jackass probably hadn't done a single thing in the couple weeks since our 'official' appointment.

I cleared my throat and began. "Since we last spoke I've had three encounters with Chaos monsters." I paused as I saw a surprised look flash over Lord Variyn's face, so Alayna hadn't told him anything after all. There was a general uproar of chatter behind me, and I suspected no one in attendance had expected as much.

I continued, going over how I'd helped slay a Chaos Wurm, presenting a piece of it—a small section of its heavy armor plates—on the ground before me. Then went on to explain about the black wyvern and how I'd assumed the Elite Dire

Bear had taken care of it only to encounter it later as I flew over House Blalor lands.

"All these incidents were outside of House Variyn you say? These are disturbing reports to hear, and I worry about the dedication of our neighboring house," Lord Variyn said, his eyes calculating but his face a mask of emotionlessness.

"All in House Blalor," I repeated. "But the wyvern moved swiftly and could easily become a threat if it chose to fly into our lands."

"And what would you do if it was sighted inside my lands?" Lord Variyn asked, his gaze bearing down at me. I didn't know what kind of answer he expected but he had to know that I wasn't a match for a wyvern yet.

"I would report its location and if confronted without a way to escape to safety I would do my best to kill it," I said, saying each word clearly and carefully all the while watching for any hint of emotion from Lord Variyn. If I said what he wanted, it wasn't clear by looking at him.

"Very well," he said, lifting his hand to his face and rubbing at his brows. This was the first sign that he'd given but what it meant I didn't know. "You are to be congratulated for your efforts. I'm sure it wasn't easy to do your class trial and tend to your obligation to me at the same time. Zander, tell me what you've done these past weeks?"

Zander was already a pale man, but he surprised me by losing a bit more color in his face and stiffening. He really wasn't looking forward to this and it showed.

"I..I uhh, I mean to say," Zander said, stumbling over his words.

It didn't help that his father called out from behind us as he struggled to find his words.

"Untangle that tongue, you vile excuse for a son," Bren

shouted. I could hear a few people around him shush him and even Lord Variyn shot a look behind us that would have given me pause. Bren grumbled something I didn't quite hear and quieted down.

I didn't think it was possible, but I felt a bit sorry for Zander at that moment. Sparing a glance to my left I saw a defeated look on his face. He wasn't quite to the point of tears, but I guessed he wasn't far off.

"Please continue," Lord Variyn said, a good-natured smile crossing his face.

"I have nothing to report. I have not encountered any remnants of Chaos," Zander said, hanging his head.

"Do not despair," Lord Variyn said, and Zander raised his head to look at his uncle. "Caldor reports Chaos monsters in House Blalor and you report none here in Variyn. While not ideal for our neighbors, it is welcoming news for us. The threat is passing us over and our efforts to deal with it have not been in vain. I propose we reconvene in two week's time and if there is no word of Chaos spreading in my lands, I will be grateful." As he spoke his eyes rested on me and I understood something.

This meeting had been a plan by Lord Variyn to declare the Chaos threat over or something to those ends. I was almost sure of it now because the look he was giving me clearly meant he didn't want to hear any more about Chaos monsters in two weeks.

I had my own calling now and had no plans of letting the Chaos threat fall to the wayside. After our little announcements were finished, we took our seats and dessert was served, a chilled chocolate pudding with vanilla wafers. I enjoyed it, but I didn't enjoy sitting next to Bren. He continued to drink and throw insults at Zander and drunkenly praise me. By the time the event ended I was all too ready to leave, but Non appeared close to the door and motioned me over just as the last guests left the hall. I turned to check and even Lord and Lady Variyn had left, but through a back door somewhere.

"What news from Merlin," Non said, he wore a neatly pressed black suit that, to me at least, almost looked like a pair of pajamas. For the first time since meeting Non his face was not emotionless, he actually looked quite tense.

"Let me remember what he said in his own words," I cleared my throat and prepared to disappoint Non. "He said, 'tell the old fool that not for all the gold in a dozen worlds and that the land and its people will be fine. Then something about the squabbles of nobles, that is as best I can remember, he didn't want to leave you a note and said that children want too much from him. Are you related?"

Non's expression darkened as I spoke and I immediately regretted tacking on the question at the end, but after a moment to right himself Non looked as passive as he normally did.

"In a sense I am, but at the same time I'm not anymore his child than you are," Non said.

I hated when people spoke in riddles, but I wasn't about to hound Non for clarification. Despite how he looked I knew he was dealing with something that was bristling his emotions.

"Anything else I can do for you?" I asked, genuinely curious if he'd figured anything new about the people who'd kidnapped and threatened me. But of course I couldn't outright say that as people might be listening.

"No, just keep your eyes open and report anything strange," Non said, barely looking at me as he turned and walked toward a wall that definitely didn't have a door. He reached a low hanging drapery and slipped behind it. I heard the smallest of clicks as he entered what must have been a secret door. He was definitely distracted if he just gave away one of his secrets while I watched.

Turning I decided to go to my room and see about tinkering with my profession. I made it all of three steps out of the room when a globe of golden light closed right over my head. It was transparent and wasn't damaging me, but when I lifted my arms to try and push it off chains shot out of the ground and entangled my hands.

Zander appeared, his eyes glowing with a faint golden light and both his hands held out as he chanted the words of a spell. I recognized one of the spells, but the globe and its purpose eluded me until I tried to take another breath and found I couldn't. I gasped struggling for air. My sword appeared in my hand, but my arms couldn't move. I stumbled back as the globe came over my head. I was relatively close to the edge of one of the doors, and an idea occurred to me.

Slamming my head as hard as I could backwards, I saw cracks begin to form all around the globe. Not being able to breathe made me manic as I thrashed against the chains and slammed my head over and over again against the door. Finally, just as the edges of my vision began to darken the globe shattered. The moment of the last strike was big enough that I gashed the back of my head on the door after shattering the globe.

Zander ended his chanting and I saw him begin another spell, probably another globe. I lurched forward and kicked him hard in the chest. He went flying backward, but finished his spell, another globe covering over my head. I had another idea this time, I began the cast for my Arcane Armor spell.

It was hard, as it was a five second cast and required me to focus. What made it hard wasn't the breathing, but the staying focused part as I kicked the shit out of Zander on the ground.

But somehow, I managed it and I felt arcane energy pour over me. As it reached my head the globe of light shattered against the translucent blue helmet that appeared.

Standing over Zander, his face bloody from my kicks and his armor scuffed from the trip he took to the ground, I cast Light Blade while holding my bonded sword. Barely perceivable light danced up the length of the sword and I raised it, ready to strike.

For his credit Zander met my gaze, unafraid and defiant. The building rage softened as I considered him. During the last part of the dinner, I noticed something. Every time Bren moved toward Zander, he flinched. If I had to guess, I'd say it was a sign that he probably beat the shit out of him on the regular. I hated Zander. A very big part of me wanted to end him here and just be done with it.

I saw Alayna's face and thought about how Bren must treat his son, before sighing and letting my blade fade away.

"I'm not your enemy," I said, turning my head and spitting blood out of my mouth.

I didn't offer to help him up, instead turning my back on him and leaving him bleeding on the ground. No sounds of casting a spell or him moving at all came from behind me. I was nearly to my room, the corridors oddly quiet when my entire body stopped moving.

No matter what I said or tried to do I couldn't. I'd literally just dismissed my Arcane Armor moments before and now Zander had cast some paralyzing spell on me? There would be no more mercy, I thought fuming as my anger rose. But it wasn't Zander that I saw walk from behind me and stop, standing in front of me.

It was Tim, the wizard bastard who worked under Lord Variyn and secretly worked against him. Memories of the three people questioning me while I was blindfolded flashed through my mind. He'd used something that blocked magic before, but it hadn't stopped my movements last time, this was something new. And no matter how hard I struggled or tried to lash out I just couldn't move.

My Lightning Strike spell was an instant cast and I focused on trying to cast it, but it had a hand movement and word component, so it failed, fizzling out before it could get going.

"Oh, clever, very clever," Tim said, lightly patting me on my cheek. "An instant cast spell so I don't have time to counter if you were a bit more advanced in your study of magic that might have worked. Did you know that the knowledge you get when you learn spells is just a variation among many? By the taste of it, that was a lightning-based attack. If you studied how to cast it and the general use of magic, you will eventually learn how to enact the spell on thought alone. The system of the Ordu will of course quantify everything, but there is more freedom than you could imagine for those who have spent the centuries required to learn."

I tried to respond but found I couldn't even speak, instead my throat made a wheezing sound.

"Oh, sorry about that," Tim said, shaking his head. "It isn't that I fear the damage your spells can do, really, I hold you here for your own protection. I've got many powerful wards placed around myself that would likely kill you when you attacked me before I could negate their effect. Let me get down to it, and you will be free to go about your business."

Tim leaned in close to my face, examining my eyes and traced his hand across my face and to my ears.

"Aw, that explains it. Where did you come across such rare items?" Tim asked, pulling one of my Masterwork Refined Mythril Ear Clasps off. "Crafted by Merlin? Could it be the

551

very same." Tim's eyes went wide, and he actually took a step back. "You entangle yourself even further than your father with powers you couldn't possibly understand. It might be prudent to end this game now."

Tim placed the ear clasp back over my ear and stepped back, taking a quick look around he sighed. "It brings me no pleasure in doing this, you were to be a useful tool and your father was a valiant man." The tip of his finger ignited with red and black energy. "This will hurt a good bit, but it's the only means I have to truly strip you of your power forever. You can't imagine what I had to do to get it."

"If it is the only one, then allow me to take that knowledge from you," a voice rang out from behind me. Tim's finger went out and he jumped backwards, startled, and looking afraid. A stream of red and black *Spark*ing energy left Tim's head and traveled past mine. Tim fell to the ground like a stiff board. He lay still, only the barest of movements from his breathing.

"The spell holding you will be released in about a minute, so don't worry," the voice said. I knew that I'd heard it someplace before but for the life of me I couldn't place it. "It's funny how time weaves and turns. I thought I would be needed further down your timeline, yet here I am. It was an interesting spell your friend had, Tim, was it? This world is rotten with my sibling's influences. They claim to be so against interfering and forcing my hand, but you know I've found countless examples of them doing much worse. The nerve of them. I've altered Tim's memory; he will believe he delivered his threat, and you went on your way. I imagine he is still very dangerous, and you should plan your actions accordingly. If not for this tiny bit of chaotic knowledge, he might have snuffed you out before anyone could do a thing. But time is funny like that, you never really know even when it seems certain things will go a specific way. Till we meet again. Be safe, Caldor, for I won't always be here."

The spell holding me in place vanished and I fell forward. Turning around I saw no one where the voice had been, and he hadn't ever moved into view. But Tim still lay unconscious on the floor, fallen from the effects of whatever that stranger had done to him. I left the corridor, heading for my room and with plans to do some drinking, when I remembered where I'd heard that voice. It came to me like a snap of the fingers.

It was the strangely dressed fellow from my very first noble's dinner, when I'd been hiding by the servants' staging area away from the repetitive questions. What had he called himself? I had it right there on the tip of my brain, but it wasn't until I turned the corner by my room that I remembered.

His name was Mah'kus and he'd drunkenly called himself a 'dead god'. Perhaps he hadn't been drunk after all. I didn't know much about gods or what they'd be like if they were dead, but whatever this guy was, he had power enough to steal spells and rearrange memories. Dead god or not, I didn't want to find myself on his bad side.

I sat alone on my bed, the thick walls of the keep and sturdy doors keeping me in a perpetual silence.

"How did I catch this being's attention," I wondered aloud, breaking the silence that seemed to be suffocating me. "And why does it care for my wellbeing, or does it?" I didn't expect answers to my questions, and none came. I found myself thoroughly distracted by the events leading up to his appearance. Something itched at the back of my head, and I remembered I'd bloodied myself.

Figuring this was the best as any time to test a new spell, I checked my health and found I was still about 30 points shy of full. I must have really knocked myself hard. Focusing on the knowledge I'd been given about the Lesser Heal spell I began the long 6 second cast. It required both speech, and movements, and a stern concentration to work properly. This was not a spell to be used mid battle.

The cast went off and I felt and saw a pleasant light rotate around me. An annoying ache that I hadn't really noticed before faded and my health pool filled to full.

"That was pleasant," I said, cracking my neck and standing. I'd decided that being alone was not what I wanted right now. Going to the kitchen I ordered some snacks and drinks to be brought to my room. Then I found a guard and located Mick, Barny, and Sam. Mick was on duty while the other two weren't, but the four of us played cards and drank well into the night.

It was exactly what I needed. I shared a very loose and condensed version of events with them and they oooo'd and aw'd in all the right places. But mostly we just enjoyed each other's company, telling jokes and insulting each other. A proper night out with the guys.

CHAPTER 53
PROFESSIONS AND ESSENCE

I awoke with a splitting headache and fuzzy memories of drinking and playing cards with Mick. It took only a few more moments for me to remember the rest of the night, dead gods, angry nobles, and psycho wizards named Tim trying to mess me up.

What was I doing staying in this keep still? I made up my mind right then that I'd find someplace else to stay in the city. Perhaps somewhere I could set up a comfortable workspace and dedicate some time to my new profession while I waited for Alayna to return. But before I did that, I needed something more now than I'd needed in such a long time.

I needed a bath.

There was no sign of 'Merlin the cook' inside the kitchens, but I had a plate given to me regardless and wolfed down a healthy portion. Even now, a week after passing my thresholds eating good food still curled my toes a bit. The overwhelming 'party in my mouth' sensation was enough that a small part of me could see myself just eating full time, growing fat and happy.

After my meal I found a servant that was willing to show me the way to the bath and prepared some of the never cooling water. At least two hours later I finished and dressed myself in fresh clothing and my armor. I wasn't expecting to need it, but with how my life had been going it seemed almost stupid not to be prepared. I'd gone from level 0 to level 12 in a short period of time, but I was still nothing when compared against the likes of Tim or Lord Variyn. The only hope I had to keep pace with my peers would be to figure out this profession and work out how to do essence collection.

There was the added benefit of course to helping adventurers like Ismene and Emory, who'd been given such a small Core affinity that leveling at the higher levels would be nearly impossible. These thoughts bounced around my head as I made my way to the street.

Where should I start or how did one even go about finding a space to rent? The only shop I had much experience with was the super shop called Gilfoy's Emporium, so I set out in that direction figuring the nice elf woman might answer some of my questions.

The air in the city was different from what I felt out in the wilds adventuring. It lacked a freshness that I took for granted, but in its place, there was a social liveliness being packed in with thousands of people. And as I walked, I couldn't help but have a bit of a bounce in my step. I was going to do some learning today and take the first steps in discovering more about my profession.

One thing I could always count on enjoying was reading and learning. It had been some time since I'd had the pleasure and it was hard to hide my excitement. I rounded a corner and sooner than I'd have thought I stood outside the expansive multicolored brick shop. The ash gray mortar was like a maze that one could follow through the colorful display and reach the black oak doors leading inside.

Stepping in I was reminded of the simple elegance that Gilfoy's Emporium had achieved. A vast open space with shelves filled with merchandise of one kind or another and a row of polished black oak checkout counters, each operated by a well-dressed man or woman.

"Welcome to Gilfoy's Emporium, Lord Caldor. We are pleased to offer you a ten percent discount on book purchases today and tomorrow. Thank you for being a specialty member, how may I assist you?" The monotone Runeforged asked. I'd been here a few times now and I kept forgetting he stood just inside the door. I jumped a tiny bit, but quickly went into an exaggerated stretch, hoping I fooled any onlookers.

"You are too quiet for your own good," I said, reaching out and patting the Runeforged on the arm.

"Please do not touch the Runeforged," Ena the elf said, wearing her signature 'all business' smile. I saw her shoulders relax a measure when she saw my face. "Excuse me, Lord Caldor, but you know the rules. Is there something I can assist you with today? Perhaps your armor needs additional repairing, or you'd like to stock up with more gems, pens and ink, or carving equipment? You are one of very few Lapidarist we've had in recent weeks."

I was about to ask what in the Wyrd a Lapidarist was, when I remembered she'd explained before, basically it just meant someone who shaped gems. I wondered how profession names worked as I'd not seen that term in the many hundreds of profession variations I'd been shown. In fact, I was pretty sure that I'd seen a profession simply called, Gem Cutter, Jewelcrafter, and even Stoneshaper—though that one turned out to be a profession that allowed you to shape stones of all kinds, gems included, to increase their natural properties and not useful to what I intended to do.

"I do need to pick up a few books to add to my collection, I've got the basics of gem cutting and shaping, inscribing, and even a book on basic enchantments, but could you help me find anything on creating gem's that collect mana and any recipe books specific for Gem Inscribing or gem cutting and inscribing separately. Really, I'm looking to get my hands on some reading materials that will keep me busy for a time, so any suggestions would be welcome," I said.

I'd learned a bit about working with merchants and I knew that they'd be more willing to help you after you'd purchased their goods. If I could find a book, or maybe three to get started, as they averaged around 100 gold per volume—though Ena claimed that they were working on an automated method that would soon drive book prices down considerably.

"Follow me and I will show you to the most popular books on each subject," Ena said, turning her simple tight black and white uniform accentuating her curves.

I went to the shelves and picked out a health potion, before heading upstairs with her. It never hurts to have another potion or two.

"You can store that if you'd like, I've made a note to add it to your final bill," Ena said, motioning to the potion I held. I did so, putting the potion away in my dimensional storage, then another question occurred to me.

"This box is a bit bothersome to carry around, do you have anything easier like a ring or a simple bag of holding that I could store it inside of?" I asked, just as Ena finished with the levers and the portal opened to the second floor, an entire level dedicated to books.

"Mixing dimensional items can be tricky, but our patented

Small Dimensional Box is able to be stored inside most dungeon created storage items. Unfortunately, there is a shortage kingdom wide, but can I offer you a specialty carrying strap or perhaps a Small Dimensional Sphere? We've found they are growing popular as of late as the edges of our box designs, while sturdy, can be a bit annoying while adventuring," Ena said, all business as usual and trying to upsell me on everything.

"Can I exchange my dimensional box for a dimensional sphere?" I asked the question sure that I knew the answer already.

"Unfortunately, no," Ena said, clasping her hands and nodding her head. "Since that box has been keyed to you, its value as spare parts is quite low. You are in luck however, the small dimensional sphere is on sale this week for only 1,200 gold, that is forty percent off the ticket price." She added the bit at the end as if that softened the blow.

The price was crazy, but what was even crazier was the fact that I had nearly twice that in gold. A thousand had been given to me by Alayna for use in the upkeep of Blackridge keep, a task that I knew I should see to sooner than later, but the broken cores, reagents, and sheer amount of weapons I'd brought back, including the magic staff, had sold very well. At last look I had 2,114 gold, 94 silver, and 42 copper.

But it wouldn't be wise to pay so much just for a small comfort, so I dismissed the idea.

"That'll be okay," I said. "Add a holding harness for the box to my bill and show me the books."

Ena nodded and I followed her down a row of books. There was a special smell that came with books old and new. This floor smelled overwhelmingly of older books, with just a hint of new smell here and there. With Ena's back turned to me

I ran my hand across the spines of several volumes, every bit about books bringing me incalculable joy.

"Here is a volume specific to Gemstone recipes. I find that it focuses a bit too much on the beauty factor of each cut and not the magical potential, but it's useful and we don't have Faddenstooder's volume, so this is the next best thing," Ena said pulling a book free from the shelf that was as thick as two fingers width, which is to say an afternoon of reading for me.

This continued for another ten minutes, and she pulled a total of 20 books free, taking them to a table and discussing further the benefits of one over the other. In the end I settled on five books, since she informed me that as well as ten percent off, if I bought four, I'd get a fifth for free. I didn't know what freedom Gilfoy's Emporium sales associates had over pricing, but I swear she made that up on the spot when she saw that I was only going to buy three books.

I read the titles of the five new books I'd purchased.
Delicate Cuts for Delicate Times, by Earnest Yumwell.
Magical Pull Theory, By Madaline Kelin.
Enchanting Hearts through Ink, by Bulldre McClarin
Gem Inscribing, and its Applications, by Theodore San
Advanced Essence Theory, by Awkland Newwald.

Three of the five books were recipe books and as such weren't extremely long, but the two theory books were massive tomes that cost twice as much as any book I'd purchased before. I ended up spending 540 gold for all five, but I considered it a bargain. My coin purse wished that the steep discounts she'd spoken about would arrive already, but never once had I regretted the purchase of a book.

There was also the added benefit that books held their value much better and could be traded for other books in the future. I spent another 20 gold to buy an empty book that had a clever design with snapping metal rings, where pages could be placed in any order that I needed. It came with fifty pages, and I figured that would be enough of a start.

After adding the cost of the potion and the dimensional box holding strap the total was 566 gold and 3 silver, which I paid happily. Now to get to the other major reason I'd come here and dropped a load of money.

"I do have another question," I said, putting my books away with my other supplies.

"What can I help you with?" Ena said, her same fake smile ready to answer my question.

"I need a place where I can study and practice my profession in peace. Do you know of such a place, somewhere I'd have privacy," I asked, giving her my best smile in return. Her smile never wavered as she tilted her head to the side just barely before answering me.

"Of course, I do," Ena said. "We have several offices that can be rented by the week for affordable fees. They are located in the basement level with employment services. Would you like to hear the options?"

"Yes please!" I answered enthusiastically. I'd hoped the over eager storefront that was Gilfoy's Emporium would have thought to try and corner every market, including office space.

"We currently have four offices available," Ena said, her eyes looking up into her head as if recalling some bit of information. "Two shared rooms, I imagine you wouldn't want those. A medium sized office, however, you'd be sharing a small kitchen area and bathroom with another office of similar size. And our Master Office Suite, which comes with a sitting room, a personal kitchen and bathroom, and an office with a desk and two large worktables. The shared rooms are 50 gold a week, the medium room 100 gold a week, and the Master Office Suite is 310 gold per week."

The prices weren't bad, and I really didn't want to share an office. My first instinct was to go for the medium sized room, but she hadn't mentioned what the office included.

"What's included inside the medium office?" I asked, biting my lip and hoping it would work for what I needed.

"A standard sized worktable and small desk," Ena said, then added raising a finger to the sky. "It is worth mentioning that the person you'd be sharing the facilities with is an enchanter and sometimes her experiments get a bit explosive. The walls have state of the art shielding so you wouldn't be at any risk, but the sound blocking enchantments aren't advanced enough to block out all of what she does."

Despite the fear of having my reading interrupted by explosions, I couldn't justify paying the sum required for the larger office yet.

"Does the medium office have a door that closes?" I asked, then clarified. "It is important that I be able to work uninterrupted, explosions notwithstanding."

"It does indeed," Ena said, her fake smile deepening.

"I'll take it," I said, taking out another 100 gold and passing it over.

"This is it," Ena said, opening the door to the office. It was roughly ten feet by fifteen feet with a comfy looking sofa taking up one wall. The desk sat across from the door, with the worktable beside it. I examined the worktable; the surface was at least twice as long and half as deep.

The wall directly behind the worktable had a sheet of wood

with many holes in it. Spread out seemingly randomly were square cups, short and long. Each were empty but I figured they were meant to hold pens and other small objects.

There were no windows, seeing as we had gone below the surface, but the light gray walls seemed pleasant enough. I was surprised they hadn't added any pieces of art or decor other than the desk, sofa, and worktable, but in a way, it made sense. If someone was to rent this long term, they'd have their own taste to consider. The chair in front of the desk was cushioned, maroon fabric pressed down by several large buttons into the wood. All in all, this place would work for what I needed, peace and privacy.

"You said there was a bathroom and kitchen?" I asked, stepping out of the room, and looking around. We'd entered out of the portal into a hallway with many doors, the one we'd taken had been all the way at the end and to the left. Passing that door was a small sitting room, two chairs, a sofa, a low to the ground table, and four doors. None of the doors had markings on them, but my office was straight ahead on the right.

It would be easy to remember as the wood for each door was a slightly different color, the one to the left of mine looking the newest, with a clear finish on a very light-colored wood. While mine was by far the darkest and most aged, looking almost like black oak.

"This door here," Ena said, pointing to the light-colored door next to mine. "Belongs to a lovely Gnome by the name of Regina Clockstein. She's a bit of a personality but don't worry she's harmless. This door here." She pointed to the door next to mine but on the adjacent wall. "Is the bathroom, it is cleaned daily but please don't go out of your way to make a mess. And the final door just there." She walked over to the door and opened it. "Is the kitchen. This cabinet here is for you to use. There are some dried foods inside that you can use, any items taken will be charged to your account. And down here in the floor is a Gilfoy's patented cold box. If you put dairy or meat items inside, they will last significantly longer. I'll leave you to it, here is the key to your office. We are open at all hours, day and night, so find me or another employee to gain access to this floor. Have a wonderful day."

And with that Ena turned and left, leaving me alone in the kitchen area. I gave it a once over, deciding I'd likely just leave and eat someplace if I grew hungry. While I knew how to cook for myself just fine, it wasn't overly expensive to just visit a nice restaurant or find a street cart nearby.

The room was only about 6 feet wide but twice as long. It had a long countertop with cabinets above and the 'cold box' set into the floor below. On the opposite side sat a basin with a lever next to a thin stone neck and a spherical appendage traveling into the ground. Inside the basin was a plug, but no water. Confused, I tried the lever and gasped. An automatic well, this wasn't too different than the keep's 'forever warm' bath system.

How fancy, I thought, chuckling as I made my way back to the office, locking it behind me.

Starting things off I had a look at my professions tab, I had given it a look here and there, but I needed to see all it had to offer.

Profession: Gem Inscriptionist, Level 1
Profession Abilities: Quality Check, Mana Infusion
Quality Check: Allows you to determine flaws in either the cut of a gem or the Runes inscribed into the gem. The more you

use the ability the more you can learn by care,
your work.

Mana Infusion: Gives you a controlled method o,
Gems, Runes, or Rune Inscribed Gems with Mana.

Both of the abilities made sense and as I focused on the.., I could see how they worked in my mind. This was important because Mana Infusion was eerily like what I'd been doing with my Aura Manipulation before I was *Sparked* and after. There was a certain finesse to it that I hadn't had, and it required a sort of two-way connection between the item I wanted to infuse and myself. So, I couldn't just pull at my own Aura and rip it about.

Next on the tab was an area that listed my 'recipes' most of which were different types of gem cuts, each one magnifying certain qualities of the gem. For instance, if I went with something called a pearl cut it would enhance Rune scripts that favored the Concentration attribute. Whereas if I did a square cut, it would amplify Strength. It was more complex than that, but as a general rule different cuts worked best for certain types of effects.

Then I had my Inscriptionist recipes. They were super basic and there were six of them. *Lesser Amplify Constitution, Lesser Amplify Intellect, Lesser Amplify Endurance, Lesser Amplify Concentration, Lesser Amplify Strength, and Lesser Mana Reinforcement.*

The final one was meant to be used first, if I understood it correctly, as a way to reinforce the gem before additional properties could be added. I decided to start doing some experimenting. Taking out my empty book and one of Gilfoy's patented self-dipping pens—that was a bit of a misnomer as it didn't need to be dipped at all and could work for several pages before a replacement was needed—I was nearly ready to start.

I laid out all my professional equipment on the worktable, organizing all manner of chisels, thin scratching tools, and so much more, into the cups and separated each side so that my Inscriptionist equipment was on the left while the gem cutting tools were on the right.

Taking out a rough piece of cloudy green fluorite I focused on the most basic cut I had, a simple cube with a step cut into the edges. I knew from a bit of light reading that fluorite was not great for holding enchantments, but it was one of the easiest minerals to carve and practice making gemstones. Taking out a polishing rag, it was one of several magically enchanted objects I'd gotten to help with my profession, I went to work.

Just by rubbing it around in the rag the rough hard edges were soon transformed into a glasslike smoothness. I could see lines running through the fluorite, I didn't know what that meant as I hadn't read very far. Holding it up to the light I could see through it nicely. Were they a sign of quality I wondered, then almost without realizing it I used my Quality Check ability.

They were cutting planes and if I cut along them the gem would shear off. Other than that, I had the impression it was a quality piece and got a second impression that it had a hardness somewhere in the middle range. What range that was or what that really meant I didn't really know.

Now that I finished getting the rough stone all polished up, something that would have required a rock tumbler—a slow and arduous task of turning a bunch of rocks together to get a smooth surface—I was ready to preform it. This required that I get it into a general shape of what I am looking for, but not the finished edges or facets.

For this I had my most precious and expensive tools, my

enchanted files. Each one was enchanted to take off a certain amount of material, it varied based on hardness, but one stroke would do the work of either ten or with my most powerful one, hundreds of strokes. I decided to start with the smallest, slowly taking away material one edge at a time. It was tedious work, but I found it gave me a chance to think, which was nice because I had a lot of thinking to do.

I let my mind run over recent events, trying to really determine how I felt about it all. It hadn't surprised me that Zander had attacked me, not really, but would he have actually killed me? Why did he hate me so much, it seemed completely unreasonable. I remembered his father's words and could guess at what set him off. With Bren praising me drunkenly and berating his son, I'm sure that had been the final straw, setting Zander off.

I really didn't want to hate anyone from Alayna's family, but Zander was making it so difficult. If I had been pushed just a hair further, I probably would have killed him. I didn't like admitting that to myself, but it was true. Those thoughts led me into the killings I'd been a part of since beginning my life as an adventurer. The Rock Eaters no longer bugged me and there wasn't any way I'd feel bad for the Gnolls, as they'd killed poor Jill, but the goblins found their way into my thoughts in the quiet stretches between events.

Sure, they'd taken Fred and nearly killed Fran and I, but why? What were they doing so far north? I realized I'd never had the opportunity to inform anyone in House Blalor about the attacks and the goblins' presence. I set aside my tools and wrote out a quick open letter detailing the events and questions Fred had been tortured for, then promised I'd figure out a way to get it to the nobles of House Blalor. Returning to my work I saw that I had gotten a 'more than rough' square formed.

Fluorite was a very soft gem indeed. I found a smaller file with a slightly harder bite and began to flatten the edges to add the step shown in my recipe. It didn't take long before I felt something click and I got a system notification gently pressing against my mind.

I'd successfully created a basic cube with a 'Square' cut and leveled my profession from 1 to 2. Looking at the gem I now got my details regarding it with my inspect skill.

Fluorite Cube
 Gem Cut: _Square_
 Durability: _10_
 Quality: _Poor_
 Weight: _7 Carats_

Well, that quality could use some work. I thought I'd done a fine job with it. Setting aside the stone I pulled out my papers and pen, looking at the Rune symbols needed for the recipes I had. Before trying to scratch them into the surface of the gem, I would practice a bit on paper. It didn't take long for me to have tried each one, as these Runic formations were the simplest there were, only a few runes each.

I focused on the Runic script for Mana reinforcement and traced the lines again. It was a very circular design, almost looking like an Order symbol, two circles, but with a twisting symbol that turned in on itself with several dots. There was a square pattern around it. The more I looked at it the more I could make out different layers to it. There was the barest of understanding behind the knowledge that had been deposited into my head and I'd need to explore that if I was ever to truly understand essence gathering.

One thing I was sure about, it would take me some time to work all this out.

I pulled free my enchanted gem tool, this one a thin metal point that would allow me to cut into even the hardest stones. Though the cube had six sides I doubted that it could hold six of my Inscriptions. That wouldn't stop me from trying though! First things first, I needed to get the Lesser Mana Reinforcement in place.

Taking up the cube I pulled out a gem clamp that I'd purchased, a bulky thing that would hold the gem for me, pressed between two stiff arms with soft cushions on each end. I turned the little wheel on it and the gem was firmly in place. Chiseling as carefully as I could, I went to work. My first attempt failed, so I moved to another of the six faces and tried again. Again, I failed.

On my sixth attempt I felt something click and with a rush of exhalation I stood, excited that I'd finally managed it. To my very untrained eyes each of the runes appeared to match, but obviously that wasn't the case, or they'd work. I inspected the gem and was pleased to see the information had been updated.

Reinforced Fluorite Cube
Inscription: *Lesser Mana Reinforcement*
Gem Cut: *Square*
Durability: *4/10*
Quality: *Poor*
Weight: *6 Carats*

.   .   .

My poor attempts to inscribe the gem had taken its toll on the item's durability, but it held together. I played with the thought of polishing the sides off where I'd made a mistake, but foolishly I'd removed the cube and couldn't figure which side was the successful one.

Instead, I made the decision to take a break and get some reading done. I was still nowhere close to being good enough to create or understand how to make a gem pull in Mana, much less Essence.

What followed was about four hours of reading, then a trip out for food, several failed attempts to create more basic gem cuts and more failed attempts at inscribing. I did make some progress here and there as I alternated between reading and cutting. My profession reached level 5 when I finally created a triangular cut and successfully inscribed it with not only lesser Mana Reinforcement, but also Lesser Amplify Intellect. I was making progress, but it would take time, and I was willing to give it time.

How many days went by I wasn't really sure, but I'd learned a number of more basic cuts and Inscriptions, when hunger called. I left my cave, jumping when another of the infrequent explosions occurred behind the door of Regina's office. I still hadn't met her, but a few times while reading I heard her door open, but I wasn't exactly looking for any inter-actions while I read.

Exiting Gilfoy's Emporium I headed for a meat cart I was growing fond of when I bumped into an unexpected trio. Grug, Beth and Adathin stood not far off eating wraps filled with delicious meats and veggies. I ordered one and stepped over to them.

"Are you ready?" Beth asked, her skin was free of any char now but remained pinkish red.

"For what?" I asked, grabbing my wrap from the vendor and taking a big bite.

"For the dungeon," Beth said, raising an eyebrow. "You said one week and you'd have a healer? We picked out a dungeon, its levels range from 16 to 23 but we've done it a few times, so you'll be totally safe."

"Oh right," I said after finishing the bite. "I need to run to the keep and grab our healer, then clean up a bit and I'll be ready. Where do you want to meet?"

"Western gate in about an hour?" Beth asked, smiling and tilting her head in a cute way.

"Deal," I said, smiling to Grug who just grunted and continued eating.

It took me ten minutes to clear up my goods and pack them away. I told Ena I'd be gone for a bit, and she refunded me a day's worth of rent, which surprised me and she told me to return anytime I needed. Then I was off to the keep with my fingers crossed that Alayna had returned and that I'd be able to whisk her away to do a dungeon run.

CHAPTER 54
FIRST DUNGEON RUN

I found her in the library sitting among a pile of books, engrossed in her studies. It was legitimately hard for me to interrupt her because I completely understood the joy of a full-on study session. Especially having just come from one myself. I made it within arm's reach of her when she looked up, startling.

"Where've you been stranger," she said, grabbing my hand and pulling me down to her. Using my much-improved body, I gracefully hopped over and landed beside her all while she tugged at me.

"Learning that my profession won't be easily mastered," I responded, leaning in, and kissing her. When I tried to pull away a moment later, her hand clasped behind my head, and we kissed passionately. I'd been alone for what felt like at least a week, so I welcomed the feeling of her body against mine, eagerly moving in closer.

After several glorious seconds, the kiss ended, and Alayna had a wicked smile on her face. "We should set up a dinner date once a week or something," she said, her chest heaving as she gazed at me. "I don't like not seeing you for so long. It is good that you've spent time working on your profession, it wouldn't be good for you to stagnate." She touched the end of my nose as she said it and I chuckled.

"I'm far too busy to worry about stagnation for like at least a hundred years. Speaking of which," I said, remembering that I hadn't shared with her the perk I'd taken. "I took the first level of Long Lived. So, assuming I'm not crushed by a monster anytime soon, I'll be around for a while."

"That's wonderful!" Alayna said, her posture straightening. "I wanted to suggest it to you, but it didn't feel right influencing your class decisions. I'm so glad you picked it, if you wait too long to pass a threshold and pick the first life extension perk, you could end up looking pretty old."

"We wouldn't want that now, would we?" I asked, laughing. "So, I need a favor and you can't say no because I kind of told a few people you'd said yes already."

I gave her my best innocent look, but she wasn't buying it.

"You told a group that I'd heal for them, didn't you?" She asked, right on the target.

"Yes, but in my defense, I told them a week ago that I'd ask you and then forgot, so they assumed I'd secured you," I said, my toothy grin acting as my only defense.

It must have worked because she laughed at me and said, "Fine, but we better leave now before my father finds out. He will find out eventually, so I hope you know what you're doing."

"So do I," I said under my breath.

574

"This Grug's favorite place," Grug the beastkin bear said, as we traveled down the road. His mastery, or lack thereof, of Common made understanding him difficult at times. "Big boats and..." His forehead scrunched and he looked to Beth and then to Adathin, signing his hands together and outward as if something was exploding. "...Grug's group know. Boom boom with big pain."

"Oh, he means the ship's cannons," Adathin said, shaking his head at Grug's difficulty.

"I guess we should tell you a bit about the dungeon then," Beth said, her cheeks rosy and temperament peppy.

We were taking a break from running, Alayna was surprisingly the slowest among us, but she kept pace well enough. She complained that she couldn't understand why they hadn't just taken horses, but Grug said he preferred to run, with Beth and Adathin siding with Grug.

"I've got it labeled as 'Pirate Dungeon', but most people refer to it as the 'Sea expanse' and it is not very popular, which is why we like it. We've run it three times now and the only reason we were in House Blalor lands was our healer wanted to try a new dungeon," Beth said, her countenance darkening as she spoke about her fallen companion.

"Why isn't it very popular?" I asked. I couldn't help but feel extremely excited. I'd heard of pirates, but only in the fictional sense as almost everyone agreed sea travel out past the coast was a death sentence.

"It can be tricky," Adathin said, cutting in before Beth could answer. "However, I think it would be wise to let you experience the details. I think we can fill you in right before if we think it's necessary. Half the fun of dungeons is the exploration after all!"

"I guess," Beth said, pouting her lips. "You'll love it,

Caldor." Beth said reaching out and putting a hand on mine. This surprised me and irritated Alayna, who harrumphed and gave me an 'oh really' look.

"I've never run any dungeons in House Attra," Alayna said, seeming to get over it rather quickly, her features softening. "What level range is it?"

Beth turned to Alayna looking as bright as ever and said, "The mobs range from 16 to 23, but don't worry, you keep us half alive and we'll get you both through it!" As she spoke, she reached out and touched Alayna's arm in an affectionate manner. I gave Alayna a look, all jest, but she must have missed it because she looked pointedly forward.

Grug didn't talk much, probably due to his difficulty in understanding and speaking common, but he kept a stalwart eye to the horizon and was the first person to give warning when the ambush began.

We were still in House Variyn lands, heading northeast to the border where House Blalor, House Attra, and House Variyn met—which I realized wasn't too far off from where keep Blackridge was located—when a pack of wolves jumped out all around us.

I had only a moment to take everything in before combat raged around me. The sun was still high in the sky, so seeing the eight or nine wolves should have been easy, but they were shrouded in a black mist that made them hard to look at. I used Inspect in that same moment, my brain just reacting and wanting to know more, but no information was given. The only other time that had happened for me was...

"Chaos monsters!" I yelled, summoning my blade in my hands, casting Light Blade over it and beginning the long cast on Arcane Armor. During the five seconds where I stood around waiting for my armor to appear, several things happened.

Grug, the seven-foot-tall bear man, reacted quickest of us all, pulling his double headed axe from his back and bisecting a wolf before it knew what hit it. Beth wasn't far behind, her bow appearing in her hand and several arrows flying free within a matter of seconds. None of the shots were lethal, but it appeared she planned that, as each arrow found a leg or someplace that slowed several wolves.

Adathin disappeared as he waved his hands about, but in his place appeared a spider the size of a wagon. That gave several more of the wolves pause, just as my arcane armor spell finished. It was a good thing because two of the bulky black misted wolves jumped in my direction. I had just enough presence of mind to fire off my Instant cast spell, Lightning Strike, while lifting my blade up to deliver a downward slash.

I'd chosen the one to my left, most likely to run into Alayna, to strike with my lightning spell, and it cried out in sudden pain as a flash of white light struck it followed by a spear of golden light. So focused on my melee attack, I wasn't able to acknowledge that awesome, one-two spell punch we'd just delivered.

As my blade descended, I realized my strike would be too slow and the wolf was likely to catch my throat. I activated the skill Swift Strike and added additional speed into my strike. It moved so quickly that I nearly lost my grip, but it worked, my sword slashed the wolf's face, splitting its nose down the middle. I let the sword fall from my hands, knowing I'd be able to call it back at any time and fired off a Firebolt into the next closest wolf.

Chains sprang up, holding that one in place as Alayna

chanted the words of the spell. I surged forward, my sword forming in my hand and struck down in an arc at its head activating Power Strike. Something strange happened as I swung my sword downward, I missed the head entirely, instead my attack dug deep into the shoulder. Releasing my grip, I lurched backwards but I was too slow, the wolf dug into my leg, and I fell.

Another wolf appeared over me as the first savaged my leg. I let loose a Lightning Strike into the back of its head and followed through with Firebolt to the face. When it lurched backwards but didn't fall, I mimicked rearing back my blade and thrusting forward, summoning my blade right before the attack would have pierced the flesh. It stabbed forward and the wolf went limp. Once more I abandoned my blade turning my attention to the red-hot pain in my leg.

The wolf shook its head, and I recalled my weapon. The sheen of light still covered it but between the pain and how I'd fallen he was just out of reach for an effective strike. So instead, I slashed my sword in his direction and an arc of white light went forth, scalping the wolf. Its ears and the skin atop its head were hanging backward in an odd angle. The wolf yelped in pain, releasing my leg and managed to take one step before a spear of light pinned it in place, killing it.

I wasn't sure how I'd be able to walk now, my shin must have broken under the powerful jaws of the wolf, because I know my foot wasn't supposed to turn that way. A golden light flashed over me, temporarily making the battle around me darken in response, and then the warmth came. This wasn't like a warm bath, but rather the warmth you feel when you wake up early in the morning and everywhere but where you lay is the perfect temperature. With that wonderful warmth came healing, swift and almost a bit brutally. My ankle snapped back into line, and I could almost feel the bone mend, with the muscles straightening back into place around it.

The abruptness of it cost me seconds, but soon I was on my feet and looking for my next target, but the battle had ended. By the looks of it not a single wolf survived to flee, and my original count had been off. Thirteen wolves were in various stages of mutilation from our attacks. Beth must have used a Fire Arrow attack, three of the wolves close to where she made her stand were still completely aflame, adding a disgusting stench of burning fur into the air.

"Good heals," Grug said, flicking blood free from his axe. He had the most amount of dead wolves around him. He also looked the most injured, but it was hard to tell with the amount of blood he was covered in. Was that all his or had he been rolling around the remains of the wolves? It wasn't immediately apparent, and I wasn't sure I even wanted to know.

I checked on Alayna, she wore her fine white silk robes that she swore offered more protection than they seemed, but I was skeptical. She didn't have a single drop of blood or even a hair out of place.

"That was intense," I said, scratching at my healed leg. The armor had held up well enough, just a small bit of fraying on the edges of the leather plates.

"I'm summoning Vash," Alayna said, pulling a blue crystal from a dimensional box at her side. She had a carrying case similar to mine. It kept the box in place with thin leather cords and was loose enough on the vertical to allow it to open enough to summon items and put them away. A second later Vash, the Astral Wolf, appeared beside her. "You should summon Ares, I bet she'd have enjoyed the fight."

I pulled free the black figurine and summoned Ares, a part of me hoping that perhaps another fight lay in our direct future. I didn't know much about using bonded creatures in dungeons, so whether or not I'd be able to use Ares was a mystery.

Ares and Vash sized each other up. They were close to the same size, but Vash lacked the intense intelligence in his eyes that Ares displayed. She clawed at him, watching his reaction, but he didn't have one. Just watching the claw that stopped right in front of him. I sent Ares a mental command to not bother the wolf, but she ignored me. Stepping closer so that Vash had to take a step backwards, which he did, but he made sure that the step brought him closer to Alayna.

"They like each other," I said in a strained voice. I did my best to sound genuine, but I knew I'd missed the mark.

"Vash doesn't care for her," Alayna said, deadpan.

I laughed and it caught on, Alayna and even Beth joining in. There was nothing better than a good laugh after a period of tense action to make you feel great.

"We aren't far from the dungeon," Beth said, reaching out toward Ares but waiting to see what she'd do. Ares tilted her head and looked her in the eyes. Appearing to like what she saw there, she nuzzled into Beth's hand.

"Oh, even Ares is a fan of Beth," Alayna muttered under her breath. I was sure Beth hadn't heard and I'd barely picked it up myself. I went over and put my arm around Alayna.

"Thanks for the heals," I said, kissing her cheek.

"You're welcome," she said, sighing as she said it.

CHAPTER 55
ARGH THERE BE PIRATES HERE!

The dungeon camp surrounding this particular dungeon was nothing more than four tents and maybe three dozen people. We'd entered House Attra lands, a new experience for me, as the border was heavily patrolled and monitored. I knew exactly when we'd passed over as there was a dead man's zone of cleared trees and brush for several hundred feet with wooden watch towers within sight of each other. A horn rang out and a group of armored men on horses approached asking our business in House Attra.

Adathin cleared things up quickly by having us all show our Adventurer's Guild crest and the guards left soon after. Once you cleared the heavy woods around the border of House Attra the terrain was mostly open plains of golden grass. On our way to the dungeon, we encountered many farmers working the fields and going about their business.

But this dungeon camp was nothing compared to the other I'd seen, of the four tents here only one looked well maintained. The ground around the dungeon was wet and there was a salty smell in the cool breeze that reminded me of the elven coast.

"You're sure we can't use Ares and Vash inside the dungeon?" I asked for the third time since Alayna had told me.

"Not since you attached her to the bonding stone, it has to do with the dungeon's magic," Alayna explained. "It causes them to revert to their stored form."

I frowned but decided not to bring it up again.

"I'll get us registered," Adathin said, walking into the well-kept tent.

"Where is the dungeon entrance?" I asked, looking around in confusion. There was a small mound of earth that the tents seemed to be centered around but I couldn't see any kind of entrance.

"This one has a bit of a strange entrance," Beth said, nodding her head along as she spoke. "On the other side of that mound of dirt there's a crack that you squeeze into. Not Grug's favorite part. And down some steps inside a big cavern is the dungeon entrance. Pretty unique really."

"I've never heard of such a thing," Alayna said, any annoyance she had with Beth seemingly gone as her excitement for the coming adventure overtook her. "Can't wait to get into the dungeon."

"No wait necessary," Adathin said, as he exited the tent. "We are up now."

The other side of the mound, which oddly wasn't a mound of dirt like I thought but more of a dirt covered stone hollow sphere, had a crack big enough for me to walk through without hitting my shoulders. For Grug this meant he had to enter and exit by turning sideways, and even then, it was a difficult squeeze for him.

"Why don't they widen the opening?" I asked, as I passed through the crack. And it was just a crack, each side had the rough and ragged look of cracked stone.

"They can't," Beth said, her tail swishing as she made it through after me. "Or at least that's what I heard. They've tried and like most dungeons, the stone area around them becomes nearly indestructible. Something to do with how dungeons work."

I expected there to be little light inside the hollowed rock, but the opposite was true. Though no lights could be seen, an ever-present glow permeated the room. Several steps into the rock was a small platform connected to a winding staircase where the stone was carved so that a person twice Grug's size could fit. Because of the curves of the stairs, I couldn't see the bottom, but I was distracted enough that I probably wouldn't have noticed.

The walls running parallel with the descending stairs were covered in depictions and runic letters. Directly to my left several circles with landmasses and water painted on them were positioned around a sphere several times their size, a sun perhaps? Lines connected each sphere to the sun, if that's what it was after all. Between the spheres I saw little triangle shapes, barely the size of the tip of my finger moving between the spheres. It was all extremely fascinating, and I didn't understand a bit of it.

I tried to understand even a single one of the runes, they were positioned around the artwork at seemingly random places. But the strangeness in their formation stopped me dead in my tracks. This was nothing like the Runic characters used for enchanting objects, either by Inscription or arcane means. I'd gotten pretty far in the *Enchanting Hearts through Ink* book, which was just a fancy title for enchantments meant to be bound to scrolls. It was my most comprehensive reference I had for runes; it held a list of all 320 unique strokes that could be used to make countless Runic formations.

None of these matched as far as I could tell. Perhaps they weren't Runes, despite looking similar, maybe they were a long-lost language. I decided to ask as much and surprisingly Grug was the first to respond.

"Is First One's words," Grug said, as if that answered everything perfectly.

Lucky for me, Beth elaborated. "From what we've heard the Runes on the wall are thought to be the ancient language of the Ordu or some civilization from around that time. Isn't it crazy how similar it looks to our Runic system?"

"It is," Alayna said, reaching out and touching the wall. The rune-like words were painted on the wall with a metallic silver sheen, while the other images had much more color. Not a single one of them appeared diminished or faded, despite how many times people must have touched them.

The stairways opened below to a large area and set into the far wall was something I recognized, a dungeon door. Two ten-foot-high doors scrawled with curving rune formations as foreign to us as the ones on the cave walls filled the edges.

"Here we go," I said, barely containing my excitement. Grug pushed the doors open, despite their size they swung inward easily. Following several steps down into a circular room, a very familiar room I realized, I followed Grug as he headed to a raised pool of water in the center.

He scooped up a handful of water, before turning and gesturing that we should do the same.

"It provides increased regeneration for an hour and heals a good portion of your health," Adathin said, when I didn't immediately step forward.

"I know," I said. "I've seen one before, this room looks exactly like the only other dungeon I've stepped foot in."

"All dungeon rest areas are the same," Alayna said,

scooping up some water in her hands and taking a long pull. "The difference starts right through that portal."

I looked up and was surprised to see something that definitely hadn't been there during my last visit. A swirling mess of lights in the shape of a door stood at the opposite end of the entrance.

"Time to cast any buffs or personal spells," Adathin said, his arms waving about as he prepared to cast a spell. I cast what I had, putting Physical Resistance on Alayna, refreshing Blade Ward, and casting the long 5 second Arcane Armor. By the time I'd done that and waited for everyone else to finish their buffs, my Physical Resistance came up, so I cast it on myself as well. I could see I'd been given various resistance buffs from the team and my health was two hundred more than it had been moments before. I could see a bit how the strength of a party could be multiplied when buffs were assigned. I made a note to look at spells I could learn to aid a party next time I had a chance.

Grug was already walking toward it and I watched in amazement as he stepped through. It was like his entire body got sucked and swirled into the mess of lights. He didn't cry out, so I guessed it wasn't a painful process, but still, that was not what I was expecting.

"Here," Alayna said, offering her hand. She must have sensed my apprehension and my cheeks went hot. I took her hand, though I couldn't help but think that I should be the one offering a strengthening hand, not her.

As one we stepped through, and I felt a pulling that was vaguely familiar. I'd felt it twice previously and each time involved the Prime Mana Shrine and visits with the Arbiter. Perhaps I wasn't as 'out of body' as I'd thought when visiting Arb.

The pulling stopped abruptly and suddenly I had to raise my hand to shield it from the sun. My eyes adjusted and my jaw dropped in utter amazement at the scene around me.

I stood, along with my party, on the deck of a massive ship. I had no comparison for the scope of it. Three massive pillars of wood were crossed by billowing sheets of white sails, at least a dozen or more of them. All around the wide deck, sun baked men and women of every race, elf, dwarf, human, even goblin, worked on rope lines. Behind me a massive orc, easily seven feet tall, yelled out orders in a language I couldn't make out, occasionally pushing other sailors or grabbing ropes and doing their work for them.

My mind couldn't wrap around the sheer scope of the vessel, but what was maybe more amazing was the water around me. As far as the eye could see there was water, the horizon ended with it and not a speck of land could be seen. I had a bit of a panicky feeling rise in my stomach as I considered what would happen if I was thrown overboard, but I steadied myself as a human with a strange triangular hat with a folded up edged and topped with a large white feather approached.

He wore a heavy long coat, and it blew in the wind revealing a ruffled white shirt and a purple sash tied around his waist, as well as a type of sword I'd never encountered before. It had a slight curve to it and a curving plate to protect the hand.

"I've got bad news and need you to tell me about your position on the matters." The grizzled voice had a noticeable drawl to it. "There be a ship hanging the black flag and the rings of Chaos heading our way. Pirates are coming." He leaned in as he spoke, adding to the dramatic flair.

"We get a choice here," Beth said, completely ignoring the man and looking at Alayna and me. "We've done it three ways so far. First, we can tell him we will help fight off the pirates, that progresses the dungeon forward and we kill mobs. Second, we can tell him we won't fight, when that happens he has you hide below and eventually you have to fight anyways but it's a harder fight. And lastly, we can kill the captain and his crew until they surrender, then use his ship to ram the other one. That particular run was difficult, and I wouldn't recommend it. Each path has different level ranges, the ship ramming one being the highest we've discovered so far."

"You really killed this guy?" I asked, looking at the grizzled face of the 'captain'. "Isn't he on our side? Seems a bit rude."

Adathin sighed and cut in. "Everything here is the product of dungeon magic, these actors are nothing but complex illusions made to release essence upon their death. However, Beth, if you remember, waiting has the same effect as saying no so we should hurry this along. I vote we help, it's the best way forward."

"I'm okay with that, Alayna?" I asked, turning to her. Her eyes still scanned the various sailors and the ship, completely engrossed by it all.

"Yeah, yeah, that's fine," she said, not taking her eyes off the sights.

"We will aid you, captain Ayre," Beth said to the grizzled captain.

"Arrright!" Captain Ayre said, reaching into his coat and pulling free his sword. "Prepare yourselves, these be dark times."

Without a word Grug turned and headed to the side of the ship. "This Grug's favorite part, cannons." He took hold of the cannon and swiveled it around pointing out to sea. I looked toward where he was aiming and was surprised at what I saw.

A ship of equal size had appeared from nowhere and was run up beside us, maybe a few hundred feet away. The wood of the ship was a deep black with gray sails and a massive black flag flying on its middle mast. The flag had the symbol of Chaos on it, and I began to worry for a moment that we'd be facing actual Chaos monsters.

"It's just a gimmick," Beth assured me, seeing where my gaze landed. "There are a few strange mobs, but mostly they're humans."

An earsplitting crack sounded and Grug hooted in glee. It wasn't the first and wouldn't be the last, as all across both ships cannon fire began to smash into the opposite ships. Beth left my side and grabbed hold of another swivel cannon; they weren't much bigger than my forearm, but they appeared to pack a punch.

I found my own, Alayna doing the same, and we went to work trying to figure out how to use it. Watching Grug I saw that he was pulling back on a lever attached to one side, so I aimed in the general direction of the ship and did the same.

Boom!

I couldn't help but laugh maniacally as my shot took a humanoid form square in the chest. I even felt a trickle of essence from the kill. All around us the cannon fire continued until the boat got close enough that the black clad pirates began to swing over on ropes.

"Time to fight!" Beth called out, her bow nocked with an arrow and ready to go.

Together we moved into an open space on the ship where we'd be able to fight freely, per Beth's instructions. The wooden floorboards of the ship were surprisingly easy to grip with my boots despite the wetness and spray of sea water coming over the edge. The clear skies had darkened and out of nowhere it looked as if it might rain.

A group of pirates ran toward us, three of them, swords drawn. I Inspected one and saw his level.

Pirate Jack, Level 15, Health 650/650

Grug rushed forward, but instead of swinging his axe he transformed before my eyes, turning into a giant bear. His mighty claw hit all three of them with a wide arcing slash and they fell backwards, not dead, only injured. I took aim at the one I'd inspected and cast Lightning Strike, the air cracked, and he took the strike full on in the face. The stun effect must have triggered because he began to shake and didn't move. I followed that up with a Firebolt, just as a spear of light and an arrow hit him. He was dead before the stun wore off.

We made easy work of the next two and Grug, still in full bear form, rushed forward into another grouping of mobs, this one had eight and was likely to present more of a challenge.

Adathin worked his illusion magic, but something was different, his strikes appeared to hurt the targets, which was new to me. I focused up, seeing Grug was busy with four targets, and I'd squared off with two myself. Back and forth I did my best to engage them with the sword, but they were obviously more skilled than me. Good thing I didn't just have my sword.

I side stepped and slashed my blade downward, releasing an arc of light at one target while holding out my hand and calling down lightning on the other. The closest one went rigid, and I took that opportunity to relieve him of his head. Using both Power Strike and Swift Strike a moment later I inflicted deadly damage. His head actually flew backwards and hit Grug's bear butt, smearing blood down his fur. Not that you'd notice, he was already covered in blood as he tore combatant after combatant apart with his animal ferocity.

Out of the corner of my eye I could see Alayna working

heal spell after heal spell on Grug. He was a very straightforward fighter, allowing his enemy to get an attack in, sometimes painfully so, and then he'd take that moment of chance to get the upper hand, or sometimes just rip the hand off. He took a lot of damage but dealt out equal amounts at least.

I caught the blade of the other pirate, he had an eyepatch but I'd tried to attack from his blind side, it hadn't worked. An arrow took him in the knee, and I used the momentary distraction to slash across his face. It wasn't lethal damage, but every little bit helped. So focused on this pirate I hadn't noticed another had flanked me.

His curved sword slashed down across my chest, my armor keeping me from getting cut. I dropped my sword and punched him in the face. It wasn't a perfect reaction but engaged as I was it was the best I could do. I wanted to try something and hoped that Alayna had her eye on me just in case I messed this up. Raising my hand above my head I slashed downward, not yet summoning my blade.

The confused pirate tilted his head to the side and didn't try to block. When I was close enough that I was sure he wouldn't be able to block I called my sword. The blade took him square in the forehead, dropping him with the same confused look still on his face.

Again, the other pirate wasn't slow to react, a dagger piercing through my armor and into my ribs. At least one broke as a flash of red-hot pain erupted in my chest. But pain was becoming a friend of mine, and I didn't mind his visits anymore. I readied the Firebolt spell, doing the hand signs, then shot out my hand to cover the pirate's face—that earned me another vicious stab to the side—but it was worth it when my Firebolt spell went off in his face, dropping him.

His dagger was still stuck in my chest, so I pulled it out. A soothing warm heal hit me then and I shot Alayna a grateful look.

The next nearly fifteen minutes were nonstop fighting and we killed just under fifty pirates before the battle seemed to pause, no more new pirates swinging over.

Captain Ayre rushed over to us, his shirt stained with blood and his sword dripping with it.

"Battles not won yet," he said, panting. "They be working strange pacts with gods of the deep. Be guarded for the sea monsters be coming."

Beth wiped sweat from her brow and filled us in. "We get about a five-minute break then the difficult mobs come over. Casters and brutes, all of them half monster and half man."

"These weren't the hard mobs?" I asked, thinking about how many times they'd gotten the best of me and how Alayna had been healing me as much as the tank towards the end. I really needed to practice with the sword more.

I checked my menus over and was surprised at how little essence I'd gained, a bit less than 15,000. We'd killed so many pirates that I was sure I'd gathered enough to add some attributes and levels. In fact, if I got this much, I couldn't even imagine the small amount the rest of the group had gotten for all this trouble. No wonder it took Emory so long to level up if all he was fighting were dungeon mobs.

"Do we collect loot now or is that later?" I asked, excited for the looting part. I knew that dungeon mobs and loot worked much differently as their body and gear were just parts of the dungeon, so I couldn't just keep a sword and take it outside the dungeon. However, from the little I'd learned, you could 'loot' a kill, a process I didn't understand yet, and get a reward of some kind. Be it gold, items, or reagents, that could be taken from the dungeon when you left.

"We can loot afterwards," Beth said. "Not enough time right now."

Sure enough, just a few moments later a chanting filled the air from somewhere on the other ship. New creatures began to swing over on blackened ropes. A group of three landed not far from us and the battle was back on.

One of the three almost looked normal, if not for a third eye in his forehead and the bird on his shoulder that looked to be quite literally growing out of him. The other two had left normal way behind. I inspected the scariest looking one, it had a huge fish-like head and rows of sharp teeth.

Shark Spawn, Level 19, 950/950

I didn't get a chance to inspect the third one as Grug took a literal bite out of his tentacled face, ending him moments later while he chewed. Alayna was chanting behind me and several chains wrapped around the shark spawn just as it went to rip a chunk out of Grug's neck. I targeted the mostly normal looking guy and cast Lightning Strike. It cracked the air and smashed into a translucent barrier that sprung up around him.

Then the chanting began, the words of which made my stomach turn and threatened to make me lose my lunch.

"Hit him hard, we can't let him get that cast off!" Adathin yelled over the din of battle. I cast Firebolt, but it hit harmlessly against the barrier. Rushing forward I kept my distance from Grug, who now fought against the shark-man. Casting Light Blade, I immediately sent out an arc of light, but it had little effect on the shield as well.

Arrow after arrow hit the barrier and it began to crack. I reached it just as the chanting went still, but I didn't stop. Using Swift Strike and Power Strike one after the other I shattered the rest of his barrier and cut the bird appendage from his shoulder. He screamed so loud that I dropped my sword and fell to my knees. It wasn't unlike the screeching that had deafened me previously, except that I was very close when it happened.

I heard yells and screams all around me as I made it back to my feet, but they sounded far away and distant. Something grabbed hold of my shoulders and suddenly I was lifted off my feet. I looked up to see a giant rotting skeletal bird flying me out to sea. Before I could do so much as lift my sword, it dropped me. I fell several feet into the cold and dark salty waters.

Releasing my sword, I swam to the surface. The ship wasn't very far away, maybe a hundred feet, but waves had kicked up and slapped violently against the side of the ship. Using all my strength I swam towards the ship, but as I neared, I realized something problematic. The side of the ship was bare of anything I could use to climb up the sides. I might get lucky and have a wave deposit me close enough to the edge, but I imagined that would entail a good bit of damage.

Looking over to the black ship I saw my chance. The sides of the ship were covered in low hanging black strands of rope-like material. I headed in that direction.

My armor and items didn't weigh me down as bad as I would have thought. The waves were a different story, picking me up and depositing me further away with each mighty swoosh of water. Several times I got sea water in my mouth, and I battled against a coughing fit while trying to stay afloat. Amidst the confusing moments I surprised myself when I hit against the black outer hull of the ship.

I grabbed hold of one of the blackened ropes only to release it a second later as it burnt my hand. The waves pushed me against them and again I felt the burning even through my armor. Clenching my teeth, I cursed my luck and checked my health. Each touch had only taken a few of my health away. Judging the amount I'd have to climb, I figured I could make it with plenty of health to spare. The swim and fight against the waters had taken it out of me though and my stamina was low. I activated my Stamina Surge skill and went to work.

Painful hand over painful hand I made it slowly up the side of the attacking ship. I imagined the sweet feeling of one of Alayna's heals hitting me, but unfortunately it never came. I wondered suddenly as I moved mindlessly up the rope, if they'd assumed I'd died or drowned. Surely, they'd dealt with that bird thing, I couldn't have been the only one to get picked up.

The thought distracted me enough that I nearly lost my grip as I turned to look out into the vast ocean. I didn't see anyone else out in the waters and against all likelihood I made it to the edge of the ship. What awaited me as I looked over the edge nearly made me jump back into the water. By my quick count there were at least twenty of the deformed and mutated fish people all standing around or about to swing over, using thicker black ropes.

All at once they moved towards me and I scanned the area looking for anything to give me the upper hand. There were large quantities, like several dozens upon dozens of barrels with some black powder spilling out of them and at least twice as many cannons and large iron balls stacked up all over the deck. I ran, my feet barely keeping grip on the thick railing, avoiding a strike here and dodging a grab there. I would grab hold of a thicker rope and rid myself of these things.

I looked long enough to call Lightning down on the closest target, then grabbed hold of a rope. It burned my hand, but I held on tight. Another man-monster was about to reach me, so I fired off a Firebolt at his face, but he ducked! The bolt of fire hit the black barrels and the next thing I knew I was flying across the gap. I hit the light-colored wood of the starting ship and spots of black played around my sight.

It was difficult to breathe, and I felt something pressing into my chest. Looking down I discovered what looked like a leg sized chunk of wood stabbed right into my chest.

"Pull it free and I'll heal him," Alayna's sweet voice rung in my ears. It was hard to see, but a fuzzy form pulled free the wood from my chest, causing significant and sudden pain, but it lasted only moments. The warmth of her heals rolled over me, and before I knew what had happened, I was back.

"That was close," I said, as Alayna threw herself down beside me to pull me into an embrace.

"You went over the edge, and they said you wouldn't be able to get back up," Alayna's words were hoarse as if she'd been yelling a lot. "I couldn't get to you, I couldn't..." Her words trailed off. I squeezed her back and then stood, taking her with me.

"I'm back," I said, hardly believing it myself. "Let's focus up, there were at least another twenty of those things on their ship."

"Not anymore," Beth said, chuckling. "You blew them to hell and back."

I followed her gaze and was surprised to find that the black ship was ablaze, one of its masts had fallen over in the middle.

"Did I do that?" I asked, trying to put together the pieces of what I'd done. "How?"

"No idea," Beth said, grinning ear to ear. "But you just streamlined this dungeon run. Normally we have to find an artifact to cleanse the ship of a curse and then use the ship to fight a big sea monster. Not sure what we do now..." Her voice trailed off as Captain Ayre approached.

"Quick thinking lad," he said, slapping me on the shoulder.

"Threats not over yet. Those foul beings were summoning a Kraken and it falls to us to deal with it. I pulled this off one of them." He held up a weather and stained map with a big red 'X' on it. "There be treasure and weapons here. What say you? We go here and seek the treasure and weapons or head straight for the Kraken?"

"Treasure and weapons," I said, everyone nodding along with me.

***

"So how do we loot them?" I asked standing over a shark-man. Beth had already reached down and opened her hand, having received several gold coins.

"Just reach down and touch it, you'll see," Beth said, moving to loot another.

I did so, reaching down and touching the shark headed man.

Do you wish to Loot Shark Spawn? Yes or No.

I sent an affirmative and, in my hand, appeared 2 gold and three teeth. Inspecting the teeth, I saw that they were 'Shark Teeth', perhaps they were used as a reagent. Going to every single corpse, I looted them all.

In total I got 249 gold, 41 silver, 8 more teeth, several eyes, a magic ring, a rusty sword, and an eye patch.

I inspected the three items to see what I was dealing with. The ring was silver with a flat blue gem that swirled inside like the crashing waves of the ocean.

Ring of the Sea's Might

+3 Strength

+3 Intellect
Durability: 25/25
Rarity: Uncommon
Weight: 6 Grams
Item Level: 19, Level Required to use: 13, Dropped by: Three Eyed Jack

The rusty sword was the same curved design as the captain had while the base damage was higher than mine, it didn't have any bonus to attributes.

Rusty Cutlass

14-18 Base Damage
Durability: 52/75
Rarity: Common
Weight: 1.2 Pounds
Item Level: 18, Level Required to use: 12, Dropped by: Marky the Sharky

The eyepatch was interesting, it didn't give many details, but the attribute bonus was tempting. It was a simple patch of treated leather attached to two strings that could be tied behind your head. A single clear gem was pressed into the inside of the patch.

Unidentified Eye Patch

Has 2 unidentified magical properties.
+9 Intellect

Durability: 50/50
Rarity: Unknown
Weight: 9 Grams
Item Level: 21, Level Required to use: 15, Dropped by: Pirate Seer

"Anyone know how to identify a magical item that won't tell me what it does?" I asked, putting all but the eye patch into my bags. Not a bad haul considering. We'd been locked out from looting the black ship as it sunk into the water, but Beth said normally there is about twice as much loot since the strongest mobs come last and give the best items.

"Let me see," Adathin said, so I handed over the eye patch. "Oh yeah, I can identify this for you. Just give me a second." He squinted his eyes and with a small flash of white he laughed. "It's a cursed item, you're lucky you didn't put it on."

"What does it do?" I asked, taking it back.

"Have a look, just don't wear it until you can have the curse removed, if you can," Adathin said, shaking his head at the item.

I inspected it again and saw it was identified now.

Sightless Eye Patch of Intellect
Cursed: If this eye patch is placed over an eye, that eye will lose all sight for an hour equal to the minutes worn. After 10 minutes of wearing, sight is lost permanently. Removing Eye Patch after permanent sight loss will result in the uncovered eye also losing sight.
Enchanted with 'Sight beyond Sight' enchantment.
Sight beyond Sight - This enchantment will allow the

user to see the flows of mana and essence that permeate the world. Doing so will allow you to cast spells 10% more efficiently and do 10% more spell damage.

+9 Intellect

Durability: 25/25

Rarity: Rare

Weight: 9 Grams

Item Level: 21, Level Required to use: 15, Dropped by: Pirate Seer

That could be incredibly useful, but now wasn't the time to play with it. I didn't mind being blind for an hour or two if I couldn't get the curse removed, but during a dungeon wasn't the time to do so. Beth let us know that the island we were traveling to was the same place they'd gone before, but normally they went there for an item to uncurse the ship, not for gold and weapons.

It amazed me that the dungeon could be so versatile and had somehow planned for each eventuality. It made you think that perhaps dungeons had a conscious mind or something, but that was silly talk.

So far, my first dungeon run was going great, despite having been thrown overboard and being stabbed and slashed multiple times, things were looking up. Those monster-men mobs provided nearly twice as much essence as the last mobs, so that was good. In total I'd earned just over thirty thousand essence. Doing a bit of mental math as we sailed toward land, I determined that Fred and Fran's take had been a little over half of mine, which set up a good idea for how much essence everyone else was getting.

I would have to look at how much total I get out of this

entire run and compare that against Alayna's take to get firmer numbers, but I am convinced that my essence collection gems would in fact change the world now. If everyone could collect essence twice or even three times as much as is standard, then leveling into the higher tier levels wouldn't be something only one in every thousand adventurers achieved. A small part of my brain was seeing mountains of gold and another equally small part felt that this change might not make the world better.

Could I teach someone else this essence ability? I knew from Warrick that most spells could be learned the hard way, through research and study, but was there a faster way when you already knew it? I wished then that I had Warrick's ear to bounce my ideas and research off of. What had happened to my trusty wizard friend. It seemed unlikely that he could be in any serious danger, he was just as strong as my father, and it had taken a world threat to take out my father.

"What's on your mind?" Alayna asked, I turned to regard her beautiful face and was surprised at what I saw there.

"Are you okay?" I asked, there was sorrow behind those purple eyes.

"Just been thinking," she said, leaning against the ship's railing and looking out into the waters. Her hair whipped up from the steady push of the sea air and she shivered.

I stepped forward, wrapping my arms around her for warmth and she melted against me.

"About what?" I asked, kissing the back of her head, and snuggling into her.

"Maybe my father was right. He sent me on a research trip, the days that I was gone, and I actually enjoyed myself and gained a good deal of essence," her voice was low and a bit sad. "I never really enjoyed researching and finding discoveries, but I did this time. And it was much safer. Maybe once you hit

600

level 15 we can both go hide away at your keep and do research together."

I gently turned her around so that I could look into her eyes. "You know that isn't what I want, and I thought you wanted this," I said, gesturing to the open sea and the vast world the dungeon had constructed.

"I thought I did too," Alayna whispered. "But we could still level, researching provides essence, just a lot slower. You took the long-lived perk, we could escape for several decades without really losing any time, discovering, and finding out new ways to benefit society."

"Why can't we do both?" I asked, wondering how small the essence gains from my profession must have been that I hadn't really noticed it.

"I've always been in the healer role, most of my family is as well, but I've never had someone die in a dungeon before. When you went over the edge and they told me that was it, no way back up. If we'd been able to summon bonded beasts, but no, not in a stupid dungeon," Alayna was beginning to ramble, and she stopped herself. "Look Caldor." She took my head in her hands. "I've never had feelings like this for someone and I didn't realize it until you were thrown overboard, but I can't..." She didn't finish, wiping away a tear and looking out into the water.

"We both understand the risk that comes with being an adventurer," I said, choosing my words carefully. "I trust that you are strong and wise enough to survive any threat we come across. Can you trust me to do the same?" I gently guided her face toward mine then added. "I'm a bit stronger than I think you're giving me credit." I meant it as a lighthearted joke, but I think she took it as a dig, because she furrowed her brows at me.

"There won't always be..." She began to say but I cut her off.

"There is always a way out of danger. Trust me to find it and I will do the same for you," I said, kissing her forehead.

"Alright," Alayna said, looking up at me with reddened eyes and suddenly grinning. "But if you go overboard again, I'm jumping in after you."

"Deal," I said, chuckling at the idea of Alayna jumping off a ship for me in her white flowing robes.

CHAPTER 56
SLAY THE KRAKEN

The island that Captain Ayre had indicated loomed in the horizon, growing ever closer as we sailed the open waters. Beth explained that normally the ride to the island was more eventful with pirate crew appearing as stowaways and attacking at random intervals, but no attacks occurred, and she reasoned we just did a better job of killing them before they could hide. The skies were a bright blue and the sun beat down on our backs as we sailed.

The fresh afternoon air chilled by the cold sea waters was relief enough to make the heat not seem so unbearable. Still, I drank a large portion of my water and snacked on some dried meat to pass the time. My experience with boats was severely limited, being on a paddle boat was the extent of it really, but I found myself enjoying the movement of such a large sea vessel. Despite the waters and the danger they likely held, I could see myself working on a boat like this, maybe sailing to the island of Avalon and challenging the hardest dungeons in the entire Wyrd.

Would Alayna be at my side? Or would she find her place

elsewhere? I cared for Alayna, maybe even beginning to love her. It was silly really, trying to understand someone else's path when I hardly knew what my life would entail in the coming years. I should focus on enjoying the now, because right now I was in a dungeon with a strong group and a woman I cared about. Now was where I was needed, where I could do the most good.

"Lay anchor!" Captain Ayre yelled. And the elves, humans, goblins, and even a few gnomes went to work pulling up the sails, dropping the anchor big and making themselves busy.

I watched as a team of burly humans worked to lower a rowboat over the side using cleverly designed pulleys and ropes. It was a sizeable boat, big enough to fit ten large men easily. Or a dungeon party and a few sailors.

We gathered together at the edge of the boat. One of the sailors, a small stringy looking goblin attached a rope ladder with wooden steps sewn into it over the edge.

"No way out of the water, huh?" I said, elbowing Beth as she passed me.

"It's true," she said, raising her hands in mock defense. "Try to find that ladder before this part of the dungeon, I bet you can't."

They'd told us they hadn't lost anyone in this dungeon before so how would they even know, I wondered. I thought to ask, but figured it wouldn't matter, I just wouldn't go over the edge again. As I stepped over the ship's railing and lowered myself, I remembered that I had rope in my dimensional box. Could I have been able to hook something using it and avoided the black ship altogether?

It all worked out for the best, I figured, sitting beside Alayna and grabbing an oar. It was almost like the dungeon wanted the ship to blow up, else why put something that could blow up so violently. I decided to make a note of the events, and what I suspected was the means of the explosion, the black powder in barrels I'd seen. My map didn't have any prior notes at all on this dungeon, so I filled in the other information as well, levels, floors, etc. Most of which was easy since this was an open-air dungeon, so no multi layered rooms and floors to grind through.

Though far less common, I think I preferred the themed dungeons like this where it seemed to contain an entire world. I wondered if the Crimson Crusades dungeon was open like this. From what I'd heard, it seemed likely.

It took several minutes of rowing to make it to shore, and I got a good look at the island as we did so. It was about a mile or a mile and half long. Almost the entire available land was filled with tall trees with wide leaves sprouting out the top like comical hair. As we got closer, I could see head-sized fruit of some kind, with yellow skin and red marbling, growing in bunches under the leaves.

The beach ran straight through the island and to the other side, a fact that you could barely make out if you caught the right angle when peering through the trees. When doing so I swore I saw a black shadow dart across my vision. I mentioned it to Beth, but she said the times before the island was just a series of puzzles and traps.

The sand was warm enough that I felt it through my boots, and I didn't envy anyone walking barefoot on it. Grug thought differently it would seem, as he lay down directly into the hot sand. What followed was several seconds of moaning and growling that made me slightly uncomfortable. When I looked to Beth she just laughed and whispered to me.

"He does this every time, he says back home they have warm beaches close to where he was raised."

"I see," I said, watching the now very sandy man bear get up. It looked like he'd added hints of blonde color into his fur and made no attempts to free himself of the sand.

"It moves every time, but in the trees somewhere we will find a cave entrance and inside is a deserted pirate's hideout. There'll be lots of traps and puzzles to solve, so stay behind me and let me work my magic," Beth said, cracking her fingers. She ran a hand up her horns and took a deep breath. "I'm ready, let's do this."

We'd gone maybe five steps into the trees when the attack began.

A spotted cat pounced atop Beth, biting into her neck. Grug moved like the wind, punching the cat in the head and stunning it. In the same second, he grabbed hold of it and smashed it across a tree, the head-sized fruits smashing down around us as a result. As each of the fruits smashed down, they exploded and sent sharp pieces of brown shell in every direction.

Another cat appeared shortly after the explosions stopped, the first cat lay still and likely dead.

"Don't hit the damned trees!" I yelled as I struggled to pull out a palm-sized piece of sharp brown shell from my leg. The stuff was tough enough to penetrate my armor and could likely be used to make armor if I collected enough pieces.

Alayna had a few bloody marks on her white robes, but she worked swiftly to send heals on Beth's unmoving body. The second cat now faced an angry Grug in bear form and it didn't look good for the cat. I inspected it while pulling a potion free from my dimensional storage and running to Beth's side.

Dire Jaguar, Level 23, 632/1050

Uncorking my potion, I poured it into her mouth and then added a small amount into her open wound in her neck. The jaguar had ripped free a good measure of her neck and softer muscle. The potion helped, I could see the muscles slowly threading themselves back together, but it would likely take a while.

"I've healed her as high as her body will go, it's going to just take a few minutes for her to regrow the missing tissue," Alayna said, joining me beside Beth.

"Heads up!" Adathin cried, a number of the explosive fruits rained down on us just as another jaguar appeared.

Alayna began to cast a spell, chanting words of power, and a translucent shield appeared around us. It likely saved Beth's life and both of us from serious damage, because three fell right in front of her shield, shattering it a moment later. Despite shattering on impact, it did its job of stopping the shrapnel.

Adathin wasn't as lucky, he was down holding onto his leg as the jaguar pounced at him.

I cast Lightning Strike and it slammed into the cat's back, causing it to go rigid. Whether from the cat being midair when it was hit or the unexpected nature of the attack as it had its back turned to me, the damage was several times more than I'd expected. The cat fell limp, atop Adathin, its body convulsing.

It wouldn't last forever so I got to my feet and rushed over. Alayna was faster, casting her golden chain spell and pulling the jaguar away from Adathin. Smart thinking on her behalf because a moment later the jaguar was all claws and teeth, lashing out. I paused, sword raised, and decided a range attack would be preferable. Slicing downward I cast Light Blade and released an arc of light in the same second. The sword continued downward, my grip releasing as it stuck in the sand, knowing I could recall it in a moment's notice.

I cast Firebolt just as the chain spell ended and the Dire cat stood. In that moment I really wished I'd purchased a crossbow and kept it loaded in my storage. It would take too long to pull free my bow and arrow at this point. The cat came at me in a flash, moving much too quickly. My blade appeared in my hands, and I cast Light Blade for the extra base damage. Just as a claw took me across the face, I activated Power Strike, piercing upward and Swift Strike to give it an extra bump of damage.

I missed its heart, and I paid the price. It was mauling me, slashing and biting into my neck. My armor impeded its ability to rip my neck out, thankfully.

I'd planned for this very situation, well not being mauled by a cat, but not being able to use my sword effectively. My hand, bloodied and in pain, went to my side and I pulled free a dagger. It wasn't attributed, but it was hardened steel and dangerously sharp. I went wild against the vicious animal, stabbing with reckless abandon. The jaguar decided my neck was too well protected and took a painful bite out of my face.

Screams left my mouth unbidden as the cat latched hard against my facial bones. If I was stabbing fast and hard before, now the blows of my arm and not even the dagger's sharp edge was likely doing damage. My mind raced unable to think of anything else but stabbing and pain. I felt a warm rush that soothed my pain temporarily, but I didn't stop stabbing. It was several painful seconds later that the jaguar finally stopped moving. However, it remained attached to my face.

As carefully as I could I opened the cat's jaws and began delicately removing tooth after tooth from my skin, until I was able to push the cat off me. Grug finished off his cat a few moments later, he'd taken a beating as well, but mostly from the falling explosive fruit with shells inside.

"Grug not liking dungeon so much," he said a second after shifting back to his bearkin form.

"I hear you," Beth said, surprising us all by sitting up while a large section of her neck still knit back together. "I've got the worst itch." She said shaking her head groggily before falling backwards half conscious.

"She'll make it," Alayna said, taking turns healing each of us. Grug's legs and arms were shredded to bits, Adathin's legs were closing up so he seemed alright, but my face was on fire, and I could feel blood pouring down my arms and legs.

Even the jaguar's back claws had done some damage, shredding anyplace between the armor that it could find. I decided that moment that when I had free time, I was redesigning my arcane armor to include a full faced helmet. The front of my face was the last thing I wanted to get chewed on.

"You look rough," Alayna said, finishing yet another heal on me.

I was the last to recover, and Alayna had to rest for several long periods between to gather more Mana. She also had to do a kind of meditative prayer to consecrate her mana, but that didn't take very long.

After maybe a half hour from the start of the cat fight, we were ready to move again, but this time much more alert. Beth kept jumping at every noise and Grug shifted back to Bear form, staying like that as we squeezed through the trees. We encountered only one more cat, which we killed with overwhelming directed force, before finding the hidden pirate hideout.

There was just one problem, it wasn't abandoned like Beth had told us to expect, in fact, it looked right busy.

"This is new," Beth explained, looking to Adathin and Grug for support.

"I think we've discovered another event path that hasn't been recorded," Adathin said, then scratching at his chin he added. "We will get a discount off our Adventurer's Guild tax for this information I think."

"Guild takes much of Grug's gold," Grug said, agreeing in his own way.

Alayna and I shared a look, neither of us had to pay a guild tax because of our positions in one of the twelve ruling Houses.

"I don't see any of the weird looking pirates," I said. We'd retreated back, just to be safe, but we had a good angle higher up. From that vantage point we could see deep into the gap where they'd made their base.

It was built between two cliffs and consisted of several wooden platforms and walkways that slowly wound downward the deeper you got. From where we were you could see four platforms and about a dozen pirates, before it turned too much to show any more.

"Caldor's right," Beth said, shrugging. "If they are the same as the ones from the boat, we could probably pull all twelve and be just fine. But there's no telling how many are hidden below. Last time we were here it went down for a good minute or so before we'd reach the bottom cave where the items we needed would be found. And there's still the chance of traps and puzzles. Remember the puzzle we had to solve to get that floor open to go down past the half level point?" She looked at Adathin asking him directly.

He nodded and pointed down into the hideout. "But if that was there, we'd be able to see it from here, remember? I think this path the dungeon has us on is less tactical and sneaky and more a straight physical challenge. I'm beginning to think that these fights mirror the choices we make, and the dungeon took us blowing the ship up as the most physically destructive path. So, it's likely we will fight more difficult monsters. I just hope the final boss hasn't gotten much stronger, it's a challenge on a good day."

Beth didn't seem convinced, shaking her head and looking down at the pirates. "I don't know."

I let out a sigh and cleared my throat. "You know what we can do to find out?" I asked with a toothy grin. "Let's go kill some pirates."

That was enough of a push to get them to agree and after some simple planning, we were on our way.

Grug was going to wait around the upper bend, just out of sight of the pirates, and Beth was going to perch up a ways, shooting arrows until she pulled a few pirates. The plan went along just fine, arrows whistling through the air, until it hit one of the pirates. Instead of turning and running it sounded an alarm, banging on some metal dish and running deeper into the base along with all visible pirates.

A heavy thumping sound started deep within the ground, and we all shared a skeptical look.

"Well that plan failed," I said, halfheartedly. No one found it amusing.

"Do we go in?" Beth asked, then shook her head a little. "What is making that freaking thumping sound!"

I could feel it in my chest and though it did no damage I felt a foreboding sense of danger approaching.

"Grug votes go kill and stop boom boom," Grug said. I chuckled at his poor grasp of Common, he almost sounded like a toddler at times, but he was a powerful ally that I respected, so I hid my laugh in a cough.

"I feel something coming," Adathin said, and I agreed with him.

"I don't know what, but it feels like something..." My voice trailed off as I tried to narrow down what I was feeling but failed.

"I say we go attack the pirates and end this," Alayna said, rubbing at her temples. The sound was obviously bugging her as much as it was me.

"Let's go," I said, and we headed down into the pirate's hideout.

Beth was right, there were still traps, but they were no match for a carriage-sized bear. A swinging spike door shattered against a powerful swipe of Grug's claws and we pushed on through, moving downward.

We found the first of the pirates just past the bend, eight of them with weapons drawn and ready to fight. They had a surprise for us as well, one of the pirates, a beastkin cat, had two jaguars at her side, making the total combatants ten. This wasn't going to be as easy as we'd hoped.

Grug caught both leaping jaguars with his mighty paws and batted them backwards. I rushed up to his side and released an arc of light at the closest pirate. Arrows flew, lances of lights and chains unleashed, while the battle raged. Adathin, for his part, seemed to be able to project illusions in the eyes of a few combatants at a time and several times I was saved by his quick thinking.

The pirates fell within a minute of fighting, they were much sturdier than the ship pirates. Only the beastkin remained, her jaguar pets dead at her feet.

"You are too late to stop the summoning," the beastkin female said, hissing at us.

"Shut mouth," Grug said, shifting back into his beastkin

form and swinging his axe in a single motion. It hit her across the chest, but still, she didn't fall. Suddenly her body seemed to vibrate, and she appeared in front of Alayna, the furthest person from her, slashing her across the face.

I turned to cast Lightning Strike as it came off cooldown, but a moment later she was back in front of Grug. Switching my focus I cast my spell, it didn't stun her. Grug traded blows with her, but soon she began to shake again, and I realized too late what was happening. Again, she moved instantly in front of the furthest party member, slashing Alayna in the gut this time.

She fell forward, yelling in frustration while casting another heal on Grug as he fought the beastkin cat. I ran to her side and began casting Lesser Heal on her. It went off just as the cat woman shimmered and I took a step back making myself the furthest away and readied my sword.

As I thought, she appeared in front of me, but I was already thrusting forward and combining my speed and damage doubling skills, I thrust right into her chest. She let out a cry of pain and stopped vibrating, going limp on the edge of my sword. I hadn't missed this time; my blade pierced her heart.

That ended the battle, and we took time to loot.

Just like I'd gotten from the jaguars above, here I got several teeth and a few gold each. The pirates gave me another rusty cutlass, and something called a blunderbuss, but its durability was zero oddly enough. The only piece worth mentioning really was what I got from the beastkin lady.

Charm of the Sleepless One
Enchanted with 'Sleepless One's Touch' enchantment.

Sleepless One's Touch - This enchantment will allow the user to remain rested without sleep. For every day that you go without sleep you add a charge to this token. You may spend a charge to inflict hex a target with nightmares for 1 week. If token exceeds maximum charges, it will be destroyed.

+9 Constitution

Charges: 0/10

Durability: 25/25

Rarity: Rare

Weight: 3 Grams

Item Level: 24, Level Required to use: 15, Dropped by: Enchantress Thress

I didn't know how I felt about inflicting nightmares on someone, but I loved the idea of not having to sleep for ten days. I'd need to get a few levels before I could use it, but I bet I'd be able to find targets for the nightmares if I really needed to. I was imagining using it on monsters and such, but then a person came to mind that could do for having some nightmares. I surprised myself when Zander wasn't the first name that came to me, but Tim, that wizard that tried to kill me.

"I've scored three pieces of a set of armor already," Alayna said, some of her enthusiasm returning after we looted our kills. "I just need two more and I'll have something to replace these stupid robes with."

"What's the armor called?" I asked, having not seen any new armor, but I'd been pretty engrossed with my own looting and inspecting.

"It's called 'Seawashed Armor of the Swashbuckler'," Alayna said, laughing. "So far it looks like a pair of stiff cloth, but it has good attributes and a set bonus that decreases the damage I take from surprise attacks."

"Can't wait to see it on you if you get the whole set," I said, trying to picture Alayna wearing plain clothes that have been hardened by seawater. I couldn't do it, so I let it go.

"There's a puzzle here," Beth said, standing in front of a pedestal set into the wooden floor.

Walking over I took a look at what she meant. I was surprised by the simple nature of the puzzle. It was a four-by-four tile grid with a single tile missing. Each tile had a series of lines on it and at first glance I guessed that all you needed to do was line them up to match.

"Seems simpler than before," Adathin said, examining the tiles. "Let me work this one out, you did the last one."

Beth huffed and puffed but finally said, "Fine." And stepped aside.

It took him two minutes and a door swung open in the middle of the platform. A ladder led us deeper, where Grug triggered three traps, but survived just fine, and we came to the stone door that Beth said held the item they needed the last time.

"This must be where our 'treasure and weapons' are," I said, mimicking the Captain's voice when saying treasure and weapons.

"Did anyone find a circular piece of stone about this big," Beth made a circle with her hands showing a circle about the size of a palm.

"Grug did," Grug said, pulling the item from someplace on his body.

It was like everyone these days had dimensional storage, Emory and Ismene were missing out.

Beth took the stone disk and set it into the round stone

door. The thumping finally stopped, but the sense of dread remained. The stone door opened, rolling into the rock, and revealing six corpses bleeding over an altar of bones and tentacles. Behind the corpses were three chests, the center most was lined in gold.

"Loot!" Grug yelled, rushing forward.

I saw Beth scrunch up as if she expected something to happen, but nothing did. Grug opened the chest and just like looting monster kills, items appeared in his hands.

"Safe?" I asked, raising an eyebrow at Beth. She shrugged and followed after Grug.

I touched all three chests and it was mostly crap drops. In total I got another few hundred gold, some bones, several cut gems and one uncut diamond, as well as a dungeon item that I didn't know what to make of.

Death's Bane (Dungeon Locked)

Dungeon Locked items can only be used inside of a dungeon and cannot be taken out.

Radiant Fire: This cutlass will burn any undead creature with radiant fire, dealing x10 damage. Any abilities used while wielding Death's Bane will have additional radiant damage added. Each use of Radiant Fire removes 1 Durability from Death's Bane.

21-26 Base Damage

+20 Constitution

Durability: *75/75*

Rarity: *Dungeon Locked*

Weight: *3.1 pounds*

Item Level: 0, Level Required to Use: 0, Dropped by: Dungeon Loot

. . .

"I think we are going to be fighting something undead," I said, and a moment later the thumping returned faster than before. If that wasn't enough, a terrible ethereal screech echoed from outside the hideout.

It turned out everyone had been given an undead killing weapon with the same limitation as mine, but with different uses. Like Beth got a bow that didn't need arrows and depleted 1 durability every 2 arrows, so with a durability of 75 she had twice as many chances than I did to inflict damage. Meanwhile, Grug was given a necklace that would absorb up to fifteen attacks per minute and granted him immunity to death touch, whatever that was.

Alayna got a staff that gave someone she healed immunity from an ability called death touch for three seconds. And Adathin received the best one yet, a scepter that allowed every third illusion he summoned to fight as if it were really there. He said he had a similar ability, but it was a once a minute thing and the illusions it would bring to life were limited.

Whatever the challenge, we felt ready. It took all of three minutes to leave the hideout and lose all confidence we'd had. The rowboat was gone, and in the sea attacking the ship was a tentacled horror. When I used Inspect, I only got a name.

Undead Kraken.

"Oh no," Beth said, taking an involuntary step backwards. "It's an undead version of the dungeon boss but twice as big."

"How will we even get to it?" Adathin asked, his voice barely a whisper.

As if in answer to his words the undead Kraken finished toying with the ship, smashing it into two pieces. It turned two red eyes to the island and began to come our way.

As it got closer, I understood the full scope of it. The tentacles were several times as wide as Grug and extremely long. How would we even begin to fight this thing?

"How did you kill the non undead version of this?" I asked, white knuckling the dungeon enchanted cutlass.

"You are supposed to ram a ship into it and then fight the tentacles for a bit, before stabbing it through an eye," Beth said, her breath coming fast.

"We got this," I said, one way or another this fight was coming to us, so we might as well be ready. "Gather all the tree fruit you can find and let's dig a hole. We can do this; we just have to be smart about it."

They agreed, all shaking heads and nervous eyes. With what little time we had, we formulated an impromptu plan. This would work, I repeated for the hundredth time in my head when minutes later the undead Kraken made landfall.

The dark clouds that threatened rain returned just as the Kraken made it to land. Seemingly hundreds of tentacles immediately shot out, smashing sand into the air and wreaking havoc. The plan started out as intended, with Grug in bear form rushing out of the tree line and slashing into a tentacle. Immediately after engaging, three nearby tentacles attempted to wrap Grug up, but he pulsed a golden light and they burst into flame, the entire length of them going dead.

Grug fled into the trees, the half alive tentacles whipping after him. Close up the Kraken was obviously undead, with large sections of its flesh just hanging free, showing exposed black flesh within. I didn't know much about sea creature anatomy, but I was surprised by the lack of bones. The tentacles hit the tree line and stopped, not able to extend any further.

The main body of the kraken pushed onto land and the next phase of our little plan started. Beth used a special ability she had, to shoot an explosive arrow right in front of the main body. She did this four times, aiming at four different locations we'd set up. I watched as they sped forward, narrowly missing the tentacles and slamming into mounds in the sand.

Perfect! An explosion rippled the very air around us, four separate piles of explosive fruit went off, hastily covered in sand. Tentacles slapped about wildly and the kraken screeched in pain, an otherworldly sound. I rushed forward throwing exploding fruit from the edge of the tree line. Each one worked wonderfully, but there were still countless tentacles moving about and ready to squeeze the life out of any one of us.

One such tentacle came from the side and scooped me up. My focus had been elsewhere, and I dropped the explosive fruit as it lifted me. It hit my pile that I'd been using and created another large explosion, the shock of which made my head ring. My left hand moved, and I spoke the words for Lightning Strike, the spell smashed down on the tentacle where I focused, several feet away. The shock of the attack passed onto me, and I hit the ground rigid from the stun.

After an excruciatingly long three seconds elapsed I made it back to my feet. I pulled my dungeon weapon free, and I cast Light Blade over it. I danced, my blade moving here and there, slashing against the tentacles that wished to ensnare me. With each strike I stepped further back, retreating to rejoin my party.

I was thankful for the Radiant Fire enchantment, each of my strikes was enough most times to bring a tentacle down. As a party we made great progress, I saw that nearly half the tentacles lay smoldering on the ground. It took me twenty strikes of the blade and three spells, before I made it to Grug's side. Meaning I had about fifty durability left on the weapon.

As a party we fought against the remaining tentacles, slowly pushing closer to the main massive head with its hardened beak-like mouth and glowing red eyes. Suddenly a jaguar the size of several carriages appeared from behind us and began slashing away tentacles. I feared for a moment that the island had set a new monster on us, but when I turned, I saw Adathin bent in concentration from such a large illusion. This must be his third and he wasn't holding back.

He maintained the illusion and brought us nearly within spitting range of the kraken before it flickered and died. Adathin slumped from the effort but remained standing.

That was the entirety of our plan, we were banking on the kraken following similar stages as the alive version Beth and company had knowledge of. The undead Kraken didn't upset, all of its remaining undead limbs pulled inward. Its eyes began to glow, and we had no time to react as a red beam of light shot out hitting Adathin.

In his already weakened state, he was too slow to dodge. Alayna held out an outstretched hand, a translucent golden sphere formed around him, blocking the beam. The shield spell was riddled with cracks, but held together. I saw a heal settle over him and he perked up. A second later one of the tentacles began to glow with a black light, red smoke wafting off of it.

The tentacle shattered the barrier around Adathin and he went flying backwards as it made contact. The black glow with its red smoke transferred to Adathin and he screamed again, in obvious pain. But something happened, a golden light pulsed from within him, dispelling the black and red.

"I think we just saw the Death Touch," I yelled over the crash of battle. "Alayna, be ready to heal anyone that gets hit by a tentacle. Beth, focus on putting those out of commission, while Grug and I go for the head!"

I hadn't meant to take charge, but no one else was giving orders and our plans up to that point had been executed. No one else had issues with it, each of them springing into action. I ran beside Grug, activating my Swift Strike to turn aside a sudden tentacle strike. The black and red tentacle flashed against my sword, not dying as they had before, but dispelling the dark effect.

Standing just in front of the kraken we were nowhere big enough to reach its eye and kill it as they'd done previously. So, I reached out a hand and cast Lightning Strike. It had the added benefit of the dungeon weapon's effect, causing the giant monster to rear back in pain. The kraken's eyes began to grow red again, this time while it looked at Beth. Grug must have noticed, because he activated an ability that caused him to rush toward Beth, intercepting the red beam.

Grug neither roared nor cried out in pain, instead just taking the hit as if it were nothing. His dungeon item working to negate the damage no doubt. I sent a barrage of Firebolts, arcs of light damage, Lightning Strikes, and Power Strikes into the kraken, but the fight continued.

The eyes flashed again, but this time they looked at me while at the same time a black tentacle slashed downward at me. Not knowing what else to do I rolled away from Grug and used my Cloak of Negation to cover myself. A heal hit me moments before the tentacle, and good thing too because my cloak did nothing to stop the black and red effect from being passed to me. It was dispelled by a flash of golden light, but for a few moments I was racked with pain so intense that my muscles nearly cramped.

The beam hit my cloak and threw me backwards, but I

sustained almost no damage from it. I really needed to use this cloak more, it was awesome.

The battle continued and we fell into a rhythm, with our weapons getting closer and closer to breaking. Beth's bow went first, I heard a violent crack and looked over in time to see her pull free her old weapon and stringing an arrow.

It was then that things changed, the kraken's entire body took on the black glow with red smoke. The eyes turned black, and they pulsed, the telltale sign that it was going to shoot a beam.

"Watch the eyes!" I yelled, trying to track which one of us it was aiming for. Adathin summoned another third illusion, this time a black griffin that looked eerily like Ares.

"It's close to death," Adathin called out. "A final blow to the eye might do it."

I took his suggestion, running over to the griffin and taking to the air. The beam shot out at us, but the illusion moved as solid and swift as the real Ares, and we twirled out of the way just in time. Bearing down on the Kraken I held my sword at the ready, it gleamed a golden light as if it knew what was coming.

The griffin flew high and to the right and I prepared to strike. We zipped downward and I activated Power Strike and Swift Strike, slashing deep across both eyes. Then turning, I cast Lightning Strike into the wound for good measure. The kraken screeched and its tentacles went wild.

Just when I thought it hadn't been enough, the creature finished its death throes and fell still.

We'd done it, we killed the kraken.

A rush of essence unlike any I'd felt before hit me then, and I had to focus in order to catch my breath.

"Gotta love the essence from finishing a dungeon!" Beth called out; she'd felt it as well then.

The illusion became just that a moment later, luckily we'd set down and I was in the process of dismounting, but I still stumbled a bit. My dungeon weapon grew hot suddenly and I dropped it. The sword turned to sand moments later, adding itself to the beach. Where the kraken had been a moment ago now sat a golden gem incrusted chest. Grug had already gone forward claiming his loot and the rest of the party were headed that way as well. I joined them and claimed my final prize from my first dungeon run. I received a sword, several pieces that were labeled as different parts of the Kraken's insides, and 819 gold! I let the sack of gold, which was hefty, enter my inventory along with the kraken reagents, then looked at my new sword.

It was in a sheath that at first glance didn't look like much. The handle was clean and made of a dark thick leather, but the pommel and guard looked like a twisting iridescent shell. The swirling shell-like material covered the length of the sword's sheath. I could tell just by the hilt and pommel that it wasn't a cutlass, which was a shame, I was enjoying using the dungeon weapon.

Instead, it had the cross style that I was used to with my Arming sword, but slightly angled toward the blade, more like a 'V' than the normal 'T' design. Pulling free the sword, which came out as if newly oiled, I saw that it was a handspan longer than the arming sword. This was a true long sword. Set into the fuller were three oval black gems. Using my profession's skills I recognized them as rare black diamonds, but they were unenchanted as far as I could tell.

The metal of the blade was white, but as I moved it the surface shifted from iridescent pinks, blues, and even oranges.

It wasn't steel, but it seemed sturdy enough. I inspected it and my jaw dropped at the attributes and base damage.

Shell Blade of the Sea Witch
3 Gem Slots
24-30 Base Damage
+13 Strength
+13 Intellect
Mana: 250/250
Durability: 125/125
Rarity: Epic
Weight: 1.3 pounds
Item Level: 29, Level Required to use: Soulbound to Caldor Miles, Dropped by: Undead Kraken

Upon further study of the blade, I noticed there was a pearl set into the end of the pommel. As I focused on it, I realized that was where the Mana was being stored from the sword's description.

"Get anything good?" Alayna asked, she was holding what looked like an oar that something had taken a bite out of on the paddle side, and inside the circular bite floated a giant glowing pearl. The oar, or staff I guessed, was covered in barnacles, and looked sea worn. "Because I got this god-awful looking staff that is probably too good not to use."

I held up my sword and her eyes went wide. "I got an upgrade, just gotta bond it and it'll be my new primary weapon," I said, sheathing the blade.

"It's so pretty," Alayna said, running her hand over the sheath.

"Yeah, it looks like a girl's sword," Beth said, poking my arm with her finger teasingly.

"Dungeon exit is here," Adathin said, getting our attention.

At the water's edge a hooded figure in worn and ragged robes, stood in a boat. Just in front of him was a pedestal with a large orb that pulsed white.

"Just touch that and it'll send us back," Beth said, likely seeing my apprehension. I followed their lead, watching as each of them touched it and disappeared in a flash of white. I went last, and before touching it stared into the hood of the figure on the boat.

The darkness was so deep that I couldn't make out a face, but as I stared a voice sounded from it.

"Take the core as an offering. You are the first to deviate from the path in a long time." The voice had an ethereal echo to it, as if it spoke from a great distance and close at the same time.

I didn't know what he meant by 'take the core' though, so I looked around and was surprised to see a very plain wooden box the size of my fist sitting on the other end of the small rowboat. Reaching down I opened it. Instead of the normal 'loot' process I was able to see inside, a rough-cut gem the size of my fist sat inside. Pulling it free I examined it.

Undead Kraken Core
Essence total: 39,150

I stumbled in surprise gripping the core close to me. My shoulder touched the spherical transportation stone and in a flash of white light I was teleported to the starting room with the pedestal containing the mana enriched water.

"What's that?" Alayna asked, she was the last person in the room, the others must have already walked up to leave.

"The dungeon gave it to me just now," I said, my eyes still wide in surprise. "It's a monster core for the Undead Kraken we killed."

"Dungeon monsters don't have cores," Alayna said, holding out her hand. I sat the core into her hand, and she must have inspected it because her eyes went wide as well. "I guess I should say, 'I've never heard of dungeon monsters having cores', congratulations!"

"Thanks," I said, putting the core into my storage. I already had an idea of what I could do with the Core. There was a certain friend of mine that was about to be power leveled when I saw her next.

CHAPTER 57
GOODBYES AND CHARACTER SHEETS

"What now?" I asked Alayna, while we waited for the party to finish paying their percentage owed to the Adventurer's Guild.

"I had fun," Alayna said, she took my hand in hers. "But and I can't believe I'm saying this, I think I am going to dig into some research and tasks my father has for me. At least for now. And who knows, maybe he won't be so mad at you for taking me to a dangerous dungeon if I dig into my work."

That killed my spirits a bit, but I knew better than to try and dictate someone's path forward. Alayna would do what she wanted, and I had a feeling I'd get her into a dungeon again, just not anytime soon maybe. "You're an amazing healer and I won't say I understand, but I respect your choice," I said, pulling her into a tight hug. "I think I have a week of study ahead of me as well. I need to do a lot of learning if I'm ever going to figure out you know what."

She shook her head knowingly as we ended our hug. "If you're going to stay in town then we should set up a running dinner date. We're still allowed to have fun, despite our responsibilities."

"Agreed," I said. "As long as we don't always go to the place with small portions. It is really good, but I need to get full sometimes." She chuckled at my jest and gestured to Grug, Beth, and Adathin as they returned.

"Grug goes home," Grug said, cracking his neck loudly and hefting his axe.

"We are disbanding our party and going our own ways," Beth said, a sad smile on her face. "But if you decide to run some more dungeons let me know, I'll be heading back to the city to sell my goods and rest for a few days."

"Same goes for me," Adathin said. "Let me know if you get any leads on some dungeons or monster hunts." He turned to Grug and patted him on the shoulder. "We're sad to see you go, Grug, but if you ever come down out of the mountains again, come find me and we can run some dungeons."

"Grug will do. Grug goes home now," Grug said, still struggling to speak Common clearly. And with that he turned and jogged off, slow at first but picking up speed as he went.

The trip back was peaceful, and we didn't have a single monster ambush during the entire trip. I took Ares and flew to Creeshaw after saying my goodbyes, hoping to run into Ismene and Emory, but Merlin hadn't seen them, and they didn't have a room rented in the adventurers hall. I was ready to leave when I bumped into a familiar face.

"I did my first dungeon run!" Creed Volkroy said, his cloak's hood still covering his face as it always did.

"So did I!" I said back, shaking his hand. "What level did you get to?"

"I pulled in enough essence to reach level 8," Creed said, smiling wide. "What level did you get to?"

"I haven't used the essence yet," I said. "I literally finished it earlier today. But I'm level 12 now, not sure if I'll get a level or two from the collected essence."

Creed studied me with a critical frown. "You are progressing swiftly. Our levels are still close enough if you wanted to run a dungeon together?" Creed asked.

"I think I need a few days to catch my breath but yeah that'd be great," I said looking around. This would be the perfect time for Ismene and Emory to appear, I thought, chuckling. "You haven't heard from Ismene, have you?"

"I talked with her and a guy named Emory just yesterday," Creed said.

I perked up at hearing that. "Do you know where they're going or where they are?" I asked.

"Ismene reached level 5 and they'd found a group willing to take them both as damage dealers. Didn't take them nearly as long as it took me. They told me that they'd invite me to the next one as they didn't have any more room," Creed said, shrugging at the circumstances.

"I'm heading back to the capital, if you see them again tell them to meet me there in a week or so and we can run a dungeon," I said, then thinking about it I added. "You're welcome to come along as well if you want."

"That'd be nice," Creed said, nodding.

I left afterwards, flying atop Ares to the capital city and back to working on my professions. But before I settled into a routine of reading, cutting gems, and inscribing them, I went to the Prime Mana Shrine to check out my essence gains and learn some more abilities.

With my dungeon adventures and not counting the core I'd gotten at the end; I was at 169,754 Essence. If I took the amount Alayna had gotten, which she'd told me during our walk back, I collected almost a third more than her. I suddenly became much less worried about keeping up with my levels and essence.

Before spending any on levels or attributes I used my new reagents to purchase two new spells and two new skills.

I learned Fireball, Arcane Missile, Damage Proficiency (Slashing), and Force Wave. There were a few defensive skills and spells I had my eye on, but this was enough for now, plus I didn't know if additional spells would become available after raising my levels, but I guessed that they might.

I assigned the essence required to level up and do my extra three attribute spread. Starting with level 13, I added 17,550 essence, then a staggering 52,935 to bring my Strength up 6 points. Then I spent 18,900 essence to reach level 14, and a surprisingly lower amount of essence to raise my Concentration attribute by 6 points, only 49,825. My higher affinity made a noticeable difference. That left me with only 26,944 essence, so I leveled up to 15 by paying a final 20,250 essence, but couldn't afford to purchase the extra attributes yet, so I assigned my 3 free attributes into Endurance and called it a day.

After all was said and done, I was left with 6,694 essence and a reverberating feeling of joy from the three increases in level. I took a final look over my menus and decided that for about a month of work I'd done well.

Name: Caldor Miles | Classification: Arcane Knight | Species: Human
Level: 15, 28,800 Essence to Lvl. 16 | Essence: 6,694 | Reputation: Rank 1, 49%
Health: 840 | Mana: 750 | Stamina: 580

Constitution: 64, Paragon | Intellect: 65, Paragon | Endurance: 38, 81%
Core: 31, Paragon | Concentration: 34, 89% | Strength: 70, 73%

. . .

My gear really did a great job in raising my attributes and I was glad to have added a new sword and a trinket to my arsenal. I went to Gilfoy's Emporium and rented the same room, my new influx of gold nearly tempting me to get the fancier room, but I held off once again.

I bonded my new sword and dropped off my armor for repair upstairs. There wasn't much damage despite the beating I'd taken, so they promised to get it back to me before the end of the next day. Then I spent the remaining hours of the night practicing the sword forms I'd learned before becoming *Sparked*. Looking back at them, I could see now that I'd been in a dozen battles or so, why they were important. Skills alone wouldn't make me a great swordsman, but technique and the application of skills just might.

CHAPTER 58
FULL CIRCLE

I entered the communal sitting room and saw that the woman I shared the office space with was out of her explosive room. Regina Clockstein a gnome in her middling years, with a no nonsense look on her face and attire befitting a queen, all silks and jewels. She sat on one of the lounge chairs, resting no doubt after a particularly large explosion had interrupted my reading quite thoroughly. Hunger drew me from my room, I planned to just grab some dry goods and retreat back to my solitude, but Regina had other ideas.

"Sit down and talk to a weary woman," she said, as I left the kitchen, dried meat in tow. About to give my best 'sorry I really can't' excuse, I thought better of it. As a powerful enchanter, at least I hoped that's why things exploded so often, I could ask her a few questions that had me stuck.

In the recent hours I'd been reading *Magical Pull Theory, by Madaline Kelin* and I found myself stuck on some of the basic enchanting concepts that the book assumed the reader would have knowledge about.

I sat on the other couch, looking across the way at Regina.

"What did you want to talk about?" I asked, figuring it would be polite to see if she had a topic in mind before I tried to pump her for information.

Regina thumbed at her chin making an odd gesture, one I'd seen her do before but wasn't sure what it meant. "No topics really, unless you are versed on Saturn's advanced Rune structure theory?" I shook my head no, having not the slightest idea what that even meant. "Thought not. Tell me about yourself, young man."

"Not much to tell," I said, scratching at the back of my head. "I'm a fairly new adventurer and I'm trying to advance my profession and understanding with gems and inscriptions."

"You made a mistake there, but young minds are so eager that they often ignore their elders," Regina said, shaking her head and a strand of her dark brown hair falling loose from the tight bun on her head. "Didn't no one tell you enchanting is the only profession worth getting?"

"I hadn't been told that," I said, smiling. Of course, an enchanter would say her profession was the best.

"Take that coy smile off your face," Regina snapped, surprising me. "It's the truth. All of the professions worth their salt are rooted in enchanting, with inscribing being a close second, as it adds stability to the transfer of enchantments to items."

"Can you cut gems with enchanting?" I asked, doing my best to keep my smile genuine, but I was annoyed at the boisterous lady now.

"Any fool can have a gem cut for them or learn to cut gems the hard way, you don't need an *Awakened* profession for such a task," Regina said, her voice calming a bit. "So tell me, how well is your study into your profession going?"

"Funny you should ask," I said, readjusting myself on the

couch to lean closer. "I've been reading a book about magical pull theory that keeps mentioning something called the stability matrix but doesn't go into any kind of detail regarding what that is, maybe you could help me out?"

Regina chuckled and grinned at me. "That's a fancy way of saying, make sure the four corners of your enchantment are stable. Enchantments need four things to work correctly. Power, Intent, Structure, Stability. Remember to PISS and you will be good to go."

I gave her a deadpan look and was sure that she was messing with me.

"I've got a book on the basics of creating enchantments that you should read," Regina got up and scurried to her room. I wasn't sure if she wanted me to follow and just as I began to rise, she returned with a thick book nearly the size of her chest. "Here it is. I have several copies, but if you want to keep it, I'll take 200 gold off your hands. Have a look at it first and let me know later if you think it's worth keeping."

"Thanks," I said, taking the book from her and setting it on my lap. "Does it talk about the...uhmm PISS in here?"

"Sure does," she announced proudly. "I can give you the basics real quick. Power first. It is simple enough; an enchantment needs some form of energy to power the effects it is trying to produce. Intent is next. This means more than knowing what you want the enchantment to do, you have to mark the structure in some way so that your markings get across the meaning of the enchantment. We use Runic formations for that as they seem to be the truest characters we have and work well. Even enchanters like me will mark items in some way, but it is usually deep in the structure of the item and not visible like the work Inscriptionists do. You following me?"

"I think so, Mana powers enchantments and Runes set the

effects," I said, trying to attach what she said to my own understanding of the topics.

"Not what I said," Regina scowled at me. "Mana is the most common energy source, but essence is used, though it be damned hard to come by, and I've known a gnome that harnessed the power of steam and another who captured lightning, though both weren't as reliable as good ole Mana."

"Essence is all around us, right? So why can't we pull it in from the world and power enchantments?" I asked, seeing if I could shake loose any useful information that would further my own studies.

"You can in theory I suppose," Regina said, surprising me. "Two issues with your thought process though. Firstly, there isn't enough latent essence floating around, its concentrated inside living beings or deep into the core of the planet. Secondly, how our bodies naturally pull in essence is a mystery that no one has figured out. Most major discoveries we have all had a skill or spell at the root of it that was gifted by the system. Without a starting point it just hasn't been worked out."

"And if someone had a starting point, what would you suggest would be worth reading to help that person figure it out?" I asked, only after saying it did I realize how obvious I sounded.

Regina tilted her head and a moment later her eyes went wide. "You didn't!" She said, standing and moving in front of me.

"I just meant hypothetically," I said, but I'd already messed up, she had me figured out.

"Do you realize the scope of change such a discovery could make?" Regina asked, her face now a mere foot from mine. "Forget powering enchantments, if someone drilled into the planet and set up a system to rotate out the items enchanted with the ability to pull in essence, we'd be swimming in essence instead of living in basically a drought. Forget what I said before boy, essence is a potent power source that is mostly ignored because of how difficult it is to procure, but the most advanced enchantments we have require it. Our methods of transferring it are crude at best, they just break the cores and hope enough essence makes it naturally into the enchantment. Being able to infuse things or gather them is the key. Its why cores are so expensive, even their dust can be a potent enchantment aid. Have you sold this knowledge yet? I'd be willing to pay a sizable amount of gold if you shared the ability with me."

I felt myself becoming more and more overwhelmed by the knowledge and the subsequent request, cursing my inability to keep a secret. Then I had an idea.

"I don't know how to share my abilities, but I could tell you all about it if you make a Binding Oath to keep it and me secret. Not forever, but until I give you the go ahead," I said, the gears in my brain turning as I thought about what I knew about a Binding Oath, basically a magical contract that would enforce its intent by magical means.

Regina's face darkened for a moment, but in the next it shifted into a deviously looking grin. "I'll sign a Binding Oath and do you one better. You can be my student and together we can work out how best to create an enchantment to draw in essence. I'll even pay you five hundred platinum if you give me first rights to patent the enchantment we create."

Something sounded too good to be true, so I didn't answer at first. Instead, going over every word she'd said and pondering on why she'd offer me such an obscene amount of gold for a patent on the enchantment. I didn't know much about patents, but I'd done a tiny bit of research after Gilfoy's Emporium kept mentioning them. There was a way to magically enforce a certain design through the system so that once a patent was laid down, even if someone discovered your same methods, they'd find that it wouldn't work, the system would keep it from accepting any energy source or at least keep it from using mana, the passage had been specific.

I also wondered how someone who rented a medium size room for studying could afford to give me half a million gold. If she was so willing to give me so much right off, it must be worth so much more. With that in mind I decided to test a theory.

"How much do you think Gilfoy's Emporium would pay for the patent?" I asked, returning the devious grin she'd had a moment before.

"Damn you," she shouted turning and stomping away before turning back, not smiling but not looking awfully upset either. "They'd give you a kingdom's worth of gold but look here young man." She returned to a foot from my face and wagged a finger at me. "This discovery is worth much more if an enchantment is worked out and I'd be the person Gilfoy would come to if he got your ability, so let's cut them out and make a mountain of gold. I can get my family to front seven hundred and fifty platinum if you go into contract with me to split the profit we get 70/30, with seventy going to me and the thirty going to you. And before you start complaining, that thirty percent will be a steady stream of gold beyond any fortune you can imagine."

My mind swirled with thoughts of gold and the things I'd be able to do with that crazy amount. It was worth bringing her in on this I decided, because if she could help me work out a stable enchantment then it would be worth it. I reminded myself that what I wanted from this was the ability to give my friends a better chance at leveling.

"I'll take forty percent and the platinum, but you have to promise me one thing," I said, biting my lip.

"I'm listening," Regina said, her expression all business now.

"I want to create inscribed gems attached to bracers that will allow adventurers to collect more essence from monster slaying and dungeon dives. If you help me learn to do that as well, then I agree and will take a Binding Oath to that effect," I said, keeping her eyes locked on mine and looking for any hint of deception, though I found none. Then remembering something I added. "Oh, and I want to be free to make and give those bracers to whomever I want without the patent requiring me to pay any amount."

"I'm amenable to all those demands, but I won't go above thirty-five percent, especially since it seems that I'll have to add you to the patent if you want to be creating your special gem. Might even need to do several patents."

"Deal," I said. It wasn't worth it to me to fight over a few gold coins when I was about to come into a massive fortune.

The rest of that day was spent in back and forth talks with Regina as we worked out the details. She wanted to bring in a select few from her 'House' to help facilitate things, but I wanted secrecy until the patents were in place and she eventually caved, saying she could get half the money without telling anyone. She also admitted that she knew of the commonly used enchantment for Binding Oaths, so we worked out the wording on both of ours and signed.

It was an odd feeling when signing one, it drew from me and, according to Regina, kept a magical blueprint of your core that would be used to enforce the promise. The contracts were magical items themselves and if they were destroyed so were the oaths, so we agreed to have them placed in a vault at Gilfoy's

Emporium that required both of us to be present to access. This took a total of two days and on the third day Regina left, saying she'd return by the end of the next day with the funds.

While she was gone, I did a bit of poking around to figure out how people kept large sums of money safe. Gilfoy offered such services, but the storage was meant for items and not gold. The Adventurer's Guild offered services as well as private banks that claimed you could pull sums from all major cities, but I wasn't sure about any of them.

While pondering over such facts I realized I hadn't picked a new perk when I leveled up to fifteen, so I made my way to the Prime Mana Shrine to do just that. When looking through the available perks I came across a new one that I knew immediately I had to take. It was called, "Arcane Asylum" and it was a perk I knew my father had before he died.

It allowed you to open a doorway into a personal space that could be used as storage or even a personal study. It was similar to Dimensional storage, except that living beings could survive inside of it for up to twelve hours. It also allowed you to bind the opening of your space to an object that other *Awakened* could access if they were given permission. The only annoying thing about the ability that I could find was it could only be used once every twelve hours, so you could spend five minutes inside and then leave but you wouldn't be able to access it again for twelve hours after leaving.

It was worth it though; it would take away any need I had for a bank or reliance on security if it was tucked away in some dimensional plane of existence.

Selecting the Perk, I felt the rush of knowledge and knew how to both bind an object and summon the door myself. Binding the ability to an object meant the cast time to open the door was almost instant, so I decided to find an object and start there. Fishing through my dimensional storage I had plenty of random objects that could work, but I wanted something I could wear and meant something to me.

I came across a ring that was one of the only possessions I had left of my father. It wasn't enchanted, I'd checked when I first *Awoken*, just a plain silver ring. Fingering it, I raised it up and readied to set the door summoning ability into it, when I got a system message.

Object is already tied to a Dimensional Space; do you wish to override? Yes or No.

"What's this all about?" I asked aloud, no one was in the garden to hear me.

I mentally sent a 'No' and decided to try using the ring. Following the steps that had been implanted into my head, I fed it a tiny bit of Mana and let it go to work. An ancient looking door with dark brown knotted wood and black metal banding appeared just in front of me. Placing my hand on the door I got a new message.

This Arcane Asylum belonged to 'Elkor Miles'. As he is no longer able to access it and you are his approved successor, would you like to claim it? (Warning, if unclaimed the space will be recycled and all objects within will be lost) Yes or No.

A surge of excitement rushed through me, and I quickly accepted, pushing the door open and going through.

I entered an expansive chamber with items and gold piled up all around. My father was never one to keep things tidy and in his personal space it showed the most. The room was at least thirty feet in length and twenty feet at its widest, but it was oval in shape, no straight edges to be found. On the furthest wall to the left there was a bookshelf filled with books, a comfy red velvet chair, and a desk. Opposite of that desk on the other wall sat three stands each with a set of armor on them.

I took a step deeper into the room and the door shut behind me. A voice spoke just in front of me, causing me to jump violently. I was glad no one was here to see that.

"Welcome son," my father's voice was coming from a pedestal just inside the door to the left, a pulsing gem the size of my head sat there. "I secretly wished you'd never have need of this room or have to endure the risks I've gone through, but I've sensed your power and knew this day would come. If you are hearing this, I've either forgotten to deactivate the gem or I've died and can't do so. I love you, Caldor. All I've done in this life is to make it a better place for Emilia and you kids. I hope that in my passing Warrick has watched out for you. In this room you will find gold enough to keep the family well fed for the remainder of their days and items I felt might help you kids along in your journey if you choose to follow my example. I wish and hope as many fathers probably do, that if you are *Sparked*, that you choose a safe life studying your profession and bettering the world through use of your minds instead of the sword. But that choice is yours to make, though I've used the study of mine to explore ways of suppressing the *Spark*, eventually the Ordu will have their way and all those with a *Spark* will be *Awoken*. I've got to go now but know that I love you and whatever path you decide to follow, I know you will excel. Tell your mother, Grace, and Gregory that I love them and I'm sorry. I don't know what killed me, but I like to hope that I died making this world a better place."

The voice cut off and the room went still. Tears rolled down my face at my father's words, just the sound of it after so long had me practically shaking. Even now he was looking after us. My father loved me and wanted only to make the world a better place, he'd said.

"I don't need to be you, father," I said, doing my best to

keep my voice from cracking. "I understand that I can take my own path. But I will emulate you and your goals. I will make this world a better place, one way or another. I love you, rest well."

I sat in the chair and pulled a book off the wall at random, but I couldn't focus enough to read it. The tears had stopped, but my mind was on my father, and I wanted nothing more than to spend some time with my family. So after I had time to gather myself up, I left and summoned Ares.

"Take me home," I said, it would be another day before Regina returned and I wanted to be with my mother and siblings.

Ares fixed me with her loving and intelligent gaze, nuzzling me lovingly. I mounted her and we flew to my home.

"We didn't expect you back so soon," my mother said, stepping outside to greet me. She read my expression in a way only a mother could and stepped forward, pulling me into a tight hug. "Are you okay?" She pushed me back and gave me a once over, seeing that I wasn't injured she pulled me back into her loving embrace. "Whatever it is, Caldor, it'll be alright."

I couldn't help it, tears came unbidden, but I got them under control before I let myself speak.

"Father, he left us gold and I heard his voice," I said, my mother seemed confused, so I continued. "This ring." I showed her the ring. "It was coded to his personal space and inside, well I'll show you, but it won't work for several more hours. He saved his voice to a gem, and I heard him speak. It's been so long I'd almost forgotten." The tears threatened to return, but I kept a stiff lip.

"You heard father," Grace said, her sweet voice coming from just behind the open door. "I want to hear it too."

"You will, all of us will," I said, seeing Gregory slip out the door as well.

Even in the few weeks that had passed, they'd changed. Grown a little taller, a bit older, and there was something else. It prickled at the edge of feeling as I regarded them both. It took me another few minutes before I realized what I was feeling. Gregory and Grace were *Sparked*, it was small still, but I could feel the power within them.

A new set of worries filled my chest as I considered that, but in this thing, I wouldn't be doing as my father had. When the *Spark* began to show I'd make sure they both got proper training and would be prepared for the day they became *Awoken*. Until that day came, I would do all I could to make the world a safer place.

The End of Arcane Knight Book 1, but not the end of Caldor's story.

LEAVE A REVIEW

Thank you for reading. Please leave a review at, My Book.

If you really liked the book, please consider reaching out and telling me what you enjoyed about it at, Timothy. mcgowen1@gmail.com.

Join my Facebook group and discuss the books at: https://www.facebook.com/groups/234653175151521/

ABOUT THE AUTHOR

 Timothy McGowen was born in August 1988 in Modesto, California. His journey into books started with reading the Goosebumps books. Later he read a novel by Terry Brooks and became hooked into fantasy/scifi almost instantly. Shortly after that he was given a school assignment to write a 5 page fiction story, and 25 pages later his story was half done. He hasn't stopped writing since.

His debut novel Haven Chronicles: Eldritch Knight has sold over a thousand copies of both ebook and audible so far. He writes Fantasy that contains a splash of scifi and Litrpg/Gamelit stories. Consider signing up for my newsletter for news on book releases as they become available.

LITRPG GROUP

Check out this group if you want to gather together and hear about new great LitRPG books.

(https://www.facebook.com/groups/LitRPGGroup/)

LEARN MORE ABOUT LITRPG/GAMELIT GENRE

To learn more about LitRPG & GameLit, talk to authors-myself included-, and just have an awesome time by joining some LitRPG/Gamelit groups.

Here is another LitRPG group you can join if you are looking for the next great read!

Facebook.com/groups/LitRPG.books

List of LitRPG/Gamelit Facebook Groups:

- https://www.facebook.com/groups/LitRPGReleases/
- https://www.facebook.com/groups/litrpgforum/
- https://www.facebook.com/groups/litrpglegends/
- https://www.facebook.com/groups/LitRPGsociety/
- https://www.facebook.com/groups/AleronKong/

Made in United States
Troutdale, OR
07/12/2023

11135105R00375